Passing THROUGH

I0587556

TICKET TO
Ride

SARAH HEGGER

This books goes to Dads and Daughters everywhere.
If you've ever watched picture perfect TV families and
thought those weren't your reality, then this book is for you.
Family is a complicated thing.

Acknowledgments

Another first for me here, in releasing a second book in a series
right on the heels of the first book. It took some writing, and let
me tell you, I will plan my time better next time.
Whew! If you're reading this, then you know that I got there in
the end.
I want to thank Penny Barber for doing her editorial magic. Her
contribution is always invaluable.

Thanks to my amazing, clever, talented and beautiful daughters,
without you I would have drifted into Instagram obscurity. And
I still don't get Snapchat. There I said it! And you can't talk back
at me about because I wrote it here.

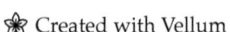 Created with Vellum

CHAPTER
One

THE BEST THING TO welcome Claire to Twin Elks stood on the porch of Winters House with his back to her. And, damn, what a back it was.

Claire took her shades off to get a better look. She had definitely not seen him around before.

In a mesmerizing stretching and bunching of muscle beneath his white T-shirt, he was hammering something above his head. Denim lovingly cupped an ass that deserved to be carved in marble.

The view was almost worth the trip to a miserable little town full of people who wouldn't spit on her if she was on fire.

Almost, but not quite.

The knot of apprehension riding her belly the entire two-hour drive from Denver expanded. Looking at the imposing Queen Ann mansion made her feel three years old and clinging to her mother's hand again. The overgrown garden had been tamed since Claire's last visit, and the exterior boards given a fresh whitewash. The house's trim and scrollwork had been painted forest green.

Porch hottie dropped his arms and tucked the hammer into his utility belt.

She couldn't sit in her car all day. She wasn't that frightened child anymore but a grown woman. A woman with needs. No, not those sort of needs—okay those as well—but other, more immediate needs like making sure she could eat. She would get out and begin her fight for those needs. In a minute or two.

Short dark hair poked out beneath porch hottie's black ball cap and clung to the sides of his sun-bronzed neck. She got stuck on his wide shoulders as she wrestled with her nerves.

A quick makeup check in the visor mirror confirmed that her war paint was still in place, but she did touch up her lipstick. Take-no-prisoners scarlet gave her a courage boost. A woman with bright red lips was not a woman to be trifled with. Her black pencil skirt and white blouse were a statement, her battle armor.

She was Claire Mathews, and she was there to save her inheritance. After all her pain and suffering, that inheritance was hers. She'd earned it.

Porch hottie turned, pushed back his ball cap and stared at her car. He sauntered down the walkway toward her car like he needed to slap a pair of six-shooters on those slim male hips.

With a last fortifying breath, she opened her car door and swung her legs out. Her favorite pair of sky-high heels hit the sidewalk with a satisfying click, and she straightened to her full five foot nine and squared her shoulders. Propping one hand on her hip, she gave the car door a nonchalant flip closed. "Good morning."

That was a good start. Her voice had sounded calm and firm.

Stopping, he made no secret of the slow journey his gaze took from her black stilettos, over her hip-hugging skirt, up her tailored blouse, and stopped at her mouth. He grinned and said in a deep voice with a light rasp, "And hello to you."

Claire lifted her chin and stamped on her urge to fidget. Even in that God forsaken town she would have expected a bit more subtlety. If he thought that caveman bullshit would discomfort her, he hadn't met Claire Mathews yet.

Which he hadn't, because she'd never seen him before. So, it stood to reason that he hadn't met her either.

Dear God, she wanted to leap back into her car and run away.

She caught herself midturn and forced herself back around. "Do you mind?"

"Not at all." He didn't look the least abashed. "We don't get a lot of women like you around here."

"Shocker!" She loaded as much derision as she could into one word. Praying she didn't hit a pothole, she strode forward. "I'm here to see Horace. Is he here?"

"Horace?" He blinked at her.

"Yes, Horace Winters." Claire spoke clearly and carefully. "The man who owns this house."

"Well…" The confusion lifted from his face and he snapped his fingers. "Of course, you are."

Claire needed to save her dwindling store of ballsiness for the real battle, for when she saw her father. She strode forward. "Indeed."

He stood in the middle of the path and impeded her progress. "He's probably expecting you. All things considered."

"What?" That threw her off balance. Horace forewarned would be Horace forearmed. And what did "all things considered" mean? She reined herself in and gave him a haughty stare. "You're in my way."

"Sorry about that." He grinned down at her, easily topping her by a couple of inches, even with her heels, and held out his hand. "I'm Finn."

Before she could stop herself, she put her hand in his. His warm, work-roughened clasp sent tingles up her arm. To hide her reaction, she added more frost to her tone. "And you're still in my way."

"I know." He kept hold of her hand. "I'm hoping to keep you here long enough to get you to talk to me."

"Subtle." She had to fight to hide her smile. Finn had cobalt blue eyes brim full of laughter and charm.

"Normally I am, but the shoes threw me off my game." He leaned in, smelling of sun and warm skin. "I've got a weakness for shoes like that."

"Those same shoes really need to get past you." *Gah!* Now he had her playing along. Most men would be giving her a creeper vibe by now, but somehow Finn got away with it. And he was distracting her when she really needed to keep it together. She went to sidestep him, but her heel sunk into the grass to the side of the path, and she stumbled.

His tanned hand shot out and cupped her elbow. "Watch yourself."

"I'm fine." Claire snatched her arm away and straightened her skirt. A clump of soil stuck to the end of her stiletto.

He cocked his head at her shoe. "Want me to get that for you?"

"That's quite all right." Claire snatched at the crumbling edges of her dignity.

He kept his face straight, but his eyes twinkled. "I'd be more than happy to sort you out."

"Really?" Somebody needed to put him in his place. It might not be her if he kept looking at her like she was a bowl of ice cream, and he had a craving. "Does this approach work for you?"

"I'm not sure." He raised an inky brow. "How am I doing so far?"

"Not good."

"Damn." He shook his head. "And here I thought I had you at hello."

She tried to stifle her laugh, but he caught it anyway and grinned.

"That's better," he said and stood to the side. "I'm sure watching those heels go will be as good as watching them come."

Claire almost stumbled. "You can't say things like that."

"Yeah, I know." He winked. "But I got you to smile, damn near got a laugh out of you, and that's better than you marching in here like Mike Tyson entering Maddison Square Gardens."

Whatever that meant. She hurried away from him before she made more of a fool of herself.

"Hey, Claire," he called after her.

Son of a bitch! He'd known who she was. Claire turned and gave it to him with a double-barrel glare.

He settled his cap back on his head. "Welcome home."

"This is not my home." No way would she ever consider Winters House her home.

"Damn straight it isn't." Her father, dressed in crappy trousers and a drab shirt, stood on the porch. Hair sticking out all over his head, he looked certifiable. And wore that charming combination of anger and bitterness on his face that Claire was sure he reserved for her. "What do you want?"

Claire forced a big smile. "Well hello, Horace." She threw her arms wide. "Surprise!"

———

Finn really liked the way Claire's ass twitched in that tight skirt as she sashayed into the house. He was less admiring of how tightly the woman was wound. She'd climbed out of her car vibrating tension.

Horace scowled at him. "Are you staring at my daughter's ass?"

"I'm not dead yet, Horace." Finn took a stroll over to the car she'd arrived in.

As entrances went, Claire's had been a good one. Very *film noir*. He got the feeling she'd planned it that way.

Claire's packaging said ball breaker, but her big green eyes screamed lost and out of her depth. It's why he'd flirted so outrageously with her. Well, that and the fact that she'd thrown him for a loop with how gorgeous she was. He had wanted to see the woman under the permafrost.

And he'd glimpsed enough to know he definitely wanted to see more.

He popped the trunk and pulled out her baggage. Matching, of course, and high quality but not quite LV. Also, there was a lot of it. He grabbed the two large suitcases, along with a smaller one and an overnight bag, and climbed the stairs to where Horace stood. "Looks like she's staying a while."

"Huh." Horace ran a hand through his hair and gave it the Bart Simpson coif. Finn caught the brief flare of hope in Horace's eyes. Like father, like daughter, all tough and crusty on the outside, but Horace hid a tried and true heart of gold. "She didn't tell me she was coming."

"Does she ever?" The bags were heavy, and Finn moved around Horace into the house.

Horace limped after him. "Nope, but she only ever comes for a day or two. Stays at Pattersons hotel so I don't know why you're playing bellhop."

Claire's heels clacked on the stairs as she climbed. She had killer legs and a fantastic heart-shaped ass that a man would have to be dead not to want to sink his teeth into. Saying so would probably earn him a slap from Claire, and Horace was handy with his cane.

Dragging his bum leg behind him, Horace trailed him up the grand walnut staircase. Stubborn old coot needed to get that hip fixed and fast. Living with pain was bullshit, but Horace was like the frog in boiling water, he'd gotten used to the pain.

Stained glass on either side of the landing threw jeweled patterns across the wood floors. It was pretty as hell and a romantic gesture from a man to his young bride. The first Horace had built the old mansion for his English bride.

Claire appeared in the doorway of Finn's bedroom. Under different circumstances, he'd be happy to see her there.

Her gaze snapped to her luggage and took a detour via his biceps. Then she looked away, blushing. "What are you doing?"

"I thought I might try my hand at stealing your bags." He gave her his most infuriating grin. Since Horace had appeared, she had all her walls back up. "I thought I'd show them to you first, so you could pick out the good stuff for me."

This time he didn't get a flicker of a smile. Instead, she leaned on the doorjamb and dangled one of his T-shirts from her forefinger. "Is this yours?"

"Yup." He put the bags down and flexed blood back into his fingers. He glanced at Horace. "Unless you've taken a liking to Nirvana."

"I'm a Christian." Horace had his miserable bastard face on, but the yearning gaze pinned on his only child made a liar out of him.

You could stir the atmosphere in the hallway with a paddle. Finn's fight reflex kicked in and he breathed deep to dispel it. Tension was a normal part of life. It didn't always mean danger.

Claire dropped his T-shirt on the floor and nudged it with her come-fuck-me shoes. "It's in my room, and I'm going to need you to move it." She waggled her fingers at the room's interior. "Along with the rest of your stuff."

"Yeah." Not going to happen. Finn picked up the bags and moved to the room opposite his. Four rooms on the second floor occupied opposite corners of the hallway with bathrooms sandwiched between. "How about we put you in here?"

"You're using my mother's room." Heels clopping across the wood, she followed him.

Finn winced for the wood under the pressure of those stiletto points. "As she hasn't used it in…" He glanced at Horace. "How many years?"

"Thirty." Horace smirked.

"Yup, thirty." Finn nudged the door open with his toe. "I figured it was up for grabs."

"You figured wrong." She got in front of him and stood with

her arms wide. "Like a lot of people figured wrong about me and this house. I'm here to set them straight."

He guessed that last bit was aimed at Horace. Poppy had told him how Claire had arrived before, breathing fire and righteous indignation about her inheritance. The same inheritance Horace had tried to give to Poppy.

Damn, things could get ugly. Adrenaline prickled beneath his skin.

"I should have known that's why you're here." Horace sneered. "Scared you're not going to get everything?"

"I'm not going to let you give it away to a stranger." Claire squared her shoulders and stuck her chin out.

Adopting a mirror pose, Horace glared back. "Don't see as how you can stop me. I'm not dead yet."

"Maybe I can't stop you, but that doesn't mean I'm going to make it easy for you either."

Claire was all ready to do battle with Poppy. Finn's former sister-in-law was as honest as they came with a heart of caramel covered marshmallow, and she would be the first one to point out the house belonged to Claire and not her. She'd already done so.

Interesting days ahead.

Finn motioned the bags and looked at Claire. "Until you two get this straightened out, where should I put these?"

The struggle played across her face, but eventually she decided she had bigger fish to fry. "This is the smallest room up here."

"Not by much." He knew because he'd measured every inch of them as he helped Hank Styles restore the glorious old Victorian grand dame to her former beauty. Under Poppy's influence, Horace had finally consented to spend money on the house. It wasn't like he couldn't afford to either. Rumor had it, Horace was loaded. Rumor also had it that was the only reason Claire ever came here.

"It's also the only one free right now." He jerked his head.

"Ryan, my nephew, is right next door, and he's convinced his room is part of Professor Xavier's mansion, so good luck getting him out of there."

Placing her bags next to the massive oak wardrobe, Finn ran his hands over the piece. Beautiful wood grain shone beneath the gentle patina of polish. Built solid and to last forever, she was a thing of beauty.

From the door, Claire watched him, and uncertainty flickered over her face. "What about the master?"

"Ben and Poppy are in there." Horace limped into the room. "The couple needs the biggest room." He stomped out again. "They're welcome to stay anywhere they like in my house."

And only Finn saw the raw hurt on her face, and only in the second it took her to disguise it and sneer at Horace.

Before he and Claire went any further though, Finn needed to set the record straight.

"Just so you know, I'm Poppy's brother-in-law. Poppy used to be married to my brother, Sean." Finn hoped she wouldn't hold that too much against him.

"Great." She smiled, but it looked forced, and her eyes told him an entirely different story. "Go Team Poppy."

CHAPTER

Two

AS CLAIRE'S EVIL NEMESIS, Poppy Williams was a severe disappointment.

Poppy stepped into the kitchen laughing at something one of the four children behind her had said. She caught sight of Claire, and her smile dropped. "Hello, Claire."

Below average height and fragile looking, Poppy had a sweet face beneath a cloud of dark, wavy hair. Dressed in jeans and a pale pink sweater, she would never have gotten the part of grasping gold digger.

She also looked like the sort of woman Claire would have liked to befriend.

Claire clung to her purpose. Poppy was a threat, and she needed to be neutralized. "Poppy."

Poppy's stamp was all over the kitchen, children's paintings pinned to the fridge, fresh herbs on the windowsill, a jug of wildflowers in the center of the scrubbed kitchen table.

Claire had come to make a cup of tea, and now she felt like she was the interloper, which was crazy, because Winters House belonged to her. Poppy wasn't even from Twin Elks. She'd only appeared a couple of months earlier. Claire gave Poppy props for having made good use of the time to get cozy with Horace so quickly.

Claire filled the kettle and put it on the range to boil. Good manners made her ask. "Would you like a cup of tea?"

"No, thank you. I was about to get the children some lunch." Poppy helped her oldest son hang his backpack on the pegs beside the backdoor. "You look well."

"Thank you." Children needed to eat, and none of it was their fault. "I can get out of your way." And then she wanted to kick herself because the only person she was ousting was herself.

"No, that's fine." Poppy supervised her twin daughters hanging their bright yellow coats.

The twins took their shoes off and stared at Claire. Identical twins, they both had their mother's dark hair and eyes, and delicate bone structure.

The silence made Claire want to fidget, and she caught herself picking her nail polish. Also red, to match her kickass lipstick. "You look well too."

Poppy managed a tight smile. "Thanks."

Poppy looked much better than when Claire had first seen her a few months back. The stress lines around Poppy's mouth had eased, and she carried a lightness around with her that hadn't been there before.

The twin wearing an adorable checked dress stared at her. "Who are you?"

"Brinn." Poppy shot her daughter a look. "If you'd like to know someone's name, you introduce yourself first."

Brinn looked momentarily abashed but recovered her grin and bounced up to Claire. "Hi, I'm Brinn." Thumb jerk at her sister. "This is my sister Ciara. We're twins."

"So, I see." Claire grew dizzy watching Brinn hop from foot to foot. "I'm Claire, and I can hardly tell you apart."

"A lot of people have that problem." Brinn pointed at her feet. "I like your shoes."

Brinn's ponytails bounced around her head as she hopped.

"Thank you." You had to like a kid who had great taste in footwear. Speaking of which, Brinn's socks had big smiley bees and flowers on them. "I like your socks."

"Ciara has dragonflies on hers." Brinn pointed at her sister's feet.

A still counterpoint beside Brinn, Ciara had joined them and watched Claire with wise eyes that seemed to see too much. "I like them because they're blue," Ciara said.

"I like blue." The oldest boy joined his sisters. His features resembled Finn's, so he probably took after his father more, but with Poppy's dark eyes. "Are you Horace's daughter?"

"Yes."

A toddler lurched toward her and fastened sticky, chubby arms around her knees. She winced for her linen skirt.

The toddler looked up at her and raised his arms. "Up!"

Claire barely suppressed a shudder as she took in the sticky, filthy hands and the green and pink smears all over his baby cheeks. But he looked so earnest she bent anyway.

"Whoa! A Sean frosting alert." Finn swept into the kitchen and scooped up the toddler. He grinned at her over the little boy's head. "I'm already hot and sweaty."

Sean shrieked and giggled and grabbed fistfuls of Finn's dark hair.

For a moment, Claire envied those chubby fists their grip on that shiny dark hair. Which was the weirdest thought she could have had. It must be the stress of the situation.

"Uncle Finn!" The other three set up a clamor for his attention.

The kettle boiled and she made her tea. Then left it on the counter. Nobody Claire knew had children. Surely that level of noise couldn't be normal? She barely contained her wince at the ear-splitting pitch.

It didn't appear to bother Finn at all as he simultaneously stopped Sean from scalping him, listened to a football story from

Ryan and expressed the appropriate admiration to Brinn for someone called Maddy's new hair ribbons.

Poppy smiled at Finn and her children as she tidied up bags and shoes. She ducked past Claire on her way to the fridge. "Excuse me."

Trying to evade her, Claire nearly stepped on Ciara. "Oh!" The idea of her heels connecting with Ciara's feet made her wince. "I'm so sorry."

"That's okay." Ciara smiled at her.

Next time she might not be so lucky, so Claire retreated to the far counter.

Poppy had a loaf of what looked like homemade bread on the counter and was slicing it. "Brinn can you tell Horace that lunch is nearly ready?"

Brinn hopped on one leg out the door and yelled, "Horace! Mom says lunch is ready."

Poppy's gaze connected with hers. Understanding flared between them, and Poppy gave her a tiny smile and an eyeroll. "I meant you should go and find him and tell him lunch is ready," she said to Brinn, who swapped legs and hopped to the kitchen table.

"I don't like ham." Ryan hung off the end of the counter edge where Poppy was working.

"Yes, you do." Poppy put ham on the bread slices. "And please stop doing that."

The mound of sandwiches in front of Poppy grew. She was now cutting vegetables and arranging them on a platter. "Ciara, please set the table. Ryan, get water glasses. Brinn, get everyone a plate."

"And one for Claire?" Brinn hopped over to the welsh dresser.

Poppy looked at her questioningly. "I've made plenty. You're welcome to eat with us."

"No. No, thank you." Those sandwiches looked delicious, pillowy and fresh and packed with ham. But she couldn't break bread with the enemy. Eating Poppy's food and then kicking her and her kids out was below even her.

Although she couldn't kick them out just like that. The kids needed a place to stay. She hadn't been thinking about them when she came here.

"You sure about that?" Finn kissed Poppy's cheek. "Poppy's bread is the closest thing to heaven you'll taste this year."

Finn's blue eyes heated Claire's skin, and she looked away to hide her reaction. "I'm sure. I had something on the drive here."

"You're missing out." Finn draped an arm over Poppy's shoulder. "When are you gonna dump that cop and marry me?"

Poppy laughed and shoved him away. A look passed between them that spoke of a private joke. "When hell freezes over."

"Just thought I'd ask." Finn stepped back and spread his arms wide. He'd put another T-shirt on, the Nirvana one she'd kicked across the hall, and the logo stretched over his chest.

Claire dragged her eyes away.

Horace walked into the kitchen, leaning heavily on a wooden cane. "What's all this noise about?"

Immediately Claire wanted to jump in and defend the children.

"Horace!" The twins ran up to him, and Ciara took his hand.

Brinn got in front of him and walked backwards. "Maddy's got new hair ribbons."

"Is that so?" Horace touched Ciara's cheek. "You okay, Mouse?"

Ciara beamed up at him and nodded.

"Yup." Brinn nodded and sent her pig tails flying again. "They're green and blue with swirly things on, and they stick up on either side of her head."

Claire knew she was staring, but she couldn't stop. She'd never seen Horace interact with children. He looked like he was comfortable doing it, and even more surprising was that the children looked like they were fond of him.

"Hey, Horace, guess what?" Ryan waited for Horace to sit and then stood beside him. "I played football at recess today." He leaned closer to Horace with wide eyes. "With the older boys and they let me play."

"Of course, they let you play." Horace nodded at him. "You've got a great arm. I bet your arm is even better than theirs."

"It is." Ryan climbed on the chair beside Horace's. "I'm a phenom. Uncle Finn says so. Ben says I should try out for the team."

Ben Crowe, the local police chief and former husband of the closest thing Claire had to friend in that town, Tara.

"Then that's what you should do." Horace caught sight of her and frowned. He turned away again.

It didn't hurt. It didn't. Only it did, and it shouldn't.

"Everybody sit down. On your own chair." Poppy carried the platter of sandwiches and the vegetables to the table and set them down. Before she sat, she glanced at Claire. "You really are welcome to join us."

To hear Tara tell it, Poppy had lured Ben into her trap, coming across all sweet faced and helpless and then working her way beneath his defenses. Tara hadn't told her that she could add Finn and Horace to the list of Poppy's conquests. Not in a romantic way, but it was clear that both Finn and Horace thought the world of her.

Finn poured three glasses of milk and a sippy cup for Sean. He then popped the cap on a beer and gave it to Horace.

"Claire?" He held a beer up to her.

Not if she wanted to stay in her skirt. "No thanks."

"Iced tea?" He peered in the fridge. "Apple juice? Milk?"

"Um…water." The rest of the kitchen watched her with interest. "San Pellegrino?"

Claire wanted to kick herself. Of course, Twin Elks didn't have San Pellegrino, and she'd made herself look like a snob.

Not that she cared what they thought of her, but she wasn't a snob.

"What's that?' Ryan sprayed sandwich over his sisters.

Brinn gave him a shove. "Eww, Ryan! Mom, tell Ryan not to speak with his mouth full."

"You just did." Poppy mopped up the damage without so much as a flinch. "And Ryan knows better, because if he doesn't, he will not be able to eat at the table with the rest of us."

Not at all bothered, Ryan chewed with his mouth shut.

Finn appeared in front of her with a glass of water. "All out of San Pellegrino I'm afraid." He raised a brow. "Also out of Perrier, Voss, and Evian."

She wanted to crawl away somewhere and hide.

"Tap water's fine for everyone else," Horace said. "Otherwise talk to Bart Grover he can get those fancy waters for you."

Bart Grover would rather tar and feather her and run her out of town. Claire took the glass and dried her hands with a nearby towel. Next, she dried the sides of the glass. "Tap is fine."

"There ya go." Finn toasted her with his beer and took his place at the table.

Now she regretted not taking the beer.

The family tucked into their lunch, talking to each other. Nobody paid any attention to her, and the familiarity tasted sour in her mouth.

Elementary school lunches all on her own. Claire Mathews with her perfect dresses and neat braids, too scared to get her shoes scuffed or her dresses ripped. Mommy would be so angry if she did. She would look so disappointed and talk and talk about how Claire should know better, and how being a lady was not something you picked and chose.

The feeling of being invisible drove her out of the kitchen, and she took her water to the front porch. New, unpainted wood contrasted with older wood along the porch railings. The intricate scrollwork was also in the process of repair. That must have been what Finn had been working on when she arrived.

A porch swing invited her to take a seat in the shade, and Claire took the invitation. Her flight to Denver had come in late, and she'd been up early that morning to make the drive.

Fall had turned the foliage around her, but the grass still maintained its green. In the old rose garden, the overgrown rosebushes had all been trimmed down in preparation for winter. The sundial in the center had been straightened.

With a push of her foot, Claire got the seat moving. A flicker of motion in the rose garden made her look over again.

Nothing.

She must have imagined it, or perhaps it had been a bird. Birds were currently arguing over a bird feeder hung from the opposite end of the porch.

Though she hated the house and everything it represented, she still felt peaceful sitting out there watching the quiet street in front of it. She closed her eyes and breathed the fresh air deep into her lungs. When had she last sat so still?

"There you are." Finn propped a shoulder against the door jamb. "Kids a bit much for you?"

Claire dodged the question. "I'm not around many children back home."

"And where is that." He sipped his beer. "Boston?"

"I'll go back to Boston when I'm done here."

His blue gaze narrowed on her.

Her evasions hadn't gone unnoticed, but she wasn't here to share her life story. "Once I sort this situation out."

"Situation?" Finn straightened and strolled over to the banister. He tested one of the new spindles. "You mean this house being yours?"

Claire appreciated his candor, but something about his manner put her hackles up. "This house is mine." Everybody in town judged her anyway. What did one more matter? Still, she avoided his gaze. She didn't need to see disapproval written all over his handsome face.

Finn propped his hips on the balustrade. "I'm sure Horace would disagree with you there. This house is still his."

"Horace makes it a point to disagree about whatever he can with me." Claire tamped down on the anger. Her mother had been trapped in an abusive marriage in that awful house, and Claire wanted to raze it and destroy those memories for her. "And you don't know anything about me or why I do what I do, so don't think that you do."

"Fair enough." He kept his face blank. "Then give me a chance to know you and make up my own mind."

She almost laughed in his face. "Why would I do that? Twin Elks made up its mind about me years ago. I don't care enough what they, or you, think of me to bother."

"I reckon that's part of your problem," Finn said.

The nerve of this guy. "I wasn't aware I had a problem."

"Really?" Finn looked at her as if he couldn't quite believe that. "You don't see that you're a little…" He waggled his hand.

"What?" Damn the defensiveness in her voice. "I'm a little what?"

"Highly strung." He grinned at her.

Too shocked to produce a comeback, Claire glared at him. He didn't even know her. Certainly not enough to make assumptions about her. That Greg had said much the same thing before she left didn't help. Right before he'd proposed they take a break. "You don't even know me."

"I don't have to know you that well to notice that about you." He raised a brow in silent challenge.

She'd accepted the criticism from Greg. He was her boyfriend, or something like that. They hadn't left things on clear terms. But Finn, who had only met her today, had no right. No right at all. "You know nothing about me."

"But I'd like to," he said.

As if she would believe that after he'd called her highly strung. "All you need to know is that I'm planning to get back what is mine, and I won't let anybody stand in my way."

He cocked his head and studied her.

Resisting the urge to fidget, Claire held his gaze. Those eyes looked like they saw way too much.

He set his beer on the floor. "Can I give you some advice?"

"No, you can't."

"Before you come in here guns blazing, take a moment." He shrugged as if he didn't care if she wanted to hear it or not. "Poppy is not who you think she is. Take some time and get to know her before you climb into the ring with her."

"Poppy will be fine. If she doesn't get in my way." Claire kept her tough-girl face in place. She'd perfected it over years, and she could rely on it. Nobody saw beyond the mask to the girl beneath, and Claire liked it that way. "You have no idea what this house cost me and my mother. I'm not going to stand aside and let it be taken away from me."

"I hear you." Finn picked up his bottle and straightened. "But I still think you're going about this the wrong way."

"Yeah?" She raised a brow at him and kept her expression stony and blank. "Only problem is, I really don't care what you think."

Finn chuckled and strolled off the porch.

Why had he thought to come out there in the first place? God that man had gotten under her skin, which she really shouldn't have allowed because he meant nothing to her. That was the only reason she wasn't going to chase after him and demand he stop laughing at her.

Ciara stepped on to the porch and gave her a shy smile.

Claire nodded a greeting.

Clambering onto the porch swing beside her, Ciara peered up at Claire. "I'm Ciara."

"That's what I thought."

"People sometimes mistake me for my sister." Ciara heaved a huge sigh. "It's because I'm the quieter twin. People remember Brinn, but me..." She shrugged. "I don't mind."

"No?"

"Nope." She shook her head, snaking her long, dark braid down her spine. "While Brinn is talking, talking, talking, I'm doing the watching."

The wisdom of that staggered Claire. "I was quiet too."

"Did you also watch?" Ciara cocked her head.

Had she? "No." Claire recalled herself at Ciara's age. "I think most of the time, I didn't want people to see me."

"Hmm." Ciara gave a Yoda-like nod.

Claire had to ask. "What?"

"I understand now." Her dark eyes brimmed with empathy. "Cecily said you were sad."

Something ice-cold slithered down Claire's spine. The name struck a chord inside her. "Cecily?"

Ciara gave her another enigmatic smile. "She said you would know her when you're ready."

CHAPTER
Three

CLAIRE DIDN'T SLEEP WELL and woke the next morning with gritty eyes and a pounding headache. She'd known before she had gotten on the plane that the trip would be difficult.

Seems that had been an understatement, and she hadn't accounted for Finn and the children. Less than twenty-four hours, and she wanted to tuck her tail between her legs and run. She had skipped dinner and cowered in her bed the night before, and despite her growling belly, she stayed put.

Above her in the nursery, Ciara and Brinn clomped across the floor like they were playing Whack-A-Mole.

The motion and noise escalated fast. Taps got turned on and off. Pipes squealed and groaned. Poppy's voice stayed calm and gentle as she woke the children and chivvied them through their morning routine.

"Ryan?" A deep bass voice that didn't belong to Finn joined Poppy's. "Find your shoes, and let's get to breakfast."

"Someone stole them," Ryan said. "You're the police. You should open a case file."

"Nobody stole your shoes," Chief Ben Crowe replied, it had to be him. "And I'm not wasting police time looking for the same shoes you lose every morning."

"Maybe we need the FBI?" Ryan sounded hugely hopeful.

Ben chuckled. "We don't need the FBI."

Their voices faded as they descended the stairs.

In the kitchen, Claire pictured Poppy making breakfast. Probably Horace would join them and Finn.

"Girls," Finn called. "Brinn? Ciara? Come on, or you'll miss breakfast."

Damn Finn and his assumptions about her. Those had kept her awake along with everything else last night. He was messing with her composure when she needed to stay focused. Even though they lived in the same house, it would be best if she stayed away from him.

Twin footsteps clattered down the stairs from the nursery.

"Where's Claire?" One of the girls asked. They even sounded the same.

"Still sleeping," Finn said.

"Will she be at breakfast?"

"Probably not." Finn's voice faded as his footsteps moved away.

"But breakfast is the most important meal of the day," said the twin.

Finn laughed, a warm, male sound that skittered down Claire's spine and made her want to laugh with him.

And that needed to stop. Right now.

She intended to avoid Finn and stay well out of the way of his charm and even more devastating opinions. Snuggling deeper into her comforter, she waited. She needed coffee, but she couldn't brave the family breakfast to get it.

Only once the house fell silent, and stayed that way for ten minutes, did she risk going downstairs.

She almost took a shower and got dressed before she went, but it was her house, dammit! If anyone had issues with her or the way she dressed, they could move out. Bravado aside though, she did concede to tossing a robe over her tank top and boy shorts.

Sneaking into the kitchen, she grabbed the full coffee pot before it could become a mirage and disappear on her. Breakfast dishes still littered the table, along with food debris that hadn't made it into mouths.

Surely Poppy could have cleaned up?

She was being a bitch, and an intolerant one at that. Poppy got four kids and three adult males through breakfast every morning. From the condition of the rest of the house, Poppy did a good job keeping it clean.

Sipping her black coffee, Claire cleared dishes and put them in the dishwasher. It wasn't like she was doing anything else anyway.

A knock at the door startled her. Tying her robe around her waist, she went to answer it.

"Bitch!" Tara Parsons nee Crowe stood on her doorstep. Dressed in skintight jeans and an off the shoulder sweater beneath an artfully open cashmere coat, she looked like she'd taken the wrong exit off the interstate. "Why didn't you tell me you were in town?"

"Hi." At last someone who didn't look at her as if she stank up the place. Claire raised one cheek and then another for a kiss. "I only got here yesterday. It was kind of a spur of the moment thing."

As in, losing her job and her boyfriend, and then getting the enormous bill for Mom's care all in one week.

"I, for one, am thrilled to see you." Tara pushed her sunglasses into her honey blonde silk curtain of hair. Stilettos clacking on the wood, she brushed past Claire and into the kitchen. "We've wasted enough time already."

Feeling at a distinct disadvantage with her bare feet and pjs, Claire trailed Tara.

"Thank you, Jesus." Tara reached for the coffee pot in a crash of gold bracelets at her wrist.

Claire handed her a cup.

"Thank you, darling." Tara gave her a grateful smile. "I

haven't had nearly enough caffeine to deal with today."

She took a sip and put the mug down on the counter with a shudder. "Ugh! Ben made that. God love the man, but he couldn't make a decent roast to save his life. It all tasted like police drama sludge."

"Well, he is a cop." Claire was enjoying Ben's coffee to be honest. Not that she'd dare say that to Tara. Tara got a mite territorial where Ben was concerned. If, say, a mama grizzly could be considered a mite territorial.

Tara shrugged out of her coat and stood with it in her hand as she surveyed the messy kitchen. "What happened in here?"

"Breakfast." Claire toyed with refilling her cup, but that would be tantamount to admitting she liked Ben's coffee, and it was far too early in the day for that sort of furor.

"Ugh!" Tara made a face. "God, I get that the woman dresses like a slob, but couldn't she clean in here before she left?"

Ignoring the conscience twinge that reminded her she'd had a similar thought, Claire said, "I'm sure she'll get to it when she gets back."

"Where is she anyway?" Eyes glittering, Tara peered about the kitchen, looking for her prey.

"Taking her children to school." Claire didn't want to see what Tara would do if Poppy showed up now. "Why don't I throw myself in a shower, and we can get coffee somewhere?"

"Fabulous idea." With evident relief, Tara shrugged back into her pale blush coat. "We can go to Kelly's little dive."

"Great." Claire liked Kelly's coffee shop, despite the fact Kelly always served up a sneer and a dollop of disdain with her coffee. Kelly was a firm member of Team Horace and Poppy.

Actually, other than Tara, the entire town was on Team Horace and Poppy.

Claire put her cup in the dishwasher. "I won't be long."

"Take your time." Tara wiggled her fingers. She dug her phone out of her bag. "I have like a hundred messages I need to respond to anyway."

After a lightning-fast shower, Claire stood in front of her open suitcase. Time demanded she throw on a pair of jeans and a T-shirt and be done with it. But going out with Tara dressed like that invited unfavorable comparison. Then again, why should she care? Sighing, she conceded that she did care. Hanging out with gorgeous, glamorous Tara could be hell on the ego.

God, being a girl came with drawbacks.

She settled somewhere in the middle for a cashmere sweater paired with jeans and heeled boots. Yes to basic makeup and no to straightening her hair.

Entering the kitchen about thirty minutes later she crashed headlong into an atmosphere tense enough to turn the air to jelly. The same atmosphere she'd hoped to avoid by getting Tara out of the house.

Poppy looked up from where she was wiping the table. "Good morning." Her tight smile spoke volumes about how she felt about Tara in the kitchen and Claire with her. "Did you sleep well?"

"Yes, thank you." She didn't want to get into the truth in front of Tara. Tara had a way of cobbling random bits of information together and drawing her own picture, a picture that had a fast and loose relationship with the truth.

Poppy nodded. "Good. Did you have breakfast?"

"Always the concerned little mother." Tara didn't bother to look up from her screen.

With a deep breath, Poppy dropped the cloth on the table and took handfuls of glasses to the dishwasher. "I am a mother," she said in that quiet, dignified way of hers. "I was just being polite."

"You know she's not a guest in this house." Tara looked up from her phone. Loathing beamed across the kitchen at Poppy.

"It's really fine." Claire jumped in. Tara spoke the truth, but Claire didn't feel it was Tara's argument to get into. "I'll get something at Kelly's."

"Oh." Poppy looked relieved, and Claire didn't blame her.

Even though Tara was the only friend she had in Two Elks, the woman could be a total bitch. Claire wouldn't want Tara and her axe grinding in her kitchen first thing in the morning any more than Poppy did.

Wait a minute! It was her kitchen Tara was in, and it was first thing in the morning.

"Try the carrot and walnut muffin," Poppy said. "Kelly is trying out a new baker."

"Muffins!" Tara made it sound like pond slime. "Claire doesn't eat carbs. How do you think she stays that size?"

"Genetics." Poppy shrugged Tara's antipathy off. "Horace has stayed slim all these years."

Claire had spent her life trying to forget her genetic connection with Horace. "I am nothing like my father."

"So true." Tara put her phone away. "Shall we?"

Poppy gave Claire a long look.

The sympathy in Poppy's dark eyes made her uncomfortable, so Claire turned and strode for the door.

Tara clippity-clopped behind her.

Once they reached the front walk, Tara let out a groan of exasperation. "I can't stand that woman."

"Poppy?" Poppy had committed the cardinal sin in Tara's book of taking Ben's attention away from her. Claire had her own axe to grind with Poppy, but she didn't share Tara's anger.

Shouldn't she though? The woman was here to steal her inheritance from her. Claire should dislike her even more than Tara did. But it was hard to dislike Poppy. So far, the reality of Poppy had refused to comply with the money-grubbing, gold-digging opportunist that existed in Claire's imagination.

Tara bleeped the locks on her car parked at the curb.

Being divorced from a local police chief wouldn't buy that set of wheels. Tara must have someone, or a group of someones, taking care of her finances for her.

Curiosity got the better of her as Claire slid into the smooth leather seat. "So? You seeing anyone new?"

"Bitch!" Tara gave her an exaggerated eyeroll. "This is me we're talking about. I'm always seeing someone new."

For as long as Claire had known Tara, that had been true. Even when Tara was married to Ben, there had been new someones lurking in the shadows. It didn't make any sense that Tara still clung to Ben like he belonged to her.

Tara recycled one man for another without a pause in between. Claire didn't know how Tara did it. Before Greg, there had been long dry spells, and it looked like Claire was entering another of those dry spells.

The look of unadulterated approval Finn had given her yesterday popped into her mind. She kicked it right out again. She needed to get it into her head that there would be no breaking bread with the enemy, and no fraternizing either. Although the idea of fraternizing with Finn left her a bit breathless.

Tara started the car, and something popular blared from the surround sound system. Claire had heard it on the radio, but she didn't really listen to modern stuff. She liked to keep it old school.

She envied Tara her ability to find men. For a girl who had been twenty-one before she'd had her first boyfriend, it didn't seem possible. Claire never had one man lined up while she got rid of another.

Exhibit: right now. If she'd had someone in her life, she wouldn't be there dealing with things on her own.

———

Kelly's Koffee Klatch had opened about three years ago and had quickly become the place to gather in Twin Elks. Along with great coffee, Kelly served fresh baked goods and a dose of cheerful sass. Except, not to her, or Tara.

Silence descended as they stepped into the coffee shop. All gazes swung in their direction, and the natives did not look friendly. Claire caught her thumb worrying the edge of her other nails and shoved her hands in her pockets.

"Tara." Kelly's wide, smiling mouth tightened. "Claire. How are you?"

"Yo, Kelly!" A man called from the other side of the shop.

Kelly glared in that direction. "Slow your roll, Vince, I'm getting there."

"But where exactly is it that you're getting? Ecuador, so you can pick, roast, and grind the beans yourself?"

Claire giggled but quelled it under Tara's furious look. What the hell? Vince was a funny guy.

Spinning on her heel, Tara looked down her nose at Vince. "Ink dry on the divorce yet, Vince?"

"You should know." A tall, dark-haired guy with clean-cut good looks, Vince sunk his chin to his chest and crossed his arms. "You always did spend more time with my ex than me."

Chelsea had cut Vince loose? Claire found that hard to believe. More Tara's friend than Claire's, Chelsea had her hooks sunk deep into her husband and liked to drag him along behind her.

Not anymore. Claire nodded to Vince. "I'm sorry to hear you're divorced."

"Thanks." Vince's dark eyes softened, and he almost smiled at her. "But we're both moving on."

"What will you have?" Kelly gave her a hard stare, clearly communicating she was not happy Claire was there and didn't give a crap if she knew it.

"Coffee. Black, please." Nobody in the coffee shop looked glad to see her. Some looked openly hostile. Twin Elks was always like that. The weight of it pressed down on her. She should have suggested she and Tara go out of town.

Except that felt like running away. Because it was running away. She didn't owe Twin Elks anything. They had treated her mother like an outsider, barely tolerating her and making her miserable. It had been partly because of their hostility that life in

Twin Elks had grown unbearable for Mom. Trapped in that house by Horace and with nobody to reach out to, was it any wonder she'd run away in the end?

Now they were under the mistaken impression they could bully her. Claire straightened her shoulders.

Her mother hadn't known what they were like. She'd arrived in Twin Elks as a new bride with some hazy notion about the welcome of small towns. Boy had that bitten Mom in the ass.

"Claire Winters." Peg Hardwhistle stormed through the door. Permed hair tendrils twitching, her blue eyes fastened on Claire like manacles. "What brings you here?"

"Mathews," Claire said. "My name is Claire Mathews."

"Is that what it says on your birth certificate?" Peg folded her arms beneath her jutting breasts.

It wasn't any of Peg's business. "I go by Claire Mathews."

"What brings you to town?" Peg had never cared about personal boundaries. If she wanted to know a thing, she asked. Subtlety would not deter her.

Claire forced herself not to drop her gaze first. "I have business here."

"Business!" Peg snorted and shook her curls. "I bet that mother of yours heard all about Poppy Williams and sent you hotfooting it down here."

Claire's mother wasn't sending anyone anywhere anymore. In fact, she barely remembered her name on good days. But these people had treated her mother abominably and didn't deserve the truth.

"Is that what you would have done?" Tara sneered at Peg.

Peg's scrutiny transferred to Tara. "Don't start on me, Tara. Everyone knows you've got a bug up your ass because Ben is getting remarried. Maybe if you spent less time being a bitch, you might have had a chance there." Peg smiled—a thing of evil incarnate. "Better luck with the next one, dear."

"Heya, Peg." Kelly grinned from ear to ear. "What can I get you? And this one is on the house."

"Pfft!" Peg flapped a hand. "You're never going to get anywhere if you keep giving everything away. I'll have one of those mocha, frappy, creamy thingies."

Kelly laughed and twiddled knobs on her coffee machine. "One mocha, frappy, creamy thingy coming up."

"You know what I admire about you, Kelly?" Tara turned her spite toward another target.

Claire really didn't get why Tara had to make a bad situation worse and braced for it.

So did Kelly. "I can't wait to hear this."

"It's how you just don't care." Tara showed her perfect teeth in a feral smile. "You walk around in the first thing you threw on this morning, and you don't care what anyone thinks of how you look."

Wow! Claire almost choked on her coffee. Sometimes Tara soared way over the line and rubbed it out behind her with her claws.

Kelly folded her arms and gave Tara a flat stare. "You want to drink your coffee or wear it, because either way you've outstayed your welcome here."

"Come on." With a nonchalant shrug, Tara glanced at Claire. "We can find somewhere better to enjoy our coffee anyway."

Hastily Claire jammed a lid on her coffee. She dug a ten-dollar bill out of her purse and put it on the counter. "For the coffee."

"God, I hate this town." Tara stood by her car, hands fisted as she breathed deep and fought for composure. "One day I'm going to walk right out of here and never look back."

"You could do that any time." Claire didn't want to rub salt in the wound, but Tara had been saying the same thing for years. "Pack your stuff and go. There's nothing holding you here."

"Poppy would love that." Tara yanked open her car door and slid into the seat.

Claire climbed into her side.

"But I'm not going to do it." Tara started her car. "I'm not going to walk out of here and let her take what she wants. Some-body has to stop her."

Having come for almost an identical reason, Claire could only nod.

Except, Ben didn't belong to Tara. They'd been divorced for years before Poppy appeared in Twin Elks. Still, Tara was her friend, and Claire owed her loyalty. "If Ben is what you want then you should fight for him."

By the time Tara dropped her back at the house late in the afternoon, Claire's mood had slid into lousy. There were reasons her mother had hated the place, and most of those reasons had taken every opportunity to tell her all about how unwelcome she was. Everywhere she and Tara had gone today, the judgy gazes had tracked them. Of course, some of that had been for Tara, but still it had stung.

Finn was working on the front porch again. He stopped and watched her walk up the front walk and on to the porch. "You were out with Tara?"

"Yes." The way he said Tara's name made her think he wasn't a fan either.

Finn looked disappointed. "You won't win many friends with that one by your side."

The disappointment thing stung, which made no sense because it shouldn't. She didn't care what Finn of the sexy body and smoldering blue eyes thought of her. "Let me go upstairs right now and cry into my pillow about that."

Finn's expression softened. "Rough day?"

"Not especially." Nobody saw past her mask if she didn't want them to. Certainly not someone who had only met her yesterday. Except, the way Finn was looking at her with empathy worried her.

The sooner she sold that dilapidated old piece of shit of a house and got the hell out of Twin Elks, the better for everyone.

CHAPTER
Four

IN HER ROOM, Claire put a call into the facility taking care of her mother.

"Hi, Claire," Doug, her mother's regular caretaker, answered the call. "How are you doing?"

"I'm okay." The facility provided excellent care, round the clock but at a price to match. Only after Mom had gone into the facility had Claire seen the true state of their finances. Mom had been living on the edge of bankruptcy for years, surviving from one payment from Horace to another.

To be honest, and she never would have said as much to Mom, the generosity of the support coming from Horace had surprised her. Mom had suggested he sent a pittance and did so grudgingly.

Yet, a fuller check into Mom's bank accounts after she was committed showed a steady payment coming in month after month and year after year, with inflationary clauses built in. Claire couldn't fault Horace's generosity or his consistency.

"So, here's the thing," Doug said, and Claire braced for it. He used that phrase when he wanted to give her bad news. "She hasn't had the best of days, and we had to give her a little something to make her sleep."

Claire wanted to call bullshit on half that statement. If they'd given Mom drugs to sleep, then she'd been impossible all day, and they'd run out of options. As they did everything they could to avoid medical intervention, she knew Mom must have been holy hell.

"All right." Claire kept her girl-in-charge voice in place. Mom's awful disease had robbed her of a mother, but fighting it was pointless. "I hope she has a better day tomorrow."

Doug sounded relieved as he replied, "I'm sure she will. The bad days don't tend to last with her. I'll tell her you called and send your love."

"Thanks."

Claire hung up and tried to ignore the girl in her who wanted to speak to her mother and touch base. In Twin Elks, where nobody liked her and everything felt like it was against her, she had wanted to hear Mom's voice and cling to the comfort it offered.

It had always been the two of them, her and Mom against the world. Now it was just her, and she needed to be strong enough for both of them.

Leaving her phone on her bed, she escaped her room and stood on the landing. Panes of stained glass painted the floor in beautiful pinks, red, yellows, and greens. The first Horace had created the stained glass garden for his English bride, so that even when she couldn't get outside because of the weather, she could always experience her rose garden.

Poor girl had only ever lived in the house for a few years and then died at twenty-four.

Poppy and her family were out, and the house fell deeply silent around her.

Without knowing why, she climbed to the third floor where the nursery was situated.

It had been designed for a large Victorian family with two bedrooms on either side of a central play area. There were two beds per room, but enough space for more if needed.

Brinn and Ciara had taken one room, and not wanting to invade their privacy, Claire walked into the other room.

A child-size four-poster stood against the far wall, its tracks devoid of curtains. They had been white and floaty with fairies sewn all over them.

She had been so young when she and Mom left that she had only a handful of memories of being there. Mom never wanted to talk about their time there, so she didn't even know which of those memories were true.

Taking a seat on the bare mattress, she let a new memory open in her mind. It had been her room, and she had lain in this bed and watched fairies dance as the breeze ruffled the bed curtains.

A large chest beneath the windows on the far side of the room had been full of her favorite toys. There had also been a bookcase on the left stacked with picture and storybooks, puzzles, coloring books, and pencils.

The bookcase was gone, but a slight discoloration on the faded wallpaper marked where it had stood.

A pink and white checkered rag rug had taken up most of the floor. Right there, to the left of the bed she had bitten into a marker and stained it green. Mom had been furious with her.

Horace had laughed. The image of her dad as a younger man firmed in her mind. Yes, he had laughed and said all artists needed freedom to create, and that it was only a rug.

Claire had sat on her bed feeling scared, and he had winked at her behind Mom's back. Then he had wrapped his arms around Mom and tried to make her laugh.

That couldn't be right. Claire shook her head to clear it, because she had to be remembering wrong.

Horace had been a harsh, angry husband. Mom had feared for her safety and Claire's. As a father, he had never had time for her or wanted her about. She had been put in that room because Horace didn't want her underfoot.

Then why could she hear the distant echoes of his deep, bass voice reading? *In a great green room, there was a telephone…"*

"Hey." Finn stood in the doorway, his shoulder propped on the jamb. "Those look like some pretty deep thoughts."

She didn't want to break the strange magic that had wrapped around her. The memories contained in her room were happy, and she didn't want to let them go. "This was my room, you know?"

"Horace said so." He strolled into the room. "We took the curtains down because they were so faded. They were pretty. Butterflies."

"Fairies," she said. "And the same fabric was there on that window seat cushion."

"One of the ladies from the prayer chain is sewing more curtains and a cushion cover," he said.

"Why?" The irrational desire to choose the fabric and make sure it was right rose in her, and she shoved it down. "Once Horace leaves, this house will be sold."

He gave her a long stare. "I don't think any of that is as decided as you seem to think it is."

"It will be." She stood and shoved the lingering sweet memories away. "Do you know what happened to the rug?"

"It had a green stain on it, but Brinn and Ciara wanted it anyway, so we moved it in there."

Claire was glad about that. Maybe they used the patterns on the rug as part of their games as she had done.

"Hank and I moved the dressing table and the chest of drawers downstairs to work on them," Finn said.

"Hank?" The names and faces of Twin Elks blurred in her mind.

"Hank Styles." Finn grinned. "Crusty old bastard. Drives a pickup that's older than God."

She didn't really remember, but she nodded anyway. "The dressing table was there," Claire pointed to the wall to the right of the bed. "It had a triptych mirror."

"It still does." Finn smiled. "It's a beautiful old piece, and we're restoring it."

Claire looked around the room again. "I don't remember a chest of drawers."

"Here." Finn tapped the wall beside the window seat. "And a wardrobe on the other side."

"Wardrobe?" A huge carved piece of furniture filled with bright, frilly, and sparkly dresses. "Are you restoring that too?"

Finn grimaced. "Unfortunately, some damp got to that one and warped it. We had to trash it."

"Oh." A stupid wave of sadness washed over her. For a wardrobe she'd only just remembered. The place was getting to her. She needed to get out of there, so she stood.

Unfortunately, she had nowhere to go.

Finn cleared his throat. "Want to see your dressing table?"

"Sure." She had nothing better to do, and the sadness was creeping beneath her facade.

Following Finn, she went back downstairs and through the kitchen door.

"Horace has got us working on all the woodwork and the furniture," he said.

It seemed a pointless thing to do, given her intentions, but she kept that to herself.

They crossed a patch of lawn and went behind the garage to the old storage sheds. One of them had been turned into a work-shop, and Finn led her inside.

"Here she is." He ran a big hand over the top of her old dressing table. The mirror had been removed, and so had all the hardware, but she still recognized it.

Claire opened the top left drawer. She had hidden her trea-sures beneath a stack of undershirts in that drawer. Bits of rocks, feathers, pretty stones that Mom surely would have thrown out if she'd found them. "This used to jam."

"I fixed it." Finn slid the drawer out and back in again. "Two of the legs needed tightening and the bottom of a couple of drawers had rotted out, but she'll be good as new when I'm done."

"I'm glad." She looked up at him, and her smile came naturally.

Finn blinked at her. "You planning to hole up in your room again tonight?"

"I hadn't given it much thought." The idea held zero appeal.

He gave her his sexy half-smile. "Want to go for a beer?"

"A beer?"

"Malted beverage, hops are also involved, best drank cold." He shrugged. "I'm off to the Elk to have one, and you could join me."

"This is not like a date, right?" Claire didn't trust his innocent look.

Finn snorted. "Don't get ahead of yourself, woman. Coming or not?"

What the hell. It beat sitting around getting bombarded by stupid nostalgia. "Okay."

———

Claire was already overdressed for the Bugling Elk, and Finn led her straight to his truck. Basically, a pair of shoes and a shirt would get you served. And in summer, Maddison sometimes waved that rule.

He shut Claire's door and climbed in the driver's side. "You ever been to the Bugling Elk?"

"Nope."

Imagining Claire's face made him chuckle. "Then you're in for a treat."

When he'd gone upstairs, he'd only done so because he heard a noise up there and wanted to see what it was.

Finding Claire sitting on the bed with a sweet pensive look on her face had snuck beneath his guard. In that moment she hadn't looked anything like the ball-buster she was reputed to be. She had looked sad, and vulnerable and lonely.

"Are you taking me to some shack?" Claire glared at him.

"Nope." The Bugling Elk was respectable enough, just odd. "I can't really describe it. You'll have to see when we get there, but the beer is cold and plentiful, and they make a great burger."

"Oh." She went back to looking out the window, seemingly lost in thought.

Finn didn't disturb her for the rest of the short drive.

As they walked into the Bugling Elk and took a seat at the large, scarred bar, Claire's expression was priceless. "Is that…"

"Apparently the largest collection of Elvis bobbleheads in the country." Finn had to laugh at her head swiveling on her neck, as she tried to take it all in.

Warren Watts had opened the bar back in the sixties and tried to recreate a pub from the village where he'd been born in England. Unfortunately, any chance of doing so tastefully had crashed headlong into Warren's Elvis obsession.

Blinking at the elk head above the ladies room, Claire said, "Are those panties?"

"Uh-huh." He waved to Maddison, Warren's daughter and now owner of the Elk.

Maddison sidled over and grinned at him. "Fat Tire?"

"You know me so well."

"And for you." Maddison's expression tightened as she looked at Claire.

"Um." Claire looked around her a bit wildly. Then she took a deep breath. "I'll have the same."

"You drink beer?" Finn had been surprised by that one.

Claire pulled a face at him. "Yes, I drink beer. When I have to."

The usual crowd was in, along with a table of faces Finn didn't recognize. They were early twenties by the look of them, and already several empty pitchers littered their table.

"Who's that?" He asked Maddison as she dropped two bottles of beer and a glass for Claire on the bar in front of them.

Maddison shrugged. "Not sure. They came in tonight for the first time. I'm keeping my eye on them."

"Is it just me or have there been a few new faces around Twin Elks lately?" Finn poured Claire's beer into the glass.

"Nope." Maddison shot Claire a hard look. "There are a lot of out of towners hanging around. I just hope they're not here to cause trouble."

As much as Finn got that Claire had made no effort with the folks of Twin Elks, he couldn't get that unguarded moment back at the house out of his head. That woman, the one who had sat in the old nursery and looked completely lost and hanging on by a thread, that woman had a soft underbelly that the town could sink its teeth into.

Focused as she was on the panty-bedecked elk head, Claire missed the attitude Maddison was handing out.

She pulled a face. "That's gross."

"Yup, and you're not the only one to think so." He gestured Maddison with his beer. "But when Maddison tried to take it down, there was an uproar from the locals."

Claire gaped at him.

"Apparently some of those panties have been up there for over fifty years, and people feel like they should stay there."

With a shudder Claire turned away. "You said they do a good burger?"

"Yup." She didn't sound like she believed him, and Finn really couldn't blame her. "I tell you what, if you're hungry, I'll buy you one, and if you hate it, nothing lost."

"You're on." Claire's eyes lit up, and she was incredibly pretty when they did. She looked younger and more approachable and like a woman he could get to know.

Finn ordered their burgers and another beer.

Claire's first one had evaporated.

Leaning on the counter, he studied her face, looking for clues as to who she was. Sure, she could do her bitch thing, and he'd seen it in action, but he'd caught glimpses of other facets of her, and he wanted more of those. "What do you do back in Boston?"

"Why?" Immediately with the hackles. He'd never encountered someone who needed a friend more but was so determined not to get herself one. Tara didn't count because Tara was nobody's friend but Tara's.

Finn kept his shrug light. "I just wanted to know."

For a drawn-out silence, Finn didn't think she'd answer, and then she said, "I'm in advertising. Ad exec for new business."

"And you like that?"

Her frown said she didn't like questions about herself. "Sure." She shrugged. "It's my job."

She motioned Maddison for two more beers. "My round?"

"Sure."

Their burgers arrived, and they both dug in.

Swirling a fry in ketchup, she glanced at him. "Actually, I don't like my job," she said. "I work for an asshole who doesn't think anyone is entitled to a life outside of her climb up the ladder."

"How did you get into it?" The burger was as good as ever, juicy and packed with flavor.

Claire moaned around a mouthful. "This is really good."

Vince walked past them and clapped him on the shoulder. "Finn." His face tightened, and he ignored Claire.

Finn wasn't going to let that fly. "You know Claire, right Vince?"

"Uh…sure." Vince glanced at him and then managed a nod for Claire. "Hi."

"Hi." Claire's ice queen slid into place and Vince beat a swift retreat.

Around the Elk, people's gazes drifted their way and lingered on Claire with various degrees of hostility. Nope, she had not made herself any friends in Twin Elks. In fact, she'd gone out of her way to get what she'd gotten, antagonism.

A roar came from the new table, and several locals glanced over with distaste.

"First I tried to be a creative," Claire said. "A copyrighter, but I wasn't good enough at it, so I went into the other side of the business."

Her cheeks had grown a bit flushed, which he suspected had something to do with the beers she'd inhaled, but it ramped up her pretty.

"Anyway." She took another bite of her burger. "I got fired."

"You did?" He hadn't expected that much honesty. "Why?"

"Technically they called it downsizing, but my downsizing lined up very neatly with my not being able to spend my weekends working anymore." Eyes sparkling, she leaned forward. Unless he was mistaken, Claire Mathews was a lightweight who got buzzed on two beers. "The asshole with no life, remember?"

He nodded. "That sucks."

"Yup." She finished her burger.

Finn finished his and wiped his hands on his napkin. "Was it your boyfriend?" And now he was on a fishing expedition, and not even doing it tactfully. "The reason you couldn't spend your weekends at work. Did he have a problem with you working long hours?"

Claire giggled, but it carried a manic edge. "Not him. He's all about his career."

"That must be why he isn't with you?" Could he be any more cringingly obvious, but he wanted to know if she was attached? He didn't do attached women. Or Horace's daughter, or women so vulnerable they were a walking train wreck. So why the hell was his head even going there?

A dark-haired guy from the new table came over to the bar and rapped on it. "Have you got tequila?"

"Sure." Maddison grabbed a bottle and lined up shot glasses. "How many?"

"Four." He turned to his table and back again. "Make that eight."

He took the tray of glasses from Maddison, caught sight of Claire and leered.

Finn gave him a look to let him know that wouldn't be happening any time soon. As in, never.

Claire sat up straighter. "Hey! We should do tequila. It's been years since I did tequila."

"Um." He needed to slow her down. "I'm not really one for tequila."

Claire pulled a face at him and tapped the bar. "Maddison."

She got an unfriendly eye in return.

Finn gave Maddison a what-the-hell look, and she flushed.

"We need tequilas over here."

Looking a lot less bellicose, Maddison poured two tequilas and carried them over with the lime and the salt. She even managed a tight smile for Claire. "Enjoy."

"Thank you." Claire gave her a full smile in return, not one of those tight-lipped grimaces she usually handed out. She salted her hand and got the lime ready. "Actually, if I could do anything in the world. I would be an accountant."

Finn nearly snorted beer through his nose. Not the answer he'd been expecting, and it made her even more intriguing.

Right now, she also seemed on a bit of tear. She took her tequila shot with a grimace and gasped.

"Why didn't you become an accountant?"

"Mother." She eyed his shot. "You gonna drink that?"

"Nope."

She reached for his and did the shot.

Finn gestured to Maddison for two glasses of water. Which made him wonder what Claire was working on obliterating from her mind.

"Mother didn't think accounting was right for me." Claire pulled a face. "Mostly she objected to how unfeminine it was. Not the right profession to catch a good husband."

Mother sounded like a real party.

"Hey." Claire's cheeks were flushed and her eyes glittering.

She pointed to where couples were shuffling around a tiny dance floor. To Elvis, of course. "We should dance."

"Sure." If it got her mind off the tequila, he was game.

When they reached the dance floor, Claire threw her hands around his neck and tucked her face against his clavicle. She took a deep breath. "You smell nice."

"Thank you." He was proud he managed a normal voice. Dancing had been a gross miscalculation. Claire was tall and they lined up perfectly, breasts to chest and hip to hip. She was also slightly drunk and plastered her long, lithe body all over him.

"So, Finn," she murmured. "What do you do?"

"At the moment I repair old furniture." She stumbled, and he firmed his hold.

"Nah ah." She lifted her head, narrowly missing clocking his chin, and peered at him. She gave his shoulders and biceps a squeeze. "You don't feel like a furniture restorer."

"Before this, I may have spent some time in the military."

"Ah ha!" She tucked herself away again. "And what did you do for them?"

Mostly trying to forget the shit he'd done for them. "I'd tell you, but then I'd have to kill you."

She giggled, far more than his lousy deflection deserved.

Hanging her head back she heaved a massive sigh. "I love dancing. I don't dance enough." Raising her head, she stared at him. "Why don't I dance anymore?"

"I'm not sure." Alcohol had lowered those thick walls she hid behind. With her beautiful eyes open and vulnerable and her face soft and sweet, she took his breath away. "Maybe you're too busy."

"No." She tucked her head back on his shoulder. "It's because I don't have anyone to dance with."

He was all kinds of a shit for being glad about that. "What about the boyfriend?"

"I'm not sure he still is my boyfriend." She giggled. "We left things kind of weird." She gave him most of her body weight. "But even before then, he didn't like to dance with me."

Fucking idiot. To miss all this sweet and sexy in his arms, the guy must be brain dead.

"Finn?"

"Yes, Claire." He lowered his head to hear her better.

Her breath huffed hot against his neck. "Do you like me?"

"I'm dancing with you, aren't I?"

"Yes, but I made you." She looked up at him and frowned. "Nobody else in this shithole likes me."

She was drunk so he shouldn't have bothered, but he liked it there, and he liked the people. "Maybe that's because you call it a shithole."

"Huh." She burrowed in again. "What would you call it?"

He gave that some thought. "A good place to find what you're looking for."

The song changed, and he adapted their pace to it. Three other couples shared the tiny space with them. One of which was Donna, a member of the infamous prayer chain, and her eyes nearly bugged out of her head when she recognized Claire.

"So, what are you looking for?" Claire asked.

If only he knew. An end to all the death he'd dealt with in his life. A way to create something instead of always destroying the things he touched. World freaking peace. "I'm not sure. Serenity."

"Huh." She stroked his bicep. "Greg says this is a break, but I don't believe people who are meant to be together take breaks, do you?"

"I don't." And he suppressed the irrational surge of relief that the boyfriend was out of the picture. Because it was irrelevant. You know what was relevant? Claire was Horace's daughter and there to get rid of Poppy. Horace's smoking hot daughter, and again, he'd stumbled back into irrelevant.

"Finn?"

"Claire."

"I really like the dancing, but I think you should take me home now." She sighed and kept dancing. "I'm tired."

He got the feeling that meant a whole lot more than just right now.

"Come on then." It was like losing a limb to disentangle her from him. He led her off the dance floor and dropped cash on the bar for Maddison. They could make good when he returned.

Outside, the crisp fall air did a lot to clear his head.

Claire followed along beside him, her hand in his. She kept hold of his hand the entire drive home, and even into the house.

In the dead silence of people sleeping all around them, he led Claire upstairs and into her room.

"Oh?" She blinked when he turned on the light. "I'm staying here now. I almost forgot."

"Can you get yourself to bed." Please let the answer be yes because putting her to bed would tax his good guy even more.

Claire swiped the air and stumbled a bit. "Sure."

Catching her against his chest, Finn stabilized her. "I'd be more convinced if you stayed on your feet."

She snort-laughed and pushed herself upright. "Me too."

"Come on then." He nudged her toward her bathroom. "Let's get you cleaned up and into bed. I bet you have a whole regimen of crap to put on your face."

"Ha!" She wagged a finger in his face. "That's what you think, but I'm a completely natural beauty." She circled her face with her hand. "I wake up like this."

"Uh huh."

She giggled. "Nope, not even close. I have a regimen and a half of crap." She adopted a voice he guessed was her mother's. "Leverage what you have, Claire, while you have it."

God, this woman had so much more going for her than her looks. He'd caught a taste of it tonight and was greedy for more. As a friend.

"Finn." She swayed toward him. "I think you should kiss me."

A surge of unadulterated lust coursed through him. His libido was one hundred percent on board with kissing her, deep and hungry.

He settled for a peck on her forehead. Being a good guy sucked so hard. "Babe, that's the tequila talking. Get some sleep."

CHAPTER
Five

CLAIRE CRACKED her eyes open and winced at the bright morning light. God, please don't let it be daylight already, please let her not be in Twin Elks, and please, please could it not be time to face the consequences of last night's behavior.

She hadn't drunk beer since college, and it had been ages since she'd eaten a burger and fries. As for the tequila, what the hell had she been thinking? She was a total lightweight in the drinking department. The occasional glass of sauvignon blanc or merlot about summed up her experience.

Rolling over, she buried her head in her pillows. If only she could stay there until they, and by they she meant Finn, forgot all about what she'd done.

She'd thrown herself at Finn and begged him to kiss her. Thank God, he'd had more sense and put her to bed instead.

And dammit! That was not disappointment she was feeling now.

From the sound of it, the family was in the kitchen. How could six people, most of them little, rival a hockey stadium full of rabid fans for volume?

Tossing herself out of bed, she stumbled into her bathroom

and brushed the yuck off her teeth. She couldn't avoid the bathroom mirror any longer.

Thick black smudges around her eyes were all that remained of yesterday's mascara. One of her false lashes was stuck to her cheek, which meant the other was probably still in her bed. Worth noting that her lipstick really was twelve-hour coverage. Not a pretty twelve hours, but still true to advertising. She ran a shower and stepped in.

A dousing with soap and water made her feel marginally better, and she grabbed a pair of yoga pants and a sweater and tugged them on.

The noise in the kitchen rolled on. She made her bed and tidied the room and then sat on her bed. Her stomach growled, and her sluggish brain begged for coffee.

Screw it! It was her house, and she shouldn't be hiding in her room. It wasn't like she could avoid Finn either. They lived across the hall from each other.

As she crossed the hallway, the door to the main bedroom opened.

Tall and broad, with a gravely handsome face, Ben Crowe stepped out.

Claire tended to view Ben through the Tara filter. Most of the time they had been married, Tara had complained about his thorough, deliberate way, and how he kept the speaking to a minimum.

Claire had always wondered why Tara was so hell bent on getting him back if she didn't even like the man.

"Claire." Ben gave her a nod and motioned her to precede him down the stairs.

Loud voices, furniture scraping, cutlery, crockery and glassware noises swept out of the kitchen in a sound tsunami, and she winced.

"Brace yourself," Ben murmured, eyes gleaming as if he was laughing on the inside.

Every child in the state of Colorado bellowed Ben's name as

he walked into the kitchen. At least, the volume level suggested as much.

Claire stood in the doorway as Ben handled it all with his quiet calm. He kissed Poppy, who was at the range cooking something delicious smelling, and then greeted each of the children in turn while simultaneously warding grubby hands from his clean and pressed uniform.

Horace looked up from the table and nodded to her. She nodded back. It beat yelling at each other she supposed.

"Claire!" Ryan caught sight of her and pointed. "Mom is making French toast with strawberries. She can make some for you too."

Volunteering Poppy's services seemed a little much, so she shook her head and sidled closer to the coffeemaker. "That's okay thank you, Ryan."

Ryan crumpled up his face. "It's because of the strawberries isn't it?"

"Eh?"

"I would have liked chocolate chips," Ryan said. "But mom says we have to have strawberries. Which I don't mind, but they're not chocolate chips."

"Uh…okay."

A hand pushed a full coffee cup in her direction, and she grabbed it and looked into the laughing blue eyes of Finn. "Morning."

"Hi." Heat flooded her face. "Thanks."

"You're welcome." Finn's grinned widened. "For the coffee as well."

Poppy turned from the range with a platter piled high with French toast and bacon. "Claire." She gave her a flawlessly polite smile. "I made plenty, and you're welcome to join us."

"No, thank you." Ignoring her stomach growl, Claire got a yogurt out of the fridge. Fat free and only ninety calories, but no substitute for French toast and bacon—she nearly whimpered—with maple syrup.

Brinn upended the jug, and the amber stream of pure ambrosia smothered her French toast.

"Enough syrup." Poppy plucked the bottle out of Brinn's hand.

Claire was with Brinn on this one. What was the point unless you could drown your French toast in a sea of maple syrup? She shoved a spoonful of yogurt into her salivating mouth.

Poppy drew closer and poured herself a cup of coffee. "I heard you were at the Elk last night."

Claire nearly spat yogurt across the kitchen. "Er…yes. Finn and I went for a beer."

"Right." Poppy gave her a flat stare and then the same to Finn. "That's what I heard."

Taking her coffee with her, Poppy sat down at the table, and Claire breathed a sigh of relief. She was quite sure Poppy had received a full report on what had happened at the Elk last night, probably with photos and probability charts. This being Twin Elks after all.

The family ate, argued, laughed, and chattered as she stood at the far side of the kitchen and sipped her coffee. After she and Mom had gone back to Boston, it had only been the two of them.

The couple of friends Claire had made at school didn't come from loud, boisterous families either. Most were single children like her, and the misfits who always stayed on the fringe of the school social scene.

Horace had also been an only child, but he seemed really comfortable sitting at the head of a large family. He answered questions, wiped faces, rescued toppling glasses, and upheld an adult conversation with Ben.

He fit in perfectly.

Finn stood up and approached her with a plate in his hand. Claire swore the devil danced in those blue, blue eyes.

"Yogurt is not breakfast." He cut a forkful of French toast and raised it to her mouth. "Come on, you know you want to."

They were still talking about French toast, right? Obediently she opened her mouth. A dribble of syrup spilled over her lips, and she licked it up.

Finn's gaze tracked the movement. "Good?"

"Very good." She couldn't drag her gaze away from his.

Finn offered another forkful, and Claire took it. Poppy made excellent French toast. Some part of her brain registered the taste as she got lost in the heat of Finn's gaze.

She didn't feel as embarrassed about asking him to kiss her anymore. Very few women wouldn't want him to grab them in a face hold and kiss the crap out of them.

Claire was willing to bet he was one of those men who owned you with his kiss—who made it his business to extract the full measure of the promise a kiss offered.

"Claire." His voice roughened. "You need to stop looking at me like that. At least while there are children in the room."

She took another bite of French toast from him and sighed. "That really is very good."

Finn groaned and squeezed his eyes shut. He murmured something to do with a daughter and a friend.

"Finn!" Poppy snapped out his name and popped the bubble between them. "I said I'm taking the children to school now."

Finn turned around and descended on the girls.

"Uncle Finn." Brinn tried to hold him off. "You'll get my dress all wrinkled.

Finn tapped his lean, tanned cheek. "Then you better give me my kiss goodbye."

"Ew." Brinn wrinkled her nose but kissed his cheek.

A giggling Ciara kissed Finn's other cheek.

Something tugged Claire's sweater, and Ryan stood beside her. "I'm going to school now, Claire."

"I hope you have the best day." Ryan had the most adorable face of any kid, ever. His dark eyes danced with good humor and life, and he had a way of focusing solely on you. His Uncle Finn had the same look in his arsenal, and it was impossible to keep them at arm's length.

Ryan nodded. "I will. I can draw you a picture if you like."

"I would like that very much." A picture for her to add to the collection on the fridge or put in her room, like she belonged to the noisy family unit. Then she felt she needed to be responsible and added, "But make sure your teacher says it's all right first. Your schoolwork comes first."

"Claire." Ryan rolled his eyes. "I'm in kindergarten. Drawing is what we do."

She'd never gone to kindergarten but had a nanny. "Right."

"Bye then." Ryan trotted off.

Poppy looked at her, as if trying to piece something together, and then went back to supervising her children. "Ryan, where are your shoes?"

"I don't know." Ryan shrugged. "Someone must have stolen them."

Claire slipped away while Poppy was herding them all out the door.

"Claire." Horace's voice stopped her as she got to the stairs.

His limp had gotten a lot worse since she'd last been there, and he leaned heavily on his cane. "When are you going to get that sorted out?"

"Do you have any idea of how long you're staying?" Horace grimaced and stopped at the foot of the stairs.

"That keen to get rid of me?" It was one hundred percent knee jerk. God, it would be so much easier if she and Horace could stop doing this to each other.

Horace shook his head. "No. This is your home, and you can stay as long as you like. But you need to know that Poppy and Ben's wedding is right around the corner, and they're getting married here. If you can't find a way to be civil on their special day, it might be better if you leave before then."

Did he think she would disrupt Poppy and Ben's wedding? Yes, he did. The look on Horace's face spoke volumes about his low opinion of her. "You're trying to hand my inheritance over to Poppy, but sure I'll be civil. I'll even put on a pretty dress and slap a smile on my face at her wedding. You bet ya!"

With a sigh, Horace turned around and limped away. "There is so much you don't know, Claire. It would benefit you greatly if you addressed your ignorance."

———

Finn ran his hands over the newly sanded wood of the chaise that used to sit on the first-floor landing and would again, once he'd restored her beauty.

Hank Styles had his grizzled head bent over Claire's dressing table as he tried to fix the intricate carvings around the mirror. Hanks big, calloused hands could work as daintily as a neurosurgeon or as robustly as a lumberjack. Hank knew wood like it was an animate object, and he was teaching Finn's dumbass everything he knew.

Since Horace had okayed the renovations to the old house, Finn and Hank had taken up working at Winters House. It was easier that way, with the amount of woodwork and furniture they were rehabilitating, and most of the tools they needed had already been in the old workshop. Finn loved the workshop smell of freshly planed wood, varnish, and beeswax. Hank wouldn't let anything else touch his beauties.

They kept the wide doors open to the crisp breeze. Fallen leaves rustled and skittered in the quiet when he stopped sanding.

Working with wood soothed Finn, especially restoring old furniture. And he needed that soothing this morning. God knows why, but his old nightmares had paid a visit last night. When he'd first gotten home from active duty, they'd come all the time, wrenching him awake and making him avoid sleep so he didn't have to experience them. The details had gotten blurrier as time passed, but the heart-stopping terror didn't change.

The call two days ago from his old CO might have triggered them. His CO had a job for him, one he was uniquely suited to. He wanted Finn to train the new recruits to his old unit. According to his CO, he had integrated back into society the most fully of his surviving squad members. That wasn't setting the bar very high. Like last night, Finn's nightmares still rolled around from time to time. Those he could deal with. His sensitive triggers bothered him more. It didn't take much to trip the switch into that dark place he was trying like hell to pull himself out of.

Accepting his CO's offer could take him right back there again. His skills, however, didn't leave him with many options.

At thirty-six, he was still way too young to pull up a bench and sit on the porch for the rest of his days. As tempting as that got sometimes. Especially here in Twin Elks where life moved slow enough to appreciate it.

Footsteps crunched on dried leaves, and Poppy poked her head around the door. "Hi."

"Hi yourself." He had been half-expecting something like this since breakfast. Poppy hadn't missed his interaction with Claire, or that he and Claire had been seen at the Elk last night. "Get the kids to school okay?"

"Yup. I took them and dropped in for coffee with Kelly after." Poppy grinned at him. "Kelly says hi."

"Did she make any inappropriate suggestions?"

Poppy chuckled. "Of course, she did."

Finn liked Kelly. The curvy blonde owned the local coffee shop and made a point of flirting with him whenever she could. Unfortunately, that spark wasn't there for either of them.

Poppy leaned a shoulder against the doorjamb and crossed her arms. "It's getting colder."

"Yup." He blew away some wood dust. "Won't be long before we get to see what winter in Twin Elks looks like."

"I always hated winter before." Poppy stared over the long lawn to the stand of trees fronting the river. With fewer leaves on the trees than in summer, the view to the river had opened up.

Finn loved that view as well. "When you were in Philly?"

"Yeah." She shivered and tightened her arms.

Guilt swiped at him. He didn't need her to tell him why she'd hated winter. After his brother's death, Poppy had worked two jobs to keep her four children fed and clothed. Winter meant money for heating and money for warmer clothes for growing children. "I'm sorry, Poppy. I should have been there."

"No." She gave him a stern look. "Your brother should have made sure we were taken care of."

Sean had been born nine years after him, a sickly baby who their mother had coddled. Blessed with robust health, Finn had never gotten as much attention as Sean.

As a boy, he'd been resentful. As an adult, he saw it for the mixed blessing it really was. Mom had spoiled Sean and raised him with a walloping sense of entitlement.

Take his marriage to Poppy as an example. Sean had thought nothing of making one baby after another and disappearing between to get his itch scratched elsewhere.

Even now, Finn didn't think Poppy knew the extent of Sean's adultery. Finn had taken him on about it once, but Sean had mouthed excuses. Poppy didn't appreciate him. He'd gotten married too young. He deserved a life.

Yeah, well Poppy had deserved a husband and a father to her four kids. After his discharge, Finn had tracked her down here to Twin Elks to offer her that. Already halfway in love with Ben, Poppy had turned him down. It was probably for the best. They hadn't loved each other.

Those years after Sean's death had been hell for Poppy. He'd been deployed and hadn't known how bad it had gotten until he had returned and seen the hovel Poppy had been living in. Mom had known and done very little.

Sean had taken the best part of Mom when he'd died.

Poppy smiled and nudged him. "Hey! Don't look so grim. It all turned out well in the end."

"If you can call it that." He pulled a face. "I mean, if you're sure you want to marry that dead beat cop."

"Hey!" She giggled and nudged him harder. "I'm so sure I want to marry that dead beat cop."

Ben was a good guy, and Finn liked him a lot.

"He tells me you turned him down." Poppy cocked her head and watched him.

Finn was grateful for the offer. "Yeah. I don't know if being a cop is for me, Poppy. I didn't want to take the job and then let him down."

Also putting a gun into the hand of a man who couldn't trust himself not to trip into his darkest place was a truly horrible idea.

"If you're sure." She gave him a searching look. "Ben needs someone he can count on."

"More trouble?"

Poppy shrugged. "Just some newcomers getting mouthy and feisty."

"Nothing Ben can't handle." Finn was sure of that.

"It seems to be happening a lot more often lately." Poppy wrinkled her nose. "I worry about him."

"I know you do." It didn't matter what he said, Poppy would still worry, but Finn tried anyway. "Ben can handle himself."

"I know, and worrying comes with the territory of marrying a cop." Sighing, she moved deeper into the workshop and trailed her fingers over the chaise. "I love this piece."

"Yeah. It's a treasure. The house is full of them."

Poppy crouched and looked at the elaborately turned legs. "Have you given any more thought to the other offer?"

He'd done nothing but chew his CO's offer over. Finn had asked for more time. He'd gotten out because he couldn't stand the killing anymore. No matter who you killed, or how justifiable the brass made it sound, blood stained after a while. It stained your spirit. "I'm still thinking about it."

"Not that it should influence your decision, but I like having you here." Poppy gave him a sweet smile. "I would like to keep you here."

He smiled back. "I like being here."

It was more than the town. It was the sense of family he had there. Poppy, the kids, Horace and now, Ben and his mother, Dot, were all part of the new family he'd stumbled into.

Mom kept her distance because she'd never been able to forgive Poppy for marrying Sean. According to Mom, Poppy had tricked Sean into marrying her, and that justified all Sean's assholery from there on.

Being here also enabled him to run interference. He loved Mom, but her grief had consumed her. She clung to Ryan and Sean as the last remnants of Sean senior. Mom used to ignore the twins completely, until Poppy took her on about it. She'd gotten better, but she still tried to keep Sean alive through his sons.

Poppy wandered about the workshop, and Finn got back to work.

"Finn?"

Here it came. The real reason Poppy had come out here. "Yup."

"What's going on with you and Claire?" Poppy felt like she owed Horace. She was one hundred percent on his side.

So was Finn, but there was more to Claire than Horace, Poppy, or any of the rest of them even suspected. "Nothing's going on with Claire."

"Oh, come on!" Poppy snorted and folded her arms. "I saw you with her this morning. The way you two looked at each other."

He shrugged and kept it light. "She's an attractive younger woman in a town where the average age is sixty-seven."

"Oh!" Poppy blushed bright red. "I didn't think of you…you know."

"And nor should you." He gave her a mock severe look. "Not that there is any *you know* going on with Claire. I just get the feeling she's not what we all think she is."

"You mean here to grab as much of Horace's money as she can?" Poppy showed her sharp teeth sometimes. She had them, especially in defense of someone she loved, and Poppy loved Horace.

"I think there is always more than one side to any story." Like Horace as he did, Finn wasn't going to hand him a free pass here. "The relationship between her and Horace is complicated. I think it gets to her more than she lets on." Plus, he'd seen the way the town treated Claire for himself. "I think a lot of stuff gets to her more than she lets on."

"And you know all this after two days?" Poppy crossed her arms.

She had a point. "It's a feeling I get. Also, when she thinks nobody is looking, she drops that mask, and there's a lot of hurt there."

"Damn." Poppy sighed. "I wish you hadn't said that. I really want to dislike her. For Horace." She shook her head. "But the kids like her, and I saw her with Ryan this morning."

Finn had seen the same thing. "And Horace is her father. It's not unusual for her to think of all of this as hers."

"Until I got in her way." Poppy grimaced. "You know she wants to pull this house down and sell it to developers." With a breath, she gathered more steam. "She wants to take all Horace's money and shove him in a retirement home."

Yeah, Claire hadn't exactly made her road here easy. "I know what she says she wants." Finn picked his next words carefully, because he loved Poppy, and he would always be on her side. "But I'm not sure even she knows what she really wants."

"Meaning?" Poppy simmered down a bit, but she still looked wary.

"Meaning this town has a lot of say about everyone and everything." He picked up his sandpaper. There wasn't a lot more he could say. "In my experience, people often have a reason for being the way they are. I'm giving Claire a chance to tell me hers."

CHAPTER
Six

CLAIRE STAYED in her room and tried to pretend she wasn't hiding out.

Shortly after breakfast, Finn crossed the lawn to the workshops behind the carriage house.

Claire sat in her window seat and pretended to read a book. Mostly she watched Finn working with an old man who must be Hank Styles.

It was only once Horace had limped into the carriage house that Claire ventured downstairs again.

The mess from breakfast remained in the kitchen. Done with trying to read, she put the dishes in the dishwasher and turned it on. Then she wiped down the range, the counters, and the table. Having come that far, she tidied the rest of the kitchen.

In the laundry, she found a pile of clothes in the hamper, plus a load in the machine and one in the dryer. She really didn't hate doing laundry, so she put the dry load in the basket, transferred the wet to the dryer and added a new load to the machine.

With her basket of dry laundry, she sat down at the kitchen table to fold. There was something soothing about the repetitive activity. Growing up Mom had done no housework. She had always employed a housekeeper.

At college Claire had been shocked how unprepared she was for even the simplest domestic task. Her roommate had called her crazy, but Claire had liked laundry best of all.

As she was folding a boy's T-shirt that must belong to Ryan, the back door opened, and Poppy stepped inside.

Claire started, not knowing why but feeling guilty as hell. "I...this was in the dryer. I didn't think you'd mind."

"Mind." Poppy gaped. "Are you kidding me? It's like my favorite fantasy. I walk into the house, and the mess is cleared away, and somebody's doing my laundry."

"Okay." Claire picked up a cotton dress, folded it and added it to Brinn's pile.

Poppy put the kettle on the range. "Tea?"

"Yes, please."

While Poppy made tea, Claire carried on folding.

Bringing their tea to the table, Poppy sat opposite her and got folding with her.

Claire picked up a man's shirt that didn't look like it would fit Ben or Finn. "Do you do Horace's laundry?"

"Technically, I housekeep for him." Poppy folded a pair of socks together. "When I first got to Twin Elks, I needed somewhere to stay when my car broke down, and I didn't have enough money to put the children and me in a hotel. In exchange for living here rent free, I took care of him. I still do."

"Right." Tara had told her the rent-free part, but not the taking care of Horace in exchange.

Poppy added another pair of socks to the done pile. "It was only ever temporary. Until I found out what else I wanted to do."

"Temporary?" As far as she knew, Poppy was here to stay.

"Yes." Poppy wasn't being exactly warm, but neither was she using that polite, formal tone. "I want to do something with gardening. I love gardening."

"Were you responsible for tidying everything up out there?"

That must have been a ton of work, along with raising four children, caring for Horace and her upcoming wedding to Ben.

Poppy shrugged. "I had some help but yes."

They finished the laundry mostly in silence, and Poppy took the clothes upstairs. Claire dug an old coat out of the mudroom that had been here since before Poppy's time and took a walk outside.

She gravitated to the old rose garden. Another legacy of the first Horace to his young bride. Sometimes in Boston, she would dream of the rose garden. Not as it looked now, but in full bloom and bathed in sunlight.

Evidence of Poppy's efforts greeted her. The unruly bushes had all been trimmed down for winter, and the paths between them were clear of weeds and overgrown grass. She'd never seen those roses bloom like they did in her dream, but somewhere in this mausoleum she had seen old photos of that rose garden in bloom.

At some point Horace must have had all the old photographs removed, because she hadn't noticed any of them hanging in the house. Also, all the knickknacks and objets d'arts that used to decorate the house. Probably upstairs in the attic. It seemed a shame to tuck them away from people.

She took one of the paths through the rose garden. It must have taken serious effort to lay it out. Built in a series of concentric rings, and cut up into segments by the paths, each section housed a different color rose. Lavender used to grow beneath the roses, and beneath that a white ground cover she didn't know the name of. Poppy would probably know what it was called.

A crisp, golden fall day surrounded her as she walked through the rose garden. A sense of belonging settled over her, and she took a seat on one of the ornamental benches facing the sundial.

A woman called her name, and Claire turned. It hadn't sounded like Poppy.

"Claire."

She looked in the direction of the voice. It hadn't been the same one as the one before. This last voice sounded like a child.

Brinn and Ciara waved to her from the front gate. Still wearing their backpacks, they must have come from school.

Dragging his backpack behind him, Ryan waved a piece of paper at her. "I got your picture, Claire."

"Awesome." She stood and walked toward the children.

"Hi." Brinn bounded up to her as she rounded the side of the house. "You were in the rose garden."

"Yes." She took Ryan's backpack from him. "Do you play in there sometimes?"

"Sometimes." Brinn gave Ciara a guarded look. "We weren't allowed to until Finn helped Mom clean up all the branches and thorns."

The bushes all looked dead now, but Claire would love to see them in bloom. Except, if things went according to plan, she wouldn't be here in summer. None of them would. Not even those roses. She stamped on the pang of regret. If it came to a choice between Mom and the roses, she would have to go with Mom.

Ciara took her hand. "Did you used to play there as a little girl?"

"I think I might have." She had distant sense memory of bees buzzing and the heady perfume of roses. But that could also have been part of the dreams.

Ciara looked at Brinn and smirked. "I told you so."

"No, you didn't." Brinn jammed her hands on her hips. "Cecily told you so."

Claire went cold.

"We're not really supposed to say about Cecily." Ciara looked up at Claire. "But it's okay because she says you know her."

And Claire had the inescapable feeling that she did. The name rang so many bells, and not only because Ciara had mentioned her the other day on the porch. Why did the twins talk as if they knew her? Why did she feel as if Cecily's presence was real to her too?

She really wanted to get to the bottom of this Cecily thing. A trip to the attic it was then.

"Don't you want to see your picture?" Standing in the middle of the path, Ryan scowled at her.

"Of course, I do." Claire made sure he saw her roll her eyes. "But let's take it inside where I can look at it properly."

Ryan eyed her as if he might call her bluff and then nodded. "Okay, then. But you need to look because I drew it special for you."

"I'm looking forward to it."

Brinn took her other hand. "Why don't you like Horace?"

God! How was that for staggering honesty?

"Um." Claire had nothing to match it. "We don't always see things in the same way."

"Like Mom and Grannie Maura." Brinn nodded. "They fight. A. Lot."

"That's because Grannie Maura is always trying to tell Mom what to do," Ciara said. "And Mom doesn't like that."

"Not many people do." Claire had no anchor in this conversation. She was cast adrift.

The carriage house door opened, and Horace limped toward them. "Are there fairies in my garden?"

Brinn and Ciara dropped her hands and danced up to him.

As she had every other time Claire had seen the girls, Brinn spoke for Ciara, "Are you here to play? Can we have a picnic?"

"Well, now." Horace pretended to give their suggestion a lot of thought. "It is a nice day. And we won't have that many nice days before it gets too cold." He slapped his hands together. "So, yes, I think we should have a picnic."

Both girls danced around him. Brinn started a song about picnics and teddy bears.

Horace watched them with a broad grin on his face.

It was not an expression Claire was used to on him. Mom had said he really didn't take to children. Maybe he'd learned to like them in his old age. It felt like shoving a rusty door open to ask, but he had the answer to her question. "Horace?"

He turned and looked at her, one grizzled eyebrow raised.

"Did I play in the rose garden?" She gestured the rose garden. "When I was little, I mean."

"All the time." Horace jabbed his cane into the soft soil beside the front walkway. "You used to build houses out of rose petals and leaves under that and wait for fairies to come and live in them."

"Look, Daddy, a red one."

"That means it's special." Horace's voice. *"It's the house the queen lives in."*

A woman giggled. It sounded like the young woman who had called her, and the hair on Claire's nape rose. But she couldn't be sure if she had really heard it or it was part of her trip down memory lane. Like yesterday in the nursery, her memories were so real to her.

Thinking about yesterday in the nursery brought another question Horace had the answer to. "Did you read to me?"

He stopped but didn't turn. "Yes. I did. *Good Night Moon*. You could recite it by heart and would always stop me when I tried to skip bits."

"Come on, Horace." Brinn waved at him imperiously. "We have a picnic to plan?"

"Horace?" She had one more question.

"Yup."

"Who is Cecily?"

Turning Horace's face gave nothing away, but there was a pleased gleam in his eyes. "I tell you what. When you want to hear about Cecily, we'll sit in the library, and I'll tell you all about what being a Winters means."

"Who's that?" Brinn pointed to the front porch.

A man dressed in a flashy suit and loafers, his hair slicked back, stood on the front porch.

Poppy stood beside him with a frown on her face. The look she gave Claire took them back to before their cease fire over laundry. "He's here for you."

"Is he your friend?" Ryan glanced up at her.

Brinn whispered, "Mom looks mad."

"Why don't you three go inside, and I can find out." Claire got the nasty feeling this wasn't a conversation the children should hear.

They ran ahead of her into the house.

"What the hell is this about?" Horace canted from side to side on his sore hip as he increased his pace.

"Claire Mathews?" The stranger approached her with his hand out. "I'm Travis Carlysle from Front Range Realty."

Damn! Damn! Damn! She had called him, once. Now Claire was afraid she knew exactly what this was about. She tried to gather all the reasons why this was for the best. Mom needed this money to stay in her facility, and with Claire out of a job that wasn't going to happen without an injection of cash,

"Front Range Realty?" Horace stiffened and scowled at Travis. "Then you must be lost."

Travis's bright white smile didn't falter in his fresh, enthusiastic face. "You must be Mr. Winters. Claire has told me so much about you."

No, she hadn't. Only that Horace was the current owner.

"I'll bet she has." Horace turned his scowl on her. "This is still my house, and if he sets foot in it, I'll get the police chief to remove him."

"There's no need to bother the police." Travis chuckled and gave Claire a conspiratorial wink.

"Too late." Poppy glared at Travis. "The police chief is already on his way."

Claire needed to take control of this situation before things got ugly. "I'm not really sure what you're doing here, Travis."

"I was in the area." He rubbed his pale, chubby hands together. "And I thought I'd check out the house. You know, start the ball rolling."

He either had the thickest skin or the thickest skull. Neither of which were doing Claire any favors right now. She motioned for him to follow her off the porch. "May I speak with you?"

Their silent, glowering audience of Poppy and Horace stayed on the porch.

Claire fought down an attack of nervous giggles. "You shouldn't have come here without letting me know first," she said to Travis.

"Yes, and normally I wouldn't." Travis stepped in and lowered his voice so only she could hear. "But I have a very motivated buyer." He gave her a weighted stare. "Very motivated."

"But the property isn't on the market." And by the look on Horace's face wouldn't be in the immediate future. Travis had made a difficult task near impossible.

Travis chuckled and winked. "Well, I know that, but we often find in my business that with the right incentive, a property can become active immediately."

"Not in this case." Claire had to shut him down and get rid of him. "And you made a mistake in coming here."

"Oh." Travis's face dropped. "Are you saying I can't survey the property?"

"That's exactly what I'm saying." She gestured for him to precede her. "And I think you should go now."

"But—"

"Now."

For a moment, his smile faltered, and then it flashed back again. "Here's my card." He palmed it like a sleight of hand magician and handed it to her. "Let's get together soon. There's a lot of interest in this little town of yours right now."

Horace's cane clicked on the path behind her, and Claire braced for it.

"This is still my house." Horace stopped beside her. "And you need to remember that before you go assuming I'll give it to you."

She'd assumed nothing, which was why she was in Twin Elks. "I'm well aware of that." Her long-time resentment simmered and spat to life. "My mother lost years of her life to you and this damn house, and now it can give her back what it owes her."

"I owe Naomi nothing." Horace met her glare with his. "She chose to leave here, and yet I supported you and her for all these years."

"Chose?" Claire couldn't believe what she was hearing. "She gave up all her choices the day she married you. She escaped from this place and ran for her life."

Horace gaped at her. "What?"

"You know, Horace, that look of surprise is so good you might even have convinced me." Claire pressed her point home. "And if I didn't know the truth, I would believe you. But I do know the truth."

She let that sink in.

Horace blinked at her and then frowned. "What is it you think you know, Claire?"

"I know everything." All the ways he had made her mother's life miserable. All the ways in which her mother had been terrorized and trapped in that awful house with that man. "And I'm not going to stand by and let you give it all away."

"You're talking about Poppy," he said.

"Yes, I'm talking about your precious Poppy." Poppy must have gone inside, because the porch was empty. "And if you think I'm going to let her have this house, you're wrong."

"She doesn't want this house." Horace grimaced. "Because I already offered to sell it to her for forty dollars and she said no."

He sneered and turned away. "What other truths do you think you might have gotten wrong?"

———

Finn sanded the edges of the fine scroll work he'd spent the last hour cutting. Damp and age had eaten away a lot of the decorative trim around the gazebo. Under Hank's grumpy but skilled tutelage, Finn had undertaken repairing it for Poppy's wedding.

From here he could see the front of the house and something was going down.

He didn't like the look of the blowup between Claire and Horace. God those two took large strips off each other, both so hurt they couldn't see the damage they inflicted.

Someone should step in and help them really see each other. Not him though. With the wedding only a few days away, he had to get this gazebo done in time for Poppy to string flowers and bows all over it.

Now Claire whirled and stormed away from Horace.

She caught sight of him and stopped. Clearly, she'd made up her mind to head his way, because that's what she did next.

Even from this distance her anger was palpable. And something else. A trace of uncertainty.

Finn had no idea what drew him to this prickly, difficult woman. Sure, she was good looking, and he was a total sucker for a long-legged blonde, but it was more than that. Claire had an edge of fragility to her, like all you had to do was break the ice to find the gentle beneath.

"I need to ask you something." She stomped up the three steps to the gazebo.

Finn took his time answering. She also had a way of bossing people around that he was less attracted to. He checked the fit of his decorative piece before answering, "What do you need to know?"

Claire had her arms folded and her toe *tap-tap-tapping* away at the floor.

Finn hid his smile. Like he said, tightly wound and missing a decent poker face.

"It's about Poppy?"

Finn put his work aside and gave her his attention.

"Horace told me something and I don't believe it."

Now he got an inkling as to what all this morning's excitement had been about. "The forty-dollar story?"

"You know?"

"Sure. Poppy talked to me about it."

Claire chewed that over and looked sour about it. "She really turned down this house when she could have bought it for forty dollars?"

"Yep." He wanted to tug her closer to him and comfort her. She might rip his throat out if he tried. "Poppy refused to take advantage of Horace."

"When did this happen?"

"Just after your last visit."

Comprehension dawned on her face. "We had a fight then too."

"You and Horace do a lot of that."

She glared at him. "I have my reasons."

"He would probably say the same." Finn knew she didn't like what he was saying, but lying to her wasn't going to help either her or Horace.

With a growl, she turned her back on him and stared at the river. "I find it hard to believe that a woman with four children, who was struggling to support herself, would turn down an opportunity like that."

"That's because you're looking for reasons not to like Poppy." He kept his tone gentle, but her shoulders stiffened. "You think she's out to steal what's yours, so you keep her at a distance." She looked so desperately alone he ached for her. She needed reminding that she didn't have to be so solitary, and Finn put his hands on her shoulders. "The irony is that if you got to know Poppy the story would make a lot of sense to you."

"I'm sure." Her voice grew bitter and brittle. "I'm sure I would love Poppy. Everybody loves sweet little Poppy."

Finn wouldn't let her be a bitch about Poppy. "Because she's special, and she has a heart of gold that's a rare find in this world."

Claire snorted and edged her shoulders out of his grasp. "Is that why you teased her about marrying Ben?" She turned with eyes glinting dangerously. "Are you secretly in love with her?"

"Nope." He wouldn't allow her to shove him away and hurt herself more in the process. "I tease Poppy about marrying me because I asked her to marry me when I first came to Twin Elks. I had some misguided notion that I needed to take care of her and my brother's kids. Make up for the rough deal my family had handed her."

"How noble of you." Claire backed away from him.

"Not really." Finn closed the distance. She could put up her barriers with everyone else, but he wanted beneath them. "It seemed like the best solution for everyone. I love Poppy, but I'm not in love with her. She's kind, sweet, capable, and clever, and I would have done my best to make her happy."

"And yourself? What was in it for you?" Her back hit a pillar and she stopped.

Finn kept coming. "I wanted to make things right, and I wasn't going to get married anyway."

"Why not?" Her breathing hitched as he drew closer. She didn't like it, but she liked having him close.

Finn leaned in. By sheer willpower he stopped a breath away from her. The last thing Claire needed right now was some horny asshole hitting on her. "I'm not the marrying kind."

Claire slid out from under his arm. "God, that's so predictable. Another man who doesn't want to be tied down."

"Some of us have good reason for that." This part of his story he'd have to get closer to her to share. "And some of us know ourselves well enough to know we're not husband and father material."

She eyed him suspiciously. "Are you sure you're not in love with her?"

"I'm sure." He leaned against the pillar and stopped himself from closing the gap. "And it's good thing she said no, because I'm no woman's happily ever after."

CHAPTER
Seven

TARA CALLED THE NEXT MORNING. "Claire, babe," she said. "Get yourself together; we're getting the hell out of this shithole for the day."

She hung up before Claire could answer. Claire lay in bed for a while staring at the intricately pressed ceiling. She didn't really want to get herself together Tara-style. Getting up and pulling on jeans and a casual shirt could get to be a habit.

God, her mother would be horrified. Claire should be horrified, but she wasn't.

A knock on her door got her out of bed. She tossed her robe on and prayed it wasn't Horace ready for another battle.

Ryan stood on the other side with a piece of paper in his hand. "You didn't look at your drawing yesterday."

"You're right." After her fight with Horace, she'd retreated to her room and stayed there until the house fell quiet. Her intention had been to sneak down later and make herself something to eat, but she'd fallen asleep. "I'm really sorry."

"You can look now." Ryan thrust it at her.

Claire tried her best, but she couldn't make sense of the colorful blobs on the page.

Ryan stared up at her. "Do you like it?"

"I love it." Claire told him. "I'm going to keep it here in my room where I can look at it every day."

"Good." Ryan nodded and went on his toes and pointed. "It's you and me. And over here are Brinn and Ciara." She could make out a head on one of the blobs. "This is Mom and Ben, and Uncle Finn and Horace. And we all live here together."

"It's a lovely picture, Ryan." In a perfect world it might even be possible, but they didn't live in a perfect world. "I love it."

"Okay." Ryan pointed over his shoulder. "Well, I got to go now and eat, and then I need to go to school."

"Have the best day."

Ryan grinned at her over his shoulder. "You too."

She got into the shower. After yesterday with Travis it seemed best to stay away from the kitchen over breakfast. The family chattered and clanged downstairs as they got their day started. Growing up an only child she had never been surrounded by this much activity. It made you aware you weren't alone.

Not that she minded being alone. She spent most of her life alone. She had her job, a few friends and she'd had Greg, but she wasn't a social butterfly. Especially lately when Mom's care had cut into her free time and her discretionary budget.

Putting her makeup on felt a bit odd. Knowing she would spend the day with Tara, she did a full face and even straightened her hair. She added a pair of heels to her skinny black pants and a button-up shirt with a trench.

When she was ready, she went downstairs for a cup of coffee.

Poppy entered the kitchen from outside at the same time and they stopped and stared at each other.

"Wow." Poppy took in her outfit. "You look amazing. If I wore that, I'd look like a hippie version of Columbo."

Helping herself to coffee, Claire had to laugh. "No, you wouldn't, but given your children I wouldn't go with the pale blue trench."

"You have a point." Poppy helped herself to coffee and added a hefty dollop of creamer.

"I didn't invite Travis here yesterday." Claire had no idea why she blurted that out, but it might have something to do with the forty-dollar story Horace had told her yesterday. As crazy as the story was, it fit Poppy more than the gold-digger narrative.

Poppy stopped and looked at her over her coffee cup. "But you did call him?"

"Yes." She didn't like explaining herself, but whether she agreed with it or not, Poppy lived here, and this would affect her. "It was more for information than anything else."

"Okay." Poppy nodded. "For the record I think it would be sad to sell this house. It's a special place."

"There are...circumstances." She didn't want to betray Mom. "Things I can't really speak about."

"That's what Finn says." Poppy sipped her coffee. "If you ever do think you can speak about those circumstances, I know we'd all like to hear them."

"Okay."

They sipped their coffee in silence, but it wasn't awkward. It wasn't exactly comfortable or companionable either. More like neutral.

That all changed when Tara cat-walked through the kitchen door. If she'd had a tail, she would be twitching it at the sight of Poppy.

"Poppy." Tara sneered and turned to Claire and then clapped. "Now, there's my girl. I was starting to worry I would lose you to the mom-jean brigade."

Poppy flipped through a recipe book, ruining all Tara's malice.

"Let's get going." Claire didn't want to sit through Tara sharpening her claws on Poppy again. Poppy didn't deserve what Tara dished out.

She hustled Tara out the front door as fast as she could.

Tara had tossed Ben away long before Poppy had arrived on

the scene. Claire knew for a fact that she'd had more affairs while Ben was on active duty than even Twin Elks gossiped about. Why Tara should resent the other woman escaped her.

Finn was on the porch, plaid shirt sleeves pushed up as he crouched and nailed a lose board down.

Tara stopped close to him, forcing him to look up the length of her legs. "Hey, Finn."

"Tara." He barely spared her a glance. Looking past her, his gaze locked on Claire. Something flickered through his gaze that she didn't catch. "You look…nice."

"Don't hold back there, Finn." Tara shifted and cut her off from Finn's eye line.

"I said she looks nice." Finn shrugged.

"I'm taking my girl out for the day, for a bit of grown up fun." Tara made it sound vaguely dirty. "Want to join us?"

"Nope." Finn dropped his head to his work again. "Have fun."

Was there a little extra swing in Tara's sashay as she made her way to her car?

Not that Claire blamed her. Finn really was all that. She turned and caught him looking at her. He gave his head a brief shake and went back to his work.

"Babe," Tara giggled as Claire climbed in and shut the car door. "That Finn Williams does not like you."

"What?" Finn liked her just fine. At least she thought he did. "Why do you say that?"

"Jesus." Tara pulled into the street with a screech of tires. "You'd think he could find something nice to say about how you looked. Even if he had to lie."

She didn't think Finn cared what she wore too much, and Claire gave a noncommittal hum in response. She was sure, however, that he did not like Tara. "What's the plan for today?"

"Shopping!" Tara trilled and fluttered a hand through the air. "Nordstrom's has got a huge sale on, and they're making way for their new line. We have to check it out. I hear they've got a new range of Jimmy's in."

Claire smiled and tried to look enthusiastic, but she wouldn't be buying Jimmy Choos anytime soon. Not when most of her salary went to keep Mom comfortable.

Tara babbled on about a new sushi place for lunch and then cocktails at some new bar, which had opened down from the mall. It sounded like a really long day ahead of her.

They had a two-hour drive to Denver, so Claire sunk into her seat and watched the passing scenery. It really was very pretty with its bright orange rock faces pushing up between the scrub brush. In summer it turned a rich, vibrant green and hummed with insect and animal life.

Fortunately, conversation with Tara didn't require much more input than the occasional murmur or grunt.

The look on Finn's face when she'd left had been perilously close to disappointment. Like he was disappointed in her. Was that because she was going off with Tara or did it have something to do with Travis and the day before?

She could ask him. That was the good thing with Finn, he'd give her a straight answer.

"What do you think?" Tara paused.

Claire realized she hadn't been listened. "Sorry, I missed that."

"God, Claire." Tara rolled her eyes. "Have you gone country slow on me?"

"Not that I'm aware."

"I said I think Poppy's using Ben because she wants a baby daddy." She snorted. "Jesus! Can you imagine foisting four kids on some man? All I can say is that bitch must suck dick like a champion."

Ick! Ben didn't look like Poppy's children were the slightest bit foisted on him. In fact, if she had just met them, she would have assumed they were Ben's children. "He's good with them."

"Of course, he is." Tara did her hand flutter thing. "Because that's Ben. He's an all-round nice guy."

"Yeah, he is." Claire had never had a problem with Ben. Like Finn he was a straight shooter and you always knew were you stood with him.

Tara made a growling noise. "When I think of that insipid woman getting all that Ben Crowe action, I want to smack something." She did. She slapped her steering wheel. "God, that man can fuck you into next week."

So much more information than Claire ever wanted to have about Ben. Then again, lucky Poppy to be getting some. Claire couldn't remember the last time she'd gotten herself some. Things with Greg had been stale for a while.

"So, speaking of sex." Tara tittered. "I met a guy."

"Yeah?" Again, with Tara and the guys. Claire had no idea how she did it.

"The sex is okay," Tara said. "But the black Amex is a definite plus."

A black Amex would make a lot of Claire's problems go away. She spoke her next thought out loud and immediately regretted it. "How much do you think Horace is worth?"

"Horace is fucking loaded." Tara gave her a hard stare. "Tell me you've got daddy's credit card with you today?"

"No." She really wished she'd kept her speculation to herself, because she hadn't been thinking about what she could get out of her father, but more of a general curiosity. "I don't take money from Horace."

Tara gaped at her. "Why the fuck not?"

"It doesn't seem right."

Tara was silent for a while, and then she said, "But everyone knows you come here and get money from him."

"It's not what everyone thinks." Claire stopped herself from saying more. Mom would hate to have her problem aired in Twin Elks. She needed the money for Mom's care and not even

Horace knew that. People liked to think the worst of her, and she didn't care enough to correct them.

If everyone else saw her as a venal opportunist, it probably meant Finn saw her that way. That disturbed her more than it should.

Tara looked like she would ask for more, so Claire changed direction. "Tell me about Mr. Black Amex."

"I can do better than that." Tara dug in her wallet. "I can introduce you to the most important part of Mr. Black Amex."

"Does he know you have that?"

"Of course, he does." Tara shrugged. "He doesn't care. Anyway, he has so much money he wouldn't notice little old me."

Claire spent the morning watching Tara spend money. And spend money. Even Mr. Black Amex had to be getting a headache at that point.

To be fair, Tara offered to spend some of it on her, but she declined. Firmly. If she wouldn't take money from Horace, she wasn't going to sponge off a man she'd never met. It did raise an interesting question, however.

Just how mercenary did people think she was?

By the time Tara had exhausted every high-end store she liked the look of, Claire's feet were more than happy to let her sink into the white leather banquette at an upscale cocktail bar Tara dragged her into.

They ordered from a waiter who almost tripped into Tara's cleavage. Tara had insisted on changing into a little black number before cocktails. Claire had resisted and now felt more like the bodyguard to her gorgeous client.

"Four o'clock." Tara made eyes at Claire. "Looking our way."

Claire very nearly groaned. Other than her sore feet, she was all peopled out. She didn't know how she had lived like that for most of her life. Of course, since Mom had been ill, her social life had slowed to a trickle.

Still, this used to be her jam.

Tara's four o'clock was a pair of suits, wearing identical too-cool-for-enthusiasm expressions, but not too cool for circling.

One of the things she liked about Finn was that he never played it cool.

She wanted to be sitting on the porch, drinking beer with Finn and trying not to get lost in those blue, blue eyes. Even if he had exhibited the unfortunate tendency to be a good guy when she had drunkenly tossed herself at him.

"Sit back, girl, and let Tara work her magic." Tara waggled her fingers. "And maybe you could undo a top button? Put on a little lipstick? Look like you're trying?"

That jerked Claire right back to the present. "What? No."

But Tara had already made eye contact.

Holy crap! Claire felt like she was watching a master class in…something. Seduction would be too subtle a word for the eye-humping Tara treated her four o'clock to. It was more like no-contact porn.

Part of her envied the confidence behind that look. It would be a nice gift to have in your arsenal.

With the predictable results.

"Hi." Suit number one leered at Tara. He indicated the shopping bags littering the floor beside the booth. "You ladies been shopping?"

Tara sucked in her bottom lip. "Maybe I'm still shopping."

His friend hung back and looked nearly as pained as Claire felt. Their gazes met for a moment and Claire had to look away before she laughed.

Meanwhile, Tara and suit one—who introduced himself as Gray—sat wedged together on the other side of the booth.

Claire made space for his friend.

Still looking a bit awkward, he slid in beside her. "Hi."

"Hi."

He cleared his throat. "So, do you come—" He looked horrified.

"Come here often?" His wry smile in response made Claire laugh.

Tara's throaty laugh drifted over. Gray had his arm over the back of the banquette and was about two inches from swinging a leg over.

Claire took pity on her guy. "I'm Claire."

She caught him with a mouthful of beer. He swallowed, choked a bit and came up coughing. "Andy."

"And to answer your original question, I've never been here before."

Andy mopped himself up with a cocktail napkin. "Me neither."

"I couldn't tell." Claire handed him her napkin to finish the job.

"Right." Andy laughed. "Because I'm super smooth."

Claire liked his self-deprecating humor. "So smooth."

"How's your drink?"

"Good." She'd barely taken a sip of her dirty martini.

Tara squealed and clapped her hand. "I love champagne."

Oh, dear.

Andy may or may not have sighed.

Not that it would have done any good. Gray was flagging down a waiter and still trying to maintain maximum eye contact with Tara.

Eyes gleaming, cheeks flushed, Tara looked to be having the best time.

"I'm not really…" Andy flushed and gestured the bar. "This is not really my thing. Gray and I work together, and he thought I should come with him."

There was something endearing about Andy. Claire thought she'd got the better suit. "Tara thought I needed to be rescued."

"How's that going?"

Claire sipped her drink. "Great."

Andy snort-laughed, and this time didn't apologize. His total lack of game made her relax.

The champagne arrived and was opened with as much flourish as Tara and Gray's combined showmanship could muster.

"Come on, Claire." Tara handed her a glass. "You love champagne."

Rather than cause more of a scene, Claire took the glass.

"Do you?" Andy asked quietly.

"What?"

"Love champagne?"

Claire gave that some thought. "I like champagne," she said. "At weddings. Maybe for a special occasion."

"Bathing in?" Andy dead panned.

Way to go Andy and that sly sense of humor hiding there. "Twice weekly."

The silence between them eased into comfortable. Andy loosened his tie. "So, why did you need cheering up?"

"Family stuff." She didn't want to bore Andy with her interminable family drama. "Why were you dragged here?"

"I'm getting divorced." Andy stared at his beer for a long moment. "Gray thought I should get right back on that horse again."

"It seems to be working for Gray," Claire said.

Gray had his jacket thrown over the back of the booth and his sleeve rolled up as he displayed a tattoo on his forearm.

Tara was being suitably appreciative.

"Yeah." Andy laughed. "He's a player. Maybe you should warn your friend."

"So is she." It looked like Claire would be driving home, and she ignored the champagne. "Maybe you should warn Gray."

"You know what we should do?" Tara whirled in her seat.

Claire's heart sunk.

"We should go dancing." Tara twined her arms sinuously above her head. She threw her head back. "I love dancing."

Gray looked like he'd found heaven. "Then we go dancing."

This time Andy did sigh. He turned to her. "I'm out."

"Oh, come on!" Tara leaned over the table toward him. "It'll be great."

Like a root canal with no happy gas. "Tara, I really think I should be getting home."

Tara's happy vibe disappeared in an instant, and a malicious look slid over her face.

Claire knew that face; it was Tara on the edge of a not getting her own way tantrum. "Hey! But you go. Why don't I take an Uber home?"

"Well, I'm not sure." Tara made a good show of protesting, but now that she'd gotten her way, peace was restored. "We girls need to stick together."

"I'll be fine." Claire managed to put the required amount of enthusiasm in her reply to bend Tara's rubber arm.

Andy kept his voice low. "How far away is home?"

"About a three hundred bucks worth." Three hundred bucks that she really didn't want to spend. Dammit, why hadn't she remembered this stuff about Tara?

"Let me give you a ride," Andy said. He indicated Gray. "We came in my car, and this gives me an easy out."

"Thanks." Claire searched for a polite way to decline. "But I can't ask you to do that."

"What if I promise to talk about my wife all the way there?" Andy said. "And my mother would never speak to me again if I let you get into a car with a stranger for two hours."

"You're not much more than a stranger." Claire had never tried to get an Uber that would take her that far. Maybe it wasn't even possible.

She dug her phone out. "It's two hours there, and then you still have to come back. I'll call an Uber."

"Then I have to go dancing." Andy looked appalled. Then his face cleared. "Hey! Why don't you do what my sisters do? They take a photo and text it to someone they trust. That way if they go missing someone knows who they left with."

Tara was already on her feet. "Are you sure you'll be fine, Claire?"

"She'll be great." Gray was taking no chances on losing out. He hustled Tara out of the booth and gathered all her packages. "Andy will make sure she gets home safe."

"Bye, babe. I'll call you." And Tara disappeared with a finger flutter and a giggle.

Andy stood up. "So, where's home."

"Twin Elks."

"Where?"

Not surprising. "A small town halfway between here and nowhere."

"You aren't going to lure me to some secluded spot and introduce me to your twelve banjo-playing brothers, are you?" Andy slung his coat over his arm.

"Nah." Claire waved her hand. "Only Leroy plays the banjo."

Andy chuckled and held his arms out. "Take your picture."

She snapped a shot of him and then stared at her contact list. The only person on there of any use to her was Horace. Everyone else was back in Boston.

Before she could overthink it, she tapped out a quick text and sent him the picture.

Andy led her to a midsize sedan, and she climbed in. "Can I, at least, pay for your gas."

"Nah." Andy started the car. "I'm going to charge it to Gray's expense account anyway."

It sounded like a good idea to her. "So, tell me about your wife."

"You know I was joking about that." He kept his eyes on the road as they slid through the city and on to the highway.

Outside of town the highway opened into a dark strip almost devoid of traffic. "I've never been out there before," Andy said.

"It's pretty. In the daylight." Andy's car was comfortable and clean, and he showed no imminent signs of being an axe murderer.

"I don't want to be divorced," Andy said.

"No?" Claire eased her shoes off. "Then why are you getting divorced?"

"Ella, that's my wife, it's her idea."

It turned out that Andy had a lot to say about his wife and his divorce, so the miles slid by. Mostly Andy was clueless about women, and she tried her best to point him in the right direction.

The car hum sent her into a daze, and she almost missed the offramp when it came up. "Here."

Andy jumped slightly. "Sorry, you surprised me."

She gave him directions to the house.

The porch light was on as he drew to a stop.

"I really can't thank you enough." Claire held her hand out. "It really was nice to meet you, and I'm glad you didn't turn weird on me."

"Likewise, Claire." He shook her hand and leaned forward. "That is one beautiful house."

"Yes, it is." In the soft lights from the porch, Winters House looked like something out of a fairytale.

Andy tensed. "Who's that?"

Finn emerged from the dark porch and headed their way.

"That's Finn." Claire opened her car door.

Andy looked nervous. "Is he your man?"

"No."

"Well, he doesn't look happy."

Poor Andy. Claire got out of his car. He was a nice guy who'd done a really nice thing.

Finn looked like someone nobody wanted to tangle with. Finn looked like he wanted to make someone else's night go very badly for them. Finn looked like the closest thing she had to a friend.

Andy drove off, and Finn glanced his way before all that seething intensity zeroed in on her. "Of all the fucking stupid, careless—"

"Hush, Finn." Claire gave in to her instinct. She closed the distance between them and pressed her face into Finn's chest. "Please don't be mad at me."

He stilled, and then his arms came around her. "I am mad at you."

"Can you yell at me later?" Claire wrapped her arms around his waist. He smelled like laundry detergent and warm skin. "I'm glad I'm home."

Finn huffed a laugh. "For future reference, if you ever want to get out of being yelled at by me, this works."

"Good." She pressed closer into his embrace and felt like she could stay there all night. Finn's presence cocooned her like a duvet on a blustery winter night. "Tara went dancing with some idiot called Gray, and Andy offered to bring me home."

"Andy?" Some of Finn's tension returned.

Claire waved in the direction of the highway, where Andy would be on his way home. "My ride. And a thoroughly nice guy whom I met tonight, and he drove me all this way home."

"Claire, baby." Finn's voice rumbled against her ear. "I can feel my mad coming back."

She pulled away enough to meet his gaze. "Let me help you out." She lowered her voice. "Of all the fucking stupid, dangerous ass things to do, getting into a car with a fucking stranger has to be one of the worst. What the fuck was I thinking?"

"That about covers it." Finn almost smiled. "I would probably have carried on for a bit longer. What were you thinking?"

"I was thinking how I didn't want to be there. I wanted to be here." She slid her hands to his chest and opened her palms over the solid slabs of muscle. "I was thinking I wished I had your number so I could have called you to come and get me."

"Claire." Her name was a soft rasp in the night. "How much did you drink?"

She recognized that tone, like she registered the accelerated beating of his heart against her palm and the growing heat in his gaze. "One drink. Not enough to not know what I'm doing."

"Good." He cupped the back of her head and tilted his head toward her.

Claire rose on her toes. She wanted him to kiss her like she wanted the next breath.

Finn brushed her mouth with his.

The touch spread through her like heated honey, and she waited for the next touch, not daring to breathe.

Finn came back for more and this time he lingered, parting her lips with his, drawing her bottom lip into the heated cavity of his mouth.

It felt so good that she whispered, "Finn," on a soft moan.

And playtime ended. Finn's fingers firmed in her hair, and he breached her lips with his tongue. There was nothing tentative about this kiss. It demanded from her and took all that he wanted.

His other hand pressed against the small of her back, pushing her against him. Full body contact that drove want into crave.

Her breasts melded into the strength of his chest. She needed more, and she rubbed against him.

"Damn." He came up for air. His eyes glittered down at her before he took her mouth again.

His hand slid down and cupped her ass, pushing her against his erection.

He was so hard it turned her knees to water. She wanted him, all of him and right now. She wanted him to drive her out of her mind.

"Finn?" Horace's voice came at them from the darkness. "Is Claire home?"

Light limned Horace as he stood in the door to the carriage house.

It didn't reach where she stood still wrapped around Finn.

Finn cleared his throat. "Yeah, Horace, she's safe. I was...er... telling her how worried about her we were."

Horace grunted. "That's not what we called it back in my day, son."

———

Finn turned from the door Claire had disappeared through and took a deep breath of the chill night air. That shouldn't have happened. He should have exercised more control. But the combination of being worried about her, the relief she was okay and Claire in his arms, beautiful, unguarded and sweet had stripped him down to base need.

Horace limped up the stairs, his threadbare bathrobe hanging open over a pair of striped pajamas. "She get home without any trouble?"

Finn nodded. Horace had brought Claire's text straight to him. They'd come up with and rejected several alternatives. "Some guy called Andy brought her all the way home."

"Nice guy."

"Yep." Finn couldn't consider the alternative without his blood coming to a boil. When he'd read that text, a primal urge to find her and protect her had taken him over. Seems his hair trigger extended to Claire now as well. It had taken twenty minutes of meditation following by a hard run through the dark streets to cool him down. "She's here and she's safe."

Horace gave him a long look. "Son?"

And Finn knew what was coming.

"Claire and I might not play nice with each other, and I sure as hell can't claim father of the year." Horace rubbed his hand over his gray stubble. "But that's my daughter, and even though she doesn't like that fact, it doesn't mean I want someone messing with her feelings."

"Understood. I won't mess with her."

Horace stared into the night. "See that you don't. She doesn't need another asshole making her cry."

CHAPTER
Eight

CLAIRE LAY in bed as the sun made the wooden floors glow like poured honey.

Horace had accused her of not knowing what she thought she knew. She'd certainly been wrong about Poppy, and trusting Tara had landed her in an uncomfortable situation. Thank God for Andy's kindness. She had already shot him a text to thank him again and knew he had arrived home safely.

The morning felt different somehow. Like the sun shone brighter, and the bed was softer. Pressing her fingers to her lips, she closed her eyes and relived the kiss.

Damn, she must have had kisses to equal it, but she couldn't think of one, and she knew for sure she'd never had one to beat it.

She tingled at the memory.

Too shaken to face him, Claire had slipped away while Finn talked to Horace. Finn had come upstairs shortly thereafter, stopped outside her bedroom for a few heart-stopping moments and then walked away. As the door to his room had shut, Claire couldn't decide if she was disappointed or relieved.

Someone knocked on her door.

"Yes." Claire struggled into a sitting position. Maybe Finn

had decided to take up where they'd left off. An all-over flush spread across her skin. If he kissed like that...

Poppy peeked around the door. "Hi. I brought you a cup of coffee. Finn said you got in late last night."

"Thank you." She'd been nothing but rude and antagonistic to that woman, and there she was bringing her coffee in bed. And it's not like Poppy didn't have her hands full getting her children out of the house. "You really shouldn't have bothered. You have enough to do."

"Ben has them all under control." Smiling, Poppy carried a coffee cup to her. "He's pretending Finn is helping, but he's probably only getting them all revved up."

Claire accepted the cup and hoped she hadn't blushed at the mention of Finn. "Thank you. I appreciate it."

"You're welcome." Poppy looked down at her feet and up again. "We were all worried when we got your text last night."

Funny thing Poppy didn't mention Tara. Claire knew, for sure, had it been the other way around, the conversation with Tara would have started with accusations hurled at Poppy. As Poppy didn't say it, Claire got there for her. "I should have known better than to go off with Tara like that."

Poppy shrugged. "Actually." She clasped her hands in front of her. "I had an ulterior motive for the coffee." She motioned the window seat. "May I?"

"Sure." A woman who brought you coffee exactly as you liked deserved a hearing, at the very least. Especially one whom you had maligned.

Poppy placed one hand on top of the other in her lap. "You and I got started on the wrong foot."

Caught mid-sip, Claire had to swallow fast or risk choking. The hot coffee scalded her throat, and she could only nod.

"The thing is, Claire, I don't know what is going on with you and Horace, but he was kind to me at a time when I really needed someone." Poppy cleared her throat. "I owe him more than I can ever repay. And I guess that makes me protective of him."

The relationship between Poppy and Horace had been the biggest reason she'd felt like Poppy would usurp her inheritance. "I know you turned the house down." Poppy deserved her honesty. "I'm not sure I'd have been able to walk away from a forty-dollar house."

"I gave it a lot of thought." Poppy laughed.

When she laughed, her eyes crinkled up, and she tossed her head up a bit. Her smile took over her entire face, and it shifted her from pretty to lovely. Tara would never be able to compete with her. Poppy's beauty came from her embracing soul. Her physical appearance only added to her appeal.

"Anyway." Poppy refolded her hands. "I can understand why you thought I might be here to take what is yours."

"I don't believe that anymore." Claire sipped her coffee to loosen her dry tongue. That kind of honesty didn't happen a lot in her life. "I know you're not part of the fight over the house between Horace and me."

Poppy frowned and stared out the window. "I do love this house, though." She looked at Claire. "I can't tell you what to do with it, but I hope you'll consider hanging on to it."

"I'm not sure I can." For so many reasons, and none she wanted to share. If she could share, they might even understand why. The house carried so many bad stories for Mom, and besides she needed the money. The last thing Mom wanted was for Horace to know about her Alzheimer's. "But like you said, Horace and I need to sort that out between us."

Poppy sighed. "I really hope you two can find a middle ground."

"Me too." She meant it as well, and that struck her momentarily dumb. Watching Horace with Poppy and her children made Claire crave something like that. But how could she trust someone who had hurt Mom like that? Unless, the truths she held as so absolute had another side she needed to hear. "I came here to get rid of you, and now I need to revise my plan."

Poppy laughed and wiped her brow. "Whew!" Then she grew serious again. "Listen, I don't expect you to want to be my friend or anything, but if we could declare a ceasefire and try to get along, it would make things easier for everyone in the house."

"Yes." Until Poppy had said it, Claire hadn't really understood how much she didn't want to dislike Poppy anymore. Poppy was kind and sweet and nothing like Tara described her. "I would very much like not to circle each other anymore. Maybe we could work on the friend thing. I mean, I won't be here for that long, but I'd like to leave knowing there were no hard feelings behind me."

"Good." Poppy flushed and stood. "I'm glad." She made a stunted gesture toward the door. "I should go and rescue Ben from Finn and the children."

"Okay." Claire smiled at her. A genuine smile that came from the heart. A weight had lifted off her chest. It brought her back to the Horace accusation. "Poppy?"

"Yes." Poppy turned in the open doorway.

"Do you know if the house has any storage? I mean, like stuff from the past."

"God, yes." Poppy rolled her eyes. "When we first came here, we had to move a lot of stuff to the attic. There were already a bunch of old furniture and chests up there."

Energized, Claire climbed out of bed. "Thanks."

As the door shut behind Poppy, she headed into her bathroom. If Horace wanted her to get in touch with her heritage, she would start with the attic.

———

Poppy hadn't been exaggerating when she said the attic was full of stuff. Running the entire length and width of the house, with only one tiny window at the east and west ends, the attic reminded Claire of every horror movie she'd ever seen.

It got marginally better when Claire found a light switch and snapped it on. Only marginally because now the space was lit by four bare light bulbs dangling from their electric cords.

God, she hoped there weren't any rats up there.

"Ugh." She stumbled through a spiderweb and spent five minutes jerking around as she got it off her. She didn't want to think about where the web's spinner was lurking. Already she swore she could feel little legs walking all over her.

Taller pieces of furniture had been covered in dust cloths and loomed at the east end of the attic. Claire peeked under a couple of cloths. She should tell Finn that he had a whole crap ton more old furniture to love back to life.

She ran her fingers over the inlay on a claw-footed chess table. The pieces lay in two small drawers fitted into opposite sides of the table.

Claire pulled it into better light. The table would be beautiful in the front parlor, in the alcove closest to the window where the morning light would catch it.

Maybe Finn wouldn't mind carrying it down there. It was a shame to leave something so lovely in the dark and dust.

A gorgeous wingback caught her eye. The upholstery was torn and faded, but that wouldn't be much of a fix. A neutral raw linen would give it a slightly more contemporary feel without taking away from any of its original beauty. Also, it would be perfect in front of the parlor fire.

Struggling a bit, she finally tugged open a wardrobe door.

"Shit!" She had opened Ali Baba's cave. Claire was almost too scared to touch all the beautiful dresses hanging inside. She hoped the mixed smells of mothballs and cedar meant the dresses weren't too badly damaged.

Pushing the door wider with her shoulder, she got closer.

The dresses weren't all the same size or period. The old photographs stacked on tables and dressers downstairs had all sorts of women in them, and it would be interesting to see if any of the dresses belonged to the women in those pictures. Also, those pictures should be hung.

She took out a high-necked sky-blue gown with a bustle. The lace at the neck had yellowed with age, but the silk held a lot of its vibrancy. Whoever had worn it had had a tiny waist and was a good deal shorter than Claire.

The dresses had been worn by women who'd conducted their daily lives in the house. In those dresses they'd laughed, cried, loved, and lived.

She flipped through a few more gowns and stopped at one carefully wrapped in muslin. Not wanting to destroy anything, she unwrapped the dress slowly.

An ivory silk dress and veil came out of the wrapping. "Oh, my." Claire traced the beautiful lace and beadwork of the off the shoulder bodice. So much time and effort had gone into the making of the dress. She could almost span the waist with her hand. From there full skirts flared.

Claire lifted it off the dusty floor and hung it on the outside of the wardrobe. She'd never seen anything as lovely. A matching veil lay over the dress.

She wanted to know who had worn the fairytale beautiful gown, and she dearly wished whoever had worn it had gotten her storybook ending.

Perhaps the woman had been related to her. There was a high probability of that, considering where she'd found the dress.

A faint whiff of jasmine teased her, and she closed her eyes. An image rose in her mind, startlingly clear in its detail. A young woman, not much more than a girl, and she was smiling, her delicate features awash with joy.

Dark, glossy hair had been twisted into an intricate hairstyle on which rested a sparkling tiara. Her veil poured down her shoulders and spread out behind her like a gossamer web.

She had been so happy. Claire was certain of it. The girl looked at her and laughed. Startled, Claire opened her eyes.

The woman was much smaller than her, more like Poppy's size, but Claire knew her from the portrait over the mantle in the parlor, and from the stiffly formal couples she'd seen in the old photos.

"Cecily?"

"*Yes,*" a woman whispered, so soft she might not have heard it.

Claire swung around. "Hello?"

Nothing but the dark, dusty cellar.

More than a bit creeped out, Claire rewrapped the dress and returned it to the wardrobe. Still, the other closed trunks and pieces of furniture called to her, and she picked up the little chess table before she left.

She carried the chess table down to the first floor and took a rest. It might not have been large, but it was built solid.

"What you got there?" Finn appeared in his bedroom doorway.

Claire's heart missed a beat.

The knowledge of their kiss crept into her bloodstream and started a slow burn.

When Claire's gaze made its way up his long jean-clad legs, over his white T-shirt and open flannel shirt, and finally found his eyes, she read the answering heat there.

"Claire?"

"It's a table," she said, wanting to beg him to drag her back into his room and give her more of what she'd only tasted the night before.

Finn walked over in his easy stroll. How could he be so sexy just walking? He crouched to look at the table. Denim stretched over his thighs.

Powerful thighs. Hard thighs.

"Aren't you a beautiful girl?" His big hands stroked the inlay and down the table legs. "You found her in the attic?"

"Yeah. There's so much cool stuff up there." She was having

trouble getting her head back to the moment. "I thought she'd look good in the alcove next to the window in the parlor."

Finn nodded. "I think you're right. Want me to carry her downstairs?"

No, she wanted him to kiss her again. Wanted him to grab hold of her and take them to the next logical step. "Sure."

God, if she could channel her inner Tara, she wouldn't be standing there with her hormones on overheat as he lifted the table with one hand.

While her inner Tara filed her nails, Finn trotted down the stairs with the table.

And what the hell? One night ago, he'd kissed her as if he wanted to possess her mind, body, and soul. He'd given her a look as if he wanted to set her panties on fire.

Then he'd walked away.

CHAPTER
Nine

FINN NEEDED SOME AIR. He put the beautiful chess table down in the spot Claire wanted it and took himself outside the house. More bad dreams had chased him awake last night. The equilibrium he needed hung outside his grasp.

A crisp fall day stayed warm under an arcing blue sky.

His old CO had called early this morning, looking for an answer. Finn didn't have an answer for him, and time wasn't providing any clarity either.

As the days went on, in fact, his thinking grew more muddled. Having Claire around was providing the wrong sort of distraction. He needed to call his therapist, or even talk to Ben. Ben had been through this. He knew the continued struggle. Still, Finn hadn't made either approach because a part of him was tired of dealing with this, tired of feeling broken. Making that call would be tantamount to an admission of failure, and he wanted to feel whole again.

This was the biggest problem with his ongoing fascination with Claire. He had nothing to offer her but a broken-down wreck with serious fucking PTSD. And they were not talking only nightmares and the shakes, but full on flashbacks, trips into his dark side.

"Hey, Finn." Dot waved from her front yard. Her massive puppy gave him a friendly bark. That thing would grow to be the size of a small pony. "Actually, I wanted to talk to you."

It was impossible not to like Dot. She had a thing for printed sweatshirts and today's read *Mother of the Groom*. "I'm all yours."

"Oh, you." Dot smacked his shoulder, which made her flyaway curls bounce. "Don't flirt with someone my age. I'm not sure my heart can stand it."

As Ben's mother, Dot sat at the center of Twin Elks, and nothing much got past her. There also wasn't a pie she didn't have her finger in. Like Ben, she had adopted Poppy's children as her family.

"How are the wedding plans going?" Dot jerked her thumb at Winters House.

Finn couldn't stop his smile. "Did Ben tell you to back off?"

"Yes." Dot's face fell. "It's my oldest son getting married, to the right girl this time, and I got sidelined."

"To be honest, I'm not sure about the other arrangements, but I finished the gazebo last night."

Dot clapped and did a little shuffle step. "That is going to be so pretty." She frowned. "I wonder how Poppy's planning to decorate it?" Growling, she punched the air. "That son of mine is so stubborn."

Finn took pity on her. "If I wanted to know what was going on, and I couldn't come right out and ask, I'd check in with Kelly. The maid of honor is neck deep in everything."

"I love you, Finn." Dot planted a smacking kiss on his cheek and followed that with a wink. "And of course, you will let me know if any information should happen to drop into your lap."

He wouldn't be able to do otherwise. Smiling, he said goodbye to Dot and got on with his walk. The houses were on larger lots in this part of town and built with distance between them.

From the porch of a seventies style bungalow Peg waved to

him. Her head bobbed as she watered the phalanx of yellow and orange flowers hanging in pots from the roof.

"You still here?" she yelled.

Finn laughed at the greeting she always gave him. "You can't get rid of me that easily."

"If you're going to hang around here, you should turn your mind to marrying." Peg brandished her copper watering can at him. "Before we have cat fights in the street."

"But Peg." He clasped his hands to his heart. "You've already turned me down and there's nobody else like you."

"You're too old for me." Peg snorted. "Did I tell you Donna is recently divorced?"

"Bye, Peg."

"Nice girl, Donna." Peg's voice followed him down the street. "Of course, she's got that hyper little boy, but you wouldn't have any trouble with him."

He waved over his shoulder.

"And she's got her mother's wide hip, but that only helps with childbirth."

Finn hurried his pace before Peg got more detailed, and he knew from experience that she would. It wouldn't have mattered to Peg if Donna stood right there.

He couldn't picture who Donna was. Poppy would know which mom was which. Not that he would be checking out Donna's childbearing hips anytime soon. Not with his head filled with a willowy blonde, who's clear green eyes held a wealth of fragility and need.

This town suited him. He'd first come here to make sure Poppy and the kids were doing okay. He'd come with his mother to mitigate the way she always lit into Poppy.

Sean had been the love of mom's life. Born sickly, he'd needed her so much as a baby and Mom had loved that. She'd needed Sean to need her. When Sean married Poppy, Mom hadn't been able to stand losing her boy to another woman.

Finn had been away for large portions of Poppy and Sean's

marriage, deployed in places he couldn't even remember the name of. It mainly blurred into one long miasma of blood, sweat, dust and gunfire. Lots and lots of gunfire. Also, sand in places sand didn't belong.

He turned left at the end of the road and waved to a couple of children throwing leaves over each other. He couldn't remember their names, but they'd been to play with the twins a time or two.

Some half-assed noble intention to do better by Poppy had brought him to Twin Elks. He hadn't expected to find something for himself.

He could breathe here. When he looked up at the sky, he saw possibilities that he'd almost given up on. Here he could be a version of Finn he liked. In this town he'd learned to laugh again and leaving it felt all kinds of wrong.

But he couldn't spend his life sitting on his ass watching the grass grow. He'd be bored out of his mind long before he ran out of money. Turning away from the house, he took the path to the hiking trails behind the town and walked his demons down.

The falling dark turned him back home without any answers, but the pressure in his chest had eased.

He got back to the view of Claire sitting on the porch with those long, long jean clad legs resting on the railing as she sipped a beer.

Her eyes were shut, and her socked foot was moving along to whatever she had playing over her earbuds. She genuinely had no idea how beautiful she was. Like this, without makeup or her armor of designer clothes she took his breath away. Skin like ivory silk covered the delicate, clearly drawn lines of her face. Her blond hair sat in a messy pile on top of her head.

From the moment he'd looked into those bottle-green eyes she'd drawn him. The enticing combination of fragility and strength, and the softness she kept so carefully shielded.

He climbed the porch stairs, and her eyes popped open.

"Hey." He leaned down and appropriated one of her earbuds. "What are we listing to?"

Her wide mouth split into a sweet smile that he wanted to taste.

"CCR," he said. "Old school. I like it."

She turned the music off on her phone and removed the other earbud. "You okay?"

"I will be." He took the seat beside her on the wooden bench.

She leaned over the side of the bench and pulled up a second beer. "Will this help?"

"That's a great start." He accepted the beer and popped the cap. The cool bite of hops and barley slid down his throat.

They sat in silence for a while. Soft night noises settled around them. The hopeful call of frogs from the river. The plaintive goodbye from a flock of Canada geese heading for somewhere warmer before the winter.

Finn sipped his beer and let the warmth of her arm touching his seep into him marrow deep. "What did you do this afternoon?"

"Nothing much." She shrugged. "There are a bunch of old photos lying around and I got the idea they should be hung."

"Yeah?" This and the attic marked the first real interest Claire had taken in the house. And damn if that didn't make him glad. "Did you hang them?"

Her husky laughter stroked up his spine. "Ah, no. I should never be allowed near a hammer."

"Is that right?"

"Yup." Her eyes twinkled at him. A light turned on in the house and turned her skin peachy. "Power tools are a hard no."

Poppy's voice rose, "Ryan! Its bath time."

Claire broke the silence. "I don't know how she does it."

"She's pretty amazing," he said. "I was thinking about my brother earlier. He was a crappy husband and father." He sipped his beer. The empty place Sean's death had left would always ache like a missing limb. "I loved my brother, but he was spoiled rotten, and he wasn't equipped to take care of a wife and four young children."

"What was his name? Your brother." She leaned in to him, her arm pressed against his.

"Sean," he said. "He was seven years younger than me."

She sipped her beer. "Is little Sean named for him?"

"Yup. Poppy was pregnant with Sean when he died."

Claire sighed and rested her head against his shoulder. "That's awful."

"It got worse." Poppy wouldn't mind him sharing. "We found out after Sean died that he'd pretty much wiped out the family finances and put them into major debt. We had to sell the house and the cars to cover his debts."

"And this is the woman who turned down a house for forty dollars?"

Her hair brushed his stubble, fine strands getting caught. He wanted to press his face into the silken mass and pull the smell of vanilla and Claire deep into his lungs. "Yeah. And marriage to a prince like me."

Claire chuckled. "Maybe you didn't ask her right."

"You're probably right." He took an exaggerated breath. "Maybe I shouldn't have started with 'Babe, it's your lucky day.'"

She shivered, and Finn put his arm around her. "Cold?"

"A little." Snuggled up beside him, her head resting on his shoulder, she fit like she should be there. Her voice grew so quiet he almost couldn't hear her. "This house is getting to me."

"Like how?" His gut murmured that here was a taste of the real Claire. The woman he had seen on the porch when he first returned from his walk.

She draped an arm over his waist. "My mom was so unhappy here. She talks about it like it was a prison, and Horace was a monster."

"But?"

"But the house is full of me," she said. "It's full of memories and stuff of people who I share a blood connection with."

"And Horace?"

"I'm still making my mind up about him." She shifted, and her thigh rubbed against his. "I feel like I'm betraying Mom by wanting to be a part of this house."

"You're already a part of this house." He hated to break the physical connection, but there was something she needed to see. He put his beer on the floor and stood. Holding his hand out to her, he said, "Come."

"Where?" She grimaced.

"I want to show you something."

The grin she gave him made him want to take the challenge. "I was always told never to go with the boys who promised to show me something."

"That only pertains to boys."

Still she didn't move, and Finn saw the need for drastic action.

He dipped and hoisted her into a fireman's carry over his shoulder.

As hard as she tried to get an objection out, she was laughing too hard and the sound made him want to thump his chest. Claire should always laugh like nobody could hear her.

"What are you doing?" Ryan appeared at the top of the stairs, all scrubbed and in his pjs.

Finn got a firmer grip on Claire's legs. "Ryan, my boy, there are times when a man has to do what a man has to do."

"You're carrying Claire." Ryan looked unconvinced. "Why can't she walk?"

"Because she was giving me a hard time." Finn winked at Ryan. "Women need to know their place."

Ryan snort-laughed at that one. "Don't let Mom hear you say that."

"Too late," Poppy yelled from the bathroom. Water splashed, and Sean giggled. "Don't listen to a word your uncle says."

"Help," Claire called. "Where's a cop when you need one?"

Ben came to the door of his and Poppy's bedroom. He propped one shoulder on the doorjamb and grinned. "Sorry, ma'am, but I'm off the clock."

Ben deserved time off the clock too. He'd been working all hours recently. There had been more trouble with local kids and newcomers.

Finn carried Claire up to the attic landing.

When he righted her, she had to cling to him as she regained her balance. As soon as she did, she punched his shoulder. "That was way out of line." Her attempt to glare at him was adorable. "And why aren't you even breathing hard?"

"All we Neanderthals are built tough." Wanting to touch her and keep touching her, he grabbed her hand. "This is what I want you to see."

He led her to the bedroom door that used to be hers and pointed to a series of horizontal scratches on the doorpost. "Hank and I found these when we were working up here."

Claire crouched and ran her hands over the notches. "Claire, three," she read. "It's me."

Older notches lined the doorpost. "The names have faded." And then she gave a cry of delight. "Horace, six." She peered up at him, eyes all huge with delight. "It could be any of the Horaces who followed the first one."

"Or all of them." He shrugged. "Hank reckons some of these go back to shortly after the house was first built."

She pulled a face. "I'm not sure why they stuck with the name."

"Me neither." Finn returned her smile. "You have to have major game when you're hauling around a name like Horace."

She ran her hands up the notches, standing as she followed the progression. "I'm glad you left them."

"See." Even knowing he was playing with fire, he slid his arms around her from behind and tugged her back to his chest. "You're already part of this house."

Leaning back into him, she rested her head against him. "Finn?"

Their bodies fit so perfectly together. He tightened his arms and sealed them closer together. "Hmm?"

"Will you help me hang the pictures?"

He nuzzled her hair out of the way and buried his face in the crook of her neck. "What pictures?"

"The pictures of my family," she whispered, moving her head to give him better access to her sweet skin. "They're all stacked together, and they should be out. People should be able to see them. I should be able to see them."

Before he lost control, he unwrapped his arms from her. Still needing to touch, he held out his hand. "Show me."

She looked like she wanted back in his arms again, and it nearly killed him to turn and take the stairs down to the first floor.

Claire led him into the formal dining room. Nobody ate in there anymore, and the massive walnut table was covered with framed pictures. "Some of these were here already." Claire picked up one and handed it to him. "The rest I brought down from the attic."

The picture Claire handed him was of a young bride dressed in a wide-skirted gown and veil. Both the bride and the man beside her—who bore a startling resemblance to Horace—had those serious faces that people used to wear for photographs. "Who is she?"

"Cecily." Claire pressed against him as she looked at the photo with him. "Winters House was built for her, and she came here as a bride." A pensive expression crossed Claire's face. "She died at twenty-four, and this Horace married again, but she loved this house, and I really want her to be part of it again."

CHAPTER

Ten

CLAIRE WAITED until everyone had left the house the next morning before she called her mother.

Doug answered again. "Hey there. How are you?"

"Good." Because her life felt too complicated to get into right then. "How is she today?"

"She's good," Doug said. "Really good. I'll hand you over."

Her mother's voice came over the line with her Kathryn Hepburn accent, but sounding strong and sure. "Hello, darling. It's been a while since I've heard from you."

"Sorry about that." Countering her mother's version of the truth only distressed her. "I've been a bit busy here."

"Are they working you too hard?" Mom tutted. "I've told you and told you, darling, there is more to life than work. Are you still seeing that nice man? I don't remember his name."

"Greg? No, we're on a bit of a hiatus at the moment." Mom didn't know she'd lost her job, and Claire worried if Mom told Doug, the facility would get nervous.

Mom sighed. "I'm not even sure what that means. Are you coming to see me this weekend?"

"No, Mom. I can't come this weekend. I'm in Twin Elks."

"Twin Elks." Mom's voice went icy. "What are you doing there?"

They'd been through it a couple of times, and it was hit or miss whether Mom remembered and how much she remembered. "I had to talk to Horace about something."

Silence stretched between them. A sharp wind tossed the tree branches outside her window.

Mom sighed. "You have nothing to talk to that awful man about. He has never been a father to you. I've told you before, he didn't even want you."

"Yes, I remember." The thing Mom didn't get when she said stuff like that was that it hurt.

Mom's hatred of Horace was so encompassing it didn't allow for anyone else to feel different. It couldn't even acknowledge that he was Claire's father. Suggesting that she might want a relationship with Horace was so far beyond a good idea, Claire wouldn't even make the attempt. She moved the conversation elsewhere. "I'll be back in a short while. I can't say how long though."

"I don't even know what would possess you to go there in the first place." Mom's voice had gone glacial. "You know what he did to me. He kept me prisoner in that mausoleum." She drew a deep breath. "Don't ask me to go into the details, but what that man put me through, no woman should have to suffer. And now you're there." She sighed. "My child is in the clutches of a monster, and there is nothing I can do about it."

"I'm fine, Mom." Her mother never did go into the details of what had happened. She hinted at abuse both mental and physical but always stopped short of an actual accusation. Claire had assumed that the reason Horace kept paying for her mother's upkeep had something to do with keeping her silent. "I won't be here for much longer."

"Good," Mom said. "It worries me that you're there."

She hated even thinking it, but she couldn't see the monster she'd been raised to see in Horace. Maybe she had some desperate, sad need for a father figure and chose to overlook the obvious. "So, what have you and Doug been up to?"

Her mother allowed herself to be diverted and prattled on for a while about pottery classes and baking.

Claire hung up about twenty minutes later.

Growing up, Claire had never questioned her mother's version of her marriage. Being in Twin Elks was changing her. This was the longest she'd ever spent there, barring the time before Mom had left Horace.

Needing to move, she got up and stared out the window. The twins were running around the garden with Dot's huge dog. Apparently, the dog had first belonged to Ryan, but Dot had promised to look after him until the family could take him.

Now Dot had grown attached to the great beast. Claire didn't know dogs, but that thing must have had a good dose of ox in him. And yet he was so gentle with the children.

Poppy appeared with a tray full of snacks and juice boxes. Being a mother seemed to involve a lot of feeding. At least with mothers like Poppy.

She tried to remember if Mom had ever made her a meal. There had always been someone in the house to do those things. And Horace must have paid for that someone because Mom had never held down a job either. Mom loved her, she didn't doubt that, but it had always been a tidy and distant love.

Sean had dirty hands all over Poppy's jeans, but Poppy didn't seem the least bothered. Instead she was pointing at Brinn and Ciara and making them laugh.

If she had children, that could be her down there in the garden. The thought rippled through her like a minor earthquake, and she didn't want to unpack it at all. She had come to sell the house and get the money for Mom.

She could ask Horace for the money. From what she'd seen so far, he would give it to her.

It wasn't Horace himself that was making her doubts grow, but the people around him. Good people loved and respected Horace. Poppy, Ben, Dot, the children, and Finn.

Somewhere between her parents lay the truth of their marriage, and she was tired of trying to piece it together with only half the story. Didn't Horace at least deserve the chance to tell her his side?

God, but Mom would be so wounded if she knew Claire was even thinking about it.

Mom need never know.

She knocked her head against the wall. She had no idea what to do.

What would Finn do?

The answer came to her immediately. Finn didn't muck about chasing his tail. If Finn wanted to know something, he straight up asked.

Tucking her resolve and a pinch of Finn-like courage close to her heart, she went downstairs in search of Horace.

Horace sat in the library with his chair turned so he could see out the window. He chuckled at something as she walked in.

"Horace?"

He turned to her, still smiling. "Those girls." He shook his head. "Poppy sure has her hands full with them."

She joined him at the window.

Ciara was chasing her sister with a water pistol while Dot and Poppy tried, unsuccessfully, to get out of the firing line.

Claire watched them for a while, but she needed to stop stalling. "Can I talk to you for a minute?"

"Sure." Horace looked taken aback.

Claire closed the library door and took the chair on the far side of the desk.

Horace raised his brow at the closed door. "This looks serious."

"I'm not sure how to start." She rubbed her sweaty palms

over her legs and tried to think of the right way to broach the subject without her and Horace getting into it. "You and Mom."

Horace stilled. His hand clenched around the edge of the desk. "Yes."

"What was it like?"

He frowned. "I'm not sure what you're asking."

"About your marriage," she said.

"Claire." Horace shook his head. "That's between your mother and me and not you and me. Whatever problems we have, have nothing to do with your mother."

"But you see that's where you're wrong." The knot in her chest unfurled a tiny bit and she wanted to cry. Some small part of her wanted a father she could love. "Mom has told me about being here, how things were between you. She told me things about you. Bad things. Things that made me not want you to be part of my life."

With a sigh, Horace covered his eyes with his hand. "It feels wrong to put this on you."

"Please, Horace." Asking him to share was like ripping the scab off a mortal wound. "It's already on me. Mom put it there, and I need to understand."

Horace went silent for a long while, his gaze outside the window. "Okay, I suppose we owe you that much, your mother and I. Why don't we start with what you think you know?"

Speaking candidly with her father, or anyone really, didn't come easily, and Claire had to stop several times to get it all out. "She said you forced her to stay in this house. Without going into details, she intimated the relationship between you was…abusive."

Horace's face went granite still.

"She said you never wanted or liked children." Claire had to breathe deep to get that one out. "She told me how cruel you were to her and me. I don't remember any of that." Claire shrugged. "But I was only about four when we left here."

Horace's eyes told of a pain she could barely face. "And this is what you think of me?"

"This is all that I know of you."

"Dear God." He covered his eyes again and stayed like that for a long moment. His shoulders lifted and fell. "If you think me capable of those things, it's a wonder that you ever spoke to me."

"That's it though, Horace. I'm not sure what I think anymore. Being here and seeing you with everyone makes me want to hear your side of the story."

He clasped his hands on the desk and sat forward. "For your honesty alone, I owe you that. First, you have to understand I loved your mother. I loved her so much I ignored the warning signs and went ahead and married her and brought her here to Twin Elks." He gestured around them. "To you, this is an old house, but to me it's my family, my history, the core of my being."

Claire didn't contradict him. She still didn't know what she planned for the house, but it was more than an old house to her now. "So, you brought your bride here."

"I did. Perhaps in my head I was mimicking the first Horace." He gave a wry smile.

"That didn't end so well did it?"

"No." Horace pulled a face. "Like I said, I ignored all signs to the contrary and brought your mother here." He took a long pause, his gaze unfocused. "Naomi hated it here. Hated it. She missed her elegant friends and her theatre and her restaurants. I thought she'd settle down after a while. I even used to take her to the city every now and again."

"You forced her to stay here?" Claire was surprised by how much she didn't want it to be true.

Horace pulled a face. "Not physically. I swear to you now, Claire, on everything I hold dear, that I did not, nor would I ever lift a hand to your mother. Not to any woman. But." He held his hand up. "I was desperate. I loved my wife, and she was leaving me and taking our child with her. I did everything within my power to make her stay. I even threatened to cut off her support if she left me."

"But you didn't."

"No, I didn't, because that would mean cutting off support to you. And it took me many years to stop loving her, and hoping she'd come back. I can't even remember when I stopped, but it was long after she'd gone."

"But you never made much effort to see me." That pain was not associated with her mother. Horace had not made much effort over the years.

"No, I didn't." Horace met her gaze unflinchingly. "And that is my abiding shame. I tried in the beginning, but it got too complicated. And I suppose I told myself that we'd have time when the two of you came back to me."

Maybe part of her had been hoping for a Disney resolution. A trunk of secret letters Horace had sent to her over the years that her mother had sent back unopened or something. But no, and Horace had been brutal in his honesty. Just an aging man who had made mistakes, big mistakes, and had no better explanation than his own flawed humanity.

Feeling like the last twenty minutes had aged her years, she stood. "Thanks for talking to me about this."

He nodded and went back to staring out the window. Sadness carved deep lines into his face. "I never stopped loving you, Claire. Even if I wasn't much of a father."

"Okay." She left, then, her head so full it felt stuffed.

It would be so much easier if she could point her finger at a villain in the story. Mom with all her bitterness had used Claire to punish Horace. And Horace had passively let her do it.

What did she mean to either of them? And did it really matter at this time in her life?

Becoming aware of her surroundings, she found herself in the middle of the rose garden. She didn't know why, but she was in the right place.

"I'm so confused," she said.

A breeze rustled through the pruned stalks of rosebushes, chasing a few leaves to her feet.

It seemed the most obvious thing to do, so she asked, "What do I do?"

Almost lost in the flutter of leaves, a woman whispered, *"Find your way home."*

CHAPTER
Eleven

CLAIRE TAPPED on Poppy's door and waited. She still wasn't sure she was doing the right thing.

"Come in," Poppy called.

Pushing the door open a bit, she peered around the edge. It felt like an intrusion to be in Ben and Poppy's room. "Have you got a minute?"

Poppy blinked at her from over the top of a book she was reading. "Sure."

"Okay." Claire pushed the door wider to accommodate her large muslin-shrouded burden. Pictures of the children covered the chests of drawers, and a uniform shirt of Ben's hung on a hanger outside the wardrobe. The room smelled of the light floral scent Poppy used with undertones of sandalwood that must belong to Ben.

She didn't know Poppy well at all, and this could be misconstrued as pushy and interfering, but Claire was going with her gut. "Look, I know it's your wedding soon, and you probably have a dress."

"I do." Poppy stood and came toward her. "What's that?"

"A dress." Claire put it on the large four-poster bed. "It's the same dress Cecily wore when she got married."

"Cecily?" Poppy frowned. "The girls talk about a Cecily."

No way Claire felt ready to share her theory, so she said, "They must have heard Horace talk about her, and there is that portrait of her over the mantel in the parlor."

"Hmm." Poppy didn't look convinced, but she peered at the bundle on the bed. "And this is her wedding dress?"

"Yes. She was tiny." Claire didn't want to offend Poppy. "Like you, and I thought you might..." She'd made a mistake. She didn't even know what she was thinking. "Never mind."

"Wait," Poppy said. "Are you thinking of wearing this to our wedding?"

"No." Nothing ventured, nothing gained. "I was thinking you might want to."

Poppy blinked at her. "Me?"

"It's too small for me," Claire said. The idea had come to her as she was sorting through the old photographs, and she'd gone with it. "But it might fit you."

"But I already have a dress." Poppy parted the muslin and peeped inside.

"I guessed as much." Claire picked up the dress. "I wasn't thinking. I had this stupid, wild idea that you might want to wear it when you got married."

Actually, she'd felt that Cecily wouldn't want her dress rotting away in an attic, and from there, her imagination had jumped to Poppy.

Frowning, Poppy unwrapped a bit more of the muslin. "Wow." She unwrapped a bit more and a bit more until finally she had bared the entire dress. Stepping back, she clasped her hands in front of her, as if afraid to touch. "It's beautiful."

"Yes." Claire had come this far. "I mean, you could try it on."

"You think?" Poppy held her hand out and snatched it back. "No, I couldn't. What if I damage it?"

"What are you planning to do in it?" Claire wanted to laugh at the look on Poppy's face. She reminded her so much of Brinn right then, half eager and half skeptical.

Poppy giggled. "Well, nothing much, but I could rip it."

"Shall we see?" Claire waved the dress in front of Poppy. She'd love to see it on Poppy.

"Okay." Decision made, Poppy whipped off her sweatshirt and wriggled out of her jeans.

Claire helped her into the dress and then started fastening the hundreds of tiny buttons down the back.

"Wow." It was Claire's turn to say it this time.

The dress fit over Poppy's waist and bodice as if it had been made for her. It was about two inches too long, but nothing a pair of heels couldn't solve.

Claire led Poppy to her full-length mirror. "Take a look."

"Oh." Poppy blinked at her reflection. "It's beautiful." Then she shook her head. "I've no right to wear this dress."

When she replied, Claire didn't know what made her so sure, but she was. "Cecily would want you to wear it. Just like she would love that you're having the wedding here."

"I don't know." Poppy's expression turned wistful. "I hadn't planned on anything this formal."

"No?" Claire finished with the last button. "Because you look like a princess, and I think every girl should look like a princess on her wedding day."

Poppy studied her reflection, still looking uncertain.

"I tell you what," Claire said. "Why don't you think about it? I'll leave it here, and you can decide when you're ready."

"Are you sure?" Poppy looked at her with uncertainty in her big brown eyes. "Are you sure you are okay if I wear this? It isn't my dress."

"It isn't mine either." Claire squeezed Poppy's shoulder. "And Cecily would be so happy to see it worn again."

———

Finn fitted the edges of wood into place. A perfect fit that gave him a soul deep sense of satisfaction. When he got the chest of drawers fixed, he'd ask Claire where she wanted it.

That morning he'd left her positioning the old photos throughout the house. Later, he'd go in and hang them for her. Maybe get one of her sweet smiles for his trouble. He wanted a lot more, but he couldn't allow that to happen.

Watching Claire get reacquainted with Winters House made him hopeful that she would stop fighting her one-woman battle against her legacy. Winters House was doing its part. The old house snuck up on you and sucked you in.

Working in the shed with him, Hank Styles was turning the replacement leg for the dressing table that used to sit in Claire's room.

"Well, you know how that goes?" Hank raised his grizzled eyebrows at Finn.

As usual, Finn hadn't a damn clue what Hank was rattling on about. Hank liked to talk as he worked. Fortunately, he didn't need more than the occasional grunt.

Finn grunted.

"Yeah." Hank gave him a meaningful look. "Man's gotta do what's in his heart."

Another grunt kept Hank happy, and he went off again.

It took him a moment to register the sudden silence as Hank stopped talking.

Hank whistled instead. "Woohee! That sure is one fine looking chickie."

Chickie? That thing flying right past Hank's head and crashing into the wall behind him would be political correctness.

Finn straightened from the dressing table and stood.

Hank was ogling a woman getting out of her car, and Finn's hair stood on end. "Jesus, Hank, that's my mother."

"Well then, son." Hank wheezed out a cackle. "You can go right ahead and introduce me."

Not on Hank's life, and Finn went to the sink to wash his

hands. He had no idea what Mom was doing there, but he needed to get into the house before she caught sight of Poppy.

Grabbing his shirt off the hook by the door, he trotted toward the walkway to intercept her. "Mom!"

"Finn." She gave him a tight smile and held her cheek up for a kiss.

Finn dutifully pecked her cheek. The familiar mom smell of talcum powder and lavender surrounded him. She'd never really forgiven him for being the son who survived, and he'd stopped hating her for it somewhere in the blood-soaked desert.

Now they were just their little dysfunctional family of two, and he did love her. "What brings you here?"

"Oh, Finn." She gave him an exasperated stare. "As if you didn't know."

"Morning." Hank sidled up beside him, a shit-eating grin all over his face. He held one calloused hand out to Mom. "Name's Hank. My ma christened me Henry though, if you're more partial to that."

Mom looked at Hank's hand as if it might bite her, and Finn had to fight to hide his grin.

Gingerly, Mom placed the tips of her fingers into Hank's outstretched paw. "Maura. Maura Williams."

"Maura." Hank engulfed her hand in his. "That's a pretty name for a pretty lady." He winked. "Finn here never told me he had such a pretty sister."

Dear God, Finn threw up a bit in his mouth.

Mom's smile looked like it might crack her face it was so tight. "Is Poppy in the house?"

And there it was. Finn bit back a nasty word. Mom had come to make more trouble for Poppy. He didn't get it, even after all this time.

He accompanied her up the walk. "Don't do this, Mom."

"Finn. You don't understand." Mom's heels clicked against the wooden porch.

It wasn't just that Mom had never been able to accept Sean's marriage to Poppy, but she also blamed Poppy for trapping Sean into marriage through pregnancy. In Mom's head, Sean shared no responsibility for getting Poppy pregnant in her senior year of high school.

Sean, always one for the easy path, had appreciated the sympathetic ear Mom had given him when being a husband and father got too real. Sean had never stood up for Poppy, and Mom had entrenched herself in the role of matriarch.

Finn held the door to the house open for her. "I'm not going to let you start any trouble with Poppy."

"You always rush to her defense." Mom glared at him, her sense of betrayal blazing at him. "I would have thought you could be more sympathetic to your own mother."

And there you had it. Now that Sean was dead, Mom couldn't let go. Poppy and her children were all Mom had left of Sean, and she was determined to keep them under her thumb.

"Hi." Claire appeared on the stairway.

As usual, Finn got that pinch in his chest when he looked at Claire. "Hi, yourself. Get those pictures put where you want them?"

"Um…not yet." She looked like she'd been up to something though. "I was busy with…never mind." Holding her hand out, she descended the stairs. "Hi, I'm Claire."

"Maura." Mom gave her an assessing look. "I'm Finn's mother."

"I see the resemblance." The Claire he knew had retreated behind a polite mask, and Finn wanted to howl for her back, but this being Mom, it might be better for her to stay behind those walls. Mom was not for the faint of heart. "I'm Horace's daughter."

She didn't even trip over that statement and Finn wanted to hug her.

"Hey, Grandma." Brinn and Ciara hung over the stair railings and peered down.

This time, Mom's smile was real. "Hello, darlings."

The psychology didn't take a master to figure out. Mom thought she could replace her lost son with Poppy's. Both boys were dead ringers for Sean, but then, so were Brinn and Ciara.

"What are you doing here?" Brinn traipsed down the stairs with a tentative smile.

They still remembered a time when Mom had treated them like second best. Finn clenched his teeth. He'd done his best to distract them, but kids were way smarter than adults.

As if sensing something amiss, Claire shifted closer to him. It worked as well; he felt better with her closer.

"Well, I missed you." Mom opened her arms. "I missed the two most beautiful granddaughters in Colorado. Maybe even the world."

Both girls rushed her and got a tight hug and a kiss.

Mom wasn't a bad person. She just got twisted in her own pain and bitterness.

The twins started chattering at the top of their voices.

"Girls!" Poppy came down the stairs. "What's all the noise —" She came to an abrupt halt and tensed.

Finn hated that Poppy threw up the defenses around Mom. Sean was to blame for not ever standing beside her like a husband. And then, after Sean's death, Finn should have made sure Poppy knew she had his support.

Claire glanced from him to Poppy, and then moved closer to Poppy.

"Mom popped by." Finn tried to lighten the mood and raised an eyebrow at Poppy. "Surprise!"

Poppy choked back a giggle and said in that tight voice she reserved for Mom, "Hi Maura. How are you?"

"Fine." Mom showed her teeth at Poppy in an attempt at a smile. "Well, actually I'm not fine, but we won't speak of that in front of the C-H-I-L-D-R-E-N."

"Children!" Brinn beamed up at him. "Why is grandma spelling children?"

"It's a test." Finn winked at her. He adored his nieces. They were so bright and full of life. Brinn was the most outgoing, but Ciara hid the wisdom of an old soul behind her quiet smile. "And you failed, because she didn't spell children at all. She spelled hippopotamus."

Hip to his bullshit, Ciara giggled and rolled her eyes at him.

"No, she didn't." Brinn pointed at him and hopped about. "You don't know how to spell."

"Yes, I can." He feigned outrage. He leaned close to Mom and whispered, "Don't start anything."

She stared straight at Poppy.

He needed to get the girls away from the Mom-induced tension. Raising both arms, he roared like a lion.

The twins recognized the game and took off shrieking. With one more meaningful look at his mother, Finn set off after them.

Finn kept one eye on the door as he played with the girls. He was glad Claire was still with Poppy, and he hoped she stayed there.

Mom appeared sooner than he'd expected. Sending the girls into the kitchen, he joined his mother on the porch.

Her pinched expression didn't augur well for her discussion with Poppy. "What happened?"

"That...that, girl doesn't care what anyone says to her. She does exactly what she wants," she said.

Meaning, Poppy had not caved to Mom's demand. "What did you want from her?"

"Really, Finn, it's not what I want." She smoothed her immaculate hair. "You act as if I came here with an agenda of my own and try to get my way. I'm thinking of my grandchildren."

Yeah, and that was always her justification. "But those grandchildren are Poppy's children."

"And Sean's." Mom looked wrathful. "She acts as if he doesn't count when they're his children."

There was so much he could say to that, but she wouldn't hear any of it. Poppy had raised those children alone even when Sean had been alive. Mom could have chosen to be a support to

Poppy, and they would have had a very different relationship today. "Tell me what you spoke to Poppy about."

"This ridiculous marriage of hers."

Everything in Finn stilled. "Tell me you didn't."

Mom smoothed her navy pencil skirt. "I don't know what you're talking about."

"Tell me you didn't come here to try to stop Poppy from getting married." Jesus, after all she'd been through, Poppy deserved some happiness in her life, and Ben gave her that.

Mom took a step away from him. "If she marries him, what will become of Sean's children?"

"They will become Ben's children, and he will be their father." She could never see that Sean's death had hurt more than only her.

"That's exactly it." Mom jabbed a finger at him. "And I don't see how you can stand there and let that happen. How can you let another man replace your brother? Usurp his role in his children's lives?"

God, there were times when he could strangle his mother. "Ben Crowe is more of a father to those children than Sean ever was." Whether she heard him or not, he had to speak this truth. "Sean was a lousy father and a worse husband. He fooled around on Poppy, left her to raise those children on her own, and in the end, left her with no money to do that with."

"Don't you—"

"Ben will never do any of those things to Poppy. He will stand by her side, support her, love her, and raise her children with her. He is twice the man Sean was, and the only person who can't see that is you."

"How dare you?" Mom quivered with rage. "How dare you speak about my son like that."

"You had two sons, Mom, and he was my brother, as well. I loved him, but I was never blind to his faults."

"Loved him?" Mom scoffed. "You were always jealous of Sean. Even when you were boys you could never stand that Sean was charming, and people loved him. You would always try to take the attention away from him."

And there it came. The bitterness she could never let go of. He didn't know why he still bothered, other than she was his mother. "I wasn't jealous of Sean, Mom. I saw who he was."

"You saw what you wanted to see," she spat. "You always resented that Sean could do anything he set his mind to."

Sean had been able to do that, but he'd lacked the follow through to complete any of the projects he'd undertaken.

"You joined the army." She gave him a look of distaste. "You ran away and played soldier, and now that's ended, you're moping around here and doing nothing. Sean would never have done that. Sean had fire and ambition and verve. He was going places."

Unlike you. Her unspoken judgment resonated between them. Even knowing she was way off base didn't make it hurt any less. His mother and her low opinion of him cut deep.

The darkness flickered at the edge of his vision and Finn sucked in a harsh breath. He needed to get it under control, right then, before he lost it. He could feel the fury creeping through his muscles, trying to own him.

The door opened, and Claire stepped on the porch. "Finn?"

He couldn't let her see the dark place, and he took off. "I've gotta go."

———

Claire didn't know what had happened between Finn and his mother, but she'd heard enough of what Maura said to Poppy to know the woman didn't hold back.

"You can't support this marriage." Maura turned to her with eyes the same blue as Finn's, but a bitterness to her face aged her. "This house is yours, and Poppy lives here like she owns it."

Strange how Claire had thought the same thing up until recently. "The children live here too, and Finn."

"I could take care of my children." Maura's mouth thinned into a slash of coral lipstick. "And Finn is hiding."

"Really? Because I think Poppy is a wonderful mother, and this is my father's house. He likes having the children here."

Maura sniffed. "You wait. You'll see what Poppy is really like when you know her like I do."

Claire doubted that. The more she got to know Poppy, the more she liked her. Maura, on the other hand, she liked less by the second, but Maura was the children's grandmother and Finn's mother. "I don't know Finn that well, but he doesn't seem to be hiding to me."

"You're right." Maura turned on her with a tight expression. "You don't know Finn that well. In fact, you don't know him at all, and it would best for Finn if you kept it that way."

CHAPTER
Twelve

FINN STARED at the row of Elvis bobbleheads arranged beside the singing carp at the Bulging Elk.

The ugly as fuck bar matched his mood.

He didn't know how Mom still got to him, but she did. She wiggled into the chink in his armor and spread salt on a still-gaping wound.

Wah! Wah! Wah! His mommy didn't love him as much as she loved his dead younger brother. He might as well add pathetic to asshole.

Maddison, the owner of the Bugling Elk, put another beer in front of him without being asked. "You got company."

"Hey, Maddison." Ben sat on the bar stool beside him. "Can I get a coffee?"

"Sure, Chief." Maddison put down her bar cloth. "You still on duty?"

"Not officially, but Marty Jensen got beat up pretty badly last night, and his friends are looking for some payback."

"Kids." Maddison snorted. "I had to kick some of those out-of-towners outta here the other night for getting rowdy. Marty going to be okay?"

"Yeah." Ben rubbed his nape. "But if you see something

brewing, I'd appreciate it if you call me. This thing could get out of hand."

"Will do, Chief." Maddison brought Ben's coffee and retreated.

The silence broke him, and Finn had to know. "Is Poppy okay?"

"Yeah." Ben chuckled. "She's mad though."

"On a scale of one to ten?"

"Fourteen."

Finn winced. "My mom can do that to the best of us."

"Poppy says your Mom has her panties in a wad about her marrying me." Ben sipped his coffee. "Know what that's about?"

"Yeah. And it's not about you." Mom would lock Poppy away if she could. "It's about holding on to my brother. If you become the kids' father, then she loses another connection to him."

Ben shook his head. "Sean will always be their father."

"Yeah, he will." Finn looked at the big cop who'd become a friend since he'd arrived in Twin Elks. Once they'd gotten over their pissing contest around Poppy that was. "But you'll be their dad, Ben. You already are and you're doing a great job."

Flushing, Ben cleared his throat. "Nah."

"Yeah, you are." Finn wanted Ben to understand that. It couldn't be easy taking on a ready-made family and the guy deserved a fucking medal for stepping up. "You spend time with those kids, show them love, are firm with them when they need it, give them your attention. That's a dad."

"They have you too," Ben said.

"True." Because Finn wasn't going anywhere. "I just can't help wondering if I'd been around more. You know, in the early days after Sean's death, whether I could have done more. Not let things get so out of hand. Poppy shouldn't have struggled like that, but I thought Mom would take care of her."

"Maybe." Ben shrugged. "Or maybe not. Horace always says

you don't get to change one thing in the past and assume that changing that one thing won't have a knock-on effect."

This is part of why he liked Horace, which brought his thoughts back to Claire.

And then his mother.

"My CO wants me to take over the training of recruits for my former unit," he said.

Ben smirked. "The unit without a name that doesn't exist?"

"That's the one." He nearly found a smile. "I was one of the best." He didn't say it to brag. "He thinks I can help them stay alive."

"You probably could." Ben nodded. "But is that what you want?"

"I'm not sure. I like the idea of being able to keep them alive." Another thing in his life on which Finn was unclear, and this cloudy shit was getting old. "I retired because I was done with war and death and destroying things. It got to where I couldn't remember whether I was one of the good guys or one of the bad guys."

"Do you know now?"

Finn had to think about that. "No." He really didn't like the answer, but there it was. "Part of me feels like that side is still inside, waiting to come out."

Ben grunted. "You having dreams?"

"Yeah."

"I still get them from time to time." Ben sighed. "Matter of fact, they showed up a lot when I first got feelings for Poppy. Ma said it was like I was growing back a missing limb. The one that gave a shit about living again."

"Huh." Finn didn't have an answer for that. "I should give my therapist a call."

"You should." Ben said. "But Finn, don't be too hard on your-self. You're one of the good guys. Only person who doesn't know it is you."

"Hey, hot stuff." Kelly Ashford, owner of a kickass coffee

shop and Poppy's friend, slid her arm around his shoulders. "Buy a girl a drink?"

Finn liked Kelly. She was good people and a straight shooter. She also flirted like hell with him, but her heart belonged firmly to her high school sweetheart. "Are you gonna put out?"

"Sure." Kelly rolled her eyes. "Try and stop me."

Poppy joined them. Her dark gaze searched his face. "You okay?"

"I feel like I should be asking you that." He should never have let Mom talk to Poppy, but short of wrestling her out of there, he hadn't known how to stop her.

Poppy smiled. "She doesn't get to me anymore." She went on her tiptoes and kissed his cheek. "She was far rougher on you today."

"She misses him as much today as she did the day he died." Poppy would get it.

She nodded. "I know, and it makes me sad for her. I don't think I could stand losing a child."

"Claire with you?" He was hoping she might be.

Poppy shook her head. "Ah, no. Last I saw her, she was wrestling a chair out of the attic. I think she's going to have some more work for you."

"What's with that?" Kelly shrugged. "Poppy says she's been hanging photos and moving furniture around."

Finn's need to defend Claire rose. "She's getting in touch with her heritage."

"Right." Kelly rolled her eyes. "But what the hell is the point of doing that if she's got one foot out the door?"

"I'm not so sure she has," Poppy said.

Kelly frowned and motioned Maddison over. "You think she won't sell the house?"

"I'm really not sure." Poppy shrugged. "But she's not what I thought she was. Finn told me that, and I didn't believe him."

"Finn told you?" Kelly turned curious eyes on him. "And has

Finn been spending enough time with Claire to get to know her better?"

"You know what, gorgeous? You talk too much." Looping his arm around Kelly's neck, he smiled at Maddison. "Get this girl a drink and let's see if that will shut her up."

"You could try." Kelly snorted. "But shutting me up has never been done before."

While Maddison got their order, Kelly nudged him. "Word on the street is you and Claire have been seen cozying up on the front porch."

"Is that so?" Life in a small town, Twin Elks specifically.

Kelly grinned. "Peg saw you the other night. She's not happy about it, FYI. She has you marked out for Donna."

You either flowed with it, or you drowned. Finn handed her a beer. "Any news on the Vince front?"

"Nah!" Kelly wrinkled her nose. "I mean, the divorce has been finalized, but it's a bit more complicated than that."

Finn tapped his glass against her. "It always is."

Poppy and Ben had slipped away to the dance floor. Twined around each other, they shuffled to the music, lost to anything but each other.

Kelly watched them and sighed. "You ever think you might want that for yourself?"

Ben looked at Poppy as if she was his entire world. It was probably the only time Finn ever saw the big guy look gentle. "Who doesn't want something like that?"

———

Claire hoped Finn was all right. She hung around downstairs hoping he would reappear.

Poppy and Ben had invited her for a drink with them, but she'd elected to stay home and watch the kids instead. Not that she had much watching to do, with them all in bed and fast asleep.

She'd already positioned the photographs where she wanted them hung, and she would have to talk to Finn to get it done. Briefly she toyed with the idea of getting out the hammer, but then took pity on Winters House. The old girl had been standing this long. She deserved to make it through Claire's visit.

Looking for something to distract herself, she wandered into the library. She liked the huge bookshelves filled with books and the fireplace that promised nights of cozy reading. Whenever Horace had been in there, the desk was littered with papers. Then Poppy would follow and tidy them all away.

Poppy must have been there last because the huge oak desk was clear of debris, and all the pens were contained in a set of leather holders.

Claire dropped into the big brown leather desk chair. It squeaked and adjusted to her weight. Maybe the first Horace had sat there and ran his empire. She should demand Finn report to the library and have him stand on the other side of the desk while she questioned him.

She snorted at her silliness and rocked the chair. She hadn't planned on staying in Twin Elks this long. This trip was supposed to have been a quick in, secure her inheritance, get some more money for Mom's facility and out again.

Now she didn't want to think about when she was going to leave.

The bookshelves were nearly full. Modern paperbacks rubbed shoulders with leather-bound first editions. Mom had never been much of a reader, but Claire liked to read. Apparently, someone else must too, because some of the paperbacks were modern titles she recognized.

She got up and browsed the shelves. She guessed by the genres that Horace was probably the reader. They both liked mysteries and history.

A small book with an orange spine nestled between an atlas and a Ken Follett. Claire pulled it out.

Good Night Moon.

Looking at the orange book brought a hazy memory into sharp focus. Horace sitting beside her ruffled princess bed with that book cradled in his large hands. His deep voice sounded in her mind as he read the familiar story.

Claire turned the page, but she already knew the words. Something dropped out of the book and skittered across the wood floor. She retrieved a photo, faded with age. It was Horace, only a much younger version. He'd married late in life and had her even later, but in the photo, he still had his dark hair and stood tall and fit.

A blond child sat on his shoulders, laughing.

It was her. She couldn't be older than two.

Mom always said Horace hadn't wanted children and hadn't spent any time with her, but the father in the photo looked like he adored the child on his shoulders.

And the little girl...

Claire's cheek itched and she rubbed it. Her fingers came away damp. The little girl looked so happy and so carefree. She looked like a child who knew her father loved her.

A noise at the library door made her look up.

"Sorry." Horace hesitated in the doorway. "I came to see if you needed any help with the kids."

Claire shook her head. "They're asleep."

"Yeah." Horace looked as if he wanted to say something, and then he shook his head. "Anyway, I won't interrupt."

The gap between the child in the photo and the woman holding it yawned. "Horace?"

"Yup." He turned.

She held the photo out to him. "Do you remember this day?"

Limping worse than ever, he stomped into the library. He really needed to get his hip fixed.

"Huh." He took the photo and frowned at it, and then he smiled. "I think this was Founder's Day. You couldn't see the parade for all the people."

"Founder's Day?" She took it back from him. There were

other people in the photo, surrounding them. "Is that like a thing here?"

"You can get run out of town for not knowing about Founder's Day." Horace chuckled. "What with you being a Winters and all—I mean, by blood."

"We founded this town?" The idea of having Winters blood in her veins no longer clawed at her.

"Not really." Horace made a face. "But to hear my grandfather tell it, we totally did. We arrived a while after the first prospectors. The first Horace quickly figured out he could make more money supplying those looking for gold than trying his hand at mining."

"Apparently, he was right."

Leaning on his cane, Horace stared at her. "You want to hear more."

"Please." She settled into one of the hearth chairs.

Horace limped to the facing chair and settled into it. "My grandfather, the second Horace, was the one who really accrued the fortune."

"Horace one must have married again, because Cecily didn't have any children, did she?"

"He did." Horace raised his eyebrows at her. "So, you worked out who Cecily was?"

"Yup." Talking about her would make her sound like a nutjob. "But I'm not sure why I think I can hear her sometimes."

Horace chuckled. "It's the Winters secret."

"I can go with that." The alternative was just crazy. "So, Horace two put us on the map?"

"Big time." He tapped the empty fire grate with his cane. "He opened a whole bunch of businesses around here: Winters Mercantile, Winters Bank, Winters Supply and Feed, Winters Haberdashers and Ladies Emporium. He even started Winters School."

She had known Winters was the big name about town but not quite that big.

"What you got there?" Horace gestured with his cane.

She tucked the photo back into the book and handed it to him. "The book you used to read to me."

"Ah." Horace cleared his throat. He stroked the cover. It still looked lost in his big hands. "You used to love this book."

"Did you?"

"Oh, yes." Horace chuckled. "I read it to you every night. Every night I would suggest something new, but every night you wanted this one." He stared at the book for a long time and then took a breath. Jabbing his cane at the decanters near the desk he said, "You drink whisky?"

"Only if it's good."

Horace raised a brow at her. "What do you think?"

"Was there a Winters Distillery?"

"Nope." He chuckled. "But there should have been."

"Maybe you should get on that?"

"Maybe I should."

Claire didn't hide her smile as she poured them both a whisky and took one to Horace.

He took a sip and gave a sigh of appreciation. "That'll fix what ails ya."

"Speaking of." Claire gave his cane a pointed stare. "When are you getting your hip fixed?"

"After the wedding." Horace flipped through the book. "Poppy asked me to walk her down the aisle." He suddenly looked guilty. "She doesn't have anyone else."

"I know." Claire thought Horace was the perfect person to walk Poppy down the aisle. "I found Cecily's dress upstairs. I gave it to her to wear. I hope she does."

"Upstairs?" Horace frowned.

"In the attic."

"Ah." He nodded. "I haven't been up there in years."

"I wonder why." Claire sipped her whisky. "Just a wild guess here, but do you think it might have anything to do with your bad hip?"

Horace snorted. "Don't be a smart ass."

Claire snorted. "I must get that from somewhere."

They sipped their drinks. The house made soft settling noises around them. The hum of oil through the heating pipes, the creak of wood settling.

"I forgot I still had this book." Horace opened it to the first page. "I wonder if kids still like being read to."

"I imagine they do." Claire let the peace wash over her.

"In the great green room, there was a telephone. And a red balloon," Horace read. He chuckled and closed the book.

Everything in Claire focused on the next words. "Read more."

Horace looked at her, and then opened the book. "And a picture of...the cow jumping over the moon."

CHAPTER
Thirteen

CLAIRE SLEPT DEEPLY that night and woke well rested. With it being the weekend, it made absolutely no difference to the children. They were up and sumo wrestling across the wooden floors at around six am.

"Mo-o-om," Brinn yelled from the floor above. Amazing how Claire could now tell which twin was which from the sounds of their voices. It helped that Ciara spoke rarely and never raised her voice. She didn't need to when she had Brinn to do it for her.

A door opened across the hallway. "What is it Brinn?"

"Ryan's in here and he's farting."

Poppy's response was loaded with I-can't-believe-I'm-saying-this. "Ryan, leave the girls alone, and if you need to go to the bathroom, do it now."

"It's not my fault," Ryan shouted. "Horace made me beans."

Claire stayed under her covers and giggled.

"Can you please stop yelling, Claire is sleeping," Poppy said.

Claire yelled back, "No, she isn't."

"Sorry."

"No worries."

Feet stomped down the stairs, surely making too much noise

for a little person. "Hey, Claire?" Ryan yelled from outside her door.

"Yes, Ryan."

"Ben's making pancakes for breakfast. Do you like pancakes?"

She snorted. "Who doesn't like pancakes?"

Ryan giggled. "Hey, Claire."

"Yes, Ryan."

"See you later, alligator."

She knew this one. "In a while, crocodile."

Finn's voice didn't enter the fray, and she hoped he'd got home safely last night.

Someone tapped on her door and Poppy peeked around. "I really am sorry if they woke you. On the plus side, Ben makes great pancakes."

Poppy smiled and closed her door.

"I'll see you in the kitchen." Claire got out of bed, because after all, who didn't like pancakes.

The morning had turned a little cooler, so she put a thick sweater on with her jeans. Makeup seemed redundant, but she scraped her hair into a ponytail.

The noise swelled up the stairs from the kitchen. All four children seemed to be speaking at once. Undercutting their shrill voices was Horace's rough murmur and Ben's deep bass.

She walked into the kitchen and nobody paid her any mind. They went right on doing what they had been doing. Helping herself to coffee, she wandered over to the large kitchen windows.

Even in the time she'd been here, the seasonal changes showed. The aspens guarding the river were almost completely bare and the grass had turned a dull shade of brown.

Someone thudded into her legs.

Sean gripped her knees and gave her a toothless grin. "Clah!"

"Well, hello there." How could you not return such an unrestrained grin? All she'd done to deserve it was show up this morning.

Sean made grabby hands at her. "Up!"

"Sean." Poppy ducked in and tried to run interference. "Let Claire have her coffee first."

"No, it's okay." Claire picked Sean up and propped him on her hip.

"Pwitty." Sean petted her hair, and Claire made a point of not thinking where those sticky little hands had already been this morning.

"Pancakes are ready," Ben said, and went past her with a large platter. "That looks good on you. You should do something about getting one of those for yourself."

Claire pulled a face at him. Honestly, she'd never given any thought to children. On some vague level she'd supposed they weren't for her. "Did Finn come in?

Spotting the pancakes, Sean wriggled to get down.

"We ran into him at the Elk." Poppy looked up from settling children at the table and winked at her. "Brinn can you tell Finn breakfast is ready?"

"But Mom, the pancakes are ready." Brinn kept an eagle eye on the platter. She already had the maple syrup at the ready.

"Brinn." Poppy gave her daughter a hard stare. "He's near the woodshed."

With a pout, Brinn made a big deal of climbing off her chair.

It was the perfect reason to go looking for him, and Claire put her cup on the counter. "I'll do it."

"Really?" Poppy smirked.

Horace stopped with his juice halfway to his mouth. "Why are you going to find him?"

Ben chuckled and winked at her. "Go get him, Tiger."

Still laughing, Claire let herself into the crisp morning.

The air smelled like woodsmoke and dry leaves. This is how she saw it. Finn had been good to her since her arrival. Maybe he needed a friend too. That was her surface theory, anyway. Deep down, or maybe not even that deep down, she would like to be more than friends.

She walked around the house, saw Finn and stopped in her tracks.

Shirtless, with only a pair of low-slung loose pants Finn was doing yoga. She recognized a sun salutation from her yoga classes, but on Finn, it looked a whole lot better than anything she'd seen. Sleek muscle bunched and stretched beneath his tan skin. He flowed from one pose into another, completely absorbed in his practice.

Even the dappled morning light was playing along and creating tempting shadows across him.

Oh my.

And then he turned his back to her, and Claire stared some more, but this time because of the network of scars marring the muscular expanse. Some of them had the precision of surgical scars, but others were bunched and ugly. It was the back of someone who'd been through a lot of pain.

Finn turned and caught sight of her. He stopped and straightened. "I didn't see you there."

"Yeah." So many questions and still so much beautiful Finn to rob those thoughts from her brain. "I came to find you for breakfast."

"And caught me doing yoga." His grin was pure charming Finn. "I promise I pump iron on odd days."

Pity for him she recognized it for the diversionary tactic it was. "Is the yoga for your back?"

He grimaced. "Sorry you saw that. It's can't be pretty."

"I'm sorry you went through that. It must have sucked."

"It did."

They stared at each other. She felt shy and tongue tied. Since she had returned with Andy that night, Finn hadn't made another move to kiss her. Yet, the way he looked at her made her believe he really wanted to, that and the way he could never keep his hands off her for long.

Finn bent and snatched a towel from the ground. "I had a couple of back surgeries."

"Okay." She had guessed that much. "What happened?"

"I ran afoul of a few stray bullets." He tried to make light of it as he rolled up his mat. "Also took one too many falls from high places."

"When you were in the services?"

Finn nodded and tucked his mat under his arm. His towel hung around his neck.

Her conversation last night with Horace had shifted things, and the peace between them last night had felt significant, like a bridge to another place. "I spent some time with Horace last night."

"Yeah?" Finn rubbed a palm over his hair and made it stick up. "How did that go?"

"It was…nice. Friendly." It might mean nothing. It might mean a whole lot more. She didn't know yet, but it was progress. "I was worried about you."

Finn stilled and his face softened. "You don't need to worry about me."

She shouldn't have said that. It had made him uncomfortable. "But I did."

"I like that you did." His tanned skin did great things for the blue of his eyes. "But I was fine. I am fine. It's part of why I do the yoga as well. It helps center me."

Claire nodded. "We should get to breakfast."

"We should." He glanced at her mouth. "Poppy also told us last night about the dress you offered her. You did a nice thing there, babe."

"Poppy is a nice person." It was hard to think clearly with him this close. And he called her babe and she hated that. At least, she'd always hated it in the past.

"So are you." He tucked a strand of hair behind her ear. "You like to pretend you're all tough and hard, but I'm on to you."

Being this close to near-naked Finn melted her resolve and a few other body parts. "You are?"

"Yup." His big, rough palm slid to her jaw. His gaze heated and held her in place with its intensity. "Inside you're all sweet and gooey like a marshmallow."

"A marshmallow?" She didn't like that so much either, but his thumb was stroking her bottom lip, and she couldn't concentrate on anything else.

"Soft and silky and sweet," he whispered, his eyes an intense blue blaze that held her mesmerized. "So fucking sweet."

Kiss me. She had never wanted a kiss more, but she didn't have the courage to close the three inches separating their mouths. It wasn't a good idea at all.

Why was that again?

Her life was so complicated right now. By what she'd witnessed yesterday, so was his. They lived in the same house, and if things went badly, it would affect everyone. She wasn't staying, and he'd straight up told her he wasn't a good relationship bet.

None of those reasons made any difference, and she stood there, her heart pounding, as Finn dipped toward her, and his lips brushed hers. "So sweet, and so beautiful."

"Finn." His name slipped out on a low needy moan.

"Right here." His mouth covered hers, firm but still seeking her permission.

Needing more, Claire licked at his bottom lip. She knew all the reasons why not, she knew it could be a horrible idea, but she just didn't care.

On a groan, Finn opened his mouth to her. His tongue slid against hers as he took over the kiss. His other hand gripped her hip and pulled her closer.

Her hands spread over the bare skin of his waist.

Possessive and consuming, Finn kissed her as if he had nothing better to do and nowhere to go. It wasn't a prelude to something else, but a destination that grew more demanding.

His cock pressed through his thin pants into her.

Feeling how much he wanted her, wanted this, went straight to Claire's head. She didn't want to hold back, and she pressed herself against him, glorying in the connection of chest to breast and groin to groin.

She lost track of the where and the when and allowed the who to own her in the press of body to body and the complete and utter possession of her mouth.

"Finn!" Ryan said from behind them. "Are you kissing Claire?"

Claire tried to hide her head in Finn's shoulder.

Finn chuckled. "Well, I was, but then you interrupted."

"Gross." Ryan made gagging noises. "Mom sent me because there aren't that many pancakes left, and she says I can't have any more until you and Claire have had some. So, you need to come now."

Claire managed to drag enough composure together to face Ryan. "Then we'll come now."

"Good." Ryan eyed them suspiciously. "I'm not leaving until you come."

Finn clasped her hand and twined their fingers together. "We'll be there in a minute."

"No, you won't." Ryan folded his arms and stuck his chin out. "Ben says that all the time, and what he means is he'll come after more kissing." His expression grew pinched. "But this is pancakes, Finn. Pancakes!"

CHAPTER
Fourteen

CLAIRE HATED CONFRONTATION, but the text from Tara had come in after breakfast. They hadn't spoken since Tara had left her to fend for herself and gone dancing. Tara hadn't even called the next day to make sure she had gotten home in one piece.

The five adults were sitting around the kitchen table finishing their coffee. Poppy and Horace were sharing the newspaper while Ben checked his phone. Finn and Ben were speaking about last night's activities.

"It might settle down," Finn said. "Everybody got what was coming to them."

There had been an incident the night before involving local boys getting pay back for one of their own being beaten up. Nobody had been arrested, and witnesses had all clammed up.

"Maybe." Ben shrugged. "But this gives me a bad feeling. I think it's escalating."

Despite their conversation, sitting here like this was peaceful and normal, almost like they were all part of the same extended family. She didn't want to leave and deal with Tara, but sooner or later, they would have to have this conversation.

Tara wanted Claire to meet her at Kelly's as soon as possible.

For a minute, she almost went upstairs and changed but couldn't really summon the energy. "I'm going out for a bit."

Looking at her from her newspaper, Poppy smiled. "Hot date?"

"Something like that."

Finn lowered his mug to the kitchen table and gave her a hard stare. "How much like a hot date?"

Poppy laughed, and Claire winked at him. "I won't be long."

She went to the front door, stopping in the vestibule to pull her coat on.

Finn propped his shoulder against the doorframe. "Wanna tell me where you're going?"

"Did you follow me out?" She pulled her hair out from her coat collar.

"Yup." He sipped his coffee. "Not liking the idea of any sort of date and you."

This jealousy thing he had going on was kind of cute. "I'm going to meet Tara."

"Why?" He frowned. "She left you to find your own way home. She's a shit friend."

Claire sighed, because even before the Denver incident, she had never been that comfortable with Tara. "I know that, and now she needs to know that."

After a moment, Finn nodded. "Okay."

"You know I wasn't asking for your permission?" His bossiness was less cute.

Finn grinned at her. "If you say so."

When she got to Kelly's, a short walk later, Claire had to suppress a groan.

Tara was sitting at one of the tables with her other bestie, Vince's ex-wife, Chelsea.

Claire hadn't grown up there, but even she knew the history between Vince and Kelly and Chelsea. Sitting in Kelly's coffee shop was the height of insensitivity and plain old petty.

"Hi Kelly." Claire didn't expect Kelly to return her smile, but she did. Kelly's smile disappeared when she saw where Claire was heading.

"There you are." Tara rolled her eyes. "And wow, are you ever going local!"

Tara said it like it was a bad thing, and Claire couldn't resist responding, "Thanks." She turned to the other woman and nodded. "Chelsea."

Chelsea was a voluptuous brunette with a face that would have been pretty if she didn't always look like she'd caught a bad smell. "Claire."

"The wedding." Tara looked at each of them in turn. "Is in two days."

It didn't take a clairvoyant to work that one out. "Ben and Poppy's wedding?"

"Obviously." Chelsea rolled her eyes.

Also, that look didn't do much for Chelsea's face.

A horrible thought occurred to Claire. "You aren't planning to go, are you?"

"Why not?" Tara sneered. "Just about the entire town is going, and I live in this town."

"I'm going." Chelsea glared at Kelly over Claire's shoulder.

"Jesus, Chelsea." Tara sneered. "Give it up already. You divorced Vince. What he does and with who is none of your business."

Chelsea scowled. "I'm still not leaving her alone with him. She's the maid of honor."

Alone seemed an exaggeration given how many people were expected at the wedding. "You and Ben are also divorced." Somebody needed to be the voice of goddamn reason. "Showing up at his and Poppy's wedding would only make a scene."

"So?" Tara grinned and made Claire's hackles stand up. "She stole Ben from me, and that means she doesn't deserve a happy wedding day."

"Ah, hell no!" Kelly stood beside their table with a cup in her hand. She banged it down on the table and coffee sloshed over the edge. "Don't even tell me you're thinking what I think you're thinking."

"Poppy didn't steal Ben from you." Claire couldn't listen to Tara's line of bullshit self-delusion any longer. "You lost him, long before Poppy even came to town."

Tara gaped at her. "That's not true."

"It totally is." Kelly glanced at Claire and then went back to Tara. "You lost him because you screwed around on him."

"What the fuck do you know?" Chelsea turned on Kelly. "It's not like you can ever keep a man."

"Girls." Peg appeared at the table. "You need to take this outside or take it down."

"This is my store." Kelly folded her arms. "I'm not taking anything outside. They can leave."

"Quite right." The town hated her enough, and Claire refused to be associated with those two anymore. She couldn't believe she'd been stupid enough to do so in the first place. "Ben is not yours," she said to Tara. "And he hasn't been for a long time. If anyone has to get real, it's you."

Peg and Kelly whipped their heads her way and stared.

"He's crazy about Poppy, and she makes him happy. Happy in a way you never did and never could. You know why?"

"Why?" Kelly was all big eyes.

Peg muttered, "Hot damn."

"Because you're the most self-centered, self-involved, selfish woman I've ever met." And Claire had her own bone to pick. "And since you couldn't be bothered to ask, I did get home safely from Denver the other night. After you ditched me and went dancing with a new man, and probably used that black Amex you got from another man to pay for it."

Tara paled. "You bitch."

"Oh, please." Claire almost laughed. "The word was invented with you in mind. You've never had a good word to say about Poppy, and that's because you're jealous."

"I don't have to listen to this." Tara stood so fast her chair toppled.

"You're jealous because you'll never have what she has," Claire called after her. "You haven't got what it takes to make Ben love you, but she has." She had to raise her voice as Tara and Chelsea reached the door. "You show up at my house for that wedding, and I'll throw you out myself."

Peg and Kelly blinked at her.

Peg found her voice first. "And I'll give you a hand taking out the trash."

Claire did her best to hide in the attic. With Poppy and Ben's wedding the next day, the Twin Elk's prayer chain had descended en masse. Their mission: to turn Winters House into dream wedding central.

Claire peeped through the porthole attic windows at the activity in the garden. Peg, with a clipboard worked a whistle and a megaphone as she got the prayer chain hopping to the outside decorations.

A flock of women harangued Finn and Hank to get final touches to the gazebo ready. It might make her a bad person, but she giggled as Hank fled and left Finn surrounded.

"Team one," Peg bellowed through her megaphone. "Let's get the organza on the gazebo."

Finn looked like he wanted to cut and run.

Peg blew her whistle, and up came the megaphone. "I specified organza, Kathy. Organza."

"I thought you might be up here," Poppy said from right behind her.

Claire started and turned. "Guilty as charged."

"I need team two to begin preparations to the dining room. Team two, report to the dining room for further instructions," Peg boomed.

Poppy joined her at the window. "Mind if I hide with you for a few minutes?"

"I don't think the bride gets to hide."

With a snort, Poppy nudged her. "If anything, you should be the one down there. As owner of the house."

"Where is Horace, by the way?"

Poppy giggled. "He locked himself in the carriage house and won't answer the door."

"Wise man." Kathy was standing at the base of a ladder instructing Finn, who was valiantly fighting the breeze and trying to drape white organza.

"How long have you been up here?" Poppy giggled as organza wrapped around Finn.

Claire joined in and laughed at the poor guy as well. She might have to stage a rescue. In a bit though, because this was funny as hell. "Peg sent me up here to look for more dinner plates."

Poppy gave her a hard stare.

"About an hour ago." Claire didn't even attempt to look sorry about it. "Hey! They don't like me, and everyone is ready to tell me why I'm such a bitch."

"Ignore them." Poppy moved away from the window and peered around the attic. "They mean well, but they can have a bit of hive mind sometimes." She turned in a circle. "Would you look at all this stuff?"

"Amazing isn't it?" Claire had actually found more dinner plates and moved the boxes closer to the door.

"Donna!" Peg blew her whistle again. "Donna, you are needed in the kitchen."

"I better get down there." Claire picked up her box of plates. "Wish me luck."

"Good luck." Poppy laughed and fell into step with her as they descended the stairs. "I came to find you to tell you I'm wearing the dress." Poppy grinned at her. "Cecily's dress."

If Claire hadn't been holding a box of plates, she would have hugged Poppy. "I'm happy to hear it."

Claire went to the dining room.

"There you are." Peg pounced as she walked through the door.

Putting the box down on the sideboard, Claire said, "There are a couple of other boxes in the attic. I'll go and get them."

"Huh." Peg gave her a hard stare. "Saw you been putting the pictures up around this place."

"Yup." Claire wouldn't have thought Peg would notice. "I think I saw someone in one of them who could be related to you."

"Probably." Peg shrugged. "My people have been here for as long as yours."

"I didn't know that."

"Of course, my people didn't make all the money and build a grand house like this."

Claire let her gaze roam the room. "She certainly is a grand old girl."

"She's a great house." Peg's gaze bored into her. "The sort of house that should be part of this community for generations to come."

And that was her cue to leave. "I'll get the other boxes."

"I'd like to see that picture some time," Peg said. "The one who looks like me."

Claire felt like she'd won a war. "And I'd love to show it to you."

"Huh." Peg looked thoughtful. "That would be…nice."

Peg looked as uncertain as Claire felt. "I'll get those plates."

"Good." As she scuttled away, Peg had the megaphone working again. "All available prayer chain members please report to the dining room. Report to the dining room immediately."

Claire almost ran into Rachel and Ann as they scurried down

the stairs in response to Peg. About Poppy's age and young mothers, they gave her looks of death as they passed.

"I hope she doesn't do anything to ruin Poppy's day," Rachel said, loud enough for her voice to carry.

Ann responded at the same pitch. "She'd better not. If she knows what's good for her."

She could have reassured them, but they probably wouldn't have listened anyway, so Claire carried on up the stairs.

"Claire!" Donna hurried up the stairs after her. "Peg sent me to help you bring some plates down."

"Thanks." Claire waited.

Donna was another of the young mothers in Twin Elks, and another member of her hate club. She drew abreast with Claire, and they climbed together. "Didn't think you'd still be here."

"Me neither." It was the truth, but now that she was there, she was looking forward to Poppy and Ben's big day. If she survived the prayer chain.

She and Donna carried the remaining boxes of plates down to the dining room in silence. Claire liked to think it was a slightly less hostile silence than the one before.

"Hey!" Kelly nodded to her and almost gave her a smile. "Do you know where Poppy is?"

"She was in the attic when I last saw her."

Kelly bristled. "What's she doing in there?"

"I locked her in." Claire had reached her limit for one day. "I locked her in the attic so I could shave her head later. Just in time for her wedding."

Kelly looked taken aback, and then she grinned. "Then it's a good thing I brought the Elmer's, because we might need to glue the veil to her bald head." She caught sight of something behind Claire, and her grin widened. "Hey, hot stuff. If all this wedding fever is giving you ideas, I'd be happy to let you make an honest woman of me."

All the women in the room turned to look at him.

Donna blushed and batted her eyes. "Hi, Finn."

"Hi." He gave Donna a warm smile, then bent and kissed Kelly's cheek. "Don't get my hopes up like that. It's not fair."

"God, you're so fine." Kelly got her hands on his shoulders and squeezed. "Why can't I get all hot and bothered over you?"

Claire had no idea why Kelly couldn't, because she was having no such trouble, and neither were a couple of other women in the room from the looks of things.

Finn turned to Claire, and she liked to think the smile he gave her was warmer than the ones he gave everyone else. The look in his eyes certainly was. "I've been sent to Grover's for supplies. I was looking for a sidekick."

"I could sidekick." She took the hand he held out to her. Her heartbeat tripped into a rapid tattoo, and her skin heated.

Because she wanted out of the house and away from the prayer chain.

Yeah, right!

———

Claire climbed into Horace's old boat of a car beside Finn. Apparently, it was all that hadn't been seconded into service yet.

It only had a lap belt, which Claire clicked into place. "He should sell this old thing."

"Bite your tongue." Finn turned in the key. "You are speaking of a vintage lady here."

Claire snorted. "A bit like his house."

The engine gargled and chugged to life, the V8 engine making a reassuring *tonk, tonk, tonk.* "So, how brutal was the inquisition today?"

"The prayer chain had opinions." With Finn, she didn't have to hide. "And they all felt comfortable sharing them."

He winced and put the car in reverse. "Ouch."

"It's okay." She made light of it. "I've got a tough skin."

Finn backed up, stopped and looked at her. "No, you don't,

babe. You walk a good talk, but underneath those come-fuck-me shoes is pure marshmallow."

"Come-fuck-me shoes?"

"Figure of speech." His grin was pure mischief. "But those shoes do give me thoughts."

Claire wasn't touching that one, and the remainder of the drive passed in silence.

They pulled up to Grover's and took up one and a half parking spots.

Peering through the windshield, Claire wished he'd gone to one of the big chain stores on the town outskirts. "I hate this place."

"Why?" Finn peered with her. "It's a great family store, and Ben always supports this place. I think he's right."

"Yeah. I get all that." Claire's judge-o-meter was all full up thanks to the prayer chain. "But this is a town store and this town doesn't like me."

Finn winked at her. "I'll protect you."

If Bart and his daughter, Mia, didn't look at her as if she was Satan's instrument of destruction on earth, Claire would have loved Grover's. It was an old school town grocer serving the needs of its community, and it was a healthy member of a dying herd.

"Finn!" Mia Grover materialized in front of them and went pale and then pink before giggling. "I didn't expect to see you today."

Finn gave her a kind, but avuncular smile. "Hi, Mia. Yup, we came in to pick up some supplies for the wedding tomorrow."

Mia's brown eyes went huge, and she wrinkled her nose. "Ooh, Chief Crowe's wedding to the widow Williams."

The widow Williams conjured up images more Gunsmoke than Poppy.

Mia glanced at her and came back for a longer look. "Miz Winters." She stressed the Winters. "We haven't seen you here in a while."

"Probably because I haven't been here in a while."

Sticking her adorably freckled nose in the air, Mia sniffed. "What can I do for you, Finn? How can I help you? Finn?"

"I have this list here." Finn acted helpless as he handed over the list.

Claire resisted the urge to hit him. He was totally taking advantage of what looked to be a monumental crush.

"Finn." Bart Grover bustled over, hands on either side of his growing belly. "Getting a few last-minute things for the wedding? Great." He rubbed his hands together. "Whole town is looking forward to it."

"I'm looking forward to it." Mia sailed past with a grocery cart. She gave Claire a hard stare. "I'm invited."

Bart cleared his throat. "That's good, Mia honey, now get Mr. Williams his order."

"Finn." Mia smirked. "I call him Finn, and I am already halfway done with Finn's order."

Bart laughed, a little forced and too loud. "Spirited girl, my Mia." He looked at Claire. "How's your dad?"

"Good." Horace was her dad, and it didn't sting as much as it had in the past. "He needs to get his hip done."

Bart tapped his belly. "You're right there. My mother got it done. Know what the first thing she noticed was?"

"No." She'd play along.

"No pain." Bart held his hands up. "No more pain. Made her wonder why she hadn't done it years ago."

"Da...Horace is being stubborn about it," she said. "But after he walks Poppy down the aisle, I'm going to see it done."

Coming past again, Mia gave them a meaningful glance. "I plan to dance at the wedding. With whoever asks me."

"Seems a solid plan." Claire gave her a smile. And then she relented. "A pretty girl like you will have lots of people asking her."

Mia did a double take, almost tripping over her shopping cart.

"Throw a couple of those cookies Mr. Winters likes in with the order," Bart called to Mia. "On us." He beamed at Claire. "Your dad started ordering those for your mom when she first got here. I guess he got hooked on them."

"For Mom?" Another way Horace kept refusing to fit into her idea of him.

"Oh, yes." Bart rubbed his palms together. "He would order all sorts of fancy stuff for Naomi. Of course, the store was my dad's then, but he'd come home and tell us all about quail eggs and caviar. Once he had lobster brought in. Fresh out of the ocean that morning."

Finn twined his fingers with hers. "We'll take that order and get going. I'm sure Peg is working on a list for me as we stand here."

"You know Peg." Bart rolled his eyes and chuckled. "I'll get that all rung up for you."

"You okay?" Finn whispered.

Not even a little. "I would be, if Horace would stay being an asshole."

CHAPTER
Fifteen

CLAIRE ARRIVED BACK at the house with Finn to find the number of people doubled. Claire might not have spent much of her childhood in Twin Elks, but she had no trouble spotting Ben's siblings.

In amongst her tall, broad sons, Dot glowed like a small sun. She even forgot to glare at Claire as she and Finn carried the groceries into the kitchen.

"Finn! Claire!" Dot flapped her hands at them. "Come and meet the boys."

The boys looked a whole lot more like men, and to a one, they were a heap of eye candy to take in. It was enough to totally fluster a woman.

"Did you all arrive together?" Finn held out his hand to a darker brother, who shared Ben's deep brown eyes but was tanned like he spent a lot of time in the sun.

"Hi, I'm Gabe." He shook Finn's hand. "I flew into LA a couple of days ago, and Mark and I came here together."

"Gabe has been working in Australia." Dot beamed up at him. "With great white sharks."

The brother Gabe had indicated stepped forward. He looked vaguely familiar to Claire.

"Mark." He shook Finn's hand.

Finn chuckled. "I know who you are, man. You guys are having a slow start to the season."

Hair of a paler brown than Ben's and Gabe's, Mark also had soulful hazel eyes surrounded by thick lashes and a pair of shoulders that screamed a physical job of some sort. Based on what Finn had said, she guessed athlete.

"Yeah." Mark shrugged. "But it's not where you are in November that counts."

Finn finished for him. "It's where you are in April."

"Hi." Gabe had turned his attention to her. "You must be Claire?"

"Hi." It came out a bit strangled.

Then Mark smiled at her, and she didn't trust her voice, so she inanely grinned in response to his hello.

"Over here is my New York highflyer." Dot tugged another son, this one even lighter haired than Mark but combined to devastating effect with Ben's coffee dark eyes.

Dressed in what Claire would lay money on were designer jeans and a custom-tailored button-up, his voice was poured cream over ice. "Otherwise known as Luke and not a highflyer, but certainly a New Yorker." He shook her hand and then Finn's.

Dot poked Luke's arm. "You're not a New Yorker. This is still your home."

Looking at his mother, Luke gave her a noncommittal smile.

"And this is my baby." Dot had another son by the arm and dragged him forward.

Dot's baby was even taller than Ben and built broader than Mark. He also had the most perfect bone structure Claire had ever seen. His face was saved from pretty by a pair of piercing hazel eyes. He was also tanned like he spent hours in the sun. Worn cropped close to his head, his hair appeared dark like Ben's.

"Rafe." He held out his hand to her and then Finn.

Dot tucked her arm through his. "Rafe is a doctor, and he's been working in Mozambique."

"Doctors without Borders isn't it?" Finn glanced at Dot and then Rafe.

Dot nodded enthusiastically. "But I'm very glad to have him back."

"She's glad to have all of them back." Ben appeared at the back of his brothers and smiled at his mother.

"Yes, I am." Dot vibrated with energy. "And I've already warned them I'll do everything I can to make them stay."

Gabe put an arm around Dot's shoulders. "How about we start with a wedding?"

"Yeah." Mark looked around the kitchen. "Where are you hiding the bride?"

"I'm here." Poppy appeared in the doorway dressed in a pretty blue and white wraparound dress. As her normal attire was jeans and T-shirts, she must have made an effort. She held up one hand like a child in school and then clasped both in front of her so tightly the knuckles turned white.

Claire wanted to reassure her she looked exactly like Poppy, sweet, pretty, and adorable.

Luke got to her first and bent and kissed her cheek. "I've been wondering who would shake my brother up. I can see why he couldn't let you go."

Poppy blushed and laughed. "Ben said you were a charmer."

The brothers greeted Poppy one by one. Ben stood beside her, his arm around her waist, and smiling like he'd won the lottery, singlehandedly brought about world peace, and declared every day Christmas.

The happiness in the kitchen was infectious and reached out and included Claire and Finn.

By the time Horace stormed in thirty minutes later, the atmosphere was relaxed and jovial.

"Is that woman in here?" Horace sidled closer to the table.

Dot chuckled. "No, Peg went home a couple of hours ago."

"Thank you, God." Horace took a seat and dropped his head into his hands. "She's going to drive me crazy."

"Never mind." Dot patted his shoulder. She looked at Claire and winked. "You'll only have to do this one more time."

"Oh." Claire flushed under all the curious gazes pointed her way. "I'm not getting married."

"Ever?" Mark blinked at her.

"Of course, you aren't." Dot smiled. "Let's get everyone fed."

Claire worked, under Dot's supervision, to get a family dinner on the large kitchen table.

Maybe it was her happiness over having her family back together, but Dot was warm and inclusive with Claire. She couldn't help hoping it was because Dot maybe liked her a bit now. Dot radiated the sort of warmth you wanted to get close to.

Brinn and Ciara wandered in and were immediately swept into a sea of new uncles. Seeming less impressed, Ryan hung back and stayed by Ben's side.

Sean stuck close to Dot but did allow himself to be passed around a bit.

When dinner was served, Claire was swept to the table with everyone else.

She took a seat beside Gabe.

Finn wedged a chair between her and Rafe and draped his arm over the back of her chair.

Gabe looked at Finn's arm then Claire and grinned. He turned his body to her. "Tell me about yourself, Claire."

"Well, I'm Horace's daughter." She motioned her father. "But I didn't grow up here. I grew up in Boston."

"I remember now." Gabe took a dish of lasagna from Luke on his left and offered it to her. "And I certainly would have remembered you if we went to school with you."

Finn stiffened and dropped his hand to her nape.

"We would have been in the same year." Claire couldn't resist giving the dragon a prod.

Gabe's twinkling eyes told her he was on to her and Finn,

and game to play along. "I would have let you cheat off my biology homework."

"What a gentleman."

Halfway through dinner, Luke tapped his wine glass and stood.

The table fell silent.

"Gabe is the next oldest brother, but he's too busy flirting with Claire to do this, so it falls to me."

Mark snorted and threw a dinner roll at him. "You just like being the center of attention."

"This from you." Ben raised an eyebrow at Mark.

The roll came back at Mark and almost hit him. Lightning-fast reflexes saved him.

"Boys." Dot sent a hard look around the table. Her expression softened as she looked at Ryan. "Don't let them teach you their horrible habits."

Ryan grinned back at her, but he had big eyes on all the brothers.

"Anyway." Luke cleared his throat. "It's been a long time since we were all together, and I can't think of a happier occasion."

Table thumps and whistles greeted that.

"Ben, you got lucky. Not only to have this gorgeous woman in your life, but she brought her wonderful kids with her." He held up his glass to Poppy. "To Poppy. If you run now, we'll understand."

More laughter and thumping.

"And now, Poppy." Luke turned and grinned at her. "We are going to take Ben away from you and give him a bachelor night."

Ben looked startled. "No, I—"

"Don't make us hogtie you." Gabe looked altogether too delighted by the idea for Claire's peace of mind. "Our brother is getting married, and we're doing this in style."

"Well, the Bugling Elk at any rate," Rafe said. "Do they still have—"

"Yes," Finn said. "Rest assured that the Bugling Elk has not changed."

"Right then." Luke looked around the table. "Shall we? Finn and Horace, you're part of this, so don't think you've escaped."

Ben looked hesitant. "I think we should help clean up."

"No, no." Dot waved her hands. "You go and have fun. Just remember, no hookers and no blow."

"Shit, Ma." Mark looked sick. "I do not want to hear that coming out of your mouth. Ever."

———

It took about twenty minutes to get all the men out of the house and the cleanup started. Claire took a dish away from Poppy. "Nope! You're the bride. Either take a seat and have another glass of wine or get your beauty sleep."

"I'm not sure I can sleep." Poppy took a seat at the table.

"Speaking of sleep." Dot rounded up the children. "Let's get this lot to bed. We all have a big day tomorrow."

Ryan shifted in his seat. "Don't worry about me, Dot. I don't need a lot of sleep."

"Go." Dot pointed up the stairs.

A woman who had raised five boys versus Ryan, no competition, and Ryan dragged his feet up stairs.

"Here." Claire refilled Poppy's glass and cleared the table. "You nervous?"

"A bit." Poppy gave a rueful laugh. "Last time I got married, I made a really bad decision. I know Ben is nothing like Sean. It's myself I don't altogether trust."

"Ben's a great guy." Claire glanced up from loading the dishwasher. Until she'd gotten to know him better, she would only have judged him by Tara's opinion of Ben.

Tara had no idea how much she'd lost out. First in letting Ben go, and secondly, in not appreciating what she had when she did. All the black Amexes in the world couldn't make Tara as happy as Poppy looked now.

Dot returned to the kitchen. "The children would like you to kiss them goodnight." With a groan, she sat at the table and poured herself a glass of wine. "Although they're all a bit revved up and it might take a while to get them down."

"They're excited." Poppy stood. "We all are."

With an affectionate look on her face, Dot watched Poppy leave the kitchen. "It was a lucky day that girl crashed into Ben's life."

"I never did hear how they met." Claire wiped down the counters.

Dot laughed. "Poppy begged Ben to arrest her."

"What?" That got her full attention.

"Poppy was driving from Philly to California and about the time she hit our little corner of the world, Sean was sick, the twins were bored, and Ryan was complaining. Poor Poppy had caught Sean's flu and didn't even know it."

Claire tried to picture it. "Sounds like hell."

"It was. Anyway, she was trying to get to Walmart so she could change Sean—who was stinking up the van—when Ryan vomited and nearly set the twins off. Poppy shot a red light by mistake, and Ben pulled her over." Dot giggled. "I wasn't there, but Ben tells me he was approaching the car, cautiously because it was an out of town plate, when this woman leaps out and begs him to take her away."

"What did he do?"

"He brought her to me." Dot gave a misty smile. "It was love at first sight for me. Ben took a little longer to come around to admitting it."

It was like something out of a romantic comedy, and Claire sighed as she wiped off the range top. "I never asked how she ended up living here."

"You didn't?" Dot raised an eyebrow. "When you came to town hell-bent on ousting her?"

Claire's face heated. "Well, it didn't look good from my perspective."

"I suppose." Dot gave her that much. "Ben was smitten, only because of Tara, he was fighting admitting as much. Peg and I made a plan to keep Poppy around bit longer. Put her in his path and see if nature took its course."

"Tara will survive." Claire filled Dot in. "She's dating some guy with a black American Express card now."

"I'm sure Tara and the card will be very happy together," Dot said with a prim smile.

Claire laughed. Dot had never shown her this side of her before. Mainly because by default, she'd landed in Team Tara. "Anyway, I don't think I'll be hearing from her any time soon."

"I reckon not." Dot sipped her wine. "I've heard the story about what you said to her from about five different people. Just for the record, you didn't threaten to pop a cap in her ass, did you?"

"Uh, no." Claire finished putting the dry ingredients back in the pantry and joined Dot at the table. "But I did tell her she wasn't welcome tomorrow, and I would personally remove her if she came."

Dot nodded. "No, you're definitely off her Christmas card list."

Claire joined in Dot's laughter.

"Tell me about the new dress Poppy said you found for her." Dot stretched her legs out in front of her.

"It's beautiful. A wedding gown that belonged to Cecily, the bride the house was built for." Claire poured herself some wine. "It looks perfect on Poppy."

Dot blinked at her. "I swear I never on my life saw this coming." She shook her head. "That is the loveliest thing to do, Claire Mathews. I used to think I knew who you were, but now I have no idea."

Claire sipped her wine. "God, Dot. Life would be so much easier if I had an answer to that question."

CHAPTER
Sixteen

CLAIRE SCORED an invitation to help the bride get ready.

Kelly already had the champagne flowing when she arrived, and Dot was tearing up.

The dress looked perfect on Poppy.

"Oh…" Dot lost the battle and wept. "You're so l-lovely, and Ben is s-so lucky to have you. And I'm so happy you're g-going to be my daughter-in-law."

"Jeez, Dot." Kelly put her arm around Dot's shoulders. "You sound really happy."

Claire held up the veil to Poppy, but Poppy shook her heads. "Veils are for first time brides."

It didn't matter how much the three of them argued, Poppy stood firm and went with fresh flowers in her hair.

Which was such a great choice, Dot went off into tears again.

Brinn swished the skirt of her pale pink dress and grinned at Claire. "I look pretty. Ciara too."

"Yes, you do." She straightened Ciara's satin sash.

Ciara heaved a sigh. "I'm only wearing this dress because it's our wedding day."

Claire winked. "Got it."

"Also." Ciara leaned closer and whispered, "Cecily is very happy."

"I know," Claire whispered back. "I can feel her."

"I'm hungry," Ryan said.

Proud of her forethought, Claire handed him a bag of apple slices and some nuts. "There'll be a lot more food later but have that until we can get you all married."

Hair slicked back and trying his best not to fidget, Ryan wore smart chinos and a white shirt. Poppy didn't like little boys in suits, so Sean wore the same. They sat down to share the snack and the twins soon joined them.

Kelly finished Poppy's makeup in peace and stepped back. "And you're done."

"Okay." After a glass and a half of champagne and the liberal application of waterproof mascara and setting spray, Dot got it together. "The children and I will greet our guests."

Brinn frowned. "But—"

"Come along." Dot got the sort of tone that made Claire nearly follow her out the door.

Poppy's children were no match for Dot.

"Five boys give you mad kid wrangling skills." Kelly shook her head. "And the Crowe boys were a handful." Then she snort-laughed. "That's what she said."

Claire joined Kelly and Poppy at the bedroom window. A steady stream of people joined the crowd on the lawn of Winters House.

White wooden chairs wrapped in tulle bows faced the gazebo. Organza drapery, fresh flowers and jar candles made the gazebo look like a romantic fairytale. Most of the chairs were already full, and Peg was supervising the addition of foldout chairs in the back.

"Is everyone from Twin Elks here?" Poppy almost pressed her nose to the glass.

"Pretty much." Kelly sniffed. "Ben was already loved by

everyone and with him marrying you, it's our own romantic miracle."

"He's so handsome and perfect." Poppy sighed.

Ben stood near the gazebo, all four of his brothers around him.

"Damn those Crowe boys." Kelly sighed.

Claire got it. "They're all so…"

"Yeah." Kelly pressed her nose to the glass. "Gabe was in the same year as me. If it hadn't been for Vince, I might have succumbed to a crush on him."

"Succumbed?"

"Believe me." Kelly rolled her eyes. "I must have been the only girl in our year who didn't."

"Poppy?" A beautiful woman dressed in a maxi dress appeared in the bedroom door. Her resemblance to Poppy was unmistakable.

"Mom?" Poppy closed the distance, and the two women embraced.

"Mom?" Claire couldn't stop herself from mouthing the question to Kelly. Poppy's mom seriously could pass for her older sister.

Kelly rolled her eyes and nodded. "It's not right. I comfort myself with the knowledge she was young when she had Poppy."

Poppy's mom held her at arm's length. "I'm happy for you, baby. You found yourself a good one."

"I'm glad you made it." Poppy hugged her mother.

If she ever got married, Mom probably wouldn't make it to her wedding, not with the speed at which her Alzheimer's was progressing.

"Doing okay there, slugger?" Kelly nudged her.

Claire didn't trust herself to speak, so she nodded.

"Heather." Kelly kissed Poppy's mom on the cheek. "You're looking great as ever. Lovely to see you."

Heather flushed and laughed. "Thank you. I wouldn't miss my baby girl's big day for anything."

Poppy threw Heather a glance, and Heather looked away. There was a story there, but it didn't look like a happy one, so it didn't belong to today.

Kelly clapped her hands. "Let's get this family married."

———

Claire was always a crier at weddings, and this one was a doozy.

Poppy made a gorgeous bride, given away by Horace with her children accompanying her to the altar.

Halfway through, Sean got fussy, and Ben picked him up.

Sean put his head on Ben's shoulder and went still.

If there was a dry eye in the garden before, there wasn't one now.

Promising their lives to each other, Ben and Poppy looked like a storybook couple. The sincere depth of their love for each other filled their vows with meaning.

After giving Poppy away, Horace had taken a seat beside Claire in the front row. She'd never pictured herself getting married, so never really thought about whether she could ask her dad to give her away.

Without stopping to question the impulse, Claire slipped her hand into Horace's.

He stilled and glanced at her but wrapped his fingers around hers.

God only knew if there would ever come a time when they could bridge the gap between them, but they could sit there and feel the connection for a few minutes.

As soon as the vows were spoken, the kissing over, Peg marshaled the troops. Tables and chairs appeared, sun parasols, tablecloths, cutlery and crockery, and food. So much food Claire didn't know who was going to eat it all.

She stayed out of the way with Horace. It gave her the perfect excuse to ogle Finn, gorgeous in a charcoal gray suit and open collar shirt. The Crowe brothers also made for eye candy, but Finn snagged most of her attention.

Peg had them all working.

"Dear God." Horace chuckled as Peg caught Rafe and Luke trying to escape and sent them off somewhere. "I've never been gladder for my bum hip."

"Indeed." Claire nudged him. "And I'm here to make sure you don't keel over or anything."

Horace's chuckled bloomed into a laugh. "Don't count me out yet, girlie. There's still some fight in this old man."

"Don't I know it." She rolled her eyes, but the atmosphere was easy between them, companionable. "Poppy looked gorgeous."

"Yes, she did." Horace smiled. "Did you find Cecily's dress for her?"

"Yup, I think I mentioned it to you the other day. I wasn't sure it was Cecily's dress."

Horace nodded. "Oh yes, it came from England with her."

"I'd like to hear her full story someday."

Horace nodded. "And I'd like to tell it to you."

A dance floor was set up on the back patio, and with much trepidation Claire saw Hank Styles take out a guitar and tune it.

Horace sighed and looked around him. "This house was made for days like this."

It was true. Children ran through adult legs. People milled in groups, talking, laughing, eating, and drinking. Even Dot's enormous puppy had joined the fray.

The house was made for days like this, and if it remained part of Twin Elks, there could be plenty more of them. Except where did that leave Mom and the cost of her care? She still didn't feel confident having that conversation with Horace, but the idea of letting the house slip out of the Winters family gnawed like a rotten tooth.

For today though, she pushed that problem aside.

"Horace!" Peg bore down on them. "Hank and his band forgot to bring extension cords, do you have any?"

"Yup, in the utility room." Horace went to lever himself to his feet.

Claire stood. "Don't worry, I got this, Dad."

They both froze and stared at each other. Then Claire turned and went to find the extension cords.

She was coming out of the utility room when a strong arm snaked around her waist and tugged her back against his chest. "Hey," Finn murmured in her ear. "You look beautiful today."

Claire leaned into the warmth and strength of his chest. "So do you."

Finn's chuckle rumbled through her. "There'll be dancing later."

"Oh?" She turned her head a bit but didn't look at him.

"Yeah." Finn nuzzled her neck. "Save all the slow ones for me."

He made her giggle like a sixteen-year-old. "Maybe." She slid out from beneath his hold and threw him a mischievous look. "It depends who else asks me."

Finn's grin in response let her know her challenge had been accepted.

In a much lighter mood, she went off with the extension cords.

Hank's band, the Sixties Stylers, proved much better than expected. Given, her expectation had not been high, but they kept the town entertained with a selection of sixties and seventies hits.

Between their sets, Peg's nephew—who also owned Doug's One-Stop Service: the place for all your car, truck, tractor, and lawn mower repairs for over sixty years—took his turn with Doug's Dancing Grooves Disco.

Luke, who smelled fantastic, smoothly maneuvered her around the floor to Santana. Then Gabe took her through the worst salsa attempt in history, which ended with them laughing so hard they could barely stand.

The Stylers took over, and Rafe and she got groovy with *Wild Thing*, and enjoyed it so much, they stayed where they were for *I'm a Believer*. Mark cut in and demonstrated that professional athletes did not necessarily have rhythm. He did have a killer body though.

Mia Grover hadn't left the dance floor yet, and she even managed a tight smile in Claire's direction.

After Mark, she needed a break and sat at one of the tables.

Kelly dropped into the chair next to her. "Whew!" She fanned herself with a napkin. "Town events are so much more fun when Dot's boys are here. They up the town hotness quotient by a thousand percent."

"Speaking of hotness quotient." She nudged Kelly in Vince's direction.

Kelly's smile dimmed. "Nah. Chelsea and his kids are here, and I don't want to make things awkward."

"Chelsea's here?" Surely Tara wouldn't…

With a shrug, Kelly said, "I didn't expect her to come either. Not after your burn in the store the other day, but I guess her desire to keep an eye on Vince got the better of her."

"But they're divorced." Claire was relieved Tara had decided to stay away. Not that she would hesitate to make good on her threat.

Kelly shook her head. "That doesn't matter to Chelsea. As long as she wins, she's happy." Then Kelly nudged her. "I see someone heading your way."

Gaze locked on her with an intensity that made her shiver, Finn stalked her.

Her voice came out a bit breathy. "He could be coming for you."

"Ah, no." Kelly chuckled. "Or my panties would be going up in flame right now."

Finn stopped in front of them and nodded to Kelly. "Hey."

"Hey yourself." Kelly stood. "And that's my cue to make myself scarce."

"You don't have to—"

Finn tugged Claire to her feet. "Dance with me."

Claire couldn't have told you what song was playing. Pressed against Finn, she relaxed into his hold and let the motion of his body guide her. She closed her eyes and got the full sensory impact of his hard chest against her breasts, the warmth of him through his shirt, the pound of his heart against her palm and the silk of his hair between her fingers. He smelled of sandalwood and fresh linen, and he moved her across the dance floor like an extension of himself.

One song drifted into another, and they stayed where they were.

Finn dipped his head, his mouth near her ear. "So, Dot is taking the kids tonight. She and Ben's brothers are going to do something special with them so Ben and Poppy can slip away for the night."

"Really?" Her mouth dried and her pulse kicked into a hard thump. With the kids gone and Ben and Poppy on their wedding night, she and Finn had the house to themselves. Of course, there was always Horace, but he stayed in the carriage house. "What are you saying?"

"I'm saying I don't want to keep fighting this. I want to do something really inadvisable. With you." He planted a hot kiss against her neck. "All you need to say is yes, Finn or no, Finn."

There really was nothing to think about. "Yes, Finn."

CHAPTER
Seventeen

THEY SEPARATED a couple of songs later. Anticipation tingling through Claire like champagne bubbles in her veins.

It still took hours for the night to wind down. Poppy and Ben left around eight to a raucous send off, complete with Just Married signs and cans tied to the car's bumper.

Having had a very full day, Sean burst into tears at the sight of his mother driving away, wailing for Poppy like his little heart was broken.

Dot tried to hold him, but he wriggled like a dying trout in her arms.

"There now, big guy." Luke took Sean from Dot and held him against his shoulder, not bothered by toddler snot and tears on his designer suit. His big hand almost covered Sean's back as he stroked. "Why don't we guys go and find something else to do?"

Sean whined a bit longer but settled down. His hand came up and gripped Luke's perfectly pressed lapel.

"Mom." Luke spoke over Sean's head. "I think the kids have had it for one day. Let's get them home."

Brinn immediately stamped her foot and crossed her arms. "No! I don't want to go home. I want to dance."

A little less fierce of face, but Ciara echoed her.

Claire stepped forward, but Rafe stopped her. "We got this."

"Hey." Mark looked at the twins. "I thought we were going to make s'mores and watch a movie together."

"Yeah, me too." Gabe stuffed his hands in his pockets. His suit and shirt looked a bit rumpled, and his hair stood up as if he'd run his fingers through it. "I was going to make some popcorn, and my special grilled cheese."

Brinn wavered and squinted at Gabe. "What's special about it?"

"I can't tell you that." Gabe looked flabbergasted that she would ask. "It's a secret."

Ciara giggled and looked at Brinn.

Still not going softly, Brinn glared at Mark. "What movie?"

"D'oh!" Mark rolled his eyes. "*Frozen*, of course."

"And then *Tangled*," Gabe said. "Of course. I love me some Maximus."

Ryan shoved his way into the circle. "Those are girl's movies."

"Oh, yeah!" Mark took a step toward him. "Do I look like a girl?"

Giggling, Ryan nodded. "Yes."

"Then you're about to get your butt kicked by a girl." Mark lunged for him, which sent Ryan shrieking down the garden. Mark looked at her and Finn. "That's my exit."

He trotted after a giggling Ryan.

Luke rocked a drowsy Sean as Gabe gathered up the girls and their backpacks.

"Have a good night." Dot surprised Claire by kissing her cheek. She spoiled the tender moment with a secret wink. "Have a very good night."

"Right, Prayer Chain!" Peg got on the loud hailer. "Let's get this cleared away."

Finn took her hand and tugged her toward the house. "I think they've got it from here."

———

Being swept away by the moment, wrapped around Finn as they swayed together on a dance floor—the candles, the romance, the music—not the same as being led upstairs with the sole intent to do the deed. It flashed neon bright, all caps in her brain. THE. DEED.

Unwelcome thoughts jeered and snapped at her. Lights on, lights off? Definitely lights off with the extra pounds she'd been adding since she had arrived in Twin Elks.

How did the etiquette work? They got upstairs and, presumably, closed the door. She would have to insist on the door being closed. Peg could come upstairs at any moment and ask where to put the extra plates. "Are you sure they won't need me?"

"Peg doesn't need anyone or anything." Finn threw her a smile over his shoulder. "That woman could lead an Antarctic expedition with a toothbrush and a whistle."

A shrill giggle, and a whole lot too much, came out Claire's mouth.

So, door closed and then what? Did she launch herself at him, or wait for Finn to make the first move? *Oh God, this was a bad idea.* Finn might think she was smooth and sophisticated. Big city girl like her. He would expect her to be the sort of girl who wore lace underwear without it disappearing up her butt crack.

They reached the top of the stairs. She wanted him; she really did.

"Donna!" Peg boomed from the garden. "Donna report to kitchen clearing detail."

Just not with Peg leading the charge in the garden.

In her fantasy, it happened organically. Say, Finn and her in the kitchen. Their eyes meet over a cup of coffee. Finn backs her into the counter. Maybe lifts her onto the counter and steps between her thighs.

Finn opened the door to his room and led her inside.

The door clicked shut behind them and made her jump.

"Get those candles out! Stat!" Peg struck again. "Dismantling crew. Move in."

It was too much, and Claire snort laughed. She couldn't help it.

Blue eyes gleaming with humor, Finn raised an eyebrow at her.

Leaning back against the door she gave in to the urge and laughed. Some of the tension in her evaporated.

Cocking his head, Finn watched her with amusement. He crooked his finger at her. "Come here, sweetheart."

"You come here." Her laughter subsided to a grin.

Finn raised an eyebrow. "I must come there?"

"Yup." She slid her hands behind her butt and pinned them to the door.

Sighing, Finn sauntered toward her, his eyes glinting with mischief. "Well, then, I don't mind if I do."

Feeling smug, she grinned at him.

Deliberately, he kept coming until he stopped when his toes nudged hers. He raised one arm and put his forearm beside her head. Bringing the other arm up, he bracketed her head.

His chest brushed her breasts. He was so close she could see the darker, indigo flecks in his eyes.

Her breath sighed out of her lungs, and she was acutely aware of the heat of him carrying the subtle scent of sandalwood on warm skin.

He pressed his forehead to hers. "I'm here. Now what?"

"Furniture crew," Peg bellowed. "Begin stacking."

Groaning, Finn leaned away from her and stepped back. He held out his hand. "Come on, Miss Mathews. Let's have a drink, and you can stop looking at me as if I'm leading you into my red room of pain."

"Pfft!" Claire came away from the door. Maybe she had been overreacting. A bit. Like a whole lot. This was Finn and before anything else she liked him. "Maybe I'm disappointed that you're not."

"Really?" He gave her a sexy little half smile. "You got a kink, Miss Mathews? I can see if I can accommodate that."

"No kinks." Finn had put his stamp on the space. Military neat, his work boots were tucked side by side beside the wardrobe. The coat hanging behind the door was a large, black parka, more function than form. A man's watch sat on the bedside table beside a book on woodworking.

"I snuck this away earlier." Finn produced a bottle of red and a corkscrew.

Claire picked up the two glasses on the dresser that he must also have snuck away earlier. "A man with a plan?"

"Or a desperate hope." Finn grinned and popped the cork.

This was more like them. Claire slipped her heels off and joined him at the deep casement by the window. She held the glasses up for him to pour. "Poppy looked beautiful."

"Poppy is always beautiful." Finn poured the red wine. "But today she looked crazy happy and that's even better."

Claire sat on the window seat and leaned her back against the wall. This room faced the garden and she had a perfect view of Peg's minions scurrying back and forth from the house. "Ben looked like he was the luckiest man on the planet."

Finn nodded and sat on the other side of the window seat. He picked her feet up and put them on his lap. He worked his thumbs into her sore instep. "The second luckiest man on the planet."

Claire swallowed her wine, relieved she hadn't snort-laughed red wine. "Smooth, Williams, so smooth."

"So, what was the scenario happening in your head?" Finn found the knot of tired muscle in her foot arch and pressed. "We get to the room and I lunge?"

His fingers were actual magic, and Claire moaned. "I hadn't gotten that far. I was still hammering out lights on versus lights off."

"Definitely lights on." He bent his head and worked his sorcery on her tired foot muscles. "You're beautiful, Claire, and

I've spent too much time imagining what you look like naked to agree to lights off."

"Oh." It came out in a breath, because what the hell else was a girl to say to something like that? And, hold the phone. "Imagining?"

"Yeah." House cats purred, leopards purred, and so did Finn Williams. Finn did it better. His hands moved over her ankles and kneaded her calf muscles. "This thing between us, babe, it's been brewing since you arrived."

"Really?" It totally had, and his magic fingers were doing impossible things to her calves. "You may have a point."

"Uh-huh."

And dear God, that smirk ought to be banned. That much confidence and charm were lethal and aimed at her.

His big hands reached her knee bend and he spread his fingers.

Claire was holding her breath, and she released it. Light gleamed on his dark hair and loved on the sharp angles of his face. "Finn?"

"Umm."

"Yes."

He looked up, blue gaze intent enough to stop her breathing once again. "Yes?"

All this hesitation wasn't going to cut it and she put her wine glass aside. Crawling on all fours she pinned him in place. "Kiss me."

"Ask me nicely."

"Kiss me, please."

Framing her face with his hands, he brought her mouth to his. He sucked her bottom lip into his mouth. "So sweet." He slanted his head and opened his mouth over hers. His tongue touched her bottom lip.

Claire opened to the invitation. He tasted of red wine and heat. She tangled her tongue with his and deepened the kiss.

On a groan, Finn met her need. Gentle was replaced with

hungry as he devoured her. His hands dropped to her hips encouraging her to straddle him.

One knee nudged the window, her other leg slipped off the bench. She growled her frustration and released the kiss.

As she stood, his blue gaze burned hot and needy.

The power went straight to her head, and she slid her zipper down.

Finn's gaze tracked the movement.

She pushed one strap down her arm and then the other.

Humming his approval, Finn stood and approached her. He spread his hands over her shoulders and then down her arms, taking the straps with him. The dress slithered to the ground, and Claire stepped out of it.

Erect, her nipples pressed through the lacy fabric of her bra.

He cupped both her breasts, his thumbs moving over her nipples.

Ducking his head, Finn put a burning wet kiss to her neck. He trailed open mouthed kisses to her ear and sucked as he caressed her breasts.

Claire needed to feel his hands on her skin, so she unclasped her bra.

Finn brushed it aside and finally put his hands on her.

Heat shot through Claire, and she arched into his touch.

His other hand spread over her lower back and pressed her against his erection. Groaning, he slid his hand down to caress her bottom and press his fingers into her soft flesh.

Claire couldn't get close enough. She rubbed against him, gasping when his cock hit the sweet spot.

Finn was wearing far too many clothes, and she worked the buttons loose on his shirt. His shirt hung open and gave her a tantalizing glimpse of hard flesh beneath. Taking her time, she pushed the placket open, like unwrapping her own special gift.

His skin burned beneath her palm, silken over the hard sculpting of his muscle. She slid her hands over his chest, and down the corrugated muscle of his stomach.

Hissing in a breath, Finn's abs tightened beneath her touch. He watched the progress of her hand, a flush riding the hard planes of his cheekbones.

"Such a beautiful man." Claire's fingers encountered his belt and unbuckled. She flicked open the clasp and then the button on his formal pants. His cock made a hard ridge against the zipper.

He groaned as she ran the back of her fingers over him. "Touch me."

"Ask me nicely."

"Please." He breathed sharply. "Touch me, baby."

Claire slid his zipper down and pushed his pants from his slim hips. Underneath, he wore black boxers that outlined the shape of him. She slid her hands inside his boxers and stroked him.

"Fuck." Finn dropped his head back, his clenched teeth creating lines of tension in his neck. "That feels so good."

Stroking him made her even more impatient, and Claire fastened her mouth over his.

Finn speared his fingers into her hair and positioned her mouth as he wanted it.

His kiss grew ravenous, demanding.

His cock flexed in her hand and Finn put one hand over hers. "Slowly." He took her hand off him and draped her arm over his shoulder. "My turn."

He slid his hands down to her breasts, kneading and testing their weight. Then he slid them down her sides, so wide they covered her ribcage. Callouses from working with them stroked her skin.

He reached her hips and hooked his fingers inside her panties and pushed them down her hips.

Needing to be naked, Claire shimmied out of them.

Bare skin to bare skin, they pressed against each other. Claire wanted to crawl inside all his hard flesh pressed against her.

Finn inserted one hand between her thighs. His fingers found her wet crevice and slid through her flesh.

Moaning her need, Claire moved against his clever fingers.

His thumb found her clit and stroked. His voice rasped in her ear. "Is this what you need, baby?"

"More." Her breath came in pants between kisses.

Finn backed her up.

When her legs hit the bed, she clambered on to it, not giving a shit about grace but wanting his body on hers, heavy and demanding.

His forearms on either side of her head, Finn came down over her. Connecting groin to groin, belly to belly and finally, chest to breasts. He framed her face and pressed his body into hers.

His mouth sought hers in a kiss that had her arching to get closer.

She opened her thighs to make a place for him.

His cock slid against her, and she pushed into the delicious friction.

"Condom." Finn reared back, breathing hard. He opened a drawer in his bedside table and pulled out a condom. He slid it over his cock, then sat back and looked at her naked beneath him.

"Look at you." He stroked one hand down her breasts, over her tummy and cupped her between the thighs. His palm pressed into her clitoris as he pushed one finger and then two inside her.

"Please, Finn." Claire writhed against him. "I need you inside me."

He increased the pressure on her clit. With his other hand, he stroked his cock. "Is this what you want?"

Nearly incoherent with need, Claire nodded. Seeing him touch himself drove her nearly insane. "Yes."

Finn removed his hand from her and guided his cock to her entrance.

Claire held her breath as he paused for a moment and then

slid inside her.

He was so hard and big, he filled her up, but she was wet enough to take him. All of him, until he was seated deep inside her.

Finn put his hands on either side of her shoulders and flexed into her. He dropped his head and watched their connection. His breath came in harsh pants as he watched himself move inside her.

Claire wrapped her legs around his back and tilted her pelvis to take him deeper.

"Jesus." Finn screwed his eyes shut. "You're gripping me so tight."

His thrusts got deeper, more determined.

Claire held on to his arms as the pace increased. The wet slap of his flesh against hers came faster.

The beginning of her orgasm unfurled deep inside her and spread through her pelvis and down her thighs. The pleasure grew in waves of intensity, and Finn moved harder and faster inside her. The pinnacle hovered within reach.

Finn's thrusts led the way, pushing her relentlessly forward until Claire tipped over the edge. Her back arched, and a low scream forced its way out her mouth.

Finn's pace grew quicker, urgent and not as deliberate as he sought release. And then he was there, his neck muscles straining, teeth clenching as he rasped a harsh groan and emptied himself inside her.

Frozen in the moment, they stayed like that. Then Finn let out a long sigh and dropped his head. He lowered himself to his forearms and pressed his sweaty skin to hers. His breath rasped in her ear as he kissed her temple, her cheek, and finally her mouth. "Claire," he whispered. "Claire."

He didn't need to say anymore. She knew what he meant. Something fundamental had changed between them in this bed. An elemental connection had been forged, and it ran so much deeper than sex.

CHAPTER
Eighteen

CLAIRE SLIPPED OUT of Finn's bed as dawn started making inroads into the night. He slept on his stomach, arms flung out. She took a moment to take a mental picture. The sheets pooled low on his back, draping his ass.

He was such a beautiful man, even with the harsh scars across his back. She ached for the pain he must have suffered to get those.

But she also needed time to get her head together.

Sneaking around his room, she gathered her clothes and slipped into the hall. Nobody was about, and she tiptoed naked into her room and shut the door behind her.

Her head was so full of Finn, and the emotions tangling in her chest made it hard to breathe.

Claire flipped on her shower and stepped beneath the spray. It was still cold, shocking her warm flesh and making her gasp. She welcomed the discomfort. It grounded her.

And then the tears came. She had no idea why she was crying, but they wouldn't stop. They came from a place inside her that had been dead for so long she'd forgotten it was there.

It was a place filled with hope and dreams and it brought a

near crippling pain. Like a door welded shut had been forced open and left her bared and vulnerable.

———

Finn waited to hear the door close before he opened his eyes. Last night had been incredible. They'd made love three times before exhaustion claimed them. He pressed his face into her pillow and drew the smell of Claire deep into his lungs.

He'd let her sneak out this morning. If she needed time, he would give her that. Once he'd surrendered to the inevitable, all his concerns had shifted into perspective. Her being Horace's daughter was only an issue if he intended to mess her around. She might not think she was staying now, but he could work on that. The only remaining nag was around him. Watching Ben last night, witnessing that much happiness, Finn had felt hope for the first time in years. Maybe he was worth loving, and maybe he did deserve that happily ever after. Or just maybe it had nothing to do with being worthy or deserving, but a whole lot more to do with opening up and accepting.

Forcing the issue with Claire at this moment would only risk pushing her away. She had so much to untangle inside her, and he didn't want to be another thread that constricted her. He could step back, wait her out, because he was playing a long game and playing it for keeps.

———

Claire showered and woke up a few hours later. Hunger drove her into the kitchen.

Hips propped against the counter, Finn was drinking coffee and staring out the kitchen window.

She stopped short of the kitchen threshold not sure what to do. The most grown up option was to stroll into the kitchen, smile and help herself to coffee. Say something not clingy but keep the door open and see where that led.

Problem being, she wasn't made that way. Under her heels and makeup, covered by her designer duds was a girl who craved commitment, needed that connection to open herself up. Casual sex had never been her thing. Sex meant something to her, and the intimacy she had shared with Finn last night had surpassed any of her previous encounters.

"You going to stand there all day?" Finn stared out the window and sipped his coffee.

He had eyes in the back of his head, and she had to laugh. "I was thinking about it."

"Anyone ever suggested to you that you might overthink things?" He turned his head and that blue gaze met hers.

Grabbing her go-girl, she stepped into the kitchen. "It might have come up a time or two."

Finn put his mug on the counter and closed the distance between them. He sauntered. Yes, he most certainly did. What other word fit that low-slung easy lope that made her feel like prey, but prey that didn't mind being that at all.

He slid a hand beneath her hair and cradled her nape. "Good morning, sweetheart."

"Is it still morning?" Her gaze locked on his gorgeous mouth and got stuck there.

"It can be." He grinned and kissed her forehead. "We could reset and go back to the moment you snuck out of my bed."

So, maybe he hadn't been sleeping as deeply as she had believed. His laughing eyes made that a definite no. "It was less of a sneak and more of a strategic retreat."

"Fair enough." He dropped a soft kiss on her mouth. "Then consider this me storming the ramparts."

Holding her face, he pulled her in for a kiss that decimated her brain function and left her clinging to his shoulders.

He pulled back and went back to his coffee mug. The mug covered his smirk, but not fast enough.

Son of a bitch was toying with her. She took his mug out of his hands and sipped his coffee. Black with a lot of sugar, she wrinkled her nose at the taste. "This is not how I like it."

"Then tell me how you like it." Finn gripped her hips and pulled them flush with his. "I'll give it to you any way you like it."

Men that made a girl laugh, kryptonite! "That is such a line."

"But it's a good one." His gaze invited her to play. "And I thought of it off the cuff."

She braced her hands on his chest, partly to keep her balance and also to keep a tiny space between them. "I'm not sure if that makes you the consummate player or just really quick."

"Claire." Finn tugged her closer until their chests collided. And his eyes were deadly earnest. "I'm thirty-seven, and I know exactly what I want. Ten years ago, I was a player, but that's not who I am today. I'm all grown up, and I don't play bullshit games anymore."

She didn't know how she felt about that. Part of her thrilled, but another part wanted to run for safety. Still, his honesty touched something real in her. "I'm not playing games either, but I am really confused right now."

"I get it, baby." He tucked her head beneath his chin and stroked the tension out of her back. "You came here with one set of preconceptions, and everything has been turned on its ass. And now you have this broken-down old warhorse humping your leg, and you don't know what to do with that either."

"Finn." She snort-laughed his name. "I promise that's not how I picture you."

He kissed her temple. "Good, because the moment I said it I regretted it." He rested his head on top of hers. "Although I'm going to lay my cards on the table here. I like you, Claire. I like you a whole helluva lot. And I really want to follow this trail and see where it leads."

"What if it goes nowhere?"

He shrugged. "Then we turn back."

Things were rarely that simple, but the moment felt golden, and she wanted to stay in it for a bit longer. "I have no idea what I'm doing."

"I get that," he said. Three words that settled deep into her being and brought calm inside her.

She burrowed deeper into him. His name sighed out of her. "Finn."

"I'm right here, baby." He kissed her head. "And I'm hungry. How about brunch?

Claire nodded, welcoming the lightening of the mood. "I think we have leftovers to feed the five thousand."

The door flew open, and Horace stomped in. He glared at Finn. "Wanna get your hands off my daughter."

"Nope." Finn grinned at him. "It took me long enough to get them there in the first place."

Horace scowled on his way to the fridge. "That's my daughter you're messing with."

"Well aware," Finn said. "And I'm not messing."

Daughter.

Such a common word.

And here was another common word that she'd never known.

Father.

For so many people that word meant picnics, broad shoulders, being carried to bed, big hands cradling your tiny one. That perfect moment when you knew the person beside you would stand tall, strong, and proud against anything that came. Deep voices rumbling through a broad chest that made you feel safe.

Horace glared at the contents of the fridge, Older, grayer, and certainly not the paladin standing strong against all comers, but still there.

Her father.

In those times she had felt alien to her mother. That some part of her didn't belong and that part needed to be sublimated, buried deep where it couldn't be found, her heart had always hoped that it could find this connection. If she traveled due west, she would find that other soul circling this life that she could find a link with.

Her chest ached. She struggled for her next breath. Tears threatened to betray her weakness, her soft underbelly. "Dad." She tasted the word. Not a big deal, right? Three letters starting and ending on a plosive consonant. "Dad." *Daddy*.

Horace stilled and turned to her. "Yes?"

"What looks good in there?" So mundane and facile, but where did you start to bridge a gap so many years in the making? There! Eight feet between them and still traversing them felt like crossing the Delaware.

Crap on a cracker. She'd become a Geico advert.

Horace cleared his throat. "Peg left her lasagna, but I don't feel that right now."

"What do you feel?" Finn joined Horace at the fridge. "Pancakes?"

"Pancakes would be great." Horace beamed at him. "With bacon."

Finn snorted. "Pancakes without bacon, what's the point of that?"

"Exactly!" Horace's cane clopped on the floor as he made his way to her side. With a sigh he eased his weight off his bad leg. He lowered his voice. "You okay, sweetheart?"

She had no good answer for that. "Can I get back to you on that?"

"Always." He took her hand. "I'm always gonna be here for you."

"Dad." Strange that the more times that one syllable left her mouth, the more okay it felt. "I have no idea what to say to that."

Horace huffed a laugh. "Me neither."

———

Later that afternoon Ben and Poppy returned to the house. The children exploded back in a frenzy of need and demand.

Claire stood back and let it roll over her.

"Claire." Ryan stood in front of her, a scowl twisting his baby face. "We have come back."

Ryan was right, they had. "Yes."

"I missed you." He barnacled himself to her legs.

How did sticky arms and a hot face pressed against you hit you straight in the heart? But they did.

"Clah!" Sean demanded she pick him up and hug him. So, she did, and drew in the sweaty sweet smell of little boy.

Mischief dancing in her eyes, Poppy looked from Finn to Claire and back again. "What did you two do with an empty house?"

"You're an evil woman." Finn leaned down and kissed Poppy's cheek. "And you're looking far too smug to judge anyone else."

While the family resettled in the house, Claire slipped away to call her mother. So much had happened and so many thoughts swirled through her mind that she wanted to reconnect.

"Claire." Doug picked up the line in her mom's room. "We haven't heard from you in a couple of days."

Guilt body slammed her. Getting caught up in Twin Elks and the people there wasn't going to help her mother. "I had to help a friend with her wedding."

"No worries," Doug said. "Only we're not having a good day today."

Actually, one of them had been having a great day. "Right. So not a good day to talk."

"Sorry, Claire." He sounded like he meant it. "When she's next lucid, I'll be sure to tell her you called and send her your love."

"Thanks, Doug." She hung up and stared at her wall for a long moment. Regardless of what happened between her and

Horace, Mom needed her. The familiar tension tightened across her shoulders.

She went to find Finn. He had a way of helping things make sense to her.

Voices coming from the library drew her.

"Poppy and I have been talking about this for a while," Ben said. "We're going to renovate my cabin and move into it when it's ready."

"We were hoping we could stay here until that happened," Poppy said.

"Of course," Horace said. A chair scraped and he said, "I'm happy for you two. A family needs its own space, but it leaves me in a bit of a predicament."

"I'm sorry," Poppy said. "But Claire's here now, and this house really does belong to her first."

Horace grunted. "This place means nothing to her."

His belief speared straight into her. Her rational side accepted that Horace had no reason to suppose otherwise. She didn't even know if she believed any different. But, last night, and over the last couple of days, the first tendrils of something good had grown between her and Horace. Now they shriveled and withdrew, and it hurt like hell.

"I think you'd be surprised," Poppy said.

Poppy said and not Horace. Poppy who barely knew her and had only really met her in the last couple of months.

"I don't know." Horace sounded defeated. "All she sees when she looks at this place is money."

"No, Horace," Poppy's voice went quiet as if she'd moved deeper into the room.

And it hit Claire that she was standing outside the room while Poppy defended her. In that room, people were discussing her feelings and coming to conclusions. Bullshit conclusions.

It felt like a bad metaphor for most of her adult life, and she pushed open the door before her brain could kick in with a warning.

Poppy, Ben, and Horace turned to look at her.

"Claire." Poppy stepped forward with her hand held out.

None of this was Poppy's doing. Funny, she'd come to oust an interloper, but the issue wasn't Poppy. The issue lay between her and her father and their dancing around each other and the truth. "No." She held up a hand to stop Poppy and face Horace across the length of the walnut desk. "Yes, I see this house as money. But have you ever asked yourself why?"

Horace frowned and clamped his mouth shut.

Ben stepped forward. "Then tell us why."

Poppy took her hand.

Mom would hate her for what she was about to do, but Horace and Naomi had made her complicit in their web of lies and deceit. They'd fought a silent war all these years with her trapped in the middle and taking shots from both sides. "You assumed my motives were mercenary. This entire town made that same assumption."

Horace used the desk to push himself to standing. "Claire, you never wanted anything more to do with me than my money."

"And that must mean I'm a ruthless gold digger?"

Horace opened his mouth and shut it again. His gaze bored into her. "What am I missing?"

"She's sick, and she's been getting worse for a long time." Stating the problem out loud stripped her bare.

Frowning, Horace stared at her. "Sick?"

"She didn't want you to know."

Poppy squeezed her hand. "Can you tell us what's happening to your mom?"

"She has Alzheimer's, and it's advanced enough that she needs a special facility."

"Goddamn it!" Horace thumped his desk. "And damn Naomi for her pride. And you've been carrying this on your shoulders and making do with the money I send you?"

Her neck felt too stiff to bend, but she gave a tiny nod. Mom would be horrified that she was sharing, but hiding didn't seem right anymore. "I earned reasonable money, and when she could still be cared for at home, we were doing fine."

"You should have told me," Horace said.

And didn't that just tear it. Anger bubbled through her and burst out her mouth. "When should I have done that, Dad? In one of your weekly calls to see if I was all right? Or perhaps I could have told you on one of your many visits to Boston to see me?"

"I—" Horace dropped his gaze first.

"Exactly!" Somehow winning the point hurt more than losing. "You and Mom made a thorough balls up of your marriage, and I'm the one crying."

Horace's expression softened as he limped around his desk. "Sweetheart."

"No." She raised her hand to fend him off. She already felt like an open nerve ending. "There are some things that can't be fixed with a hug and a cup of tea. I needed you to give a shit for so long, and you didn't. It's way too fucking late now."

CHAPTER
Nineteen

FINN GOT the details of what had happened from Poppy.

Sitting at his desk and staring out the window, Horace looked devastated. Okay, so he wasn't going to win father of the year anytime soon, but Claire had a prickly exterior that kept Horace at arm's length. Apparently, her mother had been worse, like an armored vehicle. People screwed up. Everyone did. Like death and taxes, it was one of those things you could rely on.

Poppy stood in the kitchen staring out the window. "It's cold out there." She handed him a coat. "Take this to her."

"Where is she?" He took the coat and joined Poppy at the window.

Claire stood in the rose garden, arms wrapped around her torso. "Who's she talking to?"

"Cecily would be my best guess," Poppy said.

Finn stared at her, waiting for the explanation.

"The girls talk about her all the time." Poppy shrugged. "The only Cecily I know of is the first Winters bride, the one who this house was built for."

"I don't believe in ghosts." Even as he said it, the hair at his nape stood on end.

Poppy patted his cheek. "It takes time to get used to the idea." She pointed out the window. "She needs you."

Finn opened the door to the raw cold.

"You were wrong," Claire yelled.

Finn didn't care what Poppy thought was happening, Claire was yelling at a pruned rosebush.

"I don't belong here. This isn't my home."

"Babe." He took issue with that. She did belong there. She belonged with him.

Claire spun and pinned him with hard stare. "God. They sent the Claire-tamer, did they?"

"Is that what I am?" He placed the coat over her shoulders.

She pushed her arms through the sleeves. "Thanks."

"No problem." He zipped the coat up. "I hear you and Horace got into it."

"I got into Horace you mean." Storms raged in her eyes, a swirling combination of anger, fear, and pain. "I should never have told him about Mom."

"I'm sorry about your mother." He rubbed her arms to warm her up. "That really sucks, and I understand why you kept it to yourself, but by not telling Horace before, you didn't give him a chance to do anything to help her."

"Really?" She scowled at him.

That look almost had him bailing, but she needed a true friend more than someone blowing smoke right now. "You can't hate him for things he knew nothing about."

Her silence seethed.

Finn pressed on. "I get that he didn't exactly cover himself in paternal glory when you were growing up. But you're all grown up now, Claire, and so is he. I honestly feel he's learned from his past mistakes. That man in there wants to make up for his mistakes and is waiting for you to give him a sliver of a chance."

She huffed out a dry, humorless laugh. "You're so full of crap."

That rocked him back. "Say what?"

"You're lecturing me on forgive and forget. Is that what you're doing? Or is your mother right, and you're hiding out here in Twin Elks from stuff you can't face?"

Damn. That stung. "You have no clue what you're talking about."

"Don't I?" She poked him in the chest. "Because you're so good at letting go of the past? You're still stuck in some loop that your mother fed you and still trying to prove you're worthy of being alive when Sean's dead. And I should take your advice?" She shook her head. "I might as well, right, because you're clearly not using it."

He couldn't talk to her when she was like that. Correction. He really fucking didn't want to talk to her when she was like that. Claire had a mean streak. "You fight dirty, babe."

———

Claire stood where she was as Finn stalked back to the house, hands shoved into his pockets and his shoulders hunched around his ears.

He was right. That shot at him hadn't been warranted, but he'd gotten under her skin defending Horace. It sheared too close to an open wound. Every time she came to this stupid town, everyone piled behind poor Horace. Poor Horace Winters with his bitch of an ex-wife and his mercenary daughter.

What could such a nice guy have possibly done to deserve such ill treatment?

Did they want her to write them a damn list?

"You were right." Maura stood on the far side of the rose garden, huddled in a coat. "He is stuck and staying here only makes that worse."

She must have heard a good deal of the argument. "I didn't hear you arrive."

"You and Finn were a little too wrapped up in each other."

Maura shrugged and walked toward her. "I know my son, and being here isn't good for him."

If Maura chose to believe she knew her son, then so be it. Claire didn't have the energy to set her straight. "He has his reasons."

"Indeed, he does." Maura placed her feet carefully as she walked in her knee-high heeled boots. "He and Sean never got on. He clings to Poppy to make up for that. He's never gotten over his guilt for how he treated Sean." Pain twisted her features. "None of us were ready to let Sean go."

Speaking of her youngest son's death was clearly very painful, and Claire shut her mouth rather than say something insensitive. She wasn't a mother. What did she know of the pain of losing a child?

"War changed him too," Maura said. "I could see it happening over time. Every time he came home from a deployment, Finn slipped into a darker and darker place. When he's here he can pretend none of that happened."

Claire had barely spoken to Finn about his life in the forces, but those scars must have been earned and come with a high price tag, deeper than only the physical damage. "How long was he in?"

"If Finn chooses to share that with you, that's his story to tell." Maura looked at her with distaste. "You need to earn his trust."

Damn! Maura also fought dirty.

Finn had lived an entire life with this kind of emotional drive by shooting. And now she'd done it to him as well. Things were so confusing, and she'd punished Finn in place of Horace. Like Maura had punished him for being the son to live.

It was like Maura was in her head when she said, "And you're not good for him either."

All Claire could do was stare at Maura.

"Finn likes to rescue," Maura said. "The more broken the creature, the more he needs to put them back together." She brushed the front of her coat. "And you, my dear, are as broken as they come."

"What are you doing, Maura?" Poppy joined them.

Claire hadn't seen her coming either.

"Poppy." Maura stiffened and stuck her chin out. "I'm not doing anything. I'm just giving Claire some maternal advice."

"Really?"

Claire didn't think she'd ever seen Poppy so angry. She was in full mama-bear mode, and Claire felt a flicker of sympathy for Maura. She was about to get mauled.

Stupid woman didn't see it coming and sneered. "Yes, really. I know what's best for Finn."

"Don't you go there." Poppy quivered with the depth of her fury. "You wouldn't know a damn thing about Finn if the angels came down and sang it to you."

"Finn is my son." Maura gaped at Poppy.

"Sean was your son." Poppy jabbed a finger at her. "And you treated him like he was a little lord his entire life. I should know because I inherited your creature when you'd given him an entirely inflated view of his role in the world."

Maura flushed. "How dare you."

"But don't you dare claim to know what's good for Finn." Poppy stepped right up to Maura. "You wouldn't have a clue what makes that man happy or what he needs in his life. Because if you had even the vaguest maternal fondness for Finn, you would be welcoming Claire into his life, because I have never seen him happier."

"I know what my child needs." Maura flushed.

"You know what you need," Poppy said. "And you don't want Finn, but you'll spread your poison to make sure nobody else gets him either." She turned to Claire. "Drink?"

"Hell, yes!"

They settled in the kitchen with a bottle of wine.

Poppy took the seat opposite her. "Eventful day."

"In a crappy way." Claire took a sip of her wine. "I'm

wondering if there is anyone else in Twin Elks I can fight with today."

"Maura was not your fault." Poppy's expression tightened. "I've dealt with that woman since I was eighteen, and as hard as I find it to believe, she is actually getting worse."

Claire wanted to hear more. "Yeah. What's her deal?"

"Well, she adored Sean," Poppy said. "He could do no wrong in her eyes. She accused me of getting pregnant on purpose to trap him into marriage."

"Ugh."

"Right! As if he was such a great prize in the first place. When he cheated on me, it was my fault because I couldn't give him enough reasons to stay home. When he refused to come home, it was my fault for making his home a place he didn't want to be." Poppy shook her head. "She was always telling me what I did wrong as a wife. Then as a mother. She literally called every day to tell me what I should do different."

"And Sean was okay with this?"

"Sean encouraged her." Poppy took a big sip of wine. "I should have stopped being a bitch to his mother and listened to her advice."

No wonder Poppy had jumped in enthusiastically. "And what's her deal with Finn?"

"Well, now Finn gets the worst of her." Poppy grimaced. "I don't need to tell you what a great guy he is, but Maura never saw past Sean. Finn has always loved her, but he never drank the Kool-Aid. Part of it is because Sean was born such a sickly baby, and Maura doted on him." She shrugged. "As far as I can tell, Finn was a fairly normal, energetic little boy."

"I bet he was more than a little energetic." Claire pictured a young Finn and had to smile.

Poppy looked at her in horror. "Ew! I think of Finn as a brother. I do not want to know that about him."

"Not like that." Claire's face went nuclear. "I meant he...oh, stop it!"

Poppy was killing herself laughing. "Your face."

Gathering her tattered dignity, Claire sipped her wine. Then her evil twin took over. "But if we were talking about that, I'd have to say—"

"La la la lala." Poppy stuck her fingers in her ears.

The mood lightened and they sat in silence for a while.

Poppy refilled their glasses. "When I heard Maura talking that shit, I nearly lost it." She scowled. "Finn needs and deserves someone wonderful in his life." She looked at Claire. "And I'm not sure you're not the girl for the job."

"That's not exactly a ringing endorsement."

Poppy shrugged. "That's only because I sense that you're not sure whether you want to apply for the job."

"Argh!" Claire scrubbed her hands over her face. She had so many conflicting thoughts ramming into each other. "Not knowing seems to be a permanent state for me lately."

"And this is about more than Finn?"

"For sure." She hoped there was another bottle of wine around there somewhere because they might need it. "I came here expecting to hate you and look at us now."

"If it helps, I was fully prepared to hate you too."

Claire almost snorted wine. "It does, actually. And then there's Dad and I really don't know what to make of that. Because if he isn't who Mom says he was, then that changes my relationship with her."

"Not really." Poppy tapped the table with her forefinger. "Your mom is how she is, and she's certainly not going to change now. You can't go back in time and fix things, so you may as well get okay with them and move on."

"Is that what you did?"

"Hell no!" Poppy rolled her eyes. "Did you or did you not hear me rip into Maura this evening?"

They laughed long about that one. Being with Poppy was nothing like being with Tara. Poppy was easy and real and warm. She really got why Ben had taken one look at Poppy and never looked back.

"Shit!" Poppy clicked her fingers. "I almost forgot to tell you in all the excitement." Her expression turned serious and she leaned on the table. "Horace's surgery is tomorrow. He asked Ben to take him to the hospital. I thought you should know, because I thought you might have something to say about that."

It was easy to see where she'd gotten her stubbornness from. "I most certainly do have something to say about that."

———

Finn knocked on his mother's hotel room door. When Poppy had told him about the interaction between Mom and Claire, he'd been so mad he'd had to take a long walk around the town before he could deal with his mother.

Mom opened the door and blinked at him. "Finn?"

"Hi." He motioned inside. "Can I come in?"

She watched him for a long moment. "This is about that girl."

"Yes."

Sighing, she stepped away and left the door open. "She's all wrong for you. I can't be the only one who realizes this."

"Mom." He breathed in and out hard and grabbed on to the upswell of temper. Angry people did stupid things and lost control, and someone like him couldn't afford to do that. "You have no right to say anything to Claire. You don't know her, and you sure as hell don't know anything about what's going on between us."

"I'm your mother." She squared her shoulders. "If I don't know who is good for you, then I don't know who else does."

Finn didn't know any gentle way to say it, and maybe it was time to take the gloves off anyway. He had always been so critical of Sean for not stepping in and standing up for Poppy, and now he needed to walk his own talk. "You're only my mother when it suits you."

She flinched and went pale. Her voice went soft and wounded. "Finn."

He needed to get this said. "You've been so caught up in the grief about Sean and trying to hang on to him through Poppy's kids that you forget you have another kid." It cut him to say those things. He had thought he had a handle on it, but at the end of the day, she was his mother and he did love her. "I can't begin to understand what losing your husband and then losing a child must feel like, but I do know what losing a father, a brother, and a mother feels like, and it hurts so much it changes you forever."

She blinked at him, looking fragile and brittle. "She's not right for you."

"I don't know if she is, Mom, but I sure as hell want to find out." He had to leave before it turned even uglier. "And you need to butt out. You removed yourself from my life years ago, and you don't get to jump in when it suits you."

CHAPTER
Twenty

CLAIRE ATE dinner with the family.

Finn didn't arrive for dinner and neither did Horace, but only one of them was fasting for surgery, and the other was working off a big mad. Offering to clean up, she managed to linger in the kitchen for a long while.

Still, Finn didn't come home, and she ran out of excuses to hang out in the kitchen. She managed to stretch her night by looking through more of the old photos. So many of the faces bore a resemblance to people living in Twin Elks today. She might talk to Peg about making them available to the town.

Even then, she ran out of reasons to loiter and went upstairs. Of course, she could apologize to Finn and be done with it. But that would make her a mature adult, and she'd pretty much tossed her card in the trash today.

After a long bath, she went to bed and tried not to listen for Finn returning.

She fell asleep listening, and woke to a bright, crisp day.

Dressed for warmth, she grabbed coffee in a to go cup and a yogurt. The good thing about living with a cop was that he was generally up before anyone else and put the coffee on.

Poppy had given her the details on Horace the night before

and she'd set an alarm to make sure she got up in time. She hadn't bothered to discuss it with him because—stubborn!

After her yogurt, she stepped into the sort of morning that made you believe in magic. A cool sun turned dewdrops into sparkles on all the plants and the dried grass. A light morning mist loitered in the hollows.

She got to the door of the carriage house and knocked.

"No need to pound the hell out of it." Horace yanked the door open and blinked at her. "What are you doing here?"

"I'm your lift to the hospital." Claire turned and walked toward her car.

Horace yelled in her wake. "No, you're not."

"Afraid I am." She gave him a finger wave over her shoulder. "I'm all you've got, old man, so get in the car."

In her car, she turned on the heater and cleared the condensation from the windows.

Eventually, Horace limped her way and threw himself into the passenger seat. "I didn't tell you about this."

"No, you didn't. But you were ratted out." She looked at his bag. "Have you got everything you need in there?"

Horace grunted. "I don't need much. I'm not doing the operation myself."

"Is this a hangry thing, or are you just not a morning person?" She turned into the road. They had a two-hour drive ahead of them to the hospital. They needed to find something to talk about. "How are you feeling about the surgery?"

"How do you think I feel?" He scowled at her. "Someone is about to cut me open and put their hands inside me."

"Hmm." Translation: scared as crap. "While they're digging around in there, could you ask them to look for your personality?"

Horace stilled and then barked out a loud laugh. "You got a smart mouth."

"I wonder where I get that from?" She winked at him.

"You're going to be fine, Dad. Just think how much better you can terrify the neighborhood kids when you can chase them."

Horace smiled and stared out the window. "I'm not a big fan of doctors and hospitals."

"Is anyone really?" Claire took the onramp to the highway and increased her pace to merge with the traffic. It was early enough in the morning for the traffic to be minimal. She looked around her at the growing morning. Pockets of mist haunted the valleys between the mountains. "It really is beautiful here."

"I always thought so," Horace said. "I've traveled quite a bit, but I'm always glad to come back home."

Claire wished she could have his certainty about where home was. But today was not the day to get into all that. "Did you know I had my appendix out when I was sixteen?"

"No." He tensed.

"Well, I did, and apparently, I had quite a reaction to the anesthetic." She kept her tone light. He didn't need another trip on the guilt thoroughfare today. "For days before the surgery, my friends had been telling me horror stories of people who went in for one surgery and came out missing a limb because they'd been mislabeled."

Horace turned in his seat to glare at her. "Is there a reason you're telling me this story now?"

"I'll make sure they put the right labels on you." She laughed at his disgruntled expression. "Anyway, they couldn't get me to settle until they showed me my appendix. When I woke up for real, it was in a jar taped to my bed."

The rest of the drive passed quietly with Horace napping on and off.

They arrived at the hospital and fought their way clear of the usual paper avalanche.

Finally, Horace was settled in a private room wearing the ubiquitous hospital gown.

A nurse in cerise scrubs burst through the door. "Morning, honey. Aren't you looking fabulous this morning?" She crinkled her nose in their general direction and wheeled a computer over to them. "My name is Bunny, and I'm going to ask you a few questions. Is that okay, hon?" Bunny's gaze flicked to Claire.

Claire looked at Horace. "Is that okay? Hon?"

Horace's eyes gleamed. "Give me your worst."

"You're too funny." Bunny crinkled her nose and twinkled. "Okay let's start."

She went through a lightning-fast round of questions, during which Claire found out more about Horace than she'd ever wanted to know. Basically, her dad was in great shape, even for a man half his age.

"So, here's what happens next, darlin'." Bunny took Horace's vitals. "Your doctor is going to drop by and explain your surgery to you."

"I already know about my surgery." Horace glared at her from beneath his shaggy eyebrows. "I wouldn't be here if I didn't."

"Of course not, sweetie." Bunny threw Claire an empathetic glance as she patted his hand. She enunciated slowly and carefully. "But just so you really know and understand, Doctor Grindell will be by to make sure you do." She blinded them with white teeth. "And don't you worry about a thing. Dr. Grindell is one of the best, and this is a routine surgery."

"Who's the best then?" Claire kept her face straight.

Bunny looked baffled. "Sorry?"

"You said Grindell was one of the best. I asked who the best was."

Horace grunted and his shoulders shook.

"Well, I'm not sure." Bunny collapsed into thought. "Dr. Weismann is really good, and there's always Dr. Shannon over at General." She winked at them. "But don't tell anyone I said that." She leaned in closer. "She's the comp-a-ti-shun."

With another wink, she whisked her wheeled computer out.

"Well, Dad." Claire patted his hand. "I don't know how to break this to you, but you're getting a third-rate surgeon."

Horace chuckled. "I like it when you do that."

"What?" She turned to him.

Swallowing hard, Horace grasped her hand. "I like it when you call me dad." He squeezed and dropped her hand. "Thank you for being here. I appreciate it."

Tears stung the back of her eyes, and her throat clogged. Claire was glad she was here as well. It felt like the right place to be.

Neither of them could look at each other, and she broke the moment. "I'm only here for money."

Horace huffed another watery chuckle and patted her hand. "That's my girl."

———

Finn almost got lost in corridors as he searched the hospital for Claire. The antiseptic smell made him want to gag. He associated it with pain. A shitload of pain. But Claire was in there and he wanted to be by her side.

Last time they'd seen each other hadn't been a Hallmark moment, but he had found out from Poppy that she'd brought Horace for his surgery, and he hated to think of her sitting alone in a soulless place.

Like his gaze was a programmed laser locking system, he found her the minute he walked into the orthopedic ward.

She sat alone, staring at the gray wall outside the waiting room window. This woman was going to fucking kill him. Shoulders square, chin high, she wore her fragility around her like a cloak.

Light outlined her beautiful profile and caught in the blond silk of her hair. In her pallor, the light turned her skin milk white. Moving quietly so as not to startle her, he took a seat beside her.

She turned to him and stilled. "Finn?"

"Hey, gorgeous." He tucked a piece of hair behind her ear. "How are you doing?"

He could read the way she hid her struggle behind her public face now. And then she sighed. "I'm okay. They said his surgery would be a couple of hours, but it's been longer than that."

"Recovery time can make that longer."

She nodded. "I know that. I'm just…"

"Worried." He put his arm around her shoulder and tugged her against him. "Of course, you are."

Tension drained out of her, and she leaned into him. At that moment, Finn felt ten foot tall. They stayed liked that and breathed together.

"Finn?"

He kissed her head. "Babe?"

"Are we still angry with each other?"

God, she could rip his heart out and stomp all over it with her vulnerability. He had no idea how to love a woman like this, but he was damn well going to try. "Truthfully?" He pressed his jaw against her head. "I think we're both still pissed with each other, but that can wait until we know Horace is okay."

Sighing, she tucked a hand between his knees and nestled into him. "Okay."

"Ryan sent you a drawing." He took the picture out of his pocket and unfolded it.

Studying it for a long time, she chuckled. "What is it?"

"What is it?" He gave her an incredulous look. "Clearly that blue blob is Horace and the pink puddle thing is you." Cocking his head, he tried to make sense of the rest of the drawing. "And clearly you and Horace are on an alien planet."

That earned him a chuckle. "Is everybody okay at home?"

"Yup." He liked that she called Twin Elks home. "Poppy and Ben sent their love and said they'd come up and see him tomorrow. Ciara and Brinn wanted you to know Cecily was happy Horace was sorting his hip out." For the record, he still didn't believe this ghost crap. "And Sean sent me to cheer you up."

"Thank Sean for me." She tilted her head up and smiled at him. "It's working."

Giving in to the impulse, Finn kissed her sweet mouth, lingering for a small while past comforting. "I'm glad."

"Claire Winters." A nurse in scrubs so pink they bounced off the back of his eyeballs trotted into the waiting room. "Sweetie? Your daddy is out of surgery." She wrinkled up her nose. "His surgery went great." She beamed at them like a toothpaste commercial. "Doctor will be by later to chat with you. Give us a little time to get him settled, and then you can come and see him."

The nurse bounded away again.

"That's Bunny." Claire straightened and stretched like a cat. Her breasts pressed against the front of her sweater.

He wanted to stroke the arch in her spine. "How apt."

She snort-laughed and sighed. "At least he's okay."

"Horace?" He stood and held his hand out to her. "That old coot will outlive us all."

"I'm glad he's okay." Her face softened, and for a moment she looked like she might cry.

Finn slid his hand beneath her hair and pulled her closer to him. "We all are. Would you like me to call everyone back home and let them know?"

"Yes, please." She gazed up at him with those incredible eyes, and Finn lost his way in their depths. This woman tangled him in knots and kept pulling them tighter.

One moment shoving the world and everyone in it back with both hands, the next cuddled into him like he was her lifeline, then another time turning to flame in his arms and making love to him with her soul.

He'd lost track of the real Claire.

Uncertainty flickered over her face. "What?"

"Nothing." He shook his head. "By the way, I'm not mad anymore."

She kissed him. A chaste peck that satisfied nothing. "Me neither."

"Also, I booked a hotel room nearby. It's a long drive home, and I didn't want you doing it late at night."

Mischief twinkled in her eyes, and she smirked. "Just one room?"

"Don't get ahead of yourself." Like hell he was going to book two rooms and miss spending a night with her wrapped around him. Even if it was only to sleep. "You go and find your father. I'll see you there when I've called everyone."

CHAPTER
Twenty-One

CLAIRE FOLLOWED Bunny's perky ass down the corridors to Horace's room. It meant more to her than she could express that Finn had come.

When she had looked up and seen him taking a seat beside her, her shoulders had lifted as if he took half the burden from them. Worry for Horace had kept thoughts of their fight at bay, for the most part. Still, her memory had replayed in sickening detail the things she'd said to him.

In a way, she was worse than his bitch mother. She couldn't imagine growing up knowing that your mother never saw you, only your younger brother.

Horace was watching the door when she came in. He gave her a weak smile. "Hi."

"Hi yourself." She took his inert hand in hers. "You look like hell."

"Feel it as well." Horace grimaced. "At least they gave me the good drugs."

"There is that." Relief at seeing him made her want to cry. She dropped her head and hid her threatening tears. "They said everything went well."

"Yeah." Horace sniffed. "That third-rate doctor told me as much."

She managed a watery chuckle. "But can we be sure he knows what he's talking about?"

He smiled and squeezed her hand. "Good to see you, kiddo."

"Hey, Horace." Finn entered the room. "Good to see you."

"What are you doing here?" Horace tried to frown, but he was faking.

Finn grinned. "Making time with your girl." He dug his phone out. "I have a crap ton of messages for you. Wanna hear them all?"

Horace grimaced. "Just let me know if everyone is okay."

"Everyone's okay." Finn put his hand on Horace's shoulder. "You look like you'd like to catch some shut eye."

Horace nodded and Claire felt like shit for not noticing.

Eyes already heavy, Horace looked at Finn. "Take care of my girl?"

Finn touched his arm. "You know it."

————

Taking care of her Finn-style included bullying a club sandwich ordered from room service and a couple of glasses of red wine down her. A hot shower followed, and Finn had brought her something to sleep in.

By which stage she ran out of interest in protesting the one king-size bed in the room and crawled between the crisp, cool sheets.

Flipping through channels, Finn stretched out beside her, his shoes the only thing he'd taken off.

Claire fell asleep to *American Pickers*.

She woke to a lot of hot, smooth skin spooning her. Finn gave off inferno heat and his breath huffed against the back of her neck.

His big hand spread over her belly and one of his knees was

pushed between hers. He also had an undeniable erection pressed against her bottom.

The pattern of his breathing changed. "Well, now." He tucked her closer to him. "You're awake, and clearly, I'm awake. What should we do about this?"

"You could have your wicked way with me." The offer came from some place deep inside her that needed him like her next breath.

Finn groaned and rolled her beneath him. "Baby, did I ever mention how much I like a woman who knows her own mind?"

"No." She wove her fingers through his hair, and done with talking, pulled his mouth to hers.

Finn took her mouth as if he owned it. His big body pressed her deeper into the mattress. He nudged her thighs apart with his knee and settled between her legs.

His cock lined up with where she needed him most and Claire tilted her hips into the friction. He felt so damn good, and she wrapped her legs around his hips.

Finding his way under her shirt, Finn palmed her breast, playing his thumb over her nipple. He knew exactly how to touch her, and she pushed against his hand.

"You're so hot for me." He growled and thrust against her.

Claire lost her breath in the storm of sensation. "Yes."

Straddling her, Finn sat up and pulled her top off. He lowered his head and sucked a nipple into his mouth.

She tangled her fingers in his inky silk hair. In the dark, his hair looked much darker than her pale skin. His broad shoulders loomed over her, both possessing and sheltering her. As he switched his mouth to the other nipple, Finn pushed his hand into her pants.

He slid his fingers over her slick flesh to her clitoris. "So wet." He moved his mouth down to her belly and slid her pj bottoms down.

Raising her hips, Claire helped him get rid of them.

Finn lowered himself between her thighs and opened her with his fingers.

"Yes." Claire bucked against him. "That. I want that."

"Give me that dirty mouth, baby."

She would go crazy if he didn't move. "Lick me. Put your mouth on me."

And he did, driving her out of her mind with his lips and his tongue. Finn took his time, pushing her close to orgasm and then pulling back and starting the torment all over again.

Finally, she couldn't stand it anymore and bucked against his face. "Finn! Please."

He hummed and pushed her thighs wider, and drove her fast, hard, and dirty into an orgasm.

"Wow." Her limbs noodled across the bed and she doubted she could move them. That was if she could get her brain off its pleasure high, and who the hell wanted to do that?

Finn kissed his way up her belly, her breasts, and her neck. "This demanding you is really hot."

Nobody had ever accused her of being demanding before, and she laughed. "It's new."

"I like it. You should cultivate it." Finn pressed his cock against her and kissed her. Pushing her arms up, he rested them above her head, their fingers entwined. Those deep blue eyes of his stripped her defenses. "You're beautiful, Claire."

He bent his head and kissed her, slow and deep.

Her body responded to him, and she wanted more, wanted him buried inside her.

"Finn." She writhed against him. "Now."

"Ah, not yet." He smiled against her mouth. "Bossy won't get you everything you want." He pressed hot kisses along her neck, nipping lightly at her skin. "You snuck out of my bed before I could wake you properly the other morning."

She growled and dug her nails into his hard ass. "What if I promise not to do that again?"

"I'll take that under advisement." He cupped both her breasts and looked at them. "God, I love your breasts." He kissed one and then the other, drawing each nipple into his mouth in turn. "I used to think it was all about those long legs of yours and that killer ass, but these…" He went back to her nipples again, laving and sucking until she squirmed beneath him.

Her breath caught around the word "Please."

"Please what?" His hand slid between her thighs. "Is this where you want me?"

"Yes."

"Tell me again." He reached for the side table and grabbed a condom. Fisting his cock, he rolled it on. "Tell me what you want me to do."

That made her hotter than ever. "Fuck me, Finn."

He notched his cock at her opening and pushed into her, frustratingly slowly, his head bent to watch himself join her flesh with his.

Claire whimpered as he filled her to perfection. "So good."

Finn slammed home, driving into her and drawing a guttural scream from her.

Bracing himself above her, he got serious.

His face grew taut with need. His beautiful body flexed. Sweat glistened on his muscle as he powered them both forward.

Her climax came fast and hard, rushing over her and arching her off the bed.

Finn buried himself as deep as he could and stiffened as he came. He lowered himself on her and then rolled to the side.

Claire wanted to protest the loss of him, but she didn't have the will to do much more than lie there and recover.

"Hey." Finn rolled to his side beside her. "You doing okay?"

"Better than that." She managed a smile for him. The etched lines of his face called to her, and she traced them with her forefinger. "I like this face."

He kissed her nose softly. "I like this face too."

"I'm glad you're here." She snuggled closer to his warmth.

Finn got out of bed. "Hold that thought."

In the bathroom he got rid of the condom, and then he slid back into bed with her.

Hooking an arm around her waist, he hauled her back toward him and tucked her into him. "Tomorrow's going to be another big day, we should get some sleep."

She let the warmth of him surround her and ease her. "Finn?"

"Babe?"

"When you had your surgeries, was there anyone there for you?"

He tensed, and for a moment, Claire wished she hadn't asked.

Then he relaxed and tightened his hold around her middle. "Are you feeling sorry for me?"

"Was there anyone there?"

He raised her hand and kissed it. "I had a lot of friends and army buddies walk me through it."

Maura hadn't even gone to his side when he had lain in a hospital bed after his surgeries. From those scars on his back, he had to have been in a world of pain.

She laced her fingers with his that lay on her stomach. "I would have been there."

CHAPTER
Twenty~Two

DRESSED in bright yellow scrubs with little daisies on this morning, Nurse Bunny beelined for Claire the moment she arrived in the ward.

"Oh, hon! There you are."

Claire reached for Finn's hand. Please don't let it be bad news.

Bunny's face twisted into an adorable frown. "They're driving him insane, and I don't know what to do. I tried to get them to leave, but they're not paying any attention."

"But my father is all right?" Claire needed the reassurance before she took another step.

"Oh, yes, sweetie. He's doing great. Doc is pleased with him." Bunny rolled her eyes and then frowned again. Adorably, of course. "But he might kill one of them before they go."

"Them?"

"Donna!" Peg's voice rebounded off the corridor walls. "Please take your position bedside."

Finn chuckled. "I'm going to the canteen."

"No, you aren't." She grabbed his hand in a firm grip. "You're going to go in there and turn that Irish charm on for all its worth. And you're going to get them out of there."

He tugged her back to him and landed her against his chest. "I want to hear more about my Irish charm."

"Don't make me regret saying that." She grabbed his hand and forged forward.

They reached the waiting room and Claire froze.

The entire prayer chain had taken up residence. Three members were chatting over their knitting and watching *Days of Our Lives* on the waiting room television. In another corner, the young mothers had their heads together, she guessed swapping birth or child rearing horror stories. Even Hank Styles was there, in clean jeans and a pressed shirt with his hair slicked back and neat.

"Ah, Claire!" Impressive chest leading, Peg descended on her like a battle cruiser. "We're glad you're here. I would have thought you'd be here sooner, but never mind that. I'm organizing the meal roster for Horace. Do you know if he's allergic to anything?"

"No." She'd been sitting next to Horace when he was admitted. "He's not allergic to anything, but he's not a big fan of fish."

"No fish. Got ya." Peg whipped out her phone and tapped in a note. "Favorite dishes?"

"Um...he really eats most things. He's not fussy."

"Not fussy." Peg tapped it in. "Now, any idea when he'll be released."

"They said three to four days." She was starting to understand how people felt under government questioning. "But I'll stay with him."

"Uh-huh, uh-huh." Peg could type into her phone faster than a teen on Snapchat. "We'll make arrangements for the house to be cleaned." She checked her phone. "Time's up, Donna." She peered past Claire. "Bonnie! No more than four minutes. We're on a schedule."

With an apologetic smile, Bonnie scuttled past them.

Claire threw Finn a look to get on with it.

"Peg." He got in front of her. Brave man. "Did you change your hair?"

Peg looked confused. "No."

"Stupid question." He shoved his hands in his jeans pockets and muscle flexed along his arms and shoulders. "It always looks great."

"Oh." Peg went pink and tapped her hair. "Why thank you, Finn."

"I just say it as I see it." His grin could have stripped the panties off a nun.

What a man whore. Claire raised her eyebrow at him.

Putting an arm around Peg's shoulders he turned her away from the waiting room. "Actually, if you have a few minutes, I need to chat with you." He smoldered down at her. Peg followed along like she'd lost the ability to reason. "And I know you're the only one who can help me with this."

Grateful as she was for his intervention, Claire had his number now. All that disingenuous hotness wasn't quite as innocent as it seemed. And dammit! He'd used that exact smile and those burning bedroom eyes on her when she'd first arrived in Twin Elks.

Peg didn't stand a chance.

As she entered his room, Horace threw her a desperate look.

"Hi Bonnie." Claire smiled at her. "How are you?"

"Fine." Bonnie's frost toward her still hadn't melted.

"It's really nice of you to come and see my dad." She moved to Horace's bedside and took his hand. "Would you mind, though, if I had him to myself for a couple of minutes?" She shrugged and did her best to look penitent. "I always feel like we haven't had enough time together. I know it's my fault, but…"

Horace nearly ruined her performance with his gaping.

"I understand." Bonnie leaped to her feet. "The bond between a daughter and her father is a very special thing."

"I knew you'd understand."

Bonnie leaned over Horace and enunciated painstakingly. "Take care, Mr. Winters, and get better soon. Your daughter, Claire, is here to see you, so I'll just pop along."

"Thanks, Bonnie." Claire smiled her out of the room. Then she turned to Horace and dropped all pretense. "You look exhausted."

Horace grunted but took her hand. "There are a lot of them."

"Finn's dealing with them."

Frowning, Horace cocked his head. "What can Finn—"

"Prayer chain, we're leaving," Peg called. "Ten minutes to the bus and no stopping in the cafeteria. We have snacks on the bus. I'm looking at you Hank Styles."

Claire took the seat Bonnie had vacated and pulled it up to the bed. "I brought us something." She dug in her bag and found *Good Night Moon*. "Would you like me to read it to you?"

Blinking rapidly, Horace looked down. "That's a children's story."

"I think of it more as our story." Claire said.

Dad cleared his throat. "You could read a bit."

Finn leaned against the doorjamb and watched them. He crossed his arms and jerked his head at her for her to continue.

"In the great green room…"

By the time she reached the end of the story, Horace had fallen asleep.

She put the book on his bedside table, filled his water cup, and rearranged the flowers and fruit baskets the prayer chain had brought. They were good people, just a bit overwhelming at times.

"Hey." Finn caught her arm. "Stop fussing for a minute."

"He used to read me that when I was a little girl." Her voice was thick with emotion. "It's one of a handful of memories I have of us."

Finn pulled her into a hug. "I figured it was something like that."

"He used to read me bedtime story when I lived with him."

"Did he?" Finn's beautiful deep voice had a way of soothing her rough edges.

She wrapped her arms around his waist and pressed her face into his neck. "Finn?"

"Babe?"

"So much of what my mom told me isn't turning out to be true." She couldn't look at anyone as she said that. Even saying it aloud felt like a betrayal to her mother. "He isn't anything like she said he was."

"Maybe because the man she experienced as her husband is not the same man as your father. There's only space for two people in a marriage." His heart beat steadily against her ear. "My mom used to tell Sean about her marriage to my dad. It's never good for the kid when those boundaries get crossed. Kids should never have to choose between their parents."

"Did you have to?"

He chuckled. "My mother made that choice for all of us. She and Sean were a unit, and that left Dad and me."

"You never talk about him much."

Finn shrugged. "He was a good guy. A bit absent, but a good father when he was around. He taught me to play hockey, and he encouraged me to enlist. I think he always wanted to himself, but it never happened for him."

"Did he die?"

"Yeah." Finn hugged her tighter to him. "But it was fifteen years ago now. Before even Poppy and Sean's marriage."

She glanced back at her father, now deeply asleep. "Why don't we go and get some breakfast and let him sleep?"

"Sounds good." He kissed her lightly. "You okay?"

Not the easiest question to answer. "Mostly."

"Let's start there then and see if we can improve it."

———

After lunch Poppy and Ben arrived. Poppy immediately gave her a huge hug. "You look tired."

"I am." There was something about hospitals that drained a person even though she'd not been doing much other than hanging around while Horace slept and spending time with him when he was awake.

Poppy waggled her eyebrows. "Has that bad, bad Finn been keeping you up at night?"

"Poppy." Ben rolled his eyes but looked pained and amused at the same time. Then he winked at Claire. "Has he?"

A playful Ben always took her by surprise. He was normally so contained and serious, but there was more of Dot in him than immediately obvious.

"Listen, why don't you say goodbye to Horace for the day? We'll stay with him until they kick us out. Go back to the house and relax. You can come and see him again tomorrow."

Finn put an arm around her waist. "Sounds like a good idea. We can watch the kids until you come back. Why don't you make that return tomorrow? Take over our hotel room." He handed Ben his truck keys. "Do you think you can drive my truck back?"

"Sounds good to me." Ben pocketed the keys. "Now take Claire home and don't do anything to scar my kids for life."

"So, no strip poker?" Claire widened her eyes innocently.

Ben chuckled. "Not with Ryan at least, he cheats."

As they were driving away, it occurred to Claire. "I don't mind leaving Poppy with Horace."

"Eh?" Finn glanced at her and back at the road.

"I mean, I was so angry and jealous of Poppy when I first came here, and now, I'm happy to leave her with my father. It doesn't even bother me that he will be glad to have her there."

Finn kissed her hand. "Poppy's awesome. I told you—"

She poked him. "If you say you told me so, I will make you sorry."

CHAPTER
Twenty~Three

RYAN LAUNCHED himself at her as she crossed the kitchen threshold. "Claire. Hello, Claire. We've having mac and cheese for dinner. Dot promised."

"I love mac and cheese." Her skinny jeans weren't going to make it. "And I'm sure Dot makes it really well."

"She does." Brinn bopped up to her, ponytail bouncing. "She puts bacon in it and three kinds of cheese."

"Three kinds?" That was impressive.

Ciara sidled up beside her and took her hand. There was something about that warm, small hand in hers that brought out her protective streak.

"How's Horace?" Ciara whispered.

"Grumpy." Claire smiled to reassure her.

"Horace is not really grumpy," Brinn said. "He uses it to hide his smile."

Were all kids so smart? Probably not, just these four geniuses. "So true."

"Hello." Dot greeted her with her hands held out. "You must be exhausted."

Finn tried to walk with Brinn attached to one leg and Ciara

the other. "She is. It was nice of Ben and Poppy to stay with him."

"Are you sure you're okay to look after the children tonight?" Dot frowned. "If I'd known in advance, I could have canceled my plans and taken this lot with me."

"No, that's fine," Claire said, and it really was. "Finn and I would be happy to watch them." She was learning to enjoy the sense of family the children brought with them. "And you made dinner already, so the hard part is over."

Dot snorted and rolled her eyes. "Call me if you live to eat those words."

"Will do." Finn upended Brinn and made her shriek. "Or I could toss them all out the window."

Claire didn't like him holding Brinn upside down. "Be careful with her."

"She's fine." Grinning at Brinn, Finn gave her a little shake.

Brinn giggled. "I like it."

"See."

"Just don't do that after she's eaten." Dot gathered up her things, and after kissing each child, she left.

Ryan took a seat at the kitchen table. "I'm hungry. Can we eat?"

At four thirty in the afternoon? She could pretend it was the early bird special somewhere. "Sure."

"Ryan, get some place mats." Finn put Brinn down and steadied her until she regained her balance. "Brinn, you're on knives and forks. Ciara, get some glasses. And you"—he snatched up Sean—"are going in your chair."

"Finn!" Sean patted his cheeks. "Hello, Finn."

"Hi, big man." Finn nuzzled Sean before putting him in his highchair. "Are you hungry?"

Sean nodded and slapped the tray of his highchair.

The familial resemblance between Finn and his nephews and nieces was strong enough for him to be mistaken for their father.

He also clearly adored them and was comfortable dealing with them.

Looking up, he caught her watching him and winked. "You have hungry menfolk here."

"Then they should feed themselves." Brinn tossed her head. "Shouldn't they, Claire?"

"Absolutely!" Claire high-fived her, put on oven mitts, and fetched the mac and cheese from the oven. She put it on the table far away from small fingers. "The dish is hot. Don't touch it."

Ryan immediately reached for it.

"Dude!" Finn caught his hand. "Did you hear what Claire said?"

He got busy serving the children, while Claire fetched the children some milk and beer for her and Finn. She hadn't drank this much beer since college.

Finn snagged her around the waist and drew her in for a quick kiss. "Thanks."

"You're welcome."

"Oooh." Brinn made kissing noises while Ciara giggled behind her hand.

Ryan made gagging sounds. "Ew."

"One day you're going to find some girl you want to do the same thing to." Finn gave him a gentle push.

"Or boy." Brinn raised her eyebrows at Finn. "Ryan might want to kiss boys and not girls."

Ryan dug into his meal. "I don't want to kiss anyone."

"What are you?" Finn stalked Brinn around the table. "The political correctness police?"

"Uh-huh." Brinn grinned at him. "Ciara and I will let you know our pronouns."

"You're so smart." Finn kissed the top of her head.

Brinn pointed with her fork. "Ciara too."

"Ciara too." Finn kissed Ciara as well.

When they'd left the hospital, Claire would have sworn all she wanted was a hot bath, a book, and bed. She had to be up early to go back to the hospital. Sitting in the midst of a family dinner, however, her weariness melted away. Sure, the children were energetic and took managing, but they also fed her spirit in a way she'd never experienced before.

As an only child, she'd never had noisy happy dinners. She had been accepted into this family circle as if she belonged there. Her heart gave a strong twinge. The realization body slammed her. She wanted to be a part of it. She wanted to belong there. Quick on the heels of that, came the thought she could have it for herself. She could build her own noisy, funny, energetic family.

Her gaze strayed to Finn. How much like Poppy's children would Finn's look?

He was simultaneously feeding himself and making sure at least some food got into Sean's mouth.

More importantly, why was she thinking of Finn and children and her own newly discovered desire for a family?

After dinner, Finn took the children for bath time.

"You go. I've got this." She motioned the clear up.

Finn looked at the table with a raised brow. It looked like the children had skipped the plates altogether and eaten straight off the table. "Really?"

"Sure." She waved him off. She needed time to think anyway. "I'll see you when you're done."

Taking her time, Claire set the kitchen to rights. She put the mac and cheese away and cleaned the dish. Gradually the noises from the floor above quieted down as Finn put the children to bed.

She did a lock check and then climbed the stairs. From the girls' room Finn's voice murmured as if he was reading them a bedtime story.

Claire skipped her bath and took a quick shower to get the hospital smell off her. Also, she'd ended up with mac and cheese on parts of her that baffled her. The house was silent as she finished up and put her pjs on.

A knock on her door got her heart racing.

She opened it to find Finn both arms braced on the door-frame. "Hi."

"Hi." Shyness crept through her and she had no idea why. She felt oddly vulnerable as if her earlier thoughts had opened a chasm in her defenses.

"Kids are asleep." Finn crowded her back into her room. "Now we get to do what all adults do when the children are asleep."

With that hot look he was giving her, there was no mistaking his meaning. "Finn, we can't. The children—"

"Are sleeping." He took her hand and pressed it to his erection. "And I'm one hundred percent sure I can."

This man was her catnip, her crack, her cheesecake, and she kept her hand right where it was. "Maybe we should explore this notion further."

"You go ahead and explore all you like." He backed her up until her legs hit the bed. "There's only one rule to this." He pressed her to the bed and came down on top of her. "We wouldn't want to wake the children, so you have to be as quiet as you can. And I am going to make that nearly impossible for you to do."

———

Finn nearly broke her, but Claire managed to keep it under wraps by shoving her fist in her mouth. Now she lay with her head on his shoulder, her deep breath huffing across his chest as she slept.

God he was in deep with this woman.

When she had first stepped out of her car looking like a *Cosmo* wet dream in her fuck-me heels and her tight skirt, something in him had stilled and said, *"This one."*

Through all her prickliness and barriers that same something had persisted. Now he was in over his head. Being downstairs with her and the kids tonight had put another nail in his coffin. Claire was discovering how good she was with children.

Going from the woman who had tried to climb the counter-tops to get away from them to laughing and joking with the twins. She even managed enthusiasm for Ryan's excruciating knock-knock jokes.

She gave him a sense of peace he had craved since before he retired, and she offered him a future that held hope. He could have something beautiful for him and a future filled with color and laughter.

The only other thing that came close was when he was working with Hank. Not the carpentry so much as working with the antique furniture. There was something soul soothing about taking an old piece and giving it the attention it needed.

The things he worked on came to him broken and almost destroyed. Under Hank's tutelage, he was learning to give them a new life. Not as new pieces, but as a beautiful fusion of their history and their restored beauty. The metaphor wasn't a brain twister. If he could give new life to old furniture, then there was hope for him.

CHAPTER
Twenty-Four

BY THE END of the next day of looking after Horace, Claire had a new level of appreciation for Nurse Bunny.

Horace was a horrible patient. She was about two seconds away from begging them to drug him.

He dug his spoon into his lunch and made a face. "What is this?"

"Jell-O?" It wasn't exactly mystery food. "And don't eat it if you don't like it."

He huffed and pushed the tray stand away. "Why can't I go home? These sheets are scratchy."

"Dad! You are officially the worst patient here." Claire carried his tray outside.

Nurse Bunny was bouncing down the passage, and she lowered her voice, "How is he?"

"Impossible." Claire let her take the tray. "Haven't you got something you can put in his drip?"

Bunny went into cute giggles. "Wouldn't that make our jobs easier?"

"Is there any chance they will release him tomorrow?" Claire hoped like hell being back home would improve Horace's temper.

"I'll talk to his doctor," Bunny said with a wink. "He's doing well, so I don't really see why not."

"Great." She could always push him out of the car on the way home. Just kidding. Sort of. Anyway, back in Twin Elks, she could foist him on Poppy for an hour or two, or Dot, and if neither of those worked, there was always the threat of getting Peg to babysit him.

Horace bellowed her name, and she rolled her eyes at Bunny before going back in. "What?"

"I need more water. This is warm." He gave his jug a peevish poke and nearly sent it crashing to ground.

Claire snatched up the jug. "I'll get you some more. I live to serve."

Being there made her think about her mother and how she was getting on. Before she went back, she gave Doug a quick call, only to be told Mom was sleeping and hadn't had a good day.

The tug in two directions, maybe even three if she counted Finn in the equation, yanked at her. Getting closer to her dad put her in conflict with Mom. Except Mom barely remembered her most days, so it didn't look like she would ever have to know. The dishonesty of that bothered Claire. Her parents had really done a number on her in catching her in the middle of their tug-of-war.

When she got back to Horace's room, normal visiting hours had begun, and Bart Grover had arrived. He'd brought Horace his favorite snacks, so he was looking much happier.

"Hi Claire." Bart beamed at her.

It was a marked difference from their last meeting. "Hi Bart."

"Claire." Mia gave her a tight nod, still not willing to forgive her completely.

"Okay, Dad. I'm going to leave you in good hands here." She leaned over and kissed his cheek. "Don't terrorize the nurses, and I'll be back tomorrow."

Bart and Mia blinked at her.

"Thanks, girlie." Horace patted her cheek. "I'm a miserable old bastard, but I appreciate you being here."

"Which is why I tolerate you." She patted his shoulder and left.

The drive home was long enough to make her wish she'd taken Finn up on his offer this morning and let him come with her. But Hank Styles had been around and wanted to work on some furniture with Finn.

She'd seen Finn's face when he worked with Hank. He never looked more peaceful, other than when he was in a sated sleep beside her. Maybe tonight she'd sneak into his room.

Walking into the kitchen at her house, she stopped and stared at the male bounty laid before her. All four of Ben's brothers milled about with Ben and Finn taking it into testosterone overload.

Dot reigned supreme as she directed large bodies in directions she needed them to go.

"Claire." Dot pulled her into a vanilla-scented hug that felt like home. "How is he today?"

"A miserable old goat but recovering nicely." Claire's gaze bounced from one man to another.

Objectively speaking, Rafe was the best looking in a movie star way. But Luke was no slouch there, either, and he had a layer of sophistication that left her a bit starstruck. Mark had a boyishness about him that combined with his professional athlete body, made her neurons stop firing. Gabe was the most approachable, but it came with a rough and ready bad boy warning label.

Dot whispered in her ear, "You're staring."

"Yup."

"I know." Dot patted her cheek. "They're a lot to take in. Don't be dazzled. They all still tell fart jokes."

"Hey, Claire." Gabe swaggered over with a grin. "This is a surprise home invasion."

"Ben invited them all to dinner." Dot lowered her voice. "If it's too much, we can take this over to my house."

"No, this is perfect." And it was. The drive home had been long enough to spend with her thoughts.

Gabe leaned down to kiss her cheek.

Before he connected, Finn slid into position behind her, wrapped his arms around her and tugged her back to his chest. "Babe," he murmured in her ear. "You're home."

"Yes." And it didn't matter how hot Gabe, or the rest of the Crowe boys were, because her eyes got stuck on Finn. For the most part.

Gabe's grin widened, and he took his time with the kiss on her cheek.

Finn's actions caused a few amused glances from the other brothers, and Poppy shook her head at him.

"What?" Finn put an arm around Claire's shoulder and led her to the table. He stuck his chin out and put his shoulders back.

"I missed you, Claire." Mark picked her up and swung her away from Finn.

"Me too." Rafe pulled her into a big hug that ended only when Luke took over from him.

She went with, laughing, because there was no way she was stopping them. The look on Finn's face was priceless, like he was battling his inner caveman.

"Any reason for this get together?" She finally managed to fight her way free.

"Yup." Luke handed her a glass of wine. "Mark, Rafe, and I are heading out in the morning."

Claire shot Dot a look. She hid it well, but Dot was not happy about them leaving. "And Gabe?"

"He's staying a bit longer," Dot said, and her smile came back.

"Not going back to Australia?" Claire took pity on Finn and

returned to his side. He put an arm around her waist and brought her closer.

Gabe grimaced. "Nope. Things got...er...complicated."

"His girl dumped him," Mark said.

Luke smirked at Gabe. "And as she was the daughter of the head of the research team, Gabe is shit outta luck."

"They fired you?" That sounded all kinds of unprofessional.

Gabe shrugged, but lines of tension straightened his shoulders. "Not in as many words, but Belinda asked me not to come back, and I reckon I owe her that much."

"Let's eat." Poppy bustled into the center of the kitchen. "Dinner is ready."

Dinner was delicious, as it always was when Poppy did the cooking. Again, Claire ended up eating more than she should.

Sitting surrounded by wonderful people, with Finn's arm draped over the back of her chair, she got the sweetest sense of belonging. The Crowe brothers told stories about each other and teased each other.

Dot sat in their midst and glowed with happiness.

Even usually quiet Ben joined in.

Poppy's children were effortlessly brought into the fold.

Sean was fast asleep against Luke's double folded linen shirt, drooling a little.

Brinn and Ciara played a game with Mark that seemed to involve testing his reflexes to see if they could grab a coin from his hand before he closed his fingers.

Ryan, as always, sat as close to Ben as he could get.

Ben kept his arm around Ryan's shoulder as he talked to Rafe. He'd taken on the father mantle effortlessly. She wondered if there had ever been a time when he felt daunted by taking on all Poppy's children as well as Poppy.

"You're quiet," Finn whispered to her.

Claire nodded. She didn't know how to explain what was going on inside her. She'd come with an agenda that now seemed laughable. She wished Horace was there; he would have loved it.

The old house was made to shelter large groups of people.

Without knowing why, she knew that Cecily was loving every minute. Wherever she was, she would be watching and smiling. This was the reason she'd had the original Horace build her this house.

Claire slipped up to bed a short time later. As she brushed her teeth and got ready for bed, the party continued in the kitchen.

When she left the bathroom, Finn was sitting on her bed. "You okay?"

"Why aren't you downstairs?" Classic deflection: answer a question with a question.

Finn studied her with those clear blue eyes that saw right through bullshit. "I thought I would give them some family time. Dot needs all the time she can get with her boys."

"True." She understood what made the Crowe brothers want to leave Twin Elks, but she also now understood the pull.

"What's going on, babe?" Finn leaned back on his hands. "I'm getting the feeling this is about a lot more than Horace's operation."

Claire dropped to the bed beside him. She didn't know if he would get any of it, but talking to Finn had become a habit. She wasn't exactly sure when that had happened, but there it was. "I'm confused."

"Seriously?" He snorted and took her hand to take any sting out of his reaction. "Your entire time here has been confusing for you."

She dropped on her back and folded her arms over her sternum. "I had a good time tonight."

"That's supposed to be a good thing." Finn stretched out beside her.

"I know that." She nudged him. "But it was more than fun. I felt like I belonged here. Like I fit into something."

"You do." Propping his head on his elbow, Finn looked down at her. Twining their fingers, he brought her hand to his mouth and kissed it. "There's a place for you here."

His declaration only made her confusion worse. "But what if this is not my place?"

"Like you don't belong here?"

"Yes." It hurt, because she desperately wanted to belong, but at the same time, she didn't know if she could. If she should.

Finn studied her hand, and then put it back on her tummy. "Babe, I can't make that decision for you, and neither can anyone else. If leaving here and going back to Boston would make you happy, then that's what you have to do."

"But I don't know if it would." And why wasn't he begging her to stay?

"Yeah, you do." Tension radiated from him. "I call bullshit on that, Claire You know exactly where you want to be, where your heart wants you to be. The only thing holding you back is fear."

"That's easy for you to say." His response stung.

"No, Claire, it really isn't." Finn rolled to his feet. "You're confused, and you feel conflicted, and we all get that. We're all backing off and giving you room to make your decision, but you also have to take control of this journey, babe." He ran his hand through his hair. "Your conflict affects the rest of us. Horace is on a bed of nails waiting for you to walk away from your heritage and him. Poppy is trying her best to like you and not get too attached." He leaned over her. "We all are, babe. Like it or not, Claire, people here give a shit about you, and if you leave, you're going to punch a hole through us that will take a while to heal."

She didn't know what to say, but his honesty hit her like a belly punch.

"Make up your mind, Claire." He turned for the door. "Loving someone who walks out on you sucks."

———

Finn's parting shot left her awake late into the night.

Downstairs, Ben said goodbye to his mother and brothers and he and Poppy put the kids to bed. The front door shut behind them. Poppy giggled and Ben's low murmur followed, and then they shut their bedroom door.

Throwing off her covers, Claire got out of bed. On the landing, moonlight filtered through the stained-glass windows and made shivery patterns on the floor. Horace had put those windows in for Cecily because she loved her roses so much.

Claire went upstairs past the nursery floor and up again into the attic.

She went to the pool of moonlight coming through the tiny round attic windows and sat in the chair it lit up.

Claire breathed. She opened her lungs and breathed it all in.

Around her, the old house settled and sighed. Ghosts of her family history settled around her. Nowhere in the house were they more present than in the attic. On that chaise, one of her ancestors had read a book, maybe nursed a headache or a child.

Over there in the dressing table mirror, speckled with age, someone bound to her by blood had checked his tie, or straightened his hair. In that chest, someone else had put linens away or maybe gathered treasures for the future.

For her.

She walked over to one of the bound chests and opened it. Empty except for a spare sock. A second chest was filled with old children's books that belonged in the library or the nursery, not up here gathering dust and decaying.

"Yours." The old house sighed. *"All yours."*

She lifted the dust cover off the chaise. A blanket was neatly folded on one end as if someone had just done it. Claire stretched out on the chaise and pulled the blanket around her.

"Home," her ghosts whispered. *"Welcome home."*

She must have fallen asleep because sunlight directly in her eyes woke her. Not everything in her confusion was sorted, but of this, she was sure. She was done walking away from her heritage.

She showered and got dressed, and even beat Ben to the kitchen.

Hair wet from the shower and dressed in his uniform, Ben stopped in the doorway when he saw her. "You're up early."

"Yeah." The morning had a freshness about it that made her want to embrace it. "Coffee is ready."

Ben smiled and helped himself to a cup. He rested his hips against the counter as he drank his coffee.

"So." She was glad it was Ben she would speak to first. His quiet pragmatism had a way of easing difficult situations. "I've made a decision about the house."

"Yeah?" Ben sipped his coffee, his eyes darker than the coffee he drank.

"I'm not selling it." She rushed on before he could react. "So, you and Poppy and the children, of course, are more than welcome to stay here until your house is ready."

Ben nodded and sipped his coffee. "Good."

That was it. That was it?

All her agonizing and journeying into her past and Ben nodded and said good. It put her issues into perspective, and she laughed. "You're a good guy Ben."

"Huh?" He raised a dark brow.

Claire waved him off and got herself a cup of coffee. "This house is part of me, and selling it would be like giving away that part."

"About time." Poppy bustled in with a huge grin on her face. She pulled Claire into a hug. "We all knew you'd get there."

"Did you now?" Then they'd known a lot more than she did. Claire accepted the hug while trying not to spill coffee all over the floor.

"Why are you hugging?" Brinn stumbled into the kitchen with Ciara behind her.

"Claire is not going to sell Winters House." Poppy spoke to her daughter but beamed at Claire.

Brinn rolled her eyes. "Of course, she isn't."

Ciara gave Claire a very adult smile and nod of approval.

"Sean's crying," Ryan yelled from the top of the stairs.

"I got him," Finn called and then said to Ryan. "You wanna put some pants on?"

"Not really. I like free balling it."

Finn laughed. "I hear ya."

Trying his best not to laugh, Ben deflected Poppy's glare. "He never learned that from me."

There was no more time for meaningful interchanges and introspection as they all got swallowed in the mayhem of a busy and full household getting ready for the day.

The dark spot in her day was Finn not looking at her. Oh, he was polite enough and greeted her, but he didn't look at her like he normally did, like he wanted to gobble her up or sit on the sidelines and watch her for the rest of the day.

His blue eyes were glacial, and a sharp reminder that she may have sorted out part of her life, but she still had another mountain to climb.

————

Twin Elks relieved her of any need to tell Horace the news. Claire had no idea how the news beat her to the hospital, but it did.

When she got there, Rachel was sitting beside Horace, and she stood when Claire entered.

"Oh, Claire." She got another hug. They were big on hugging in this part of the world. "I heard and we're so happy you're not selling Winters House."

Horace raised an eyebrow at her. "Something you'd like to tell me, daughter?"

"I'd like to have the chance." She disentangled herself from Rachel.

Rachel beamed at them both. "Winters House is so much a part of our community. I can't imagine the town without it."

"Quite right." Peg bustled in, wreathed in smiles. "The Good Lord knows we've had our issues with you, Claire, but you have shown your true colors now."

Horace raised an eyebrow at her.

"I told Poppy and Ben I wasn't selling the house this morning."

Stilling, Horace studied her. "Any particular reason why?"

"It's my home, my heritage." She felt shy admitting this. "It's a part of me."

"Quite right." Horace squeezed her hand. "It took you a while to realize that."

"Now, Horace." Peg shook a finger at him. "Don't be lecturing her. There is no space for I told you so between a parent and a child."

"Peg." Horace kept his gaze on Claire. "I'm gonna ask you real polite to get your butt out of here."

Peg snorted. "That's not polite, Horace, but I'm going." She waved at Rachel. "And you're coming with me. I'll spread the word, don't you worry, that the Winters House crisis is over, and that you'll be receiving visitors when you're back home."

"She has her uses," Horace said as Peg bustled out. He crossed his hands over his belly and stared out the window.

Claire stared out the window with him. For such a momentous moment, neither of them had much to say.

"The Winters legacy," Horace said, still staring at the other side of the hospital out the window. "It's bigger than the house."

"I thought as much." She didn't have all the answers to what her future looked like yet, but she was done running away from fifty percent of her ancestry. "I thought you could share some of it with me while you recovered."

"You staying that long?"

"I thought I might."

"Huh."

A pigeon fluttered to the sill outside the window and strutted its stuff. Another pigeon joined him.

Horace breathed deep. "No wonder there are so many of them."

Claire had to laugh.

"It's right, you know." Horace watched the pigeons. "You learning about your legacy. I'm real glad, Claire. Real glad."

"Same." She took his hand and held it. "I feel like I've wasted an awful lot of time."

"We can't think like that." Horace looked at her. "We don't get to cherry-pick the parts of our past that we change and assume the now would still look the same except for that one small piece. We are where we are, and we can only look forward."

CHAPTER
Twenty-Five

FINN TAPPED the last joint into place with Hank hanging over his shoulder.

"Gentle like," Hank crooned. "Like you're pleasing your lady. Ease her into it, persuade her where you want her."

Hank's breath tickled Finn's neck. "Seriously, Hank." Finn glanced over his shoulder. "Personal space? You're starting to weird me out."

Chuckling, Hank straightened. He pointed his chin at the join in the old rocker Finn had put together. "You got a real way with the wood. My pa used to say anyone can learn to work with wood, but there's some what's got the way with them." He sniffed and shoved his hands in his coverall pockets. "I got that way with me. You do too."

"Thank you." Rare as they were, a compliment from Hank was to be savored. Finn wished he were in a better frame of mind to do so. The news about Claire and Winters House had thrown him this morning. He was in deep with her, and her confusion frustrated him. He wanted to yell at her to find what she wanted and grab that thing. And he wanted that thing to be him and their future.

It had taken him this long to consider the possibility that he could have what he'd secretly always wanted. That he could love, and he was worth loving back. Now that he'd made that decision for himself and found the one, he wanted to have that with her. He wanted her all in with him.

Hank rocked on his feet and sucked his teeth. "Thought mebbe you might be thinking of sticking around."

Finn made a noncommittal noise. Hank liked his gossip and wasn't always partial to the facts. The less you gave him the better.

"Seeing as that honey of yours is sticking around."

There you had it. Finn ran his fingers over the join, looking for any rough spots. "She didn't say she was sticking around forever."

"Is that what's souring your milk this morning?"

Finn wasn't about to take love advice from a man whose idea of courtship involved a Bud six-pack and a set of glow-in-the-dark condoms. "What's with all the chatting?"

"Darn it!" Hank stamped his foot. "I'm trying to offer you a job here. You keep stroking on that wood, and I'm liable to change my mind."

That got Finn's attention, and he straightened so fast he almost slammed his head into the tabletop next to the rocker. "What did you say?"

"A job." Hank sucked his teeth. "Working with me in the shop. Permanent like." He sniffed. "I got more work than I can handle. It's coming in from all over, what with there not being that many of us that can do this anymore."

It took Finn's head a moment to catch up. In addition to specialized carpentry, Hank had a workshop at the far end of town where he repaired and refinished furniture. He had told Finn that he used to make some furniture as well, but that he'd stopped that after his nephew left Twin Elks, and Hank didn't have any help.

Finn had started working with Hank as something to do

while he got his head together. It had never occurred to him to turn his hobby into something more.

The idea took root. "Let me think about that, Hank." He stood and dusted sawdust from his pants. "But I'm thinking I buy in and make it more like a partnership than me working for you."

"Partnership." Hank puffed out his cheeks. "There you go getting ahead of yourself and all."

Finn knew better than to react. Hank liked to bark, but for the most part, he was toothless. "I have some money set aside, so I could buy in. Maybe we could get to making some new stuff while we're at it."

Hank pulled a face. "New stuff." He huffed. "What do you know about making new stuff? I taught you a coupla things, and now you're all set to take over the world of furniture manufacture."

"I have a way with wood." Finn couldn't resist. "You said so yourself."

Hank went red in the face. "Now listen here, you—"

"Excuse me." A man stood in the workshop doorway. Finn put his age at a few years younger than him. Dressed in what Finn would bet were designer duds, with a haircut that cost a whole lot more than the five-dollar trim he got on Main Street from a cousin of Kelly's, the man reeked of money and snobbery. "I'm looking for Claire Mathews."

There you had it. That was the thing Finn had guessed he might say but had still hoped to be wrong about.

"You a friend of hers?" Hank had gone full country bumpkin on the guy. Even adding a hitch to his coveralls for effect.

The newcomer looked like he smelled something bad. Now Hank could be ripe on occasion but not that bad. "I was given to believe she would be here."

"Is that right?" Hank was having such a good time Finn let him roll with it. "And who exactly was it that gave you to believe such?"

"Eh?" The man blinked at him. Finn had to admit that if the guy had asked for anyone else, he might have stepped in, but a green-eyed monster had him by the balls and was hanging on tight. This guy looked exactly like the sort the Claire who had stepped out of her car in her killer shoes would date, and Finn wanted to rearrange his pretty face for him. And muss up that two-hundred-dollar hairdo he had going on.

"Who told you Claire would be here?" He interpreted Hank for the guy.

"Oh." He looked affronted by the question. "Her mother. Look, is she here or not?"

"Not."

Hank shook his head. "Nope."

"Are you sure?" He tugged a smartphone out of his perfectly pressed pants and consulted it. "This is the address I was given."

"If you can find her, young feller, you can call me a liar and spit on my grave." Hank grinned.

"But this is Winters House?" The guy took a careful breath. "The home of Horace Winters."

"Yep." Hank grinned.

Finn nodded and tried like hell not to laugh.

The guy made a noise of exasperation. "Then I do have the correct address, and Claire is staying here."

"Well now." Hank looked at Finn and opened his arms wide, a man on whom the light had dawned. "If you'd'a started by asking if she lived here, then we would have said yes. Ain't that right?" Hank looked to him for corroboration.

Finn couldn't give it. He wouldn't have told slick dick anything without hearing more of why he was here and what he wanted with Claire.

"So, she is here?" The guy gritted the question through a tight jaw.

"She is living here." Hank enunciated slowly. "But she ain't here now."

The guy made a strangled sound. "Do you have any idea when you are expecting her back?"

"Nope."

"A guess?"

"Hmm." Hank looked at him and frowned. "Now yesterday she came back late afternoon. Day afore that it was full dark before she got back. What do you reckon?"

Hank's playtime was over. Finn stepped forward. "I didn't get your name."

"Greg." The guy stiffened and squared off. "Greg Halburton."

"Halburton?" Hank tapped his chin. "Any relation to the Halburtons over in Rattlesnake Gulch?" He turned to Finn. "Now that Debbie Halburton can wrestle a greased hog down faster than you've ever seen."

"No." Greg looked like he might puke. "Is there anywhere I can wait for Claire?"

Hank grinned. "Yep."

Greg waited.

Hank kept right on grinning.

Greg almost growled. "Would you care to tell me where?"

"I would." Hank nodded.

"You can wait on the porch." Finn pointed him in the right direction. "Just as soon as you tell me what you want with Claire and why I should let you wait for her."

Greg drew himself up tall. "I am her fiancé."

"Well shit," Hank said as Greg stalked away. "That can't be good."

Finn clenched his fist. "No, it fucking can't."

———

Relieved to be home, Claire parked behind Horace's tank of a car. Horace would come home tomorrow, and that would end her long trips to and from the hospital. She also had an inkling he was going to be fairly impossible as a patient.

The last of the twilight lovingly bathed the old house in rose gold. The beauty of it filled Claire with serenity. Now that she'd conceded defeat, the house welcomed her home, ready to comfort and shelter her.

Her feet ached, and she slipped off her heels before walking to the house.

Greg sitting on the front porch sipping a beer made her stop. Short of her mother sitting on the porch, Greg ran a close second for the last person she expected to see.

"Claire." He put the bottle aside and rushed toward her. "Thank God."

She didn't react fast enough, which was how she ended up being swung in Greg's arms with him trying to work his tongue into her mouth.

She turned her head. "Greg. Could you put me down?"

He did but kept his arms around her. He gave her the smile that always used to work wonders on lowering her guard. "You look beautiful. Did you miss me?"

Finn lounged in the doorway and raised his brow at Greg's question, as if silently demanding she answer for both him and Greg.

"What are you doing here?" No, she hadn't missed him. After her first few days here, she'd barely even thought of him at all.

Greg's expression blanked, and he took a step back. "I hadn't heard from you, and I was worried."

"Really?" Greg had put them on hold with the ruthless efficiency of a scalpel, citing the need to make a clean break as the reason. She was tired, hungry, and that beer in Finn's hand looked really damn good. Finn looked even better.

With Greg following she climbed the porch steps and stopped in front of Finn. "Hi."

"Hi." No noticeable thawing from this morning. Perhaps even a thicker layer of frost. "How's Horace?"

"Doing better. He comes home tomorrow."

"Great."

"I think so."

Finn stared at her, not giving an inch, physically or emotionally. His silence made her want to chatter.

Gaze locked on her, he sipped his beer. "Met the fiancé, by the way."

"The what?"

"Claire." Greg came up behind her. "Can we go somewhere and talk?"

She really didn't want to. "What about, Greg?"

"Us." Greg gave Finn a pointed look. "Somewhere private."

"Don't get yourself hot and bothered about me, Sparky." Finn sipped his beer and straightened. "I've seen and heard enough."

"Finn." Claire wanted to stop him and explain, but he kept walking. Dealing with Greg was probably a better first step. She dropped her shoes on the porch and grabbed Greg's beer and took a long swallow. "You drove all this way, so talk."

"Really, Claire." Greg gave a stilted chuckle. "Perhaps we could start with basic civility and you invite me to sit."

She waved him toward the porch swing and propped her ass on the railing.

Greg hitched his trousers to protect the crease and sat. "And since when do you drink beer?"

"I love beer." She finished the bottle. "I've discovered a new liking for it."

Greg stared, planning his point of attack. He crossed an ankle over his knee and spread his arms on the swing back. "It's pretty here. You never mentioned that before."

"Mostly because I was doing my best to get out of here as fast as possible," she said. With the dark, the temperature was dropping, and she hugged herself for warmth. Greg was not getting an invitation inside. "Can we get to the part about what you're doing here?"

"You've been gone for weeks," he said, a hint of censure in his tone. "None of your friends have heard from you. God knows, I haven't heard a murmur."

That was too much. "You as much as told me not to contact you after our breakup."

"Would we say it was a breakup?" Greg looked thoughtful. "Or more of a break. As in taking a break."

Claire hugged herself tighter. She might need to yell for a sweater if he didn't get to the point soon. "I took it as a breakup, and none of your subsequent behavior suggested otherwise."

His expression grew regretful. "You're right. I wanted out at the time, and I spoke before I'd thought it through properly."

"Yes, you did." It had hurt like hell. "You broke up a three-year relationship without any warning, and then refused to speak to me. You even left me notes with a friend about picking up my stuff."

"I was wrong, Claire." Oozing sincerity, Greg leaned forward and spread his hands. "It didn't take me long to realize I'd made the biggest mistake of my life."

"How long?"

Greg blinked at her. "Eh?"

"How long did this realization take? I was in Boston for four weeks before I came here, and you seemed fine with the decision then. I've been here for two weeks, and now you're here."

He frowned. "I can't pinpoint an exact moment. It was more a growing realization."

"Like a fungus?" Something suspiciously like a suppressed laugh came from the house.

"What?"

"I asked if the growing realization was like a fungus?"

"Claire," Greg whipped out her name with his done-playing-around tone. "I can see you're in one of your moods and aren't taking this seriously. You need to come home with me. You don't belong here. All you've ever said about this place has been that you hated it and had no time for your father. People are worried about you." He took a heavy pause. "I am worried about you, and so is your mother."

Ah! There it was, the missing piece of the puzzle. "You saw my mother?"

"Doug called me and said she was asking for me." Greg stood and adjusted his pants crease. He was particular about that crease. Even gave their dry cleaner precise instructions on how he wanted it. "I went to see her."

"You know she's not all there." Mom had loved Greg. And Greg had always been kind to Mom.

Greg sniffed. "I know that, but she was perfectly lucid during my visit. She is concerned about how much time you're spending here. She is also near frantic that your father is keeping you here against your will."

"He's not." Claire stood, not wanting him to loom over her. "I'm staying because I want to be here."

"I find that impossible to believe." Greg stepped closer to her. "You need to come back to where you belong. To your life. Even if that life doesn't include me. I'm here for you, not for me or even us."

"Right." *God, how had she fallen—and stayed fallen for so long— for this guy?* He was cold and rigid, and she could write his understanding of her on a pinhead. "I'll come back when I'm ready, and not before then. You see, Greg, this is my life. I'm living it right this second. I didn't put it on hold when I came here."

"What are you talking about?" Greg took her arm. "It took me all yesterday to fly to Denver and hours of driving today. You're making no damn sense."

"Sparky." Finn's voice was a low snarl from the doorway. "I've got no problem with you per se, but you get your fucking hand off her."

Greg dropped his hand and whirled. "Who are you?" He

turned back to her. "Who is he, and more importantly, who is he to you?"

"I tell you who I'm not." Finn strolled forward, leashed violence in every powerful line of him. "I'm not the prick who comes down here claiming to be her fiancé."

"You said that?" Claire gaped at Greg. Also, Finn like this was a bit scary and whole lot sexy.

Greg flushed. "I exaggerated, but I didn't think he and his yokel buddy would let me see you."

Finn looked at her and raised a brow. "You done here?"

More than that, and she nodded. "I'm done."

Stalking Greg, Finn smiled ferally. "That means you're leaving."

To give Greg his due, he considered taking Finn on and standing his ground. In the end, he made the right decision and scuttled for his car. "I'll call you."

"Don't," Claire called back. "I think your idea about a clean break was the right one."

She stood beside Finn as Greg climbed into his rental and backed into the road. "Were you eavesdropping on our conversation?"

Finn snorted. "Damn right I was."

CHAPTER
Twenty-Six

AFTER DINNER, Claire went to the library and put in a call to her mother.

"She's right here," Doug said and handed the phone over.

There was so much she wanted to discuss with her mother, but instead she asked how she was.

"I'm good," Mom said. "I started a new puzzle yesterday. A thousand pieces."

"Wow! That should keep you out of trouble."

Mom snorted. "As if anything could keep me out of trouble. Are you still in Twin Elks?"

"Yes." She hesitated and then hated herself for it. For as long as she didn't speak her truth she would be caught between her parents. "Dad had his hip done, and I'm staying until he's better."

Mom's silence shrieked down the line. "I see."

"I'm trying to get to know him better." Perhaps she shouldn't have said anything. With Mom's memory, she need never have known, but the lie felt too heavy for her to keep carrying.

Mom sighed. "He is your father. I suppose you have a right to know him."

"I know you hated it here, hated him. But I don't." Claire risked another step into the forbidden.

"I didn't hate it or him," Mom said, and she sounded sad. "I was young and foolish, and Horace and I were never suited. He swept me off my feet, and when I came down again, it was to discover how different we were."

Claire sat frozen and tried to process that. Mom had never said anything like it before. She didn't understand why or where the change came from. "You always spoke about Twin Elks and Dad as if you hated them."

"I know." Mom's voice grew defensive. "I had one child, Claire. I was not going to lose her to that place. When you're a mother, you'll understand."

When she was a mother? Claire had only recently admitted that possibility to herself. Greg had been a hard no on the children thing, and she'd thought she was too. If she did ever become a mother, would she be entitled to make her fears a part of her children's realty? She didn't think so, but then, being a mother had never been anything she'd given much thought to, and what did she really know anyway?

She let the conversation slide along more familiar lines and away from dangerous territory.

The door opened. Finn came in and gave her a questioning look.

She motioned to him that he should stay, and he perched on the edge of the desk and waited while she finished her call.

"Your mom?" He indicated the phone.

"Yeah." Claire stared at the phone as if it could provide insight into the conversation she'd had with her mother. "Apparently she doesn't hate Horace or Twin Elks anymore."

Finn pulled a face. "Yeah. I can't be much help on the mom thing. Given who mine is."

"I feel like I'm trying to live in two worlds simultaneously." She looked out the window into the night. With the weather driving everyone indoors, the street was quiet. "I know what you think."

"Yeah?"

A lone squirrel high-wired the telephone cables. "You think I should make a decision. That the way to stop that is to choose."

"Pretty much." He spoke from right beside her. Turning her chair so that she faced him, he crouched at her feet. "I also understand that's a lot easier said than done."

When had he come to mean so much to her? She looked into his beautiful face and realized how much she really cared what he said. Finn Williams had become a factor in her decision making, and she couldn't pinpoint how or when that had happened. "What should I do?"

"I can't tell you that, babe." He cupped her cheek. "And I'm sorry I was such an asshole about it before." He stood and tugged her into his arms. His head rested against hers. "The problem is that you've gotten under my skin, and just the idea of you leaving puts me in a shitty mood."

His confession squeezed her heart. "You've gotten under my skin too."

"Now comes the part I really don't want to say."

"Then don't." Fear trickled icy droplets down her spine. "Let's stay here and pretend everything is perfect."

He chuckled, but without any real amusement behind it. "I think you've had your life flipped on its ass," he said. "You arrived here in your sexy skirt with an iron-clad set of beliefs about yourself, your dad, this house, everybody who lived in Twin Elks, and that's been eroded." He kissed her temple. "I think you need to clear your mind. Make a decision with a fresh outlook. The change happened to you and not this town, or even this great house. You need to take that change back to where you started and see what that feels like."

"What are you saying?" She was very much afraid she knew exactly what he was saying.

Finn sighed and kissed her head. "I'm saying you should go

back to Boston and see how you feel there. If you still want to be there instead of here. I think you need to discover that for all our sakes; yours, mine, Horace's, even Poppy and Ben and the kids." He growled. "Even for that asshole who just left. Find out where you want to be, babe."

"What if it's not here?" She had to ask.

Finn's arms tightened around her. "Then we'll miss you." His voice dropped to a hoarse whisper. "I'll miss you most of all."

Intimacy throbbed between them, stained by a growing sadness. Claire looped her arms around his neck and kissed him.

The familiar and intoxicating taste of Finn surrounded her.

Finn groaned and molded her to him, his kiss ravenous and slightly desperate, as if he needed to absorb her. He broke away breathing hard. "Be with me. Tonight."

She didn't know where she wanted to be from tomorrow onward, but for tonight, the decision was easy. "Yes."

————

Claire worked with Poppy to get everything ready for Horace the next day. As he shouldn't be alone in the carriage house while recuperating, they moved Ryan upstairs into the room that had been hers when she was little and moved Horace into the main house.

"Do you think he'll manage the stairs?" Claire was feeling anxious and antsy. Her conversation with Finn last night ate at her serenity. Finn was right. She did need to discover where she wanted to be, before she sunk deeper roots into Twin Elks that would need a painful extraction.

Poppy rubbed her back, as she would one of her children. "He'll be fine. Besides, he will probably have everyone in the house running around after him."

After moving Ryan, they went to fetch what Horace would need from the carriage house.

Claire had barely been in the carriage house because she had always seen it as Horace's space. Built at the same time as the main house, it shared the same rich wainscoting and wooden floors.

Horace's nasty mustard-colored recliner and seventies-style plexiglass coffee table did their best to ruin the room, and along with the plush pink floral rug under the massive television, almost did the job.

Poppy sent her a speaking look. "I know. I get in here once a week to clean, but he won't hear anything against the furniture."

"It could be beautiful in here." Mentally she catalogued the furniture she'd found in the attic. Some of it might need Finn's touch, but it would make the carriage house a charming cottage.

The thought of Finn's touch set off a different set of memories. Memories of last night and this morning when Finn had done more than touch.

Poppy chuckled and nudged her. "I'd love to know what you're thinking about right now."

"Nope." But her face heated, and she followed Poppy down the hall.

"There are two bedrooms, each en suite down here," Poppy said, over her shoulder. "Horace uses the one, and the other is stuffed full of crap he doesn't know what to do with."

While Poppy found a suitcase for Horace's stuff, Claire pictured the carriage house as she would do it. Really, someone should have a word with Horace about how he lived. She had an inkling of how much Dad was worth, and yet he surrounded himself with thrift store furniture.

Then again, those things weren't important to Horace. Despite his wealth, he lived a simple life. He loved his books, his sports on television and being with Poppy's children. If she did leave, she would make him more comfortable. And he could protest as much as he wanted. Poppy might not be able to get him to do what she wanted, but his daughter had inherited his streak of stubborn.

"I'm going to fix this up." She helped Poppy add clothes to the bag. "The attic is filled with beautiful things."

Then she stopped. If she left Twin Elks, she would need someone else to fix the carriage house. Another person would make sure all the attic treasures saw the light of day.

"What is it?" Poppy studied her.

Not ready to talk about it yet, Claire waved her off. "It's nothing."

———

Finn and Ben brought Horace home from the hospital later that day. Claire ignored his grousing all the way up the stairs. They got him into the bedroom they'd gotten ready for him.

"Don't see why you had to move Ryan." Horace sank to the bed. The journey had taken it out of him, and he looked pale and exhausted.

Claire helped him ease into bed. "I wanted you close enough to make your life miserable."

"Figures." It lacked Dad's usual bark. He looked around him. "It's been a while since I lived in this house."

Claire slid his shoes off. "How long?"

"Not really sure." He frowned. "It just got too quiet in here. This is a big house, and it keeps a big silence."

She knew what he meant. "I'll get Finn to help you get changed."

Horace grunted, and then took her hand. "What is it?"

"Eh?" His perception shook her.

"You've got a bug up your ass." He jabbed a finger at her. "Best to let it all out."

Claire sighed and sank to the bed next to him. "Why don't we wait until you've rested?"

"Uh-oh." Horace shook his head. "I'm really going to hate this, aren't I?"

"Maybe." She didn't know the answer to that question. Part

of her sensed Horace didn't want her to go and would miss her if she did. "I need to make a decision."

Horace grunted and nodded.

He looked pale, and Claire helped him to inch back on the pillows.

"I can't keep living in two worlds," she said as she unpacked his bag from the hospital.

Horace frowned. "What does that mean?"

"It means I have to decide where feels most at home to me. On the one hand, I have Boston, and I've lived there all my life."

"And on the other you have this." Horace arced his hand through the air. "This house and your history."

Claire looked at her father. Her father. He wouldn't be around forever, and they'd missed so many years already. "And you."

"Well." Horace blinked and cleared his throat. "You know you will always have a place here. There's not much to do around here, but it's not like you need to work if you don't want to."

"I want to." She perched on the edge of his bed. "But I lost my job before I came down here. It's why I needed the money for Mom."

Horace grunted. "You know there is always the foundation."

"Foundation?"

"The Winters Foundation," he said. "It runs a number of charities. And then there are our investments and business interests. I keep an eye on them, but I have some smartass suit in Denver who runs them day to day. You could take your place on the board."

"I don't know anything about foundations and investments," she said. But she had taken a business degree.

"You could learn." Horace grimaced as he tried to shift his leg. "I bet you didn't know anything about advertising until you learned."

He was right, but he was also tired and needed rest. "I'll think about that as well."

"You do that."

She went to the door and called for Finn before returning to Horace. "Finn thinks I should go back to Boston and see what I feel about it."

"Finn should mind his own goddamn business." Horace scowled.

Finn entered the room in time to hear him. "Now my feelings are hurt."

"Crap!" Horace glared at him.

Finn grinned back. "Let's get you squared away, and then I challenge you to a chess game."

"You're on." Horace snorted. "Nothing gives me greater pleasure than kicking your ass."

"You can try." Finn moved to the bed to help him.

Over Finn's shoulder, Horace's gaze met hers. His eyes told her he understood. He didn't like it, but he understood. "When do you leave?"

She wanted to collapse into tears. This trip hadn't been supposed to be this hard. She was supposed to come down here, toss Poppy out on her ear and leave again. She'd thought a week tops, maybe a day more if Poppy proved difficult, and she had to get the lawyers involved. "In a couple of days." Then she spoke to both men in the room. "But if I decide to stay in Boston, you won't get rid of me that easily."

Neither man laughed, they both looked at her with a knowing patience. Visiting Twin Elks when she could find the time was not the same as making her life there.

"Anyway." Horace broke the silence. "I contacted that place where your mother lives and made sure they would bill me from now on."

"Dad." Mom would hate that.

Horace made a cutting motion through the air. "Claire Cecily Winters, you are my daughter, and my only child. I have more money than God, and if I choose to spend it taking a load off your shoulders, you can't stop me."

"The full name, eh!" Finn whistled. "He means business."

Mom would never know, and part of her predicament could be laid at the feet of Mom's stubbornness. God, to be free of the burden of paying for the facility. The relief gave her vertigo. "Thank you."

"You're welcome." Horace managed a tight smile.

Claire walked to the door so Finn could settle Horace, but before she left, she needed him to know. "And I will be redecorating the carriage house before you move back in."

"I don'—"

"Horace Anthony Winters, you are my father, the only one I have, and if I want to make sure my father lives comfortably in beautiful surroundings, you can't stop me."

CHAPTER
Twenty-Seven

A WEEK later Claire ran out of excuses not to go. The carriage house looked lovely, and as soon as Horace could look after himself, he would move back in, and he didn't need her fussing over him anymore.

On her last night, they invited Dot and Gabe over for dinner. Brinn and Ciara didn't try to hide their sadness. When they said goodnight, both girls cried and hugged her and made her promise to come back again.

"I will." She kissed each girl in turn. She just wasn't sure for how long. If her life was in Boston, it would mean getting a new job and settling back into her life.

Ryan hid behind Poppy. "You mustn't go."

"Ryan." Poppy cupped his face. "Claire has to go, and you need to say goodbye.

"No." Ryan pulled away from Poppy and ran up the stairs.

"I know how he feels." Poppy put her arm around Claire. "We're all sad to see you go, but some of us do understand why."

Claire was sad too, like she was cutting into her own flesh and making herself bleed.

She would be leaving first thing in the morning, and she climbed the stairs to say goodbye to Horace.

"You do what you have to do." He cleared his throat and looked away. "You don't have to make anyone happy but yourself, you hear me?"

"Yes, Dad."

He coughed. "This time. Having you here. Best time of my life." He cleared his throat again. "Best time ever."

She was really going to miss him. Being with her father, in their house, felt like the closest she had come to herself in years.

So why was she leaving? It wasn't the first time she'd asked herself this question. As sad as it was, she was leaving because she had to. She needed to decide where her life was and what she wanted out of it. Finn was right, she couldn't make that decision with only half the information. "I'm going to miss you, Dad."

"Same." He patted her hand. "It's been right having you here. But whatever you decide, let's make sure we stay in contact more. That you come and visit more often."

"That I can promise." She never wanted the distance to build between them again.

Horace scowled. "Now go and say goodbye to that man of yours."

She stood and kissed his cheek. "Bye, Dad. I love you."

He stilled and then whispered, "And you. I love you too."

Finn was waiting in her room, already in bed. She and Finn had never spoken of their future, but this was like a glimpse into the possibility. If she stayed in Twin Elks and let their relationship grow, they would become a couple, and explore where this thing between them went.

He put his book down and watched her. "Come here."

Claire tingled at the rough desire in his voice. No matter how many times they came together, she was always ready for more.

"What did you have in mind?" She climbed on the bed and straddled his hips.

Finn gripped her hips and pressed her against his erection. "I'll give you a clue."

His cock pressed against her, and Claire moved on him.

Groaning, Finn speared his hands in her hair and pulled her down for a rough kiss. His tongue invaded her mouth as his other hand slid under her shirt and fastened around her breast.

With a roll, he changed their positions but continued to grind against her. "I want you to remember this. Remember me."

"I'll always remember this." Claire ran her hands over his back, pressing her nails into the hard ridges of muscle.

Finn got rid of her clothes as fast as he could. Buttons popped, and seams ripped, but they both wanted no barriers.

She was ready for him already, and she wrapped her legs around him. "I need you inside me."

Finn got the condom on and thrust inside her.

Claire arched under him to take him deeper.

Then he stopped and framed her face with his hands.

She writhed beneath him, desperate to feel all of him.

"Whatever you decide, make sure it's what you really want," he said. "If you decide to live in Boston and that your life is there, then this is goodbye."

"Why?" There didn't seem to be any give in his stance. It sounded so final. They should have had this conversation before, and now they were out of time. "We could still see each other. It's so much easier now to have long-distance relationships."

His face grim, he shook his head. "That's not for me, Claire. I'm in this thing between us all the way, and I need you to be in it with me."

"What do you mean?" She didn't want this to end.

"I mean I'm in deep, Claire. Now is not the time to say all that's in me, but if you come back, we'll talk about what it means."

"That's not fair."

He withdrew and thrust again. "Yeah? Well I reckon I owe you one for leaving me here in limbo."

Then there was no more talking as Finn made love to her. They fell asleep, but Claire woke a couple of hours later and reached for him again. Just before dawn, he woke her and took his time.

When she woke again, Finn was gone. She dressed and picked up her bags. Brinn and Ciara hugged her again. Ryan butted her in the tummy and gripped her tight. "I'll miss you."

"I'll miss you too." Behind Ryan, Poppy stood with Ben's arm around her. Sean was in Ben's arms, and beside him, Brinn and Ciara looked mournful. They had come to mean so much to her. More than she could verbalize, so she turned and got into her car.

Horace waved from his bedroom window.

She drove away, Winters House in her rearview mirror until she turned the corner, and they all disappeared.

———

Gabe was a good guy, Finn liked him, but he sucked at building, and no way was Finn letting the man near the power tools. That made him think of his conversation with Claire, and his chest ached.

He had joined Ben and Gabe up at Ben's cottage. Ben wanted his help in assessing the work to be done. For the most part Ben, intended to do the work himself, which would take years. Ben didn't know this yet, but Finn intended to help him with it, and whoever in Twin Elks he could bully, beg, or cajole into it.

After they were done, they sat on the deck with a few beers. The view was incredible, and Finn could see why Ben had chosen this spot.

"Have you heard from Claire?" Ben kept his gaze on the mountains in the distance. Between them and the mountains, red rock formations all slanted on the same diagonal across the undulating terrain.

"Nah." Finn ignored the jab in his chest. "But I didn't expect to."

"Why not?" Gabe stared at him. "I thought you two were a thing."

Who knew what they were? "We are. Kind of. She needs to make up her mind what she wants."

"Ah." Gabe nodded.

Ben glanced at him. "Do you know what you want?"

"Yep." He sipped his beer. "I want to be here. I want to put down roots."

"Really?" Ben gave him one of his rare smiles.

"I'm going into business with Hank Styles."

Ben sipped his beer and then murmured, "Well, damn, that's good news."

"But what if your lady doesn't want to be here?" Gabe voiced the question that tormented him.

"I can't live in a city again." And Claire was probably the only thing that would get him considering that. "I need what I find here. The peace. The sense of family. Poppy and those kids will always be my family."

Ben nodded, because he got it.

"Not me." Gabe shook his head. "As soon as I can line something up, I'm out of here."

He wanted to ask Gabe what had happened with the girl and the job in Australia, but he wouldn't pry. Gabe would tell him if and when he was ready.

"I don't get how you could send her away," Gabe said. "If things were really good between you, why let them go?"

"Because we need to want the same things," Finn said. "Look at what happened to Claire's parents. They were in love. It took Horace years to get over their breakup."

Ben looked at him.

Something about the way Ben was looking at him put him on the defensive. "What?"

"Nothing."

"No, I want to hear it."

"You say you're all in, right?"

"Yeah." Finn didn't think he was going to like where this was going.

Ben shrugged. "All in is all in."

"I wasn't." Gabe stared at the view. "All in, I mean. With Belinda. My ex. That's why she broke up with me, because I wasn't all in. She wanted to get married, and I didn't."

"Huh." Finn wanted to demand Ben explain himself, but he was also not sure he really wanted to hear the explanation. "Why not?"

"She wasn't the one." Gabe shrugged. "I'm not even sure there is a one for me."

Ben chuckled and sipped his beer. "Yeah, that's what I said."

"I really hate when married people do that." Gabe nudged Ben with his foot. "You get all superior and smug. Some of us don't want to get married and do the whole picket fence thing."

"Sure." If anything, Ben looked even smugger. "And some of us don't know our ass from our elbow."

CHAPTER
Twenty-Eight

CLAIRE DROPPED her bags inside the front door of her apartment. When had it gotten so small?

The air inside smelled stale and musty, and she opened a window. Street noise drifted in. The hum of car engines, the thump of techno music from a car parked below her building, people walking by and talking, the distant wail of a siren.

It had all been so familiar to her. The soundtrack to a life she had thought she wanted. She heard children's voices and went to the window. Two young boys followed a woman, who could be their mother, down the street, arguing and shoving as they went.

She called Poppy to let her know she'd arrived.

"Hey." Poppy's voice flooded her with a sense of loss. "You got home in one piece?"

"Yup. Just got in." She wandered into her kitchen. A fine layer of dust lay on the countertops. On her window ledge, the straggly fresh herbs had died in their pots. "How is everyone there?"

"Well, Ryan has decided that he'd rather follow in Mark's footsteps and become a hockey player. He's taken up residence in Horace's room all afternoon and has them both watching the hockey channel."

"Is Dad okay? Taking his pain medication?"

She heard the eye roll in Poppy's voice. "You know your father." She deepened her voice. "Just get me a whisky." She went back to her own voice. "He's decided to wage his own war against opiates."

"The girls?"

"They've been outside for most of the day. We're having a mild one today, and I thought they should take advantage of it. This will be our first Twin Elks winter."

Claire had never spent the winter in Twin Elks. She'd bet it was pretty.

"We miss you," Poppy said. "All of us."

Suddenly, Claire was angry with Finn for making her do this. She said goodbye to Poppy and ended the call.

Restless, she cleaned her apartment and caught up on her laundry before going to bed.

The next morning, she called a friend.

"Claire." Kristy answered the call. "Is that you? We thought you'd dropped off the edge of the world."

Twin Elks did feel like a whole other planet. "Nope, just seeing my father."

"Sweetie." Sympathy filled Kristy's voice. "Was it horrible?"

"No. It was…" And she didn't have a description for the rollercoaster she had ridden in Twin Elks. "Anyway, I'm back and still unemployed."

"Then we have to do lunch." Kristy had married a wealthy financial guy a few years back. The first thing she'd done when they returned from honeymoon was quit her job at the same advertising agency Claire had worked at.

"That would be nice."

"I'll round up the girls." Kristy giggled. "We want to hear all about your adventure." Then she whispered, "You didn't hear this from me, but Claudia is boning her personal trainer."

"She just got married." A week before Claire had lost her job. In fact, Claudia's wedding had preceded Claire's final argument with Greg about moving in together. She had wanted to, he not so much.

And thank God for that.

"I know." Kristy giggled. "It's too delicious. But you know nothing."

"Right."

"Good," Kristy said. "Phresh at noon?"

"I'll be there." She hung up. That gave her a few hours to kill. After her shower, her hair and makeup done, she put on a wool tailored slip dress. The dress had gotten snugger since she'd last worn it. A pair of black stilettos completed the outfit.

Looking at herself in the mirror, she felt a bit more settled. This Claire was also part of who she was. Maybe she didn't need to be one or the other but could find a way to be both.

After grabbing her purse, she went to her regular nail salon. Her level of grooming had slipped while she was in Twin Elks and her roots would also need doing. Once her nails were done, she made an appointment with her stylist for later that day. She couldn't see Mom with roots showing.

When Claire arrived at Phresh, Kristy, a waiflike beautiful redhead, was already seated at their regular table. She stood and enveloped Claire in a waft of perfume. "Claire. You look…great."

Not by Kristy's standards she didn't, but then, Finn had never had a problem with the way she looked. "I've gone full country."

"We can fix that, sweetie." Laughing, Kristy gave her a perfume drenched hug.

Claire didn't want to be fixed, so she gave a noncommittal shrug and sat.

The waiter hovered. "Can I get you something from the bar?"

"What do you have on tap?"

Kristy gaped. "Beer? Sweetie, you really have gone full country." She turned to the waiter. "Two martinis. Grey Goose. Dirty."

It wasn't worth fighting over. Finn would hate the restaurant with its clinically white walls broken up by large photos of fresh produce. Behind Kristy, the cross section of a strawberry looked a bit obscene. "Anybody else joining us?"

"Bad news there." Kristy wrinkled her nose. "Apparently, Claudia has Botox scheduled, but I just came from the salon, and she wasn't there." Kristy winked. "So, I guess Botox is now a euphemism for getting some sweaty trainer love. Patty has a thing at her kid's school. Some world fair day or something." Kristy leaned forward. "Get this. Patty baked a cake for it. Patty. Baked." Letting that sink in, Kristy sat back. "I swear she didn't buy it or get her housekeeper to do it."

"Jennifer?"

"Working." Kristy pulled a face. "That girl works way too hard. She needs to get out more."

Jennifer had a mortgage to take care of, but Claire didn't say anything.

The waiter put their martinis down.

"So, it's just me." Kristy spread her hands wide. She ordered a salad, which she would probably only pick at.

Claire ordered the same.

They sat for a moment, the white tablecloth between them. Sharing her Twin Elks experience would mean nothing to Kristy. "Tell me about what's been going on with you."

Kristy prattled on, interspersing her stories with gossip about mutual friends. None of whom had called her while she'd been in Twin Elks.

Her phone rang, and Kristy motioned her to answer it.

"Claire." Greg sounded pleased. "I just found out you were in town."

That didn't take long. "Yup."

"Dinner? Tonight?" He sounded sure of her agreement, and she nearly refused, but they needed to finish the conversation they'd started in Twin Elks. She was here to put things in order, get her head straight. Like it or not, Greg was part of that package. "Sure."

"That's my girl." He chuckled. "Meet me at Rafaels?"

"Sure."

"Eight thirty?"

They ate much earlier in Twin Elks, with the kids needing to get to bed. She'd gotten used to it and would probably be starving by eight thirty. "Sure."

"See you there." His voice deepened. "Glad to have you back where you belong. You had me worried there for a moment."

Claire hung up, and Kristy pounced. "Was that Greg?"

"Yes."

Reaching across the table, she grabbed Claire's hand and squeezed. "That must be agonizing for you. I know it's not my place to say, and I love you like a sister." Kristy hadn't spoken to her sister in over five years. "But Greg was seen with Amy Kennett."

"The blonde?"

"Not a blonde at all." Kristy rolled her eyes. "And fat."

The most noteworthy thing about Kristy's news? Claire didn't care.

———

Her stylist managed to squash her in on a cancellation, which meant cutting her lunch with Kristy short, but as they'd exhausted all conversation about an hour in, it didn't bother either of them.

She rushed from the restaurant to the salon, where the condition of her roots and ends launched a thirty-minute conversation she'd rather not have had.

Her heels had gone past torturous, and her belly thought her throat had been cut as she rushed from the salon to meet Greg. This used to be her life. Always rushing somewhere. Finding importance and value from the sense of being constantly in demand.

Finn would be sitting with a beer outside the workshop, maybe wearing his coat if the weather was cold, but he and Hank ended nearly every day with this ritual. They wouldn't be talking much or rushing anywhere. They'd watch the sun go down, let the day and any stresses go, and move into the night.

Greg was waiting for her at a table by the window. He stood and went in for the kiss again.

"Stop." Claire put a hand on his chest. "This is not where we are."

"Claire." His look was reproachful. "I've explained this to you. I want us to get back together."

On the table, he had a bottle already opened and two glasses poured. What she had to say really wouldn't take an entire meal.

"Just a minute." She found a waiter. "I'll have the green salad and the clam linguine. To go."

Greg's face broke into a grin. "In that case, I'll have—"

"He's not ready to order," she told the waiter and then motioned Greg to sit.

She took the seat opposite him and sipped from the glass closest to her. The wine was good. Not as good as beers on the porch with Finn, however. Her heart gave a dull throb.

"Greg." She took another sip for courage. "You need to hear me when I tell you that we're over."

"But—"

"You're not listening." She raised her hand to forestall him. "When you suggested a break, I thought there would never be a time when I'd get over you."

He smiled and tried to capture her hand on the table. "But you don't have to. I'm back. You wanted to move to the next level, and I agree." He took a deep breath and beamed at her. "You were right all along. We should move in together."

"No." She grabbed for her shredding patience. She didn't want to hurt him, but his thick skin was making it very difficult.

"I was wrong, and you were right. We weren't at that point, and we never were going to be. What we had worked on a level, but that was a superficial level and that suited both of us for a while."

He looked sulky. "But now I want more."

"But I don't." She kept her tone gentle. "At least not from you."

Greg reared back, a flush on his cheekbones. "This is because of that hillbilly asshole isn't it?"

"Finn and I...are not up for discussion." She forged ahead. "This is about so much more. It's about being in Twin Elks. It made me aware I was only half alive."

"What does any of this have to do with us?" Greg looked confused.

"Nothing." She stood. "Because there is no us. Not anymore."

Turning from the table, she left without looking back. The waiter had her order, and she paid and left. After picking up a bottle of wine on the way home, she let herself into her apartment.

The sterile silence rushed out to greet her. She had no idea when she had become so accustomed to the noise and activity in her house. And it was her house. She checked her watch.

Right now, the kids would all be tucked up in bed and fast asleep. Ben and Poppy would be sitting in the kitchen having some adult conversation before they went to bed. The kitchen range would be keeping the cold out.

Would Finn be with them or would he be sitting upstairs with Horace?

Her appetite gone, she put her pasta in the fridge and opened the wine. She picked at the salad unenthusiastically but gave that up as well. In her bedroom, she changed into a pair of yoga pants and a T-shirt.

Finn loved yoga pants. His eyes always lingered on her ass when she wore them.

Looking for distraction, she finished unpacking her bag from

Twin Elks. The note was at the bottom of her case, and she almost missed it.

Not recognizing it, she opened it.

She didn't recognize the handwriting as belonging to Poppy or Finn. It was far too legible to be Horace's and far too beautiful to belong to either of the children.

If you love something set it free.

A prickling at her nape made her need to rub it away. Before she could talk herself out of it, she dialed Poppy's number.

"Claire." Poppy's voice brought Twin Elks rushing back to her in a welcome, warm wave of home. "How are you doing?"

"I'm fine." She searched for a clever way to get the information she wanted. Then again, this was Poppy, and she didn't need to beat around the bush. "I want to ask you one question about Finn."

Poppy breathed in and said a tentative, "Okay."

"I need you to be absolutely honest with me."

"Oh God, I hate it when people say that," Poppy said. "Are you sure you want my honesty? Before you ask."

"I need it."

Poppy took a deep breath. "Go for it."

"Would Finn be the type to think he knew what was good for a woman better than that woman herself."

Poppy's delighted laughter peeled down the line. "He absolutely would."

CHAPTER
Twenty~Nine

CLAIRE DROVE up to see her mother two days later. She'd spent those days doing what Finn wanted her to, exploring her former world. A couple of halfhearted calls from the remainder of her friend group, with vague suggestions they get together, ended any guilt she felt about not spending time with them.

She missed Thai food, fresh bagels and the neighbor's cat, who dropped by for a can of tuna and a cuddle in the evenings.

She didn't miss the busy and the rushing, and the noise made her head ache. She missed the beautiful stores with their creative window displays, but she had no particular urge to spend money in them.

Yesterday, she'd checked her bank account to discover Horace had been doing more than she'd asked of him. She loved that he thought of her, but they would need to have a chat about boundaries and her independence.

Everything was so new with them. They were both guaranteed to make mistakes.

Doug let her into her mother's room with a big smile. "Well, hello stranger."

Mom sat in her chair by the window. She looked no different from the way she had always looked. Her hair was beautifully styled, and she wore a classic Diane van Furstenberg wrap dress and heels. Her makeup was flawlessly applied, and the smile she turned on Claire could have welcomed a head of state. "Darling."

"Hi, Mom. You look great." Claire took the hand extended to her and kissed her cheek.

Doug stood behind Mom and smiled. "Marcie comes in three mornings a week and makes our girl look wonderful."

"Have you gained weight?" Mom studied her with a slight frown.

She should have known Mom's eagle eye would miss nothing. "A bit."

"Huh." Mom looked at Doug. "She'll need to lose that now. It becomes so much more difficult at my age."

"I think you both look great." Doug went the diplomatic route.

Claire took a seat opposite her mother. "It seems like ages since I've been here."

"It has been." Her mother inclined her head. "I had a visit from Greg the other day."

"He told me." She glanced at Doug, who nodded. Today was a good day. "He tracked me down in Twin Elks."

Mom frowned. "I thought he broke up with you. You could have knocked me over with a feather when he arrived at my door."

"He did break up with me." Claire waved to Doug as he let himself out. "Then he changed his mind."

Mom sniffed. "I hope you told him what he could do with that idea."

"I did." Claire grinned at her mother. "He didn't take it too well, but he'll get used to the idea."

Mom gave her a keen look. "Who is he?"

"He?" But her flaming cheeks gave her away, and Claire laughed. "I'm not really sure, but I like him a lot, and I want to see where things with him go."

"And he lives in Twin Elks?"

Claire couldn't hold Mom's gaze; she felt guilty as shit. "Yes."

Mom looked out the window for a long while before she spoke. "I loved a man enough once to follow him to that town." She turned back to Claire with her perfectly composed mask back in place. "Just be sure you know what you're doing."

"It's not only Finn that draws me there." God, she didn't want to hurt her mother, but she needed to explore the other half of her, understand who she was when she had the full puzzle box of pieces. Finn had been right about that too. "I thought I might live with Dad for a bit. Get involved in the family trust."

"Did you?" Mom raised a perfectly sculpted brow. "And what if that doesn't work out?"

She didn't have a good answer for that. "Then I'll deal with that when it happens."

"Claire." Mom gave her an exasperated look. "It's not like you to put yourself at risk like this."

No, it wasn't, but perhaps that was the problem with the life she'd been living thus far. Because whatever else happened, she knew her father loved her now. And if things didn't work out with Finn then she was still close to where she wanted to be. "It's not that much of a risk."

"Well." Mom sighed. "Don't come crying to me when it doesn't work out."

After that, Claire changed the subject. Her mother would never see Dad any differently. In her head, she'd been dragged off to live somewhere awful and kept prisoner there. It was way too late to change her now. They talked about small things until Doug came back with her mother's lunch tray and Claire left.

As she was leaving, Mom reached for her hand and clung.

Mom had never clung to her. Claire was even more surprised to see tears in her eyes. "What is it, Mom?"

"Don't leave me." Mom tightened her grip. "I don't want to lose you."

"You're not going to lose me." Claire sat down again.

Over Mom's shoulder, Doug shrugged.

"If you go there. To Twin Elks." Mom's voice shook. "How do I know you'll come back?"

So much fear filled Mom's face that it tugged at Claire. This was the real truth behind all the years of vitriol. Fear that Horace would lure Claire away from her. "I'm never going to leave you, Mom." She only had one mother, flawed or not. "Having a relationship with my father won't change how I feel about you."

"He was always so much better with you than I was." Tears tracked mascara down Mom's cheeks. "He could always make you stop crying, and when he came home, you always gave him the biggest smile." Her breath hitched in a sob. "I didn't know what to do with you. I would stand beside you, and I loved you so much, but I didn't know how to make you stop crying, or how to make you smile."

Shock held Claire still. She had never seen this side of Mom. Never even suspected for a minute that Mom doubted herself. "Then why did you take me away?"

"I loved you, and leaving you wasn't an option. I told myself that if I had you to myself, then you would love me." She swiped at her cheeks. "And I really did hate that place."

The last part surprised a laugh out of Claire. "I don't know why, it's beautiful."

"I was young." Mom blew her nose. "I felt trapped."

A kernel of an idea bloomed in Claire's mind. A crazy idea that she dared not repeat to anyone, but there anyway. "Do you think you would still hate it now?"

"I don't know." Mom rubbed her hands on her dress. "It's lunch time. Isn't it lunch time? Where is Doug with my lunch?"

"Right here, Naomi." Doug handed Mom a damp washcloth. "Let's get you cleaned up, and then we can have lunch."

"Okay." Mom nodded, docile as a child, and wiped her face. "What day is it?"

"It's Wednesday, Naomi." Doug took the washcloth and

finished wiping her ruined makeup away. "Which means pasta for lunch."

Mom looked up at him like a trusting child. "I like pasta."

"And it looks good today." Doug helped her to her feet. "It's lasagna with a green salad. That's your favorite."

"Yes, it is my favorite." She turned to Claire and smiled. "Hello. Are you here for lunch?"

———

It took another week or so to arrange to have her apartment packed up and put on the market. Saying goodbye to her friends took hardly any time. Keeping up her lifestyle had cost money she had needed to keep Mom comfortable, and she had put distance between herself and her social circle. Most of them had moved on with their lives even before she'd gone to Twin Elks.

Funny, she'd believed that once she got the money out of Horace, she would come back and pick up her friendships where she'd left off.

Friendship was what Poppy offered, and what she could build with Kelly, and Dot.

After all the agonizing, the decision to go back to Twin Elks was remarkably easy. The only problem she hadn't solved was what to do with her mother, and she needed to talk to Dad about that.

After giving her apartment key to the landlord, Claire stepped into the cab to the airport and didn't look back.

———

At Denver International, she rented a car and drove straight through to Twin Elks. Dusk was falling as she hit the outskirts and drove past the Walmart Poppy had been trying to reach that day she'd fallen out of her car in front of Ben.

Only a few people were out in Winters Park, and they were

all bundled up against the cold. Slowing down, she waved to Bart and Mia as they were packing up for the day.

Kelly's Koffee Klatch was already closed with a dim back-light illuminating the stainless-steel display fridges. So many of the buildings along Main Street were empty. She would have a word with Dad about that and see if they could find a way to encourage people back to Twin Elks.

She turned into her street and slowed to a crawl. The turrets of Winters House were etched against the sky. Warm yellow light spilling from the windows beckoned her. It was unbelievable that there had been a time, a few weeks ago, when this house had represented nothing more than a quick cash infusion.

She chuckled to herself when she thought of the extent of her former plan. Arrive back in Twin Elks, demand Horace sell the house and put him into a care facility. The idea of Horace in any sort of facility went to show how dumb that plan had been.

The gates were open, and she turned into the driveway and parked between Ben's cruiser and Finn's truck. Delicious smells enticed her toward the kitchen. Stopping on the porch, she peeked through the window.

There they all were, and her heart filled.

Horace sat beside Ryan. She had no idea what they were talking about, but it looked deep. Baby Sean perched in his high-chair between Poppy and Ben, who divided their time between him and the other children.

Brinn and Ciara sat on either side of the one person she couldn't look at yet. Brinn was chattering away, and Ciara nodding along with her.

The chair she had usually sat in was empty.

And then she looked at Finn, and her heart did a weird twist. The kitchen lights cast a sheen on his dark hair and created shadows on the strong lines of his face. Finn's beauty was far too rugged to be considered handsome in the same way as Greg. It was a beauty that owed its attractiveness to harsh lines and rugged appeal, to the laugh lines around his eyes, and the stern set of his jaw. And those eyes. So blue they could rival the sky.

She couldn't wait another minute to greet them all, so Claire entered the kitchen.

Brinn spotted her first and shrieked, "Claire."

A body barreled into her as Ryan got to her first and fastened his arms around her hips.

Brinn grabbed one hand and Ciara the other.

"You're back." Brinn grinned at her. "Did you miss us?"

So much. "Yes, and I think you've all grown."

"It's the good country air," Brinn said and nodded sagely.

Ciara beamed up at her and didn't need to speak to convey how she felt.

Next, Poppy barged through her children and clasped her in a huge hug and whispered in her ear, "I expected you days ago."

"It took a little longer than I thought."

"Claire." Ben leaned over and kissed her cheek. "You should have told us you were coming. We could have picked you up from the airport."

"I wanted to surprise you," she said.

Ben gave her one of his rare smiles. "It worked."

All the time aware of Finn in her peripheral vision, she looked past him to Horace. "Hey, Dad."

"Claire Cecily Winter, you get over here and hug your father." Horace pounded his cane against the floor.

Claire did as she was asked, and Ben helped Horace to his feet so he could hug her.

"You've gotten taller." Claire looked up at him.

"It's the operation." Horace had the biggest grin on his face. "The doctor tells me it's because I'm standing up straight."

She smiled back. "Good to know."

"How long are you back?" Horace didn't believe in beating around the bush.

Neither did his daughter. "I don't know. Indefinitely, and we need to find a solution for Mom. If I'm going to be here, then I need her closer."

Horace rolled his eyes. "I would have thought the solution was obvious." He waved his cane outside. "We have an entire carriage house out there for your mother and a caregiver."

"Funny you should say that." The apple really didn't fall far from the tree.

And then she ran out of distractions. The others melted away as she looked at Finn. "Hi."

"Hi?" He raised a brow at her. "That's all you have to say?"

Claire's heart double-timed it. Things were so unsettled between her and Finn. "I thought it was a good beginning."

"Really?" He shoved his hands in his pockets. "That's the best you can do after walking out on me and now waltzing back in without saying a word."

"Did I walk out, or did someone push me out?" He needn't think her being there meant she would take his crap.

Finn smiled with his eyes but kept his face straight. "Semantics."

"Oh, I don't think so." She stalked him across the kitchen. "And I think you have some explaining to do."

"Is that right?" He met her halfway and slid his arms around her. "I can't wait to get started."

CHAPTER
Thirty

ANY CONVERSATION between her and Finn was cut short by the noisy demands of a family dinner. The children all wanted to speak to her. At the same time. At full volume. In the weeks she'd been there, she'd developed the knack of simultaneously holding three or four conversations.

After dinner, Finn made coffee, and Poppy took the children upstairs for baths and bedtime.

"So." Dad added a drop of whiskey to his coffee.

Claire gave it a pointed look. "Should you be doing that?"

"Should you nag like an old woman?" He motioned at the bottle, and she nodded and pushed her cup closer.

He took a sip and sighed his pleasure. "Now we can talk. Tell us why you're back."

Finn took the seat next to her, his arm over the back of her chair.

"I went back to Boston to see how my old life fit." She met Finn's gaze. "And it wasn't so much that it didn't fit, as that it didn't fit me as well as being here does."

"That's a big change of heart you had there, girl." Horace raised his wiry eyebrows. "Seems a mite sudden."

Shifting in his chair, Finn crossed his arms and dropped his chin to his chest.

"It's not like I could never survive there, because I have for most of my life. It's more like I feel more like me here."

"Huh." Horace sipped his coffee.

"You said something about managing the trust. I'd like to know more about that. Also, more about the family investments."

Horace nodded. "That I can teach you."

Finn's silence wore on her a bit.

"And your mother?" Horace met her gaze squarely. "You think she would agree to moving back here?"

Claire shrugged; she really didn't know. "She's not that aware of her environment outside her room. Still, I think the move might be really traumatic for her."

"Well, if she can't, we'll have to make sure you get out there to see her often," Horace said.

Before they went much further, Claire needed to set him straight. "I'm not asking you to bankroll me."

"I'm not offering." Horace snorted. "If you stay here, you'll do it on your own two feet. Work your pampered, manicured fingers to the bone."

"Damn right I will."

"Damn right."

"I noticed the extra money in my account." She raised her brow.

Horace raised his. "Gonna make a federal case of it?"

"Maybe."

"Pfft!"

Poppy came back into the kitchen and winced. "I'm sorry, Finn, the girls asked if you could say good night."

"Of course." He stood and kissed Claire's head. "We'll talk later."

"Well." Horace maneuvered himself to his feet. Even in the short time she had been gone, he'd gotten a lot more mobile.

"I'm heading upstairs to bed. I'll see you all in the morning." He touched her shoulder as he passed. "Good to see you, girlie."

"Good to see you too." And she'd never thought there would come a time when she could say that and mean it.

Claire walked to the front porch with her coffee. Too restless to sit, she leaned her shoulder against a column. Full dark had fallen while they had dinner, and the rosebushes were nothing more than short skeletons sticking out of the ground.

She crossed the lawn to the rose garden and walked to the sundial in the center. Wind sighed and toyed with tendrils of her hair. Claire knew she wasn't alone.

"I came back."

"Good. This is where you belong."

"I know that now."

The rational part of Claire's brain insisted that she freak out. She was standing in a deserted garden having a conversation with a spirit. She didn't even believe in ghosts.

"We are lonely." A breeze sighed through Claire's hair. *"Do what I never could and fill this place with children and love and laughter. Make our legacy happy."*

The sadness of Cecily's tone brought tears to Claire's eyes. It was filled with a sort of yearning that was hard to comprehend. She understood Cecily's yearning. How Cecily was waiting and pushing back a growing despondency. "I promise."

It might have been a trick of the light, but for a second, Claire almost made out a form in the dark.

"Hey." Finn spoke from right behind her. He slid his arms around her. "What are you doing out here?"

"Saying hi to an old friend."

Finn snorted. "Now you sound like Brinn and Ciara."

"Children know a lot more than we give them credit for."

He made a noncommittal noise and pressed his cheek to the top of her head. "I'm really glad you're back."

"I get it, you know." She felt lighter now that she could

commit to a course. "You sent me away because you thought it was for my own good."

"Was I wrong?" His tone came just shy of smug. "You came back here, and now you know what you want."

The smugness annoyed her. "Yes, but you didn't have the right to manipulate that outcome. If we're going to build something here, it's going to take honesty."

"You're right." He tucked her under his chin. "I treated you like a child, and that isn't right."

She settled into his embrace. "Greg did that, and I didn't like it."

"Did you really just bring up your ex? I thought we were having a moment here."

She laughed. He could always make her laugh.

"Babe." His voice rumbled through her. "How about we take this moment upstairs?"

She couldn't think of a better idea, so she turned and took his hand. They let themselves into the house.

Ben and Poppy's soft voices came from the kitchen.

They didn't speak as they climbed the stairs together. Only when Claire had closed her bedroom door behind them did Finn make a move.

He pulled her into his arms and kissed her, softly and gently, as if he was exploring her reaction.

The taste, feel, scent combination hit her hard and she clung to him. Missing him had been hard. As if he was a base need, and some part of her had been dormant.

He broke the kiss and rested his forehead against hers. "Do you remember what I told you before you left?"

"That if I came back you were all in?"

"That's the one." He cupped her face. "Let me make this an official declaration. I want it all, Claire. I want the everyday and the special occasions. I want to grow this thing between us and take it all the way." He gazed into her eyes, his expression fierce and demanding.

His intensity made her shiver a little. "What does that mean?"

"You know what that means. It means I'm all in. All. In."

Claire raised her mouth to his. "Me too."

"Babe." He squeezed his eyes shut. "I'm gonna hold you to that."

Enough with the talking. Claire kissed him with all the pent-up feelings of the last few days.

Finn responded like flame to tinder and bent his knees and picked her up. He crossed to the bed, dropped her on it and came down on top of her. He undid her top button. "I missed you." He bent and kissed the skin he'd revealed as his fingers moved to the next button. "Too much." Another button, another kiss. "More than I thought I would." A few more buttons until they were all undone and he pushed her shirt open.

"Let that be a lesson to you." Claire tugged his sweater over his head. He was moving too slow for her.

Finn spread his hand over her belly. "You're really not going to let that go, are you?"

"Not yet." She slid her hand over his glorious corrugated belly and unsnapped his jeans. "Now might be a good time to mention that I'm a sulker."

"Really?" He hissed as she gripped his erection. "That means I'm going to have to work really hard to put you back in a good mood."

"Uh-huh." Claire nodded as she stroked him. Her need for him clamored through her. She wanted more. "Finn?"

"Baby." He lowered his head and kissed her belly.

"I need you."

He planted hot kisses on her belly. "I know exactly what you need, baby. I've got everything you need right here."

And he really did.

———

Finn woke while it was still dark outside. Claire's breath huffed softly against his neck. She was a cuddler, his girl. She liked to tangle as many of her limbs with his as she could before she fell asleep.

It made him hot as hell, and not only the good kind. He guessed he'd have to learn to sleep with one leg out of the covers, because having her wrapped around him was too damned good.

This was what he'd been searching for since his discharge. Later he would wake Claire, make love to her again, and then they would go downstairs and join the breakfast mayhem. After breakfast, Claire would probably want to spend some time with Horace in the study, and he would go out back and work with Hank.

The old guy was still holding out on a full partnership, but Finn would wear him down. It would be good for both of them.

Maybe he could sneak back to the house for lunch. Catch Claire alone somewhere in the house and make up for lost time.

"Mom!" Ryan bellowed from the hallway. "Ben. I can't find my backpack."

A door opened, and Poppy whispered, "Ryan, keep your voice down."

"But Ma, I need my pencils."

"Mo-o-om." This time is was Brinn. "Ryan is in our room."

Claire stirred beside him. She pressed her face into his chest and came up laughing. "I'd almost forgotten this part."

"How is that even possible?" He pushed the tangle of blond hair from her face and kissed her mouth. "Good morning."

"Mom!" Ryan sounded like he was right outside the bedroom. "I'm going to say good morning to Claire."

"No, Ryan!" Poppy's shout came too late, because the bedroom door flew open.

Ryan appeared at the side of the bed. "Hey, Claire. And Finn. Did you have a sleepover?"

"I'm so sorry." Poppy appeared in the door, all sleep tousled and clutching a robe.

Finn laughed and threw himself on his back. Okay, so strike a line through items one and two on his agenda. "No worries."

"Come on, Ryan." Poppy got a firm grip on his hand and dragged him out. At the door, she turned and winked at them. "Breakfast is in only thirty minutes."

As the door closed, Claire collapsed on his chest, still laughing. "What's your view on children?"

Finn rolled her to her back. "As of right this minute, I'm gonna have to give the idea a veto." Before any of the other stuff that came with all in, he wanted to revel in having her where she belonged. "But I reserve the right to revisit this discussion in the future."

CHAPTER
Thirty-One

CLAIRE DRESSED CAREFULLY for her date with Finn. Strange to think after all they'd been through that it was their first date. Still, late as it was, what girl didn't want to look good?

She chose one of her old-life dresses, a black sheath that skimmed her curves and ended well short of her knees. She paired it with a great pair of heels and took extra care with her makeup and hair.

"Wow." Brinn was all big eyes when Claire walked into the kitchen. "You look gorgeous."

"Gorgeous." Ciara grinned and nodded. Then she giggled. "And so does Uncle Finn."

Gorgeous was exactly the right word to describe Uncle Finn. He cleaned up great in an open-necked shirt and blazer with black pants. "I would have gone with a tie." He grinned at her. "But this is Twin Elks, and it might put everyone in shock."

Finn came closer, kissed her cheek and whispered in her ear, "Double wow."

"Have fun you two." Poppy grinned, almost vibrating with excitement. "And don't be home too late."

"No worries." The expression in Finn's eyes left her breathless. "I'll have her home and in bed by nine."

Ben flinched. "Little ears?"

"Sorry about that." Finn said, looking anything but. "Shall we go?"

There was only one real restaurant in Twin Elks, so it was no great surprise when Finn took her there. "Next time we'll take this to Denver and spend the night."

"Next time." For now, she was so glad to be back, she wasn't that keen to leave again. "I've never eaten here."

"Finn," a rotund, balding man greeted them at the door. "Don't you two look nice? Are we celebrating?"

Finn kissed her knuckles. "Not today, Miles, but one day soon."

Claire had never met Miles and his wife Lillian, but they'd moved to Twin Elks three years earlier and opened the Grove. Other than them, there was Dolly's Diner or the Roadhouse as far as eating out in Twin Elks went. Of course, the Bugling Elk made one helluva burger, but she'd never felt welcome there.

Miles led them to a table by the window. White tablecloths contrasted with the dark wood floors and exposed-beam ceiling. "This is nice. I've never been here before."

"It's a bit of a surprise." Finn took the seat opposite her. "If my mother wasn't such a snob about where she ate, I might never have found it."

Claire didn't want to think what Maura would make of her and Finn, so she pushed it from her mind.

After ordering a bottle of red, Finn handed the wine list back to Miles. "So." He leaned his elbows on the table. "Tell me about Boston."

"I thought we'd covered that."

"I never did get the details on Greg." Finn's expression darkened.

Claire couldn't resist a bit of teasing. "Careful there, Finn, or I might think you're jealous."

"Busted." He grinned and kissed her palm, his mouth hot on

her skin. "I nearly drove up there and helped you make up your mind."

She shook her head at him. "And just when you were forgiven."

"I'll make it up to you." And Finn's grin promised her all sorts of after dinner delights.

The food was good, and the company even better. Claire left the restaurant feeling truly happy for the first time in ages.

Finn took her hand and led her to the car. A sharp breeze carried a hint of winter and scattered leaves across the sidewalk. At the car, he turned her toward him. "Claire." He tucked a piece of hair behind her ear. "When I came to Twin Elks, I wasn't expecting anything like you to happen to me."

"Me neither."

He laughed, his teeth a flash of white in the dark. "Yeah, I got that distinct impression."

"I've changed my mind since then." She slid her arms beneath his jacket.

He kissed the top of her head. "Let's go home."

"Home." She tasted the word in her mouth.

Finn's muscles tightened. His tone packed a warning that made her shiver. "Claire."

"What?" She followed the direction of his gaze.

It took her a moment to recognize the four young guys approaching them. They'd grown so much in the years since she'd been coming in and out of Twin Elks. "It's the Rivers boys and Blake Schaeffer." Try as she might, she couldn't remember the fourth guy's name.

"Get in the car, Claire." Finn radiated tension completely at odds with the situation.

Claire tried to laugh him out of it. She'd never seen Finn like this. "They're local boys."

"In the car." Finn's gaze had gone stone hard, his face etched in ice.

Claire moved for the car.

The four guys were about six feet away.

"Hey, Claire Winters?" Darius Rivers stepped forward. He'd gotten really tall. Even with her in heels, he had four inches on her. "Or is it Mathews?"

"It's both." The boys seemed weird to her. The smell of alcohol hit her. "Anyway. Nice to see you."

"Is it though?" The other Rivers boy stepped closer. "That's not how we hear it. We hear you don't wanna be here." He jeered and looked at his friends. "In which case, we'd like to extend our invitation for you to get the fuck out of Twin Elks."

Claire didn't think she'd heard right. All the aggression couldn't be coming at her.

Finn balled his fists. "You need to step back."

"You and me don't have any drama, Finn," Blake said. "But I've got issue with the company you keep."

"Too bad." Finn stepped in front of her. "Now back off."

"Or what." The one whose name she couldn't remember laughed. "You ready for all of us? Old man. We don't need people like her coming here and thinking they're better than us."

"You're going to get hurt." The menace in Finn's voice made her hackles rise.

Claire touched his back. It was rigid beneath her palm. "They've been drinking, Finn. Let's go."

Darius Rivers crowded closer to Finn. His brother, Gideon, bracketed his shoulder with no-name guy on the other side. "You threatening me, Finn?"

Claire stared at the four guys in shock. They were deliberately antagonizing Finn. She dug in her purse and found her cell.

"What are you doing?" Blake lunged for her and knocked her phone out of her hand.

Claire made some noise of shock, and her phone clattered to the ground.

Bodies surged on Finn.

Darius gripped her arm, but before she could do anything, his hand was gone.

Moments compressed into sounds of flesh hitting flesh, grunts of pain and then pleading.

And Finn. Finn always at the center of it, moving so fast she could barely track him. Darius went down fast, hitting the sidewalk with a sickening thud.

Finn spun, grabbed Gideon and sent him face first into the car.

No-name tried to make a run for it, but Finn grabbed him by the hair and yanked him back. Three punches to his stomach, and No-name hit the road on his knees.

That left Blake, and Finn rounded on him.

Blake stepped away from Finn, arms raised, his gaze terrified. "Finn, please man. I didn't touch her."

Finn didn't seem to hear him but closed on him.

Blake didn't look nearly as tough now. He tried to run, but Finn caught him.

"Please." Blake tried to cover his head with his hands.

Then Claire saw Finn's face and her blood ran cold.

He wasn't angry. He wasn't anything. His face was completely devoid of emotion, and his eyes as empty as a machine. In that moment, the person inhabiting his body was not Finn.

Blake was crying and trying to get away.

"Finn." He scared her, but she couldn't let him do that. "Finn, stop."

Claire screamed Finn's name as he hooked his arm around Blake's neck.

Blake's face turned red, his feet scrabbling as he tried to get free. Eyes pleading with her, he scratched Finn's arm.

"Finn." Claire lunged for the grappling pair. Finn had to stop. She touched his shoulder. "Finn."

That frigid, empty gaze swung to her. It was like he wasn't even seeing her.

"Finn." With shaking hands, she cupped his face. "Finn. It's me, Claire."

The mist cleared in his gaze, and he really looked at her. "Claire."

Blake choked.

"You need to let him go, Finn. You're strangling him." Her voice shook around her plea, and she had to fight the urge to cry.

Finn glanced at Blake. Releasing him, he leaped away from Blake. "Fuck."

"You're fucking crazy." Blake helped Darius stand.

Claire didn't take her eyes off Finn. He'd gone very pale. "Just go," she said to the guys without looking at them. "Get away from him."

Looking at the four guys, Finn grimaced. He pushed his hands through his hair and clung. "What did I do?"

"They were hassling us." Claire didn't dare touch him again. He looked completely freaked out. "And you…"

She didn't know what Finn had done, because she'd never seen anything like it. Cold, clinical, and detached, he had disappeared into a place so dark she couldn't follow him there.

"Jesus." Still clutching his hair, he sank to the sidewalk.

Not knowing what to do, Claire called Ben.

"Hey!" Ben answered the phone with a laugh. "Why are you calling me on a date? Finn not—"

"Can you come?" Ben was the first person she could think of.

Ben's tone changed. "What happened?"

"It's Finn." His head was lowered and his hands hanging between his legs. He looked completely defeated. "He needs you."

While she waited for Ben, Claire crouched in front of Finn. Around them, people had gathered outside the restaurant. Voices she couldn't identify kept asking what had happened, but Claire didn't have answers for them. She really didn't know.

Worse, she didn't know what was happening now, but Finn was locked tight somewhere, and she couldn't reach him.

"Finn?" Blood oozed from his cracked knuckles. She reached for one of his hands.

Finn jerked them back. "No."

"I don't know what to do," she said. "What do you need from me?"

After a long silence, Finn raised his head. "I need you to stand back."

"Why?" It felt wrong to put distance between them when he was like that. He needed her, and she wanted to be there for him.

Finn looked tortured. "Please."

What else could she do? She stepped back and felt like the worst kind of coward.

Ben's cruiser pulled into the parking lot, and he climbed out.

Just looking at his tall, broad shouldered form approach, Claire knew everything was going to be all right.

"Miles." Ben nodded to the restaurateur. "How about we get everybody back to their dinner?"

"Right, Ben." Miles nodded and herded people back into the restaurant.

They filed back slowly, looking over their shoulders and speculating.

Ben waited for them to be out of earshot before he asked her what had happened.

Claire did her best to describe the events.

Ben crouched in front of Finn. "Finn." He clapped a hand on Finn's shoulder. "Is that how it went, buddy? Did it happen like Claire said?"

Finally, Finn raised his head and turned his tormented gaze on Ben. "I could have killed them."

"Nobody died here, Finn." Ben spoke quietly and firmly. "In fact, they're all long gone."

"I couldn't stop." Finn shook his head. "I reacted to the threat, and I couldn't stop."

Ben frowned and studied him. "But you did stop."

"They were stupid punks." Finn shook his head. "I know a hundred ways to deescalate a situation like that. All I had to do is get Claire in the car, and it would have been over."

Ben glanced at her for corroboration.

"I took out my phone," she said. "One of them knocked it from my hand and tried to grab me."

"And Finn?"

"He…" Claire didn't want to make things worse, and she was left speechless.

Ben nodded. "I see." He got to his feet. "I'm gonna ask you to come with me, Finn."

Claire couldn't believe it. Ben was their friend. He lived in the same house as them. "It wasn't his fault. He didn't start it."

"Finn?" Ben looked down at him.

Finn got to his feet and held out his hands for the cuffs.

"No." Claire got between them. "This is insane. You can't be arresting him."

Ben motioned Finn to the cruiser. "I'm not going to cuff you, dude. Get in the car, and let's go for a ride."

Claire tried to stop them and grabbed Ben's arm. "Why are you doing this?"

Ben turned to her, his face grave. "Do you trust me, Claire?"

"Yes." At least she had until that moment.

"Then let me take him with me." He glanced to where Finn had climbed in the cruiser. "Let me take him with me and help him wrestle his demons."

CHAPTER
Thirty-Two

FINN STUDIED his hands as he sat across the desk from Ben, who was talking on the phone to the four guys involved.

"Good news." Ben hung up. "None of the guys are interested in pressing charges. There's been a lot of tension between newcomers and local kids lately. They were drunk, didn't mean to scare Claire, and now they're sorry."

After Ben had made it clear that he knew who the aggressor had been. "Great."

Face expressionless, Ben studied him.

Finn went back to looking at his hands. The things he could do with those hands used to keep him up at night. The things he had done had put him in counseling for months. He'd come to Twin Elks to escape that life, but there was no escaping when the monster was within.

"Wanna tell me what's going on?" Ben sat back in his chair and folded his arms behind his head.

Finn didn't care to at all. "You should get back to Poppy and the kids."

"The best part about being married to Poppy is that she would agree I was exactly where I should be right now." For Ben it was the equivalent of a lecture.

"What do you want from me, Ben?"

"I want you to come the fuck out of that dark hole in your head and talk to me." Clearly not intending to go anywhere, Ben propped his feet on his desk.

"Am I under arrest?" He didn't need to stay there though.

Ben pulled a face. "Don't be a dick."

It nearly made him laugh, and he was being a dick. He shouldn't bottle things up; his counselor had been quite clear on that. "You saw what I did tonight."

"Yup."

Finn waited for more, but Ben had used his word allotment for the day and stared at him.

"I could have killed them, Ben." His wry laugh served in place of a sob. "If Claire hadn't called me off, I would have."

Ben nodded. "Then it's a good thing she was there."

Shit! Ben must have been messing with him. He was a smart guy. Too smart for that dumb as crap statement. "That's not the point."

Ben grunted.

"What if Claire hadn't been there?" Then he named the monster roaring at him. "And what if next time it is Claire?"

"Here's what I know." Ben stared at the ceiling, looking strangely relaxed next to Finn's turmoil. "Four guys came at you and your woman. One of them made a grab for Claire, and you stopped him." Dropping his chin to his chest, he looked at Finn. "Could you have resolved it with words? I don't know. I wasn't there."

"Regardless." Finn wanted to tip Ben off his squeaky chair. "My reaction was out of proportion with the incident. Those guys weren't trained. I could have disabled them without beating the shit out of them."

"Maybe." Ben shrugged. "Or maybe they could have gotten the jump on you."

Finn was tired of word games. "What's your point?"

"Neither of us can say for sure what might have happened.

We can only deal with what did happen." He dropped his feet and sat up straight. "And that reality is that four guys attacked you and Claire, you fought them off, and nobody is badly hurt."

Wouldn't it be great if Finn could believe that and leave it there? But he couldn't. What had happened to him had brought all his shit into clear focus.

He was the wolf amongst the sheep, the vulture flying with the sparrows, and he couldn't pretend anymore. The ache in his chest expanded into his stomach and made him want to puke.

It had been such a beautiful dream while it had lasted. The idea that he, Finn Williams, could live a normal life, work a normal job, and marry the girl he loved and have children.

Ben stood. "Let's go home. Claire must be worried sick about you."

Well, at least he could fix that for her.

Claire sat in the window seat with a view of the road. It had been hours since Ben had driven away from the restaurant with Finn.

"Claire?" Poppy tapped on the door.

"Come in."

Poppy opened the door and stepped into the room. "Ben texted to say he was on his way home."

"Is Finn with him?" Claire didn't like the look on Poppy's face.

Poppy shook her head. "Sorry, but Ben said he went for a walk."

That nasty sense of foreboding slithered down her spine again, and she needed to talk, or she would go crazy. "I think he's going to do something."

"Like what?" Poppy perched on the end of the window seat.

Claire moved her legs to give her more space. "I'm not sure. But that look in his eyes."

"He never talks about his service." Poppy touched Claire's

ankle, a small maternal gesture to say she was there, like she would comfort one of her children. "I always got the feeling there was much more there than he ever spoke about."

Headlights came down the road. "He scared himself tonight."

"And you?"

"Truth?"

Poppy nodded.

"He scared me a bit too."

Headlights arced across the ceiling and lit Poppy's delicate features. She looked out the window. "That's Ben."

But not Finn. She didn't need Poppy to say anything. "I'm fine." She forced a smile for Poppy. "Go and be with your man."

"I think you're lying." Poppy cocked her head and studied her.

The bald honesty made her laugh. "You're right, but I don't think I can talk about it anyway."

"Fair enough." Poppy stood. "As long as you know I'm here if you ever do want to talk about it."

"I know." And she did. Life got so weird sometimes. She'd come to Twin Elks fully prepared to hate Poppy, and now she counted Poppy as the truest friend she had.

"Finn loves you." Poppy patted her knee. "I know he does."

All Claire could manage was a nod, because she wanted to break down and cry. Even with the foreboding, she didn't doubt Finn's love. But if life had taught her one thing, it was that love was very rarely enough.

She didn't know how long she sat there, but eventually, she got cold enough to have a shower, put on her pjs, and climb into bed.

The next morning, she woke with the sun shining in her eyes.

It was later than she normally slept, and she stumbled out of bed. Concern for Finn chased her into the shower and through teeth and hair brushing. She pulled on sweats and a long-sleeved T-shirt that belonged to Finn and went downstairs.

Breakfast was almost over, and the kids were gathering back-packs and shoes.

"Hey, Claire." Brinn and Ciara greeted her with their normal sunny smiles.

It was hard to be moody with all that light beamed at you, and she smiled back. "Have a good day, girls."

"I intend to." Brinn nodded and then heaved a big sigh. "Although I can't take responsibility for the behavior of others."

Fighting to keep her face straight, Claire said, "Too true."

And then the wisdom of that statement smacked her, and the sadness swooped in again.

Ryan bounded up to her. "Hey, Claire?"

"Yes, Ryan."

"Guess what?"

"I couldn't possibly."

Ryan puffed out his chest. His eyes shone. "I'm trying out for football today."

"Really?" He seemed too young for that. Ben and Horace said Ryan had a helluva throwing arm, but he was so small. "What about hockey?"

"And waste my potential?" Ryan rolled his eyes at her.

Poppy nodded and gently tugged his head back. "Do me favor, big guy?"

"Oh-kay." Ryan looked suspicious.

"Don't grow up too fast." Poppy gave him a kiss on the fore-head and turned away.

Ben was waiting for Poppy with a quick hug and a murmur in her ear.

That was what Claire craved, the effortless warmth and intimacy.

It's what she thought she and Finn had, or might be building.

"Morning." Finn strolled into the kitchen. He didn't look any different and went through the normal morning mauling from his nieces and nephews.

He also didn't look at her or walk over and give her a kiss or whisper something naughty in her ear.

And what the hell? She had sat up for hours, and then lain awake for a few more worried about him, and he'd been in the house all along.

Poppy herded the children out the door. "I'll walk you to the bus." She turned to Claire. "And I thought I might drop Sean off with Dot and stay a while." Her smile looked a bit tattered. "Today is her baking day."

Ben grabbed his to-go mug. "I gotta get going."

And the kitchen was empty.

Finn propped his hips against the counter. "Well, that was subtle."

"Where were you?" He needn't think he could toss out a joke and slither away. They needed to talk.

Shrugging, he fetched a mug and filled it with coffee. "Nowhere particular. After I left Ben, I went for a walk."

"All night?"

"No." He stared into his coffee. "About a couple of hours. I didn't want to wake you when I got back."

"I wasn't sleeping." Claire wanted to yell at him, shake him, anything to get through the strange calm that blanketed him. He stood right there and looked like her Finn and sounded like her Finn. She'd bet if she got close enough, he would even smell like her Finn. Then why did it feel like her Finn was slipping through her fingers?

The silence stretched seconds into hours. Finally, he sipped his coffee, grimaced and put it on the counter next to him. "I called my CO last night. Commanding officer," he said.

That did nothing to allay the creep of unease. "I know what a CO is."

"Of course, you do." He adjusted the mug on the counter.

"Dammit, Finn." Claire couldn't stand the silence anymore. "What did you do?"

"I told him I would accept the position he offered me."

For all her impatience before the silence, she would have chosen it over that decision. It hung like a noose in the space between them.

Claire put her head in the noose anyway. "What does that mean?"

"It means I will be training future mes." Folding his arms, he stared at her, his fiery blue gaze daring her to challenge him.

She snatched up the gauntlet. "You agreed to train other people to do the very thing you hate about yourself? Explain to me how that makes any sense."

Finn shrugged. "It's what I am."

"Bullshit." She'd never met that man, but she knew this one. "You're Finn Williams, uncle, brother, friend, and lover. You're adored by your nieces and nephews. Poppy thinks you hung the moon. Ben calls you friend, and so does Horace, and neither of them use that title lightly."

Finn dropped his chin to his chest and stared at the floor.

"And I—" She almost lost her courage, but she had to give it all she had. "And I love you.

His spine jerked straight. "Jesus, I wish you hadn't said that."

If she'd hated his last ice breaker, that one was a whole scale worse. His response to her telling him she loved him punched into her, and for a moment, she forgot how to breathe. Then she sucked a breath into her starved lungs and that was way worse.

"Claire." His blue eyes reflected the pain raging inside her. It was hard to look at him, but she made herself do it.

He stepped toward her. "Please, don't look at me like that?"

"Like what?" she whispered.

"Like I've betrayed you."

A sob burst out of her and changed into a bark of hysterical laughter. "Isn't that what you're about to do?"

"Claire." He closed the distance until he stood in front of her. His hands were balled into fists by his side. "You've gotta understand."

Did she? She didn't see that working for her.

Finn gripped her arms. "What happened last night, that's who I am. I can't change that."

The words made sense, but their implications floated like dust motes in the air. Dust motes with clinically sharp edges that would carve grooves through her when they eventually alighted.

"I'm a killer." His hand tightened. "Nothing will ever change that. I've been kidding myself. I lost control of it."

"Get to the point." She had a few shreds of dignity left, but if he drew it out much longer, she would implode and beg him not to do it.

"The point is that next time it could be you or one of the kids," he said, his voice raw and hoarse.

Funny, it didn't help at all that he was hurting himself as much as he was hurting her. She could see it in those beautiful blue eyes that he meant every word coming out of his mouth. Not only that, but he believed them, and he meant to act on them. "Is this where you tell me it wouldn't be fair to me to ask me to wait for you?"

"Not in those words." He winced. "But I guess so."

No, he didn't get to do ambiguous. "You guess so? I'm afraid that's not going to work for me. Yes or no, Finn? In or out? Are you with me or is this over? Are we over?"

His nod looked like it might break his neck. "We have to be over."

"You know, I don't see that." She forced a brittle laugh out. She wouldn't break. She refused to break. Too late; she was already broken. Shattered like the porcelain dolls in the attic against Finn's obdurateness. "But I'm not going to beg you to change your mind." She had to get out, but she stopped at the kitchen door. The hurt raged in her, demanding she draw blood in return. "Interesting that you made me confront my demons, yet you're asking me to agree as you give in to yours."

Finn dropped his head.

Claire turned for the stairs. "You made me trust you, Finn, yet you can't do the same for yourself."

CHAPTER
Thirty~Three

CLAIRE MADE it to her dad's room. Her hand shook as she knocked. The contained sobs threatened to tear her apart.

Sitting by his window reading, Dad stood the moment she entered. "Sweetheart?"

Shaking her head, too overwhelmed to speak, Claire headed for the comfort he offered.

Dad opened his arms and held her while she cried. She appreciated that he didn't ask any questions but kept providing the tissues.

When she had no tears left, she crawled into the armchair opposite Dad's.

Taking a seat, he looked at her over the top of his glasses. "Tell me."

"It's Finn."

He shook his head. "I guessed as much. Want to tell me about it?"

"He's leaving."

Dad nodded. "Because of what happened last night?"

"You know about that?"

"Small town." He shrugged. "If it helps, everyone is firmly

on your side and Finn's. They say those stupid kids caused the entire thing."

Unbelievably, she had more tears to shed. "It makes no difference because that's not what Finn believes."

Dad waited.

"He doesn't think he started it, but he scared himself when he lost control. He says he's a monster, and the only place he belongs is back with his old unit."

Snorting, Dad folded his glasses and put them on his book. "Stupid shit."

Succinct but true. She blew her nose. "He's not listening to me."

"Of course, he isn't." Dad huffed. "In his head, this plays out as him making a courageous and noble sacrifice. That boy loves you," he said. "He's got some boneheaded notion that this is for your sake."

"You sound so sure of that."

"Why do you think I talked myself into not going near you or your mother for all these years?"

Claire ached a bit for all of them. "Stupid shit."

"Tell me about it." Horace shook his head. "Want some advice from an old man?"

"If that man is you." She'd never had that sort of relationship with Mom, and having Horace there took some of the edge off her pain.

"Actually, it's more of a confession."

She nodded.

"We've already established what a stupid shit I was. I wish I could tell you I got smarter after that, but I think I actually got stupider." He stared out the window. "It didn't take long for my noble sacrifice to start sucking and not making much sense. But by then you two had been gone for six months, and I wasn't sure of my welcome anymore."

How she wished he'd at least tried.

"I let a little more time pass while I cowered in this big old house. Eventually, so much time had passed that the chance of being welcomed back was about zero."

"You could have tried."

Horace nodded. "Yes, I could have, and I should have. But I was a coward. For as long as Naomi didn't tell me no for sure, I could cling to this tiny hope." He looked down at his hands on his lap. "After a time, the hope died as well."

Claire didn't get it. "Dad, how is this horribly sad story going to help me?"

"See it as a warning." His eyes fierce, he looked at her. "Right now, Finn isn't thinking straight, and talking to him won't do any good. Let him go. Let him feel the consequences of his actions. But take this time to decide if he really is for you. And if you decide he is, then a moment of sacrificed pride is a whole lot better than a lifetime of regret." He grimaced. "I know this from experience."

"What if I do that, and he still doesn't want me?" All her rejection fears clouded her thinking.

Horace shrugged. "What if he does? What if a little courage could win you your heart's desire?"

"I'm scared."

"Of course, you are." He patted her knee. "And I can't promise you happily ever after. Maybe he'll never work this out for himself. Maybe he never really loved you in the first place, and this is just a convenient exit clause."

Claire winced. "You really suck at this comforting thing."

"You have a point." Horace chuckled. "But it will be worth it if I can save you from making the same mistakes I did."

———

It didn't take Finn long to pack his stuff. He had always traveled light anyway.

Claire hadn't come out of Horace's room all morning, and he wanted to spare her having to see him again.

Already the bedroom felt empty, like he'd never been there. He'd been happy in his room, found that illusive peace. Even if it was only for a few weeks and had been snatched away, he'd still had it.

The door flew open, and Poppy stormed in. "What the hell are you doing?"

"I'm going to contract to my unit as an instructor." He picked up his bag.

Poppy stood in the door and folded her arms. "Because you're such a monster and you don't trust yourself around Claire or the kids?"

"Yup."

"You're such an idiot." Poppy stalked him and poked him in the chest. "And you're going to lose everything good in your life."

"I'll still see you and the kids." He couldn't mention Claire, not yet. His room was flooded with memories of her. Memories of them tangled in his sheets, making love, laughing, talking.

Poppy poked him again. "How good of you."

"Come on, Poppy." She had to see he wasn't doing this for his sake. "You weren't even there. You didn't see what I became."

"No, you come on, Finn. And before you forget, I've been on the receiving end of one of your self-sacrificing moves. I didn't like it then, and I don't like it now."

She didn't know what she was talking about. "Meaning?"

"Finn." Poppy stamped her foot. "You offered to marry me when you didn't love me, so you could look after me and the children."

He had done that. "It was the right thing to do."

"It would have made everyone unhappy. Imagine now that I'd said yes, and Claire had still come to Twin Elks. Only in this outcome, we're married." She gestured between him and her.

"And you fall hard for Claire, but it doesn't matter because you're married."

"I would never cheat."

"No, you wouldn't." Poppy's face softened. "You would just be the most miserable man on the planet."

He didn't see the connection. "You said no, so this is a nonissue."

"And if I'd said yes?"

"I would have married you."

"Exactly."

Call him obtuse. "What are you saying?"

"You get these things in your head, Finn. You make up your mind about something and not hell or high water can shift you. You entrench yourself in your own bullshit thinking."

He snorted. "Nice!"

"Correct me if I'm wrong." He wouldn't dare anyway. In her current mood, Poppy would punch him. "But at the time you offered to marry me, you believed you would never find someone to share your life with?"

"Right." At the time he'd been thinking he would never get married, never meet the girl who could bring the light to his darkness. An inkling of understanding dawned. Still, this was different. "I made a mistake."

"Like you're making a mistake now," Poppy said. "You make these sweeping decisions about your life and your happiness and you're not that good at it."

Her bluntness made him huff out a laugh. "That was one occasion."

"Really?" She glared at him. "What about your mother?"

"My mother?"

"You've decided she's too fragile to love more than one son. You never tell her how much it hurts when she treats you like it should have been you and not Sean. You even threw yourself right into the mouth of death because you decided she was right."

Finn wanted to force her to take those words back. She couldn't be more wrong. Mom had loved Sean best, so he had gravitated to Dad. When Dad had died, he'd done what his father had asked and taken care of Sean and Mom.

But had he?

Under his watch, Sean had died, and before that, he had screwed up his marriage.

"You weren't responsible for Sean." Poppy cupped his cheek. "Sean made shitty decisions all on his own. You are also not to blame for Maura being such an idiot. You never did anything to make her not love you. I'm a mother, and there are times when my kids drive me mad, but I wouldn't know how to not love them." She shrugged. "Besides I think Maura loves you as much as she loved Sean. She relies so much more on you. If she faces that, however, she has to face how she feels like she failed you both."

Thus far, her dissection of him wasn't enjoyable. "But I am responsible for what I did to those boys. They were barely older than teens, Poppy."

"Some of it you are." Poppy nodded. "But while we're handing out blame, let's give some to Uncle Sam, who put you in places and circumstances that demanded those sorts of skills from you. And let's put some blame on those guys. They provoked you."

"Nobody forced me to join up."

"And you knew exactly what you were getting into when you did?"

"Maybe not exactly."

"You take on the weight of the world, Finn." Poppy grabbed his shoulders. "And you carry it around. You even proposed to me to make up for how bad a husband Sean was. And now you're going to let those burdens take the best thing that ever happened to you away."

"Yes, I am." Their conversation needed to end because he didn't like her implications. "Because it's the right thing to do.

Because I won't take the chance with Claire or you and your kids that I might snap. Because it's what I have to do. Take responsibility."

"Oh, Finn." Poppy hugged him. "You're so damn stubborn, and it's going to cost you."

CHAPTER
Thirty-Four

CLAIRE AVOIDED GOING into Finn's room for as long as she could. Taking pity on her, Poppy went in and changed the sheets and cleaned it.

Finn's absence hung over the entire house.

When he made the football team, Ryan burst into tears. "I want to tell Finn."

"Why don't you call him?" Poppy hugged her son.

Ryan pressed his face into her stomach. "But he won't come and watch me play."

"Maybe he can come to a game or two," she said. Over his head Poppy glanced at Ben across the dinner table.

Ben's jaw tightened, and his fingers whitened around his cutlery.

"When is your first game?" Horace ruffled Ryan's hair. "Because I want to make sure I get there."

"I dunno." Ryan stared at his plate. "Coach didn't say, but I have a letter for Mom."

"We'll put your schedule on the fridge." Claire kept her voice chipper. "That way none of us will miss a game."

"Except Finn," Ryan whispered.

And she had nothing to say to that. Because nobody had heard a word from Finn.

Ciara heaved a sigh. "Cecily is sad."

Cecily wasn't the only one. Claire pushed food around her plate. She kept herself busy while she did what Dad had advised. This time she needed to decide if despite everything, Finn was still worth it.

She couldn't ignore common sense that stated if a man wanted to be with you, he would be. If she went after him, would she really ever know if he would have chosen her in the end?

In the meantime, she made plans to move Mom to Twin Elks. Amazingly, when she'd brought it up to Doug, he'd been all for the idea. "She'll be better surrounded by family."

Claire wasn't sure Mom would consider Horace her family, but she needed to be closer. She'd spent most of her life separated from one parent, and she refused to do it anymore.

If the carriage house didn't work out, Dad had offered to buy Naomi a smaller house nearby, or even get her into a retirement community about an hour away.

Missing Finn never really went away, and she tried to fill her days. Fortunately, the Winters family had extensive investments, foundations, and shareholdings to keep her from obsessing too much during the day. She and Dad spent hours every day as he went over all of it.

She also kept bringing things down from the attic and breathing life back into the mansion. The furniture she left where it was, as it reminded her too much of Finn.

Hank Styles moped around the workshop as if he'd lost his best friend.

Even Dot had lost some of her bounce.

Finn was so stupid to turn his back on all of these wonderful people. He called himself a monster and a killer, yet he couldn't see what others did.

Hank saw their shared passion for working with wood and a

younger man to continue his legacy. Dot saw a man she considered a sixth son. Ben missed his friendship. The twins missed the way he would chase them and wrestle with them. Ryan missed the best connection he had with his dead father. Poppy didn't say much, but Finn was the closest thing she had to a brother, and she both missed him and wanted to kick his ass. Even Kelly missed him. Although Claire suspected that had a lot to do with how easy on the eyes Finn was. Mia Grover had wept on her shoulder and suggested they hold a sleepover vigil for their mutual loss.

They were about to sit down to dinner when Peg knocked and poked her head around the kitchen door. "Ah, Claire. Good. I caught you."

"Hi, Peg."

The rest of the family greeted her.

Horace sat up straighter. "Come on in, Peg."

"Would you like to join us, Peg?" Poppy always made enough for more mouths.

"Thank you, but no. I have a pot roast simmering. I came by to speak to Claire." She motioned at the porch outside the kitchen. "A word. If you don't mind."

Claire exchanged glances with Poppy, but she went. There weren't many who would deny Peg.

Outside, the winter chill had made its way to Twin Elks, and Claire hugged her arms to herself. She'd lost weight since Finn had left, and she seemed to be cold most of the time.

"I won't keep you long," Peg said. "I just popped by to assure you that the prayer chain is aware of your situation."

"Um…okay." She didn't really know what else to say.

"The Finn thing." Peg winked at her.

Claire managed a nod.

"You're one of us now, Claire." Peg clapped her on the shoulder. "And we look after our own." She leaned forward and lowered her voice. "The prayer chain is dealing with this."

"I see."

Peg gave an evil chuckle. "No, you don't. But you will." She gave Claire a knowing look. "Never underestimate the power of the prayer chain."

———

Finn sat in his crappy efficiency apartment and flipped through TV channels. He'd gone all that way, even met with his old CO, and then run out of momentum. Still in the manila envelope, his contract sat on the cheap, plywood coffee table.

He'd been in a funk for three weeks, and people were starting to get pissed at him. His CO had called at least four times to find out what the holdup was. He should be out there looking for accommodation, but he couldn't seem to move away from *Nat Geo Wild*.

He checked his watch. Twin Elks was an hour behind him, so right now the kids would be coming back from school. He really hoped Ryan had made the football team. Grabbing his phone, he fired off a quick text to Poppy.

She came back instantly. *He made the team. His first game is this weekend. Sad that his Uncle Finn won't be there :(*

Shit! And he'd made a promise to Ryan. Sean had broken all his promises to his children, and now Finn was doing the same.

Tell him I'll make sure I make one soon.

Will do.

And then because he couldn't stop himself. *Everybody good?*

Okay. You?

Not an easy one to answer. *Doing okay. Met with CO. Have my contract.*

Congratulations? Even by text, he could see the challenging look Poppy would bend his way.

He didn't know why he needed her to know, but he did. *Haven't signed yet.*

Why?

Poppy had kids, she could play blink all day, so he blinked first. *How is she?*

The three dots appeared and went away. The screen stayed the same for a long while, and then the three dots reappeared and disappeared again.

He should never have asked. Finn tossed his phone on the coffee table. He'd lost his right to know how Claire was when he left her.

Ping.

Finn dived for his phone, missed, and sent it skittering under the television cabinet.

"Shit." He leopard crawled to the cabinet and reached underneath. It was a tight fit for his arm, but he got hold of the thing.

I don't know what to say. Poppy had texted.

Dammit! He was putting Poppy in a shitty position, dividing her loyalties.

He put his phone down.

Then picked it right up. Poppy would deal, and he dialed her number.

"Finn." Her sweet voice bridged the miles and made him feel connected to Twin Elks. "How are you? Really?"

"I'm shit, Poppy." The relief at not keeping things all bottled up washed over him. "I miss her like fucking hell."

Poppy sighed. "Then you know what you have to do."

"I can't." Because his paralysis extended beyond signing that contract. "Can you just tell me how she is?"

"She's okay. She misses you too." Then she said, "I don't know whether to tell you the next part."

Every muscle tensed. "Tell me." Fear snaked through him. "Is she hurt?"

"No, nothing like that." Poppy cleared her throat. "But she has been seeing a lot of Gabe Crowe."

Those tense muscles tensed some more. "What for?"

"I think he makes her laugh. Makes her forget she's sad."

"Motherfucker." Finn clenched his phone. It hadn't even been

a month, and fucking Gabe had made his move. Finn remembered the way Gabe had flirted with Claire at the wedding.
Come around to the house and flirted with her right in front
of him.

"Finn?" Poppy sounded anxious. "Are you still there?"

"I'm here." More growl than words. "I gotta go."

He hung up before she could respond.

Gabe Crowe with his trust-me smile and easy-come-easy-go
way. Finn would like to rearrange his face for him.

What did that asshole think he was doing with Claire? The
dick-weed didn't even intend to stay in Twin Elks.

Finn's conscious twinged, but he shut it down. He'd done
what he did for Claire's good. Not to try to talk his way into her
pants.

The thought of Claire with Gabe nearly made his head
explode. The fury built in his chest until he had to get out.

Ripping open his door, he stopped short.

On his doorstep, his mother stood with her hand raised to
knock.

"Mom."

"Finn."

She was as immaculately dressed as ever, in a skirt and
blouse, not a hair out of place, makeup perfect, but something
about her felt different. Off. "Are you okay?"

"Of course." She gave him her plastic smile. The one she
reserved for members of her bridge club and golf four-ball. Just
before she beat the crap out of them. "May I come in?"

"Sure." Her being there made no sense. Firstly, how had
she found out where he was? And then, why was she
there?

Mom looked around his apartment with a look of distaste.
"This is rather...dingy."

"It's temporary."

Fiddling with her purse strap, she walked to his window and
looked out. "Poppy told me you were here."

That answered one question, but Poppy talking to his mother didn't make any sense. "She called you."

"Yes. She told me about Ryan's football game."

"That was nice of her."

"Yes." Mom grimaced. "Not that I approve of Ryan playing such a violent game."

No. It had taken Dad to persuade her to let him play hockey. "Mom." He couldn't do a session of Poppy bashing. "She's a good mother."

"Yes. She is." She tensed. "Not like me. A much better mother than I was."

He couldn't believe what he'd heard. "Mom?"

Without looking at him, she waved her hand. "Don't bother to deny what we both know."

Finn needed to sit down, and then he remembered his manners. "Can I get you anything? Something to drink?"

"A glass of water would be fine." She turned and looked at him. "I suppose you're surprised to see me."

Finn pulled a bottle of water from the fridge and poured it into a glass for her. "I wasn't expecting you."

"No." She took the water and wrapped both hands around it. "Did you do it yet?"

"What?"

"Reenlist."

That's why she came? "I'm not reenlisting. I'm going back as a contractor." He indicated the envelope. "Or I should be. My contract is in there, but I haven't signed it."

Mom sagged and water slopped on the floor. "Good."

"Mom?" He took her elbow and guided her to the sofa. A nasty suspicion whispered in his ear. "Are you sick?"

"No." She put the glass on the coffee table and took a tissue out of her purse and dried her hands. "I really am fine."

"Sure?"

She almost smiled. "Very sure."

She had such a forceful personality, it was often hard to

remember that she was a physically petite woman. Sitting on his butt-ugly, brown-and-yellow couch with her shoulders stooped, she looked vulnerable and fragile.

Her hand shook as she rubbed her forehead. "I hoped I would be on time. To stop you."

If he had speculated as to what brought her, that would have been bottom of his list. "You want to stop me?"

"Finn." She pressed her fingers to her mouth. "I don't want you to go back there. I'm not sure I could do it again." Her breath hitched, and she took a moment before she spoke again. "I know you don't like me interfering in your life, but I'm here to ask you not to do it."

"Why?" He had nothing else.

"I never slept," she said. "All the time you were deployed. I never slept. Every time the phone rang, I was worried they were going to tell me you were injured. Or worse. Every knock at the door."

He didn't know this woman. He'd never heard anything like that from her. Sean had always been the son she lavished with her love.

"After Sean…" She still couldn't say the word. "It got worse. Because you were all I had left." Her breath hitched.

She was crying. It floored him.

"Sean and I were very close. I couldn't help it. He needed me so much when he was a baby." Tears ran down her face, putting rivulets in her makeup. "I used to walk the floor with him night after night when he couldn't settle. I used to sleep beside his crib and listen to him struggling to breathe."

"I know that, Mom." Some of those nights, he would have given anything to have her sit by his bed and read him a story. But it had always been Sean, and it still was. He didn't see any reason to sugar coat it. "Sean was your favorite, Mom."

"Sean was the one I knew best." She nodded. "I was comfortable with him. I know a mother is not supposed to say this, but I understood Sean, and he understood me. You were like a foreigner."

Shit. After all this time, it still hurt.

"I adored you," she said. "But I couldn't relate to you. I didn't know how to show you how much you meant to me."

"I was just a kid, Mom. Maybe an energetic one, but still just a kid."

"I was raised by women, you know."

He did know something like that. His mother had been raised in a house with his grandmother and great-grandmother. Somehow there had never been any men around.

"Until I met your father, I had only known men in passing." She gave a little laugh. "I had certainly never interacted with any little boys before I had my own. I didn't know how to handle you. Sean was so much easier."

To be fair, he had been a rowdy little shit. Always knee deep in something and wading through the thick of the action. He had constantly come home with rips in his clothes and skinned knees. "Sean was more like you."

"Yes, he was." She patted her cheeks dry and took a deep breath. "Not a day goes by that I don't miss him."

"I know, Mom." He eased on to the sofa next to her. "Me too."

"Ryan and little Sean look just like him."

"They do."

She sighed. "But they're nothing like him in personality."

"No." Blaming her for spoiling Sean served no purpose. Maybe Sean would have turned out like he did anyway.

"You think I don't know that I was part of what ruined Sean," she said.

His day had officially drifted into the *Twilight Zone*.

"You never say so, but we both know it's true." She looked at him as she said it. "Part of the reason Sean was such a terrible husband was because I spoiled him. Never forced him to be accountable for his actions."

The pain had carved itself into her face, and she had suffered enough. Losing a child was enough pain for anyone. "You did what you thought was right."

"I smothered him with love. I gave him all the love that I couldn't give to you."

Finn felt that one too. "I would have been happy to take the love."

"Don't you think I know that?" More tears streamed down her face. "I look at you and I see such a good, strong man, an ethical one, and a kind one, and I know I had nothing to do with any of that. No, you did that on your own."

"Mom." He wanted to bawl like a baby. Not for one moment had he thought his mother looked at him and saw those things.

"I came here to beg you not to go back to that life again." She tucked her tissue into her purse. "I came here to tell you that I know I failed you, and that you don't think I love you as much as Sean, but you're wrong. Your life is as valuable to me as Sean's was. I've already lost one son; I don't want to lose another."

He had nothing, so he just blinked at her. "It's not an active deployment position."

"I know." She nodded. "I asked Poppy, and she told me what you're doing." She cupped his cheek. "But darling, if you join again, you'll lose yourself. You're such a peaceful, loving soul. You're too gentle for what it is they want you to do."

"Mom, you don't know—"

"And I don't want to. All I know is that I said goodbye to a beautiful child, and they gave me back a haunted man. Be happy, Finn. Find what makes you smile and do that."

"I'm not sure I can."

"Yes, you can." She held his face between her palms. "You're a good man, Finn, a wonderful one who any woman would be lucky to have. I didn't do a good enough job letting you know that, and it's my failing and not yours. You are so worth loving, Finn. You deserve all the love this world can give you."

He and Mom had never had anything approaching that sort of conversation. "Is this because of Claire and me?"

"It might be." She stepped away from him and drew a big breath. "In my opinion, she isn't good enough for you." She shrugged. "Yes, I know. You don't have to say it. I did the same to Poppy." Squaring her shoulders, she gave him a fierce look. "But nobody will ever be good enough for you, Finn."

He nearly laughed. Never had he thought to be dealing with her maternal blind spot turned his way. "Mom—"

"But I will try." She held up a hand. "I will learn from the past and do better. I only want you to be happy."

Another suspicion raised its head. "Have you been talking to Poppy?"

"Don't be ridiculous, Finn." She patted her hair back into place. "You know Poppy and I don't speak."

CHAPTER
Thirty~Five

CLAIRE NEVER THOUGHT she would see both her parents in the same zip code. Five weeks after she got home, Mom moved into the carriage house with Doug. He took the second bedroom and they had Donna come in to give him days off.

Mom walked around the carriage house touching things. She picked up a Royal Dolton figurine. "This is pretty."

"There are a lot of pretty things here, Naomi," Doug said.

She gave him a vague smile. "Hmm. I know this place."

With no idea how to handle Mom reacting well, Claire glanced at Doug. The breakdown they had braced for over the move to Twin Elks never came. But it was early days yet.

"You used to live here," Doug said. "A long time ago."

"Yes, I did." Mom looked out the window. "I know this garden."

"You used to spend a lot of time in it," Claire said. "Maybe you could take a walk outside when the weather is nice."

"Maybe." Mom patted her cheek. "This is my house? All of it?"

Claire nodded. "Yes."

Then Mom smiled. "Good." She settled herself in a floral linen armchair. "I think we should have tea now."

"I think that's a great idea," Doug said. "Should we invite Claire to tea?"

Mom smiled at her. "I would like that."

After tea, Claire went back to the main house. They had decided they would introduce the notion of Horace being there slowly.

He and Peg looked up from where they sat at the kitchen table as Claire entered.

"How is she?" Dad got up. He moved with such ease, it was hard to remember his painful hobble. "Settling in?"

"She seems fine." Claire poured herself a cup of coffee. "Doug says we can still expect a few turns, but so far, so good."

"Huh!" Peg shook her head. "I never thought I'd see the day when Naomi came back to Twin Elks."

Horace chuckled. "Me neither."

"Thanks for making this happen, Dad." Claire gave him a hug.

Dad patted her back. "It's all good."

"Well now." Peg got to her feet. "I think I need to get going."

"I'll walk you out." Dad offered her his arm. "You never know what could happen between here and your house."

Peg giggled. Yes, Peg, giggled. "Horace, it's just down the road."

"Then that's how far I will escort you."

As the door shut behind them, Claire finally got it together. Had she just seen her dad flirt with Peg? That hip operation had him moving forward in lots of directions.

Which brought her around to herself. Mom was safely installed, and now it was time to sort the Finn situation. Five weeks, and she still ached for him as much as she had the first day he'd left.

If Dad was taking control of his life and moving forward— even if that was with Peg—then it was time for her to get off her ass.

She left the kitchen and went to her room.

A disturbing thought wormed into her brain. If Dad and Peg started dating, maybe more, would Peg be in the house with her bullhorn?

The mental images were too horrible to dwell on.

On her bed, her bag lay open, and she had only to put a few more things in it, and then she could be off. It didn't matter who was right or wrong. She loved Finn, and she was damn sure he loved her. She was betting her pride and her heart on that being true.

She'd given him his damn time to get his head out of his ass. Now it was time to make his options clear to him.

"Hey." Poppy spoke from behind her. "You still doing this?"

"Yup." She folded a linen shirt and packed it. The same shirt she'd been wearing when Finn first kissed her.

With Poppy, Kelly and Dot, she'd spent hours of chatting to get to this point. Her new girl posse was behind her decision.

"And why was that again?" Poppy sounded weird.

Claire folded a sweater. "Because I love him, and it's worth bending to make this happen." Poppy knew that, and Claire turned to face her.

And stopped.

Finn stood next to Poppy in the doorway.

"Hey." He gave her his gorgeous crooked half smile.

"Hey?" He looked as beautiful as ever. She'd forgotten the pure, deep blue of his eyes. "Is that it? After you walked out on me?"

"I'm getting to the other part." He stepped into the room.

Poppy gave her a smile and left, closing the door behind her.

Her knees felt weak, and Claire sat on the bed next to her suitcase. She had been on her way to him, and now Finn stood in her room. He had come to her, but she didn't know why, and she didn't want to wait another minute to find out. "Are you here to stay?"

"I hope so." He stopped in front of her and crouched at her feet. "If you'll have me."

"Just like that?" He was missing a few steps in the reconciliation process.

"Well, first I thought I'd grovel." He took her hands. "And beg your forgiveness for being such a stupid dick and hurting you."

"That's a good start," Claire said. Over the last five weeks, her anger had been replaced by sadness that he couldn't see how good what they had was. And okay, a residual trace of anger that he had thrown that all away. "How can I be sure you're back to stay this time?"

"I can tell you that I am," he said. "But you have no reason to believe me. I went to Hank first and bought into his business. I'm here to stay."

"Do you love me?" Because at the end of the day that's all that really mattered.

Finn kissed her hands. "More than I can say."

"Then I'm all in."

The joy on his face couldn't be faked. "Just like that?"

"Maybe not just like that." She wouldn't be her if she let it go without a smidge of retribution. "You're not off the hook on the groveling thing yet, and I'm still a sulker."

"Understandable." He rose to eye level with her and put his hands on either side of her hips. "I love you, babe. I'm so sorry. I never wanted to hurt you, and I ended up doing it anyway." He wiped his fingers over her cheeks. "Please don't cry."

"I'm not crying. Much." Claire sniffed. "I'm finding it hard to believe that you're here."

"Believe it." He kissed her softly. "And believe that here is where I'm going to be for the rest of our lives."

Claire kissed him back. "I want you to know that I'm totally okay with that."

Epilogue

A HALF-MOON FLIT in and out of the streaming clouds. The ozone crispness of coming snow scented the air and stiff winds blew in the laden clouds. A lone owl sat atop the squat fifties cube of the Twin Elks Public Library and hooted for his mate.

Inside, the old oil radiators clanked and coughed out heat from the boiler buried deep in the basement.

Light crept out from beneath the door to the meeting room and lit the bottom of the beanbags in the reading nook where every Thursday librarian Sally Klemper did a story hour for local children.

Chairperson addressed the meeting. "Let's make this quick tonight. It's cold as hell, and I want to watch the new season of *Your Best You.*"

Secretary perked up. "Does that start tonight?"

"I love that show." Social Media tittered. "I would love to be on it. Did you see the promo with that new girl, Blythe? The diet and exercise one?"

A flurry of conversation broke over the group.

"Let's come to order." Secretary tapped her gavel on the desk. "I second Madam Chairperson. Let's get this done and get out of here."

Treasurer shook his head. "You know you can just TVO that show, right?"

"Look who's all techno wizard." Counter Intelligence cackled over her knitting.

"Back to business at hand." Secretary glared from beneath her row of iron-gray curls. "Treasurer, would you like to report on the matter of Winters House?"

"I would." Treasurer grinned and looked smug. "I can say that Winters House is now safe for at least another generation. Also, there is reason to hope that matters are progressing positively toward yet another generation of Winterses."

"Oh, that's lovely." Communications dabbed at her eyes. "We're all so happy for you."

Treasurer grunted and dropped his chin to his chest. "Thank you."

Everybody clapped, and nobody louder than Social Media, who added a cheer. "Hear, hear."

A breeze played through everybody's hair and ballooned the maroon, polyester drapes.

"Must she." Secretary shuddered.

Treasurer shrugged. "She's happy."

"Madam Chairman?" Secretary turned to the head of the table. "I believe you have news for us?"

"Yes." Chairman fidgeted in her chair. "I believe we have an opportunity to bring another of our former young folk back into the fold."

"You mean Gabe?" Social Media blushed.

Chairman nodded. "He's staying."

"Temporarily," Treasurer said. "He has no intention of staying forever."

"Oh, you." Chairman chuckled. "Where you see a problem, I see an opportunity."

Secretary nodded. "Quite right! I declare Operation Veterinarian open. Second?"

"I second." Social Media went a deeper shade of pink.

Communications tittered. "Hear, hear."

Treasurer raised his hand. "I agree."

Counter Intelligence added another row of purl before she looked up and said, "For sure. Let's keep family where they belong."

"Right." Secretary straightened. "Last item on the agenda. Operation High School Sweethearts."

"Oh." Communications' hand shot in the air. "I can take that one."

All gazes swung her way.

She preened before she said, "I can report that there have been some developments in that matter."

They all looked at her.

She flushed. "Well, that's it. He goes for his coffee every day, and they chat."

"That's what they've been doing since she came back to Twin Elks." Social Media gaped at her. "Is that all you have?"

"No." Communications straightened in her chair. "There have been meaningful glances. Frissons."

Secretary snorted. "Frissons?"

"Frissons." Communications insisted.

"Well." Secretary rolled her eyes. "If that's it, let's close up by reiterating our purpose."

Everyone straightened in their chairs and recited, "We are committed to the revitalization of Twin Elks through the active encouragement of growing our community."

"Before we go." Social Media got out a sheaf of papers. "I have my report."

"It's not on the agenda." Secretary puffed up. "You know it has to be on the agenda. We have rules here."

Social Media glared at her. "I know that, but I want to give my report."

"But *Your Best You* is starting in five minutes." Chairman consulted her watch. "Tell us quickly, dear."

"I've started a campaign, which I think we need to discuss. A way of attracting the right element back to Twin Elks."

Secretary heaved an impatient sigh. "Next time. We will discuss this next time."

"Fine." Social Media stuffed her papers back in her bag. "And I will do my own thing until you find the time to discuss it."

Chairman patted her hand. "Get it on the agenda, dear."

Social Media and Catering were the last to leave.

"What did you do?" Catering cocked her head and studied Social Media.

Social Media smirked. "I may have started a rumor or two."

"What rumor?" Catering leaned forward, eyes alight with anticipation.

Social Media giggled. "You'll see."

There are currently four books in the Passing Through series. If you want more of Twin Elks, Colorado—the town where love comes to stay—check out book #3 in the series, Walk On By. The series order is Drove All Night, Ticket To Ride, Walk On By, and Running On Empty.

———

Get Walk On By

She's lost love.
He's lost hope.
They'll find together where they never expected.

Since high school, Kelly Ashford's heart has belonged to one guy, her high school sweetheart, who got away—which doesn't explain why now she's all grown up and her sweetheart is free; Kelly can't keep her hands off gorgeous, funny Gabe Crowe.

Gabe Crowe is back home in Twin Elks, but he's not staying. Twin Elks holds nothing but bad memories for Gabe, and he's leaving town—just as soon as he can tear himself away from the oh-so-tempting Kelly.

Can Kelly and Gabe find a new way forward, or is their connection just passing through? And must the Twin Elks prayer chain once more do that magic they do so well?

Chapter One

Some things never change. Unfortunately, the Bugling Elk in Twin Elks, Colorado, was one of them. Gabe had traveled as far as his passport could take him, lived away from Twin Elks for over fifteen years, and he could say, with certainly, that it remained one of the ugliest bars he'd even been in.

"Gabe Crowe. And still pretty." Maddison Watts, the Elk's owner and barkeeper, leaned her elbows on the counter. "Beer?"

"Whatever's cold and on tap." The beer there was always good and cold.

A white spangled Elvis suit with yellow armpit stains still watched over the bar. Elvis bobbleheads, allegedly the largest collection in the state, were right where they'd been when he last saw them, stacked up next to the singing carp, which he'd lay money still did an eerie version of *Take Me to the River*. A couple more pairs of panties might decorate the elk head hanging over the women's bathroom, but Gabe didn't want to get any closer to check it out.

The characters in the bar hadn't changed any either.

Ronnie Falkirk, well into her eighties and still working dispatch for Gabe's brother Ben, sidled up next to him. "Well, well, well." She waggled her shocking copper-colored head and eyed him with a sharp brown gaze nearly buried beneath layers of blue goo. "Look who's back in town."

"Hey, Ronnie." Gabe expected no less. He'd gotten out of Twin Elks for college and came back as rarely as he could get away with. "You look good."

"No, I don't. I'm older than dirt." Ronnie cackled and winked at him. "Your mom sure must be glad to have you back."

Guilt double-tapped him, and Gabe hid his wince behind a sip of beer. "Yup."

"She missed you." Ronnie layered more guilt on. "Missed all

her boys, really. Other than Ben. Of course, he didn't go anywhere." She whistled and wheezed out a laugh. "Got himself a nice little family now, Ben has."

"Yup." Gabe had returned for Ben's wedding a few weeks back. At the time, he had every intention of getting back to Australia as soon as he could. Funny how life laughed when you were making plans.

————

For first dibs on news, deals, and giveaways, and so much more, join the @Home Collective

Or if Facebook is more your thing, join the Sarah Hegger Collective

Anything and everything you need to know on my website http://sarahhegger.com

About the Author

Born British and raised in South Africa, Sarah Hegger suffers from an incurable case of wanderlust. Her match? A hot Canadian engineer, whose marriage proposal she accepted six short weeks after they first met. Together they've made homes in seven different cities across three different continents (and back again once or twice). If only it made her multilingual, but the best she can manage is idiosyncratic English, fluent Afrikaans, conversant Russian, pigeon Portuguese, even worse Zulu and enough French to get herself into trouble.

Mimicking her globe trotting adventures, Sarah's career path began as a gainfully employed actress, drifted into public relations, settled a moment in advertising, and eventually took root in the fertile soil of her first love, writing. She also moonlights as a wife and mother. She currently lives in Ottawa, Canada, filling her empty nest with fur babies. Part footloose buccaneer, part quixotic observer of life, Sarah's restless heart is most content when reading or writing books.

Praise for Sarah Hegger

Drove All Night
"The classic romance plot is elevated to a modern-day,
wholly accessible real-life fairy tale with an excellent mix of
romantic elements and spicy sensuality."
Booklife Prize, Critic's Report

Positively Pippa
"This is the type of romance that makes readers fall in love not
just with characters, but with authors as well."
Kirkus Review (Starred Review)

"What begins as a simple second-chance romance quickly
transforms into a beautiful, frank examination of love, family
dynamics, and following one's dreams. Hegger's unflinching,
candid portrayal of interpersonal and generational
communication elevates the story to the sublime. Shunning
clichés and contrived circumstances, she uses realistic, relatable
situations to create a world that readers will want to visit time
and again."
Publisher's Weekly, Starred Review

Hegger's utterly delightful first Ghost Falls contemporary is what other romance novels want to grow up to be." – Publisher's Weekly, Best Books of 2017

"The very talented Hegger kicks off an enjoyable new series set in the small Utah town of Ghost Falls. This charming and fun-filled book has everything from passion and humor to betrayal and revenge." – Jill M Smith, RT Books Reviews 2017 – Contemporary Love and Laughter Nominee

Becoming Bella
"Hegger excels at depicting familial relationships and friendships of all kinds, including purely platonic friendships between women and men. Tears, laughter, and a dollop of suspense make a memorable story that readers will want to revisit time and again."
Publisher's Weekly, Starred Review

"...you have a terrific new romance that Hegger fans are going to love. Don't miss out!"
Jill M. Smith – RT Book Reviews

Blatantly Blythe
"Ms. Hegger has delivered another captivating read for this series in this book that was packed with emotion..." Bec, Bookmagic Review, Harlequin Junkie, HJ Recommends.

Nobody's Fool
"Hegger offers a breath of fresh air in the romance genre." – Terri Dukes, RT Book Reviews

Nobody's Princess
"Hegger continues to live up to her rapidly growing reputation

for breathing fresh air into the romance genre." – Terri Dukes, RT Book Reviews

"I have read the entire Willow Park Series. I have loved each of the books … Nobody's Princess is my favorite of all time." Harlequin Junkie, Top Pick

Also by Sarah Hegger

Urban Fantasy

The Cré-Witch Chronicles

Prequel: Cast In Stone

Vol l: Born In Water

Vol ll: Purged In Fire

Vol III: Raised In Air

Vol IV: Cradled In Earth

Vol V: Joined In Spirit

Sports Romance

Ottawa Titans Series

Roughing

Hooking

Contemporary Romance

Passing Through Series

Drove All Night

Ticket To Ride

Walk On By

Running On Empty

Ghost Falls Series

Positively Pippa

Becoming Bella

Blatantly Blythe

Loving Laura

www.ingramcontent.com/pod-product-compliance
Lightning Source LLC
Chambersburg PA
CBHW071155100726
47908CB00002B/389